THE
RESURRECTION
OF
ANNE HUTCHINSON

THE
RESURRECTION
OF
ANNE HUTCHINSON

ROBERT
RIMMER

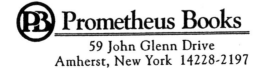 Prometheus Books

59 John Glenn Drive
Amherst, New York 14228-2197

Inquiries should be addressed to
Prometheus Books
59 John Glenn Drive
Amherst, New York 14228–2197
VOICE: 716–691–0133, ext. 207
FAX: 716–564–2711
WWW.PROMETHEUSBOOKS.COM

08 07 06 05 04   6 5 4 3 2

Library of Congress Cataloging-in-Publication Data

Rimmer, Robert H., 1917–
    The resurrection of Anne Hutchinson.
    ISBN 0–87975–370–6 (hardcover : alk. paper)
    1. Hutchinson, Anne Marbury, 1591–1643—Fiction. 2. Massachusetts—
History—Colonial period, ca. 1600–1775—Fiction. I. Title.

PS3568.I4R47 1986
813'.54   86–25472

Printed in the United States of America on acid-free paper

If in the manner of men, I have fought with beasts at Ephesus, what advantage is it to me? If the dead do not rise, let us eat and drink, for tomorrow we die.

Paul speaking to the Corinthians (I, 15:32)

INTRODUCTION

Less than a year ago, a woman who called herself Anne Hutchinson achieved international fame for a few weeks. Claiming that she was the same woman who had been banished from Boston in 1638, three and a half centuries ago, she was featured on several major national television shows and was the cover woman on *Time* and *Newsweek* magazines.

While the pros and cons of her resurrection and the theory that she is, or was, in the vanguard of a Second Coming of Jesus Christ have been examined endlessly by the popular media, as well as most religious journals and newspapers, at no time did this Anne Hutchinson give the media much information about her transition from the dead to the living, or about her relationship with Bob Rimmer.

Probably no one would have paid much attention to her claim except for the curious fact that, although she could be seen by all who personally beheld her (and as I can personally attest was a very beautiful woman), no one managed to capture her image on photographic film or videotape.

Many skeptics were sure this was the result of a cosmetician's trick make-up, and not because she was the "soul" image of her former self. Nevertheisss, this strange phenomenon lent widespread credibility to her claim that she had returned from the dead, and it made her warning that God Himself had purposely restored her to earthly life quite believable. Millions of people were obviously influenced by her claim that God's answer to the insanity of nuclear destruction of His people was for them to engage in a kind of Thoreauean "civil disobedience."

During the short time that she was a *cause celébrè,* Anne was accompanied by Saul Dremler, a young man who was about to enter his first year at Harvard Law School. Despite the possible adverse affect on his future career, Dremler made it quite apparent that this woman had turned him, a Jew, into a fervent believer in resurrection. Indeed, he indicated to all who would listen that the appearance of Anne Hutchinson on earth might herald the coming of a new Messiah.

Up to this time, her first "disciple," Bob Rimmer, has remained in the background. Although she always referred to "Dear Robert" as her protector and said he was responsible "because of his love for me" for her resurrection, neither Anne nor Bob Rimmer have revealed many of the intimate details of her previous life, which Rimmer claims she confided in him.

It should be noted that Rimmer gave what he calls a "sermon talk" about the banishment of Anne Hutchinson and her brother-in-law, John Wheelwright, at the First Parish Unitarian Universalist Church in Quincy, Massachusetts, three months before he met the "real Anne."

In this sermon Rimmer said, "In the past few months, having completed a new novel, I've gone a step further. I've adopted Anne Hutchinson. I have suggested in a previous book that, if you have very shallow genealogical roots or if you're just lonesome, it's fun to adopt an ancestor. All you have to do is to pick out someone who lived many years ago and rescue them from oblivion. Blow off the dust of time and bring them back to life. If you do, you will own them. And you may be sure that somewhere their spirits may be trembling with delight. Anne is the first female ancestor I have adopted—and I must admit that I've fallen in love with her."

But now, with Anne Hutchinson, the question arises whether Rimmer is slowly passing into what may be described as a psychiatric "no-man's land." Has he, in fact, gone beyond Luigi Pirandello and tried to merge a living, but unknown, woman into the personality of a historical personage?

As you will discover, we gave Mrs. Hutchinson a very thorough physical examination at the Hedman Psychiatric Institute. Rimmer believes that the results, especially our failure to get clear chest and bone X-rays and her strange responses on electrocardiograms and electroencephalograms, confirm the supernatural existence of the woman. And, of course, her strange disappearance after fourteen days on earth adds to the mystery.

Now, after many months of therapeutic counseling, Rimmer still insists not only that Anne Hutchinson was resurrected but that she will return again, and that the woman he has written about is not a figment of his imagination. When I finally convinced him that he should write this book as a form of therapy, he was afraid that he would reveal aspects of her days with him and her previous life which would shock many people. But then he decided that when Anne does reappear, she will not be ashamed, nor would she be penitent for her loving nature. But when his wife, Emily, and I read the manuscript, we warned him that many of his readers would believe that the story he has told reflects a dangerous flight from reality.

Despite our fears, the book is now in your hands. This is the "true story" of Anne Hutchinson, which she told to Rimmer in her own words. It will no doubt startle many historians, who will deny that Anne could have been the kind of loving and highly sexed woman he describes in the Puritan New England of her day. In addition, Rimmer has included a slightly modernized version of Anne Hutchinson's actual trials, which are nearly impossible to locate in most libraries. They are the only words that Anne Hutchinson ever spoke (or wrote) that have been preserved—until now. Rimmer believes that they not only confirm the reality of his own experience and affair with Anne Hutchinson, but reflect the kind of woman that she really was, or is.

I have known Bob Rimmer for many years as a friend and physician. While I am sure that he is not an atheist, I am quite certain that, prior to this experience, he did not believe in an afterlife or a God who took any personal interest in human affairs. But now he insists that the world has not seen the last of Anne Hutchinson. Whatever constituted the twentieth-century reality or illusion of her will coalesce again. In the meantime, if you come to love her, as he does (whether his story is fantasy or he has moved beyond our concepts of reality), you may also want to ask this lovely lady: "Anne Hutchinson, where are you now?"

David Z. Hedman, M.D., President
The Hedman Psychiatric Institute

1

Am I losing my mind? Have I finally crossed over the bridge from reality and taken up residence in the fictional worlds that I have been writing about for the past twenty-five years? Have I become a split personality talking to a figment of my imagination—a woman with a totally different personality who lived long ago?

Tuesday, the day after I drove my wife and three of her women friends to Logan Airport, a cold northeaster started to blow. The sleety rain, changing to snow, encapsulated me in the loneliness of our ten-room house, which extends from the front hall several hundred feet in two directions. A little concerned at leaving me alone for two weeks, while she took a packaged tour of European museums with her painting group, Emily had kissed me goodbye nervously and given me last-minute instructions on feeding the cats and watering plants in her greenhouse. Then, laughing, she told her friends: "Bob won't really miss me. He's having an affair with Anne Hutchinson."

I was responsible for her little joke. A few months ago, when we were sipping our second before-dinner martinis at the Gazelle, a restaurant on the top floor of an office building in Quincy that overlooks Boston Harbor to the north, I told Emily that I had agreed to give a sermon at the United First Parish Unitarian Universalist Church. *Sermon* was Keith Munson's word, not mine. Keith is minister of this church, and he was aware that I had recently "discovered" Anne Hutchinson and that I was fascinated by her. My subject was to be "The Banishment of John Wheelwright," who had been the first minister of First Parish. Back in 1637, when this occurred, Quincy was known as Mt. Wolleystone.

Keith is well aware that by most church standards I am not a religious man. Most of my life I have avoided organized religion. I told anyone who asked what my religious beliefs were that I was both a Humanist and a Tantric Hindu. I believe in worship of the *lignam* and *yoni*. Emily didn't mind if I used the words because she knew that most people weren't aware that they meant penis and vagina.

Feeling the toe-curling effect of two martinis, I had tried to get Emily interested in the history of Quincy. "I told Keith that I was much more

5

intrigued with Anne Hutchinson that with John Wheelwright. He was her brother-in-law, you know, and with her husband, Will, and their family, she arrived in the Massachusetts Colony a year before Wheelwright did."

I waved out the dining-room window toward the hills of Quincy, the Neponset River, and Milton a few miles away on the western horizon. "Three centuries ago, Anne lived in this area. When she was excommunicated by her church she probably sailed in a skiff from Boston and then rowed up the Neponset River, over there. A few days later she walked some sixty miles through the woods to Rhode Island to meet Will, who had gone off ahead of her with the family.

Before she was banished, the Hutchinsons were one of the most respected families in Boston. When they arrived in the Colony, the General Court, headed by John Winthrop and Thomas Dudley, gave Will six hundred acres of land at Mt. Wolleystone and later appointed him surveyor and "alloter" of acreage to new arrivals. Land was given to the original founders of the Massachusetts Bay Colony under the charter signed by King James and then was reapportioned to new colonists based on their commitment to the Colony and their economic standing. No land was allotted to anyone who was not accepted as a member of the church. Some of the Hutchinson land was probably on the site of this building where we are sitting right now."

I knew that Emily wasn't too interested, but she listened to me patiently. "I never did understand why she was banished," she said, "or why you're so intrigued with her."

"I like fiery women," I said. "That's why I married you. And I enjoy rebellious people—especially women." I grinned happily at her. "I hope you won't mind, but to tell you the truth, I've fallen in love with Anne Hutchinson."

Emily just smiled. She was used to an author's hyperboles. She knew that I had been in love with many women during our long marriage. But she had survived. Anyway, Anne Hutchinson had died nearly three hundred and fifty years ago. This obviously wasn't a dangerous extramarital attachment.

But little did either of us know what was about to happen. Somewhere in Paris—maybe, right now in the Jeu de Paume—Emily is probably enjoying the French impressionists firsthand. But I'm sure she would be quite surprised to discover that I am not living the monastic existence that I assured her I would. Or is it possible that Emily is involved in this insanity? Am I the victim of a practical joke engineered by her and our friend Dave Hedman?

I gave the sermon—really a lecture—on Wheelwright nearly a month ago, and I told more than two hundred people who heard me that they should read the two trials of Anne Hutchinson. The first was before the General Court of the Massachusetts Bay Colony on November 7 and 8, 1637, when she was formally banished. The second trial occured later, in March of 1638, when she was excommunicated by the First Church of Boston after having been kept prisoner for six months in the home of Joseph Weld of Roxbury. Since the transcripts of the trials are not generally available, I decided that I would transcribe them into more modern English and put them in a screenplay format. I also suggested to my listeners that, since the three hundred and fiftieth anniversary of these trials was close at hand, perhaps we might find a modern Anne Hutchinson in the congregation who would help us reenact them. It must have been obvious to whoever heard me that I was infatuated with Anne. Thinking about it now, as I write this, I remember that at first I was convinced that some woman—aided and abetted by Emily and David—could have decided to bring my daydreams to life.

Even before Emily had left for Europe, I was busy retyping the trials, modifying a word here or a sentence structure there and adding some descriptive actor's directions to make the trials more understandable to modern readers. And I was wondering why some astute producer of a television series hadn't recognized the potential for a dramatic weeklong series about the Massachusetts Bay Colony and John Winthrop's utopian Boston—"a city upon a hill." His patriarchal dream of the good life, lived according to the law of the Scriptures, had nearly been undermined by America's first feminist—Anne Hutchinson.

Tuesday evening, momentarily absorbed with the potential of being a bachelor for two weeks, but at the same time feeling a little lonely, I lit a fire in our living-room fireplace, poured myself a healthy hooker of brandy in a big snifter glass, and started reading over my previous day's typing. Outside, as I searched for modern meanings for words and phrases like "scruples," and "being privy to the ground of things," and "good estate," the rainy sleet pounded on our open-rafter living room, providing a doomsday accompaniment to the solemn words of the magistrates and ministers who had word-whipped Anne Hutchinson with their theologies so many years ago.

Soothed by the crackling fire and the cozy smell of the brandy, I must have dozed. I awoke with a start. A cold chill warning of imminent danger ran down my back and legs. Someone was pounding on the front door, and I could hear a faint cry of "Help me! Help me!" I looked at my watch. It was nearly eleven P.M. By this time Emily was five hours in the air over the Atlantic. No one I knew, or whom Emily knew, would possibly come calling at this time of night. I had read recently of robberies committed by burglars who had used a "Help me" or "My car is broken down" as a foil to gain entrance to a house. Switching on the outside pole lantern, which illuminates the front steps, I peered out the window beside the front door.

A totally naked, wild-eyed woman, sleet slashing against her face and breasts, was clinging to the iron railing beside the door. Her long, dark-blonde hair was whipped with rain around her face and shoulders. There was no car in the driveway, nor anyone in the street beside her. She might be a decoy. I fully expected a gunman to appear beside her, but what choice did I have? Alone, she'd soon die of exposure to the freezing night. I opened the door. Sobbing, she collapsed in my arms. "Thank the dear Lord!" she sighed. "Aye, the rain must have put the fire out. The Indians are gone. Pray that they come not back." Fainting, she slid onto the front hall floor.

In a state of shock, I carried her across the living room and laid her down on an oriental rug near the fire. For a moment I thought that she was dead, but then I could see the slow rise and fall of her breasts. Who in Hell was she? I guessed from lifting her that she weighed about a hundred and thirty-five pounds. She was only a few inches shorter than I am. Five foot seven, I guessed.

I ran into the bathroom to get a towel to dry her, and grabbed my terrycloth bathrobe. When I got back, her eyes were still closed. She was not young, but her body was firm with only a slight curve to her stomach. There were no operational scars. Her breasts were large but not sagging. Her nipples, extended from the cold, suggested that she had suckled more than one child. Her pubic hair was lush and grew more profusely than might be expected on a woman who I judged to be in her late forties. Her fingers were long, and her fingernails cut square. She wore no nail polish. Strangely, untypical of American women her age, her underarms were unshaved, and her well-shaped legs were covered with fine blonde hair.

In the meantime, while I was admiring her eye-pleasing body and her large, chiseled face with no make-up, I was vigorously rubbing her down with the towel. At the same time I was wondering if I should telephone the police. What could I say to them? I was in an embarrassing position. Who would believe me? How could I convince anyone that a naked woman whom I had never met had arrived at my house in the middle of the night? Almost shouting at her, "For God's sake, don't die on me!" I lightly slapped her cheeks. Shivering violently, she finally opened her eyes. They were big, wide apart in her face, Caribbean-Sea green, and so enticing you could happily drown in them.

Sitting up and sobbing, she clung to me for a moment and then she pulled away. "Who are you?" she demanded. "Where am I?" Then, aware that she was naked, she covered her breasts with her arms and inched away from me. "Oh, dear God. What have you been doing to me?" she sobbed.

Even more bewildered than she was, I dropped the towel on her. "Not a damned thing!" I assured her angrily. "You came here—uninvited. I didn't ask you to come."

"Who are you?" she repeated.

I told her my name and she shook her head. "I know not your name," she said and then her eyes widened and her mouth opened with surprise. "Aye, you must be the one who—" She clasped her hand over her mouth and didn't finish.

"Must be the one who what?" I demanded.

"Please," she begged me, "do not ask me. Methinks it is a revelation.

Where am I?"

"Quincy, Massachusetts," I said, sarcastically, sure that she knew where she was.

"Quincy? I remember that name. Edmund Quincy. His farm was nigh to us at Mt. Wolleystone." She sat up and grasped my arm. "You said Massachusetts. Is this the Colony? How did I get back here? I was in Dutch territory. Nieuw Netherlands." Lost in thought a moment, she stared past me, and then she moaned. "Oh, God, oh, dear Jesus Christ, what have you done to me? Why did my children have to pay for my sins?"

She was now sobbing hysterically, but I didn't feel very sympathetic. I had listened to her in total disbelief. The few things she had said and the names she used had alerted me. This woman know her colonial history. If this was one of Dave Hedman's practical jokes, he had gone too damned far this time. I grabbed her shoulders and shook her roughly. "I suppose that you're going to tell me that you are Anne Hutchinson," I yelled at her angrily.

"Aye, Sir," she said. I knew that I had frightened her. "That is my name."

"Yeah, and my name is Adam." I scowled at her, thinking that she really did look like a voluptuous Eve. "I'm sure that you know your name." I decided to put an end to this game. "What else do you know? What was your maiden name? What was your father's first name?" I was certain that it was unlikely that anyone impersonating Anne Hutchinson would know that.

"My father's name was Francis Marbury. My mother's name was Bridget." She responded without hesitation. "My husband, Will, died in Portsmouth, on the Island, eighteen months ago."

"What Island?" I demanded.

"The Isle of Aquiday. Some call it Aquidneck."

I knew that Aquidneck was the Indian name for what was now Newport, Rhode Island. "Eighteen months ago?" I shivered, wondering if I had been invaded by an occult spirit from the underworld. "More likely three hundred years ago," I said, backing away from her. Whoever had primed this woman had done a good job. The thought occurred to me that she might be some giddy woman who had heard me speak and decided "to become" Anne Hutchinson. So I asked her if she had heard my sermon on Wheelwright at the First Parish Church. She was bewildered. "I know you not. Do you mean Johnny's church? Is this Mt. Wolleystone? Poor Johnny. He is in Piscataqua. They made him leave the Colony five years ago. Six months before I did. He could not tolerate Master Wilson or Master Weld, either."

"Who is Johnny?" I demanded, still trying to trap her.

"John Wheelwright. He is my brother-in-law. He married Will's sister, Katherine." She got to her feet. Staring a little dizzily at me, she grasped the edge of a chair and slid into the bathrobe that I held out for her. She stared around the room, aware for the first time of the lighted lamps. "This fireroom is exceedingly bonny and warm," she said gratefully and bent over to look at one of the bulbs in a table lamp. "But the light hath no flame. Please, good Sir"—tears were gliding down her cheeks—"if this be Heaven, my children must be here—and Will."

"This is not Heaven," I said coldly. I decided that I had no choice. If Dave and Emily had cooked this up, I might as well play the game. Pretty soon a noisy gang of their friends would arrive with this woman's clothes, and I'd discover, as they pounded my back hilariously, that I had been hoaxed. "Whether you went to Heaven or Hell is not known," I said a little harshly. "Presumably, you and your children were scalped by the Indians." I scowled at her. "But right now *you* seem to have your head on straight."

She shuddered. "Uncas did not scalp me. He murdered my friend Miantonomo. Two days later he tomahawked Francis, Will Collins, Anne, Mary, William, Susanna, and Zuriel, all my poor children, while I watched. Oh dear God, it was awful. I thought my heart would jump out of my body—and then I fainted."

She was sobbing now, but I was still wondering if she were one of the best actresses I had ever seen.

"What happened to you?" I asked.

"Methinks the savages were a little afraid of me. Master Winthrop convinced Uncas that I was a very evil spirit. They brought me back to their camp. They made a huge pile of faggots and stripped me naked. They tied me to the pyre and then danced for hours around me." She buried her face in her hands and moaned. "I knew I was being sacrificed to their god. Then they set me afire with maize and sticks. I must have fainted."

"You died like Joan of Arc," I said, thinking for a second that that would make sense. That was the way Anne Hutchinson would have wanted to die—a martyr.

This Anne, tears coursing unheeded down her cheeks, was once again staring at the light bulb, hypnotized by it. Before I could tell her not to, she touched it quickly with her finger. "'Tis hot!" she squealed. "But all the fire is inside. Be there no candles in Heaven?"

"Only electricity," I said, wondering, if no one came, what I was going to do with her. If she weren't a friend of Dave's, maybe she was an escapee from some kind of mental asylum. I was certain that by morning she would be headlines in the *Boston Globe*. The radio and television programs would be interrupted as her keepers mounted a search for her. "Tell me where you come from," I said soothingly. "I'll drive you back there."

"I told you. Before it happened, I was building a new home in Dutch territory." She shivered. "If this be Mt. Wolleystone I cannot stay here. I'm sure Master Winthrop or Master Dudley would hang me or have me whipped on Boston Common." It occurred to me that the Puritans had actually hung Anne Hutchinson's friend Mary Dyer on the Common, but that was quite a few years after Anne had been burnt.

"They can't hang you," I told her cheerfully. "They're all dead."

"Then this must be Heaven," she said softly. "Who are you?" Her widely spaced, dreamy and hypnotic eyes never left my face—as if she were trying to penetrate my skin and find her answers there.

"I can assure you that this is not Heaven," I told her. "To my knowledge I haven't died yet—not in this century, anyway. As for you—with a little luck, and if you stop running around bareass in the snow—you may even live to the twenty-first century." I laughed at her bewilderment and thought: this lady is a superb performer. "And just for the record, there hasn't been any Second Coming of Jesus yet," I told her, "so you can be first in line."

She shook her head, her gaze both penetrating mine and going beyond me. Finally, with a little sob she said, "I never believed that the sown body could return in the flesh. Only the soul is immortal."

I couldn't help smiling. "Let's stop kidding each other," I told her. "I just rubbed you down. Whoever you are, your soul has a very substantial female covering."

2

Whoever this woman was, it was apparent that she was going to spend the rest of the night in my house. I was reluctant to call the police. The sexual overtones of telling them that a naked woman had rung my doorbell and veritably moved in was not only embarrassing but was unbelievable. But how could I tell her that she must leave? I spent the next half hour trying to get her to admit that she was either playing a joke on me or that she was a patient of some kind who had escaped from a mental home. But to every question that I asked her, she shook her head pitifully and kept repeating, "In sooth, I know not why I am here. All I know is that I am Anne. The last thing I remember is the Mohegans—there were fifty or more of them—and then Uncas, their leader, threw his torch on the corn husks. Flames surged around my face. I screamed, and my voice echoed over and over again growing fainter and I could not hear myself anymore——"

I listened to her dubiously. I hadn't completely rejected the idea that I was the victim of a plot which Dave and Emily had carefully contrived to jar me out of my "affair with a lady long dead." But I had to admit that not only did this woman's style of speech resemble that of a seventeenth-century woman, but her accent was definitely early American English. She spoke with a rolling Shakespearean sound to her words that made them seem like a warm caress. I was certain that no sane woman would carry a joke this far, nor play the part so well. But slightly insane? Of that, I was not so certain.

She had arrived at midnight, with the only option left to her being that of sleeping in a stranger's house—and in a stranger's bed. Not that I expected to go to bed with her, or even wanted to. I was convinced that she was an "author lover." Like teenagers who tag after rock-music stars—they called them groupies when I was young—she was probably one of many lonely older married women who "discover" an author, read everything that he has written, and then falls in love with him sight unseen. Such women are a complete mystery to the men who married them. They live in a fantasy world equal to any novelist's. Over many years I had encountered quite a few of them. One or two had become so obsessive that it hadn't been easy to divert them back to reality or convince them that "despite what I wrote," I was probably no better in bed than their husbands.

What could I do? Huddled in the corner of the sofa, she stared at the dying fire. Tears were glistening on her cheeks and now she was murmuring, "Dear Jesus, I pray Thee, tell me why hast thou brought me here? What am I to do?"

"I don't know what Jesus is going to tell you," I said a little acerbically, "but I think you should go to bed. There's a guest bedroom. You'll be perfectly safe. Tomorrow after you've had a good night's rest, we'll figure this out." I stood up and reached for her hand. She took mine, and I could feel her trembling as I led her toward the bedroom.

Passing the kitchen, it occurred to me that she might be hungry, and I asked her. She nodded appreciatively. "If you could spare some pudding or porridge," she said, "or even an apple."

I opened the refrigerator door and she stared at the lighted inside in open-mouthed astonishment. "God keeps winter in a box and He lights it without a flame." She spoke in a hushed voice. Then she saw the fruits and vegetables. She pointed excitedly at the oranges. "Might I please have one? I have not eaten one for many years. They are very good for scurvy."

While she was peeling an orange, I showed her a box of oatmeal. "There's no pudding or porridge," I said. "But I can make you some warm cereal, or you can have a hamburger, scrambled eggs, a roast-beef sandwich, or a chicken leg."

She grabbed my arm. "Please, good Sir. Must you speak so fast? You use strange words—*electricity, hamburger, sandwich*—and you say negatives strangely. Sometimes I understand you not." She smiled and hoped that she hadn't offended me. "You are exceedingly generous," she said with an anxious expression on her face. "I hope that you have more food in the cellar. What month is this?"

"It's March 24th," I told her and pointed out the window to the backyard that I had lit with a floodlight. "As you can see, spring will be a little late this year. The rain has turned to snow."

"We must eat sparingly," she said. "Many months will pass before you can replenish your stores." Like a child unable to make up her mind and wondering aloud if I kept a cow, she decided on cheese between bread and a glass of milk. She examined the sliced bread carefully and shrugged. "If this be bread, it feels like cotton. Can you eat it?"

I offered to toast it for her, but she shook her head and murmured something about warming it in the fireplace and that that was really too much trouble.

"What do you know about me?" she asked as she ate the sandwich and sipped the milk, obviously relishing it.

I was on the verge of telling her that she, in truth, was a total stranger to me. But instead I poured myself another hooker of brandy, and I decided to play whatever her game might be.

"Not as much as I'd like to," I told her, trying to sound sincere. "I'm a writer of stories. I finished a novel a few months ago called *The Immoral Reverend,* and I made a passing reference to Anne Hutchinson. I decided then, when I had nothing else to do I would try to learn more about her."

"That is an exceedingly strange title for a book—*The Immoral Reverend.*" Her eyes were questioning pools surrounded by a tiny smile that lit her face and lips.

I shrugged. "Anne Hutchinson was convinced that a lot of reverends—ministers—in the Massachusetts Bay Colony were immoral. She insisted they preached a covenant of works, and that they weren't true ministers of God."

She sighed and shook her head. "That is so, but 'tis difficult to understand you." She shrugged. "Doth not your reverend believe that God loveth us all? No matter what we may do, I am sure His Spirit is within us."

"You may be right," I said. "But if you're talking about a covenant of grace, I'll warn you in advance—no one gives a damn about that anymore." I ignored her pained expression and continued. "Most people don't even know what grace means today." Once again I tried to convince her that she had not awakened in Heaven nor could I believe that by some miracle she had been resurrected. I told her that if she wanted to play this game it was more entertaining than Scrabble or Trivia, a new game that had swept the country.

She shook her head. "I know not those games."

"You'll have to face it," I insisted, "we are now living on the edge of the twenty-first century. There isn't much left that is immoral any more." I laughed. "A lot of people wouldn't even believe that my reverend is sexually immoral."

"Sexually?" She stared at me with a puzzled look.

"He enjoys sleeping with other women in addition to his wife."

She laughed softly. "Oh, I understand. He is not truly sleeping. Adultery is against the law. Is he a Ranter or a Familist?" My skin was suddenly crawling with goose pimples. No one except perhaps a few antiquarians and religious scholars, certainly not a crazy woman, could possibly know anything about a long-forgotten, seventeenth-century religious group who called themselves Familists or the Family of Love. Had this woman sitting opposite me really returned from the grave? It was ridiculous, I told myself. Anne Hutchinson's fleshly body had long ago turned to dust. Whatever remained of her on earth was nothing but undefined energy.

But I couldn't help myself. If this were a game, I wasn't quitting now. "I often wondered about you," I told her. "You told John Cotton at your excommunication trial that you *abhorred* the idea of a community of wives—wife sharing. But supposedly that was what some of the Familists did."

It was her turn to be surprised. She avoided my question. "You have read my trials? Were they printed in England? Roger Williams told me that

Governor Winthrop and Master Weld had written a book about me and my brother-in-law, John Wheelwright."

"Winthrop's first book was published in England in 1644," I said. "For nearly a century you were forgotten. No one knew that a transcript of your trials existed. Then nearly a hundred years later the governor of Massachusetts, Thomas Hutchinson, who was your great-great-grandson and a great-grandson of your oldest boy, Edward, found a copy of your examination before the General Court of Massachusetts and published it."

I grinned at her. "Poor Thomas didn't know whether to approve of you or not. He was a Tory. If you had lived another hundred years, I'm sure you and he would have been enemies. He was on the British side in the Revolutionary War. He would have looked upon you as a rebel. The rebels in Boston hated poor Thomas. He finally fled back to England before they could murder him." She listened to me with a blank expression on her face, and I realized that Anne Hutchinson could not have been aware that some of the seeds she had sown had flowered into a rebellion against the King of England. I shrugged. "No one knows where Thomas Hutchinson found the manuscript of your General Court trial."

"I know who wrote it down," she said, quite excited. "Robert Keyane. He did not fancy me much. Later in March, when they brought me before the church, I saw him once again recording everything that was said in the big pulpit book that Master Wilson kept under his chair." She shuddered. "Casting me out was Master Wilson's greatest triumph."

"That book was lost, too." I told her. "Even Thomas Hutchinson wasn't aware that a transcript of your church trial existed. But a man named Ezra Stiles, who was a minister and president of Yale College, copied it from church records in 1771. It was finally published by the Massachusetts Historical Society in 1888. It wasn't until then that a new generation discovered that your friend, John Cotton, had pulled the rug out from under you."

Anne—I had decided, insane or not, to use her name—was now testing a dish of vanilla ice cream that I had spooned out for her. "Sweet angel snow," she murmured as she ate it. Then once again tears were flowing down her cheeks. "Prithee, forgive me. I am not usually so weepy." She tried to smile at me, but it was a forlorn smile. "I have only now remembered. I am fifty-two years old. You mentioned Edward. If this truly be another century, they my son Edward is dead, too."

"Not only Edward," I said thoughtlessly. "But the man I just told you about, your great-great-grandson, Thomas Hutchinson, died several hundred years ago."

"My whole family is dead," she sobbed. "If I am truly alive—why? Oh, why me? Oh, dear Jesus, I was a loving woman but not a wicked one. If this be not Heaven, then it must be Hell." She shivered and stared at me. "Are you Satan?"

I shrugged. "I don't really know. I guess I'm a sinner too. Maybe I sold my soul to the devil like your friend Captain John Underhill. I enjoy women but they always seem to get me into trouble." I was grinning and trying to cheer her up. But I wondered how she would respond to that name.

"Do you mean Jack Underhill?" she demanded. "Hath he, too, come back from the grave?"

I shook my head. "Not to my knowledge."

"For a long time I was very angry with Jack," she said. "He did not truly hate the poor savages like Governor Winthrop and Master Dudley did, but he helped massacre hundreds of them in Connecticut. He wrote a long story about it and he was a hero—they made him captain of the militia in Boston. Governor Winthrop was most agitated with Jack when he signed a petition protesting the banishing of poor Johnny."

"Johnny who?" I asked, once again testing her.

"John Wheelwright. I told you he was my brother-in-law." She shrugged. "That was not the end of Jack's troubles. Jack was a Familist. He practically admitted it to Governor Winthrop. Jack left of the Colony before they hung him. He went to Piscataqua and finally became the governor of New Hampshire."

"I read in Winthrop's *Journals* that Jack liked women too," I told her. "Winthrop wrote in detail about Underhill's affair with the cooper's wife. Presumably, when the cooper was making barrels, Underhill arrived to give her religious instruction. But when her husband came home with the constable, the front door was locked. Underhill claimed they weren't fornicating," I laughed, "just playing together."

Anne smiled at me and shook her head. "Will always said that Jack was a beard splitter."

"What do you mean by a beard splitter?" I asked, even though I had a pretty good idea.

She giggled and said, "A man given to wenching. Jack could not settle down with one lady only. A year ago he decided that living in Dutch territory was safer, too." She sighed. "He had originally come to the Island. But Master Winthrop and Master Dudley were trying to take over Providence and Aquiday. They called it the Isle of Errors. We felt certain that it was no longer safe for heretics. Six months ago Jack clomped onto my farm. He had only then arrived by horseback. I fed him and after the children had gone to bed, he told me that ''tis too cold to sleep alone.'" She shrugged. "I agreed— but I told him only if he were on his feet at four o'clock in the morning and would chop some wood and help me make soap." She smiled at me. "He stayed an entire week and helped me mightily around the place. Perchance he will come back from the dead, too. Methinks you would like Jack."

This conversation was going beyond reality. But I couldn't help myself. I looked around the kitchen apprehensively, afraid that Underhill might suddenly materialize. Some people actually believe that people can return from the dead in astral bodies. Free from gravity, they float from one place to another. With a little bit of luck, you could have a unique new adventure and even bed down with unsuspecting women.

But Anne's body was no will-o-the wisp. I couldn't wave her into oblivion. "It's really time to go to bed," I finally told her. Obediently, but reluctantly, she followed me into the guest room. I turned on the light, but when she saw the twin beds in the lonely room, she clung to me. "Please, good Sir. Do not leave me. Where dost thou sleepeth?"

Surprised that she had suddenly switched to calling me *thou* instead of *you,* I pointed down the hall. "You have nothing to fear," I told her. "I won't bother you. There's no one else in the house. My wife is in Europe."

"Thou say this be March. Hath the New Year begun?" she asked. "When is Conception Day?"

For a moment I was bewildered. Then I remembered the Puritans had used the Julian calendar. March was the first month of the year. In late March, the Passover, when Jesus was conceived, was the official beginning of the new year.

I told her again that it was March 24th.

"That means that thy wife cannot return here until May."

It took me a few seconds to grasp her reasoning. Then I realized that she was thinking of the spring migration from England to New England that had brought several thousand people to the colonies in the early 1600s. Sailing the Atlantic in those days wasn't feasible until the summer months and often it took as long as twelve weeks. I wondered if Anne was planning to take Emily's place and be my surrogate wife. But I didn't voice the question.

"My wife will be flying home in ten days," I told her. I was quite certain that no matter what else happened, Anne wouldn't be here when Emily returned. Going to bed with a dead paramour was one thing, but as spooky as that might sound, I was sure that I couldn't have two wives—even if one had just been resurrected from the grave.

But Anne didn't understand me. "I know not what you mean. Your wife can fly? Perchance she will fly in here directly."

I assured her that was quite unlikely. "She can't flap her arms and fly," I said. "We have machines that have wings. Emily will fly home in one of them in about ten days."

"Hast thou ever slept with another woman?"

"We agree that we can love more than one person."

Anne clapped her hands. "Thou soundest like a Familist. Is this a Family of Love?"

"You haven't told me whether you are a Familist or not," I countered.

She smiled, "Until I know thee better, I dare not say. But I do abhor sleeping alone. Please, wilt thou sleep with me? I am very frightened."

I shood my head. She certainly wasn't acting like any Anne Hutchinson whom I had read about. "I don't think that that would be wise."

"Please, Sir, thou doth not need to fornicate with me. But should thou desire to, thou canst love me and thy wife too." She smiled brightly at me. "When she returneth, I shall thank her and tell her that I love her, too."

I was sure of one thing: I was a man. She might be a poltergeist come to haunt me, or a resurrected woman still cold from the grave, but her sea-green eyes imploring me, her sweet face tilted toward mine as she clung to my arm, and her very complete and erotic female body that I had massaged back to life were hard to resist.

Anyway, I should have known that it wasn't easy to argue with Anne Hutchinson and win. "Thou told me that thou knew not as much about me as thou wouldst like," she said as I hesitated. Her voice was suddenly warmer and even more throaty than it had been. "To sleep with a woman is to know her." She chuckled merrily. "In bed a woman doth not hold her tongue."

"Who else have you slept with besides your husband and Jack Underhill?" I asked, giving up and letting her follow me into the master bedroom. She didn't answer me, but everything that I had read about Anne Hutchinson had led me to believe that she had been a very moral woman and spent all of her free time reading Scripture. In addition, as a mother of fifteen children, she had presumably been monogamous. But there were several question marks in her life—John Cotton, for one, and Harry Vane. But I assumed that her relationship with them had been lovingly platonic.

Happily surprised with the king-sized bed, she tested it. "No feathers," she said. "It is almost as firm as the floor." She grinned at me. "There is room enough for a whole family in this bed or a Turk and all his wives." I saw her eyes searching the room. "But first, I must piss. Where is the chamber pot?" I showed her the bathroom, and she peered into the toilet shaking her head. "I cannot piss or shit in fresh water."

Laughing, I flushed it and tried to explain that the incoming water would flush her piss or shit through pipes into a sewerage-treatment plant, and ultimately, I was sorry to tell her, into Massachusetts Bay.

Smiling at me, she gathered the bathrobe about her and squatted on the toilet. "I need not now to make a stool," she said shyly, "but I remember my momma told me that Cardinal Woolsey had three miles of lead pipe installed at the Queen's palace at Hampton Court to bring in fresh water, and the Queen had a stool that flushed water." Anne laughed, "But she liketh it not because it wet her arse. My momma told me that everyone at the Court had their own closet stools that were covered with satin and velvet. The palace had eighteen hundred rooms, but after awhile it stank so bad the Queen had to move out. The Queen had her own stool grooms. Methinks she liked those boys to wipe her bum."

"What queen are you talking about?" I asked.

"Elizabeth. I was eleven years old when she died."

Thinking she wanted privacy, I walked toward the bedroom but she grabbed my hand. "Please," she wailed. "I am afraid. Do not leave me." It occurred to me that modesty about one's body and its functions did not arrive in America until Victorian times. Quite practically, Anne and Will Hutchinson had shared the same chamber pot, and she had emptied the slops in the morning.

When she finished, I pointed at the roll of toilet paper. She examined it curiously and pulled out a long piece. "Bum paper?" she asked and marveled as she dried herself. I turned the faucet on the bidet and she squealed with surprise and put her hand into the warm spout of water. "A biddy, with warm water," she said in awe. Facing me, she sat happily over the spout. Staring at the soap I handed her, she said, "But it is so hard and white." Then she soaped herself vigorously. "Thou must have a well in the cellar with a fire going," she said. "If this be not Heaven, then it is a miracle."

I handed her a towel and she kissed my cheek. "Thank thee, dear Robert," she said. "Thou art very nice to me."

I scowled at her. "Before I decide whether I'll sleep with you, finish what you were going to say when you first saw me and said you must be the one who——"

"Thou tellest me that thou hast read my trials?"

I nodded.

"I was banished because I had revelations. But it was true. Many times I knew what would befall me long before it happened. When Uncas applied the torch to the pyre that they had built around me and the flames were searing into my brain, I saw thy face and I knew that thou wouldst come to save me."

I looked at her incredulously, unable to control the goosebumps crawling up my spine. "You mean that you saw me three hundred and fifty years ago?" I tried not to let her see that she was giving me the cold shivers. "That's ridiculous."

She sighed. "I saw thy face but I knew not who you were or that I would live again."

Still naked, shivering, she crawled into bed. "Dost thou wear a night dress?" she asked. I shook my head, but offered to give her some pajamas that I never used.

"Methinks it is warmer to sleep together naked," she said. "Please, dear Robert, do not fear me. Undress and come to bed."

Nervous because I now had a considerable erection, I finally slipped in beside her. She was neither frightened nor embarrassed. "Why art thou afraid of me?" she asked, and without waiting for an answer she snuggled in my arms. To my surprise, her fingers encircled my penis. "This is nice," she murmured. Long ago Will and I used to sleep like this." Then she perched on her elbow and stared at me with a loving expression. "Thou makest me baffle-headed," she said softly. "Who art thou? I know thou lovest me."

"How do you know that?" I asked, suddenly feeling suspicious again. I was sure that Emily must have told Dave that I was having an affair with Anne Hutchinson, and Dave, bursting with laughter, had suggested that one of his patients—a lonely widow, perhaps—volunteer to bring my daydream to life.

But when I questioned Anne further about her revelations, her answer was frighteningly believable. "Often Christ Jesus hath given me revelations. Before Uncas threw his torch on my pyre I heard a voice tell me, as it had many times before, 'Thou willst not die. Thou still hast work to do on this earth. When the time is ready your beloved Jesus will come for thee.'"

Smiling at me, Anne kissed my lips. "Dear Robert, thou art my beloved too. Methinks Jesus knew I would find thee." She stared at me puzzled. "I keep thinking I know thee. Thou remindest me of Will. Tell me why thou lovest a woman whom thou hast never met. Tell me all thou knowest about me."

3

By this time I was no longer sleepy, but I had decided that I wouldn't tell this woman—at least not yet—that I had spent the last three months reading everything I could find that had been written about her, or that I had copies of most of the books in the house. If she were still here tomorrow and I was still as confused about how to get rid of her as I now was, she could stay and read about herself in a collection of biographies, novels, a narrative poem, and one full-length play. She could even read John Winthrop's *Journals* and learn what was going on in Winthrop's mind while he was dealing with the problems she had caused in the Colony.

Lying next to her in bed, I still didn't believe that she was really Anne Hutchinson. I might believe in ghosts—or even in reincarnation—but *resurrection of the dead!* Even the resurrection of Jesus Christ, to my mind, was a myth promulgated by our ancestors, who equated man's death and rebirth with the fertility patterns of nature. This woman obviously knew a great deal about Anne Hutchinson's life and times, but it was the kind of information any good actress could acquire before playing a part. I was still waiting for her to say something that would reveal unconditionally that she was a twentieth-century woman.

While I was thinking this, I was aware that Anne was staring at the ceiling with tear-filled eyes. She seemed to be as bewildered as I was. "Did you ever hope to live again?" I asked her. "To be born again and see what life would be like a few centuries from now? Benjamin Franklin did. When a seemingly dead fly, that had been held in suspension in a bottle of Madeira he was drinking, suddenly came to life, he told a friend that he wished he could be like that fly and see the world a hundred years from then."

"I know not Benjamin Franklin," she said. "But I knew that my soul was immortal. I am much troubled. My body seemeth to be a fleshly body, but I know that cannot be. Why am I here?" She sighed. "It troubles me too that you do not believe I am Anne Hutchinson."

Then Anne murmured in my ear, "It troubles me, too, if I be my soul, why do I have such fleshly feelings." She leaned on her elbow and smiled at me. I was aware that, flesh or not, her clear skin seemed to cast an indefinable

21

glow across her face. I couldn't help myself. I hugged her and she giggled. "I may be dreaming but thy pillicock pressing against my belly seems real enough. Put it inside me and it will feel better for both of us."

For the next hour we transcended reality together. She was a most affectionate and lusty lover, kissing and biting my lips and cheeks and shoulders, rolling on top of me, and arching and squatting on me so that I could disappear into the warmth of her breasts and the depths of her vagina at the same time. Then with a moan of delight, rising to a scream of abandonment, she climaxed and stretched out full length on top of me in my arms. "I am sorry that I was so noisy," she whispered. "Will was befuddled when I screamed. He said I would wake the children, but I told him the girls knew he wasn't beating me, that we were begetting children."

I was learning one thing. If this really was Anne Hutchinson, Puritan or not, she was an enthusiastic lover. "Tell me about your early life," I whispered to her between kisses. "No one knows very much about that."

"Sweetheart," she said, "thy dear cock is still agog in my queynte."

I laughed and told her not to worry, I wasn't sleepy, and I could last, even if she couldn't.

"Most times I was too afire for Will," she smiled. "My fire put his out too quickly."

Before she peaked a second time in a flesh-churning yell of ecstasy, her fingers slashing my back, I thought she might put my fire out temporarily, too. Begging me to forgive her, kissing the welts she had made on my back and shoulders, she smiled tenderly at me. "Women my age aren't supposed to be so whorish. Poor Will. After we came to New England, he had to work so hard that he finally just wanted to hold me—and not beget little ones."

"You had fifteen kids," I said. "That would seem more than enough. Did Will want so many children or did you?"

She laughed. "How doth a woman such as me not have babies? Sometimes Will would spill his seed."

"Wasn't that against the law?" I asked. "God slew Onan for masturbating."

Anne shook her head. Even while she was talking, her vagina was still gently squeezing my cock. "You do not understand Scripture. God slew Onan not because he spilled his seed, but because he would not follow levirate law and marry his sister-in-law." She shrugged. "I read in a book in Papa's library that during the twenty-four months that a woman suckles a child, a man can thresh inside her but will not winnow." She shook her head. "Alas, it worked not for me. I taught my children to drink milk from a cup when they were six months old and pretty soon I was quickly fertile again. I tried a sponge." She laughed. "But the only thing that ever worked was not swiving. Anyway, it doth not matter. I loved children and so did my Will. They came easily and none died at birth."

"Do you remember their names?" I asked, thinking that was a test no imposter could pass.

"Most certainly I do." Once again she was on top of me slowly undulating her buttocks. "I desireth not to lose thee," she grinned at me. "I was married to Will August 9, 1612, in England. And all my children but the last were born before we sailed for the New World. Edward was born in May 1613. My first Susanna was born September 14, 1614. Richard came in December 1615." She smiled. "Will was careful with his seed for the next year. Faith was born in August 1617. Bridget arrived January 15, 1619, and Francis on the 24th of December 1620. Elizabeth was born in 1622, but poor little William died in June 1623." She sighed. "The same year, 1630, my first Susanna, sixteen years old, and Elizabeth, nine years old, both caught the plague and died. I was only thirty-eight, but I wanted to die too."

Lost in her memories, she was silent a moment. "All my other children lived." She shuddered. "Except those that the Mohegans murdered. When I moved to New Netherlands, there was Samuel, who was born December 1624. Anne came two years later in May 1626, Mary in 1628, and Katherine a year later in 1629. Our second William was born September 28, 1631, and our second Susanna arrived two years later on the 15th of November 1633. Susanna was born four months after John-Luv had left for New England along with my first son, Edward. He sailed to America with Will's brother, Edward, and Ed's wife, Sarah. Finally, in New England, Zuriel, my dear little rock, was born in Boston in March 1636."

"You life was filled with Johns," I said, and although I knew the answer, I asked her which John this was.

"Thou knowest many things about me," she grimaced. "It was not John Winthrop or John Wilson. Those two Johns hated me." She smooched my lips fervently for a moment, and then she chuckled. "Methinks they knew I was no Puritan in bed. But I had three Johns who loved me. Johnny—John Wheelwright, my brother-in-law—John Underhill, whom I called Jack, and John-Luv—John Cotton." She sighed. "I was desolate when John-Luv left for New England. But I knew that he wanted me to come to America too. That's why he agreed to oversee Edward when Edward decided to go adventuring with him in the New World. That was in 1633, a year before Will and I and our family sailed for New England."

"Cotton was married," I said, determined to find the answer to something that had bothered me ever since I had "adopted" Anne. "Did he love you too? Like this?"

She stared at me with a faraway expression and didn't answer for a moment. My cock had left her nest. Lying on her side, her face against my chest, she was holding it tenderly. "When we were alone, I always called Master Cotton, John-Luv," she said quietly. "He loved me but he always felt guilty about it. Breaking the law made him all a-mort."

"You mean dejected?" I was fascinated at this revelation. If it were true, it explained why Anne Hutchinson had uprooted her family in Alford, England, and made the dangerous trip to America. It wasn't only that Cotton was her religious mentor, he had been her lover as well.

"When our love for each other passed beyond our love of the spirit within us, John-Luv was very worried. He prayed to Jesus to forgive him, especially after he married Sarah. And I prayed with him." She smiled. "But not so hard. I told him that we both loved Jesus. Loving each other, we did not hurt anyone and Jesus was forgiving. But he told me that we must also face our own conscience."

By conscience, I knew she meant Cotton's Calvinistic beliefs in the Scriptures, but I still wasn't sure whether she actually meant that she and John Cotton had made love. "Tell me about it," I urged her.

"Not now," she said. "I hath not done my duty." To my surprise she slipped down in the bed. Laughingly she held my limp cock erect and put it in her mouth.

"I didn't know Puritan ladies did such things," I gasped as she expertly brought me back to life."

"Some Puritan ladies, like Margaret Winthrop and Anne Bradstreet, probably did not." She was happily wiggling me back inside her. "But I was never a real Puritan lady. Papa saw to that."

For the next ten minutes, with bedsheets a heap on the floor, oblivious to the sleet and snow splattering against the window, Anne proved that, alone with her man, no matter how she might have appeared in public, she was in her words "a romper," "a cream pot of love" and very good at "rantum scantum." With her heels and hands kneading my "arse," I exploded inside her. Seconds later, with a long happy moan, she hugged me as I collapsed against her breasts. She soothed my back with her hands. "Thou needeth to sleep," she whispered, "and so do I." And we did—entwined until morning—deeply aware of each other even as we found new sleeping positions.

I awoke slowly, trying to recall the night before. I was certain that I had dreamed her. But there she was wide awake watching the snow swirling against the sliding glass window walls. She pointed to the digital clock. It was eight o'clock. "How doth it count the hours and minutes?" she asked.

"Electricity, dancing across positive and negative poles," I said, wondering how she would react if I flipped the remote switch on the television. But I decided against it. I was sure that the television or radio would either shock her out of her wits—or if she coped with them too easily then this was no resurrection but a glorious hoax.

I was much too pragmatic to accept her as the real Anne Hutchinson, but I had to admit that whatever her game might be it was adding an interesting dimension to my life. I gestured at the blizzard outside and told her that I was happy that she was here beside me and not frozen to death in the snow.

Sighing, she agreed, and said, "If there is no cow in the barn to take care of—and thou hast no other duties—we can stay in bed for another hour. If thou desireth, we can fuck again," she chuckled. "And thou canst tell me if thou still lovest me."

I asked her if she really understood that this was the twentieth century. She shook her head. "I know not what to believe. Papa liked to think of the future, but when I got dreamy Will would tell me the future will take care of itself." She smiled. "If I could have conceived so far ahead, I would have been certain that Christ Jesus would have returned by now."

"But you knew that the world had existed thousands of years before you or Jesus were born."

She nodded. "Most people—even Momma—believed that God created the world in seven days, and then made Adam and Eve, but when I was fifteen, I told Papa I was not so sure. Papa only laughed and told me I must keep my thoughts to myself—or between me and him."

"That's one reason I adopted you for an ancestor," I told her, laughing. "I like women who talk back to men."

"So that thou canst conquer them?"

"No. Because women who stimulate my brain, stimulate my pillicock and make me aware that I am a man. Your father must have been an exceptional man not to get angry with a daughter who challenged him."

"Momma was afraid that he treated me even better than my older brother, another John who loved me. Papa had been married before. His first wife died and left him with Susanna, my stepsister. But Susanna was married before we left Alford and Papa moved us all to London."

Rambling on, Anne told me that her father, Francis Marbury, had lost his parish at Alford and went to the Marshalea Prison because he had defied Bishop Aylmer and denounced many Church of England ministers who, he insisted, "were guilty of the death of many souls as have perished from the ignorance of their ministers who had been ordained by the bishops who knew they were unable.

"All that happened in 1578," Anne continued. "My papa was a young man, but many years later when I was born he was still a silenced minister. He was always in and out of trouble with the bishop. Then suddenly, when I was fifteen, he was given a small church in London—St. Martin's. The Bishop suddenly liked him because he was not a Puritan. Although he detested stupid ministers and priests, he was not against the bell, book, and candle ritual."

Anne smiled. "Papa used to tell us that Bishop Aylmer had been very furious with him. He told the bishop that many of the ministers couldn't even read the Scriptures or write their own names, but they thought they were

Jesus Christ nonetheless. The bishop called Papa an 'ass and fool.' But Papa knew he was telling the truth. He went to prison because of what he believed." She shrugged and a tiny smile crinkled around her eyes. "Like father, like daughter. My mother, Bridget, came from the Dryden family. She had earls in her family who could trace their ancestry back to Charlemagne. Her father was John Dryden, Esquire, but he was a Puritan. His grandson, who was named after him, wanted to write poetry and plays. His grandfather was not very happy about that."

"Your cousin, John Dryden, became a playwright and a well-known poet," I told her. "When he was older—to stay out of trouble with the King—he changed his religion and became an Anglican. You can read some of the plays that he wrote, if you'd like to." I was thinking as I said it that this woman probably knew more about seventeenth-century English literature than I did.

Clapping her hands excitedly, she said. "I love plays. Sometimes I pretended that I was an actor. When I was sixteen Papa took me to the Blackfriar's Theater. I met Master Shakespeare. The first time Momma was very upset. I was her second child. My brother John was two years older. But when I was five I could read more than he, poor dear. Like me, Momma had divers babies, but when I wasn't helping her with them I was reading all of Papa's books. But Papa told Momma that it was all right. Besides the Geneva Bible and an old Wycliffe Bible, Papa had Master Chaucer's *Canterbury Tales* and *Troilus and Cressida* and a collection of plays by Master Shakespeare. Papa was not too happy that I read them or that I read *Doctor Faustus* by Master Marlowe. Papa told me that they were all dissolute men and wenchers. Master Marlowe was killed in a brawl when he was young."

Anne sighed. "I can see that you have many books in this house. Papa had two hundred and thirty-four books with bindings and many others without. I counted them, and I read most of them. I never could speak Latin very well, but I read Caesar's *Gallic Wars,* some Cicero and Horace, and all of Ovid and the love poems of Catullus and Tiberius. Momma could speak French and she told Papa that Queen Elizabeth had learned to speak French. So she taught me. She laughed, "It came in handy when I met Harry Vane."

I was listening to her in amazement. It never occurred to me that Anne Hutchinson might actually have met William Shakespeare. Why had none of her background surfaced during her trials? I questioned her, certain at last that I had found her Achilles heel, but her answer was very convincing.

"Quite a few people in the Colony knew that I had read divers things but I was in trouble enough. Finally, not even John-Luv knew that dear Harry Vane gave me all the books that he had brought with him to Boston or that some nights Will and Harry and my children read Master Shakespeare's plays together." She paused, obviously reminiscing. "Papa told Momma that if women like Queen Elizabeth and Queen Anne could watch plays performed at court and Henrietta Maria, King Charles's wife, could even act in them in the palace, then, although he didn't approve of most of the silly stories, he wanted his daughter to be as good as any woman who was ruling men."

Anne smiled. "I was very pretty then and Papa enjoyed it when his little princess disagreed with him. He told Momma that King Charles should have married me instead of Henrietta Maria."

"What was Mr. Shakespeare like?" I asked, still dubious.

"He selected me from the crowd," Anne smiled. "It was at the winter theater, Blackfriar's, not the Globe. It was the tenth time I had been there and they were performing *The Taming of the Shrew*. I had seen six of his plays, and four of Master Jonson's. Papa took me twice a year with my brother, John, and once with Will Hutchinson to see *The Honest Whore,* a play by Master Dekker. That was the year before Will and I were married. I was nearly nineteen when I met Master Shakespeare. He and Master Jonson and Master Dekker came to see their own plays, and they were apt to ask people watching how they liked them. Sometimes they even acted in them."

"I can't believe that there were many women in the audiences."

Anne laughed. "There were quite a few wearing masks. Papa said they were whores. But Papa never took me dressed like a woman. I was disguised as a boy. I wore stockings, breeches, and a wool cap. But that afternoon, between acts, Master Shakespeare walked up to our bench and stared at me. He was about forty-five. I had big breasts even then. But they were strapped down and I was wearing a little pillow betwixt them to make my entire chest look big.

"'I wrote this play,' Master Shakespeare said to me. 'Dost thou like it?' I nodded and did not dare to speak. He touched my cheek with his finger, and said to Papa, with a hearty laugh. 'If this be a lad his beard is a long time coming. Perchance he could play Kate.'" Anne chuckled. "I never lived it down. Will did not see that play but I read it to him. He wanted me to tell Master Winthrop not to worry, that he had tamed Kate." She giggled. "But Master Winthrop would never have known what I meant. Master Winthrop had many, many books, but I am certain that no one in the Colony except me had Master Shakespeare's plays. Papa bought them in St. Paul's Churchyard. When he died they weren't listed in his will so Momma said I could have them."

"Living in London, you must have been aware of what was happening in England." I was thinking—leaving aside the religious implications of reincarnation, historians and television talk-show hosts would jump out of their skin to actually talk with someone who had walked on earth in the seventeenth century.

"Momma knew everything that was going on at the court and with the royalty," Anne said. "Especially when Elizabeth was queen. I knew that the kings and queens paid lip service to the Sciptures, but Puritans they were not. They did what they desired and repented later. Long before I was born Henry II of France had two mistresses, Diana of Poitiers and Lady Fleming. He wanted to make France and Scotland one country by marrying Mary Stuart from Scotland to his son, François. They were only about sixteen. François finally became king. But he died before he was twenty. Mary was Catholic, and she did not desire to live in Scotland. John Knox was the Presbyterian minister there at that time. He liked not Mary or any royalty. He wanted to keep women in their place."

Anne was leaning on her elbow, her breasts dangling provocatively close to my face as she continued to talk.

"Momma told me that Queen Elizabeth—they called her the Virgin Queen—finally decided not to marry. She promised Mary to unite the throne of England with Scotland if Mary married again and produced an heir. Mary had many suitors, but she married her cousin Henry Darnley. But Lord Darnley was a weak man and he drank too much. He was jealous of Mary and was positive that David Rizzio, Mary's advisor and secretary was her lover. Then Mary got pregnant. Was it Rizzio's son or Darnley's? Darnley was involved in a plot to murder Rizzio. Mary was so angry that she moved out of the castle, and moved in with James Hepburn, the Earl of Bothwell. Then Darnley, who was acquitted of murdering Rizzio, was murdered himself and everyone was sure that the Earl had done it. Bothwell was arrested, but Mary produced his acquittal and married him. Elizabeth was not much pleased about this. Before long, even though Mary loved Bothwell, the Pope annulled her marriage to him and told everybody that Bothwell had raped her."

Anne shrugged. "Mary had many enemies, but they convinced her that if she married the Duke of Norfolk, whom she had never met, everything would work out. But by now Elizabeth was angry, and she had Norfolk thrown in the Tower of London." Anne shook her head disgustedly. "You can understand now why Thomas Hooker, a Puritan, was sure that the destruction and end of England was imminent. And I believed him. It became even worse. Four years before I was born, Elizabeth arrested Mary and her executioner chopped off Mary's head. But then, Elizabeth had no choice. Mary's son, James, became king of England and Scotland. When Elizabeth died, James was thirteen years old. Many people called him Solomon, the son of David—meaning David Rizzio. James told Elizabeth before she died that he would deeply resent his mother's death but that didn't stop Elizabeth. Elizabeth died when I was eleven, but everyone knew what was happening at court.

"When James became king" Anne said—and it was obvious that she enjoyed an audience—"he told the scholars to translate a new version of the Bible. Papa said it was because James thought that the Geneva Bible did not properly establish the divine right of kings. James died in 1625." Anne chuckled. "Actually he loved men better than women, but he managed to begat an heir with Queen Anne, a Danish princess whom he married. Their son, Charles, became king. James was a Protestant, but Charles married Henrietta Maria, a Catholic girl, and he restored all the papal ritual to the Church of England. He appointed Thomas Laud as archbishop, and soon the country was overrun with pursuivants reporting back to Charles and to the archbishop any minister who was preaching without a surplice or who did not make his congregation kneel or did not use a wedding ring to perform a marriage." Anne shrugged. "That is why many of the Puritan ministers went to New England. If they had stayed in England, they would have been hung from the gallows. Some of them became Separatists and went to Holland, and I was thinking I might go there myself and join them. But I did not for a host of other reasons."

On her elbow, Anne was staring at me with tears in her eyes. "I liked London. It was such a big city. Papa said more than two hundred thousand people lived there, and so many things were happening all the time. It was beyond compare. Hast thou been there?"

I nodded. But you wouldn't recognize it now. The Thames is still there, and St. Paul's and the Tower. But it is very much bigger now. Millions of people live there."

"Millions?" Anne's voice echoed mine. "I cannot conceive millions." She kissed me passionately, but she was trembling and snuggled against my neck. "Dear Robert, I am frightened. Tell me why I am here? I keep remembering my poor children. Why didst God bring me to life without them? What art thou going to do with me?"

4

How could I answer Anne's questions? I tried to tell her that she was the believer in Jesus, not me. I knew that Jesus had said, "He who believes in Him who sent me has everlasting life . . . has passed from death to life." But as for me, I told her, "I always have believed that when I'm dead I will be dead forever, you rascal you."

She didn't laugh, or think that was funny. "Jesus told the Jews," she said, 'Do not marvel at this: for the hour is coming in which all who are in their graves will hear His voice and come forth—those who have done good, to the resurrection of life—and those who have done evil to the resurrection of condemnation.'"

I shrugged. "But three hundred and fifty years ago, you were quite sure that your mortal body would never be seen again." I hugged her. "Whoever you are, you are a very pretty woman and obviously a very loving woman. I don't feel guilty. You're obviously old enough to have known what you were doing last night and this morning. But whoever you are, I'm damned sure that I haven't been making love to the noncorporeal spirit of Anne Hutchinson. You are a live female with your heart throbbing and your vagina ready. If I really believed that it was possible, after some three hundred and fifty years, that you could be reconstituted in exactly the same physical body that you inhabited at the time of your death—and that by some wild chance your atoms would suddenly coalesce on my doorstep in the middle of a noreaster—I would bow down to the Lord shivering and beg his mercy and

She looked at me solemnly and then brushed my lips with hers. "I know not whether my body be a mortal body or why I am here." Her hand wandered over her face and her breasts as she spoke. "Perchance you perceive me as a corruptible body and I seem to function as a mortal body—but in truth this may be the hour Jesus spoke of, and the person you seem to behold as me is really a spirit."

"That's silly," I said. "Do you know how many people are alive today on this planet?" Four billion or more. Do you know how many have lived and died, since you died?" I shook my head. "The number is astronomical. Prob-

30

ably a trillion. If the millennium is here, are they all going to hear God's voice and come to life? The world will be so crowded no one will be able to sit down. There will be standing room only."

She smiled sadly. "Thou art telling me that resurrection is not possible. But are not all those people living, dying, being born—are they not a continuous resurrection of the Spirit? I understand not your big numbers, but since the Holy Ghost dwelleth in everyone and God hath created me and you, is it not possible that God hath the power, if he desireth, to re-form the dust of us and re-create us?"

"But why you?" I demanded. "And why am I involved? Why hasn't God done it before?"

"How dost thou know He has not?" She smiled, "But who would believe anyone who tells you 'I have returned from the dead.' Perhaps God likes to juggle. Perhaps I am here because I doubted such a thing happened. Perhaps I am here because thou loveth me. Like Paul in the Scriptures, John Wilson was afraid that people would eat, drink, fornicate, and never work for their salvation if there was no resurrection." She shrugged. "But that is not true." She was silent for a few minutes as we both tried to unravel this impossible dream. Then she said, "Papa told me that one thing he cherished about Papists is that they knew God had a sense of humor." She laughed. "Master Wilson certainly had not one."

I grinned and told her that she was going to be very surprised to discover that three centuries later she was now outnumbered. There were more than three million Papists in Boston and what was more, the Pope had recently appointed a new bishop, who told all the Catholics, "After Boston, there is only one place to go—Heaven." But I assured her that Boston wasn't Heaven.

"For the moment," I said, "the weather is cutting us off from reality. It's time to break our fast."

There was plenty of food in the house, and I had to admit that although I was snowbound with a very religious woman, at least her indwelling spirit was most affectionate and loving. I didn't tell her that it occurred to me that if she were really resurrected, God had answered one problem that had baffled ministers and philosophers for centuries. If Anne truly was in the vanguard of a great awakening of the dead, then the good Lord had sense enough not to start people all over from birth. On that basis, Anne had been lucky that she died rather early in life. A world full of four score and ten grandmothers and grandfathers would be difficult to cope with.

I was also sure of one thing: Hugh Hefner would be very happy to have this Anne pose for a *Playboy* centerfold. As a fifty-two year old, she had aged in the style of many female cats, who despite numerous litters remain lean, agile, and ready for fertilization long after all their ova are gone. Anne could compete with any of the occasional fifty-year-olds to whom *Playboy* occasionally condescended and showed in nubile full color.

I was sure of another thing. If by some amazing throw of the dice that had restored the dissipated energy of a body long dead and Anne had reappeared on earth, I needed to come to terms with the idea gradually. At least, I thought, this is only Wednesday morning. I still had twelve days before Emily returned and the top blew off.

Right now, in a very real sense, I was living with a child bride. Her fifty-two-year-old body and brain were in top shape, and she could make love as well or better than some seven generations of ladies who had succeeded her on earth, but could she, or any seventeenth-century brain, cope with three hundred and fifty years of future shock? Permanent death for most people might be easier to accept than the horror of rehabilitation into a world they had never made nor could ever conceive.

Before I left her to make breakfast, I reintroduced her to the bathroom. Last night she hadn't noticed her reflection in the big mirror that flanked one wall. Now she stared at her naked self with some surprise, and her eyes filled with tears. "I know that I am Anne Hutchinson. But I do not remember this woman's body that I now inhabit."

I stared at her astonished. "You mean you don't recognize yourself?" I was suddenly totally suspicious again. "What did you look like?" I knew that, unlike the cases of Winthrop, Cotton, Wheelwright, and Harry Vane, no one had ever painted or drawn a portrait of Anne or Will Hutchinson.

She shrugged. "I have not seen my face since I left the Colony to live on the Island. When Edward brought some of our things from Boston, my looking glass had disappeared. Neither my sister Katherine nor Mary Dyer had one. She smiled. "Wouldst thou remember how you looked if thou had not seen thy face for seven years? I am older, I think. My face is leaner." She lifted her breasts with her hands. "These are bigger and not so firm. Methinks I am me and no mistake."

I found her a toothbrush and toothpaste and showed her the shower stall and the bathtub. She quickly grasped how to control water, but washing with me "in the rain" did not appeal to her. Tubs she knew. She told me that once or twice a month when the men were all out of the house, the ladies heated water in the kettles over the fire and washed all over. In the summer she bathed in a freshwater pond near her farm in Mt. Wolleystone not far from the Chevi Hills. "It was close to the Hutchinson farm," she said. "Will and I washed there in warm weather while the children swam and played naked in the sunlight."

Anne spat out the toothpaste that I gave her and asked for salt, which I produced from the kitchen. When she got in the tub she was ecstatic. With her breasts floating in the warm water, she held up a washcloth and laughed. "Even in the winter, I used a cloth for my parts and made Will use one too. But many Puritans washed not much, nor did royalty. Momma said they poured perfume all over themselves to cover up the stink." She crinkled her nose. "At my meetings I told everybody that they must always be prepared. God desireth us to arrive in Heaven clean in body and in spirit." The whiteness of the soap continued to amaze her. She tasted it and spat it out. "It looketh fine enough to eat," she said apologetically.

She stayed in the tub while I showered and shaved, a process that reminded her of Will, who pared his face with a much bigger open razor. "Will did not have a beard like Master Winthrop wore," she said. "It was too much trouble."

I gave her a towel and when she picked up the salt to brush her teeth, I complimented her on what seemed to be a complete set of white teeth without cavities. "Papa saw Queen Elizabeth once," she said. "He said that her teeth were almost black from eating too much sugar and chocolate. I guess it is fortunate that I never overly fancied sugar."

Waiting for her in the kitchen, I saw the newspaper boy trudge through a drift to leave the morning *Globe*. Retrieving it, I turned the pages quickly, but there was no mention of a missing woman. Thinking that if she were an escapee from some mental home, it might not have made the morning papers. I turned on the radio to wait for the news. Wrapped in my bathrobe, carrying a hairbrush she had found, Anne pattered into the room shyly, looking in all directions. "Thou must have friends who have come?" she said. Then she noticed the sound was coming from the radio.

"My friends all live in that little box," I told her facetiously.

"Electricity?" she asked with raised eyebrows, obviously attributing all miracles to that word. "Yet I knoweth not what that is."

"Yes, you do," I told her. "Brush your hair fast." I tore some small pieces from the newspaper. "Hold your brush over the paper." She did and the paper jumped and clung to it. Her face was a broad smile. "Magnetism," she laughed. "I know that."

"More or less," I said. "Lightning is a better example."

She nodded, "It is God challenging us, reminding us that He is in Heaven."

I shrugged and tried to explain that God or someone had let men learn that the sound of voices and pictures of themselves could be transmitted by currents through the air. I knew that in the seventeenth century they had used windmills to grind the grain and saw wood, and I told her that windmills and water falling and huge fires burning could all make electricity. "With electricity we can send our voices and pictures of ourselves around the world. We no longer have to wait months to know what is happening in England or anywhere. If the queen, who is Elizabeth II, gets a pimple on her neck, everyone in the United States will know it a few hours later."

The station was now playing rock music, and Anne held her hands over her ears. "I never heard such noisy music. Canst thou stop the electricity?" she pleaded. "It maketh my brain go prittle prattle."

When the radio was quiet, Anne asked me what was the United States. I laughed. "Well, as you know, it all started with the American colonists coming here seeking religious freedom. Many of them, like you and Roger Williams, believed that you should be able to think for yourself and believe what you wished to about God and salvation and grace. But of course, you were banished because you believed in freedom of speech. But the King and even John Winthrop realized that too much freedom was a very dangerous idea. If people didn't obey the laws, good or bad, the Colony wouldn't survive. I know that at your trial, Winthrop told you that you had to obey the Fifth Commandment and honor thy fathers, who were the State, and history records that you, bless your heart, didn't agree with him. A hundred years later, most people in the colonies and in America didn't think like Winthrop did either. They signed a Declaration of Independence and went to war against England and King George. They drove the king of England's soldiers out of America. It was a long war. A Revolutionary War." I grinned at her. "One of the reasons that I fell in love with you is that you were one of the rebels who helped start it."

"Dost thou still have a governor?"

I nodded, "Yes, and a big State House with a statue of you standing in front of it."

Smiling, she shook her head. Obviously she didn't believe that anyone had made a statue of her. "This time methinks I will hold my tongue. I told Will before he died that we should all stop making rules and laws. We should teach people to believe in God. Then we do not need magistrates."

I grinned at her. "The truth is you were probably America's first anarchist. But I don't know whether you really believe that we can get along without man-made laws."

"Dost thou believe in God?"

"Sort of," I said and hugged her. "I believe in the God that is inside your heart and behind your smiling eyes."

Anne was happy with the suggestion of bacon and eggs for breakfast and assured me that it was a woman's place to scramble the eggs. The thinness of the bacon, the milk "in a box" and particularly the bread popping up in the toaster fascinated her. *Electricity* was fast becoming her favorite word. When it created a bright ring of fire on the stove, she thought it was most beautiful. She pointed to the living room. "Thou only needeth a fireroom to keep warm and enjoy friends," she said. "And thou needest no tinder box if the fire dieth."

She examined a fork, touching the prongs with her fingers. "Methinks I heard of this tool," she said. "Master Winthrop had one sent to him by a friend in England, but he never used it." She ate her eggs with a spoon and remarked that I must be very rich to have silver and so many plates.

I made some coffee, which she said she had tasted. "Twice a ship brought some coffee beans into Boston, but they cost many pounds and we could not grind them like this," she said. "But if thou hast some cider in the cellar I would desire that."

I remembered that for many years the Puritans, and even John Winthrop, wouldn't drink water, fearing that it might carry some disease. A hundred years later our forefathers, like John Adams and Benjamin Franklin, were only able to face the world after a flagon or two of hard cider. I told her that although I had some beer, today most people didn't drink alcohol with breakfast—except for occasional champagne breakfasts. Thinking that whatever else this might be it was certainly a time for a celebration, I opened a bottle of champagne. She tasted it gingerly and it tickled her nose. "Methinks this will make one more boosey than canary or rum," she said, but she finished her glass and grinned sheepishly at me. "Now I am not so much at sixes and sevens."

"Why are you nervous?" I asked. "Don't let my doubts about you worry you. I'm happy that you're here and I don't care whether you're a spirit or not."

"That doth not worry me," she said. She opened her bathrobe. "If any of thy friends arrive, how canst I meet them like this?" She smiled. "I looked at your wife's clothing but methinks they will not fit me, and even if they did I would not be so forward as to wear them. If thou hast some cloth, like wool or linen or cambric, and a needle and thread, I can make a gown."

I knew that she was quite a few pounds lighter than Emily, but the real reason that I didn't go searching in Emily's closets and drawers for things like bras and panties and even shoes was that when Emily came home, she'd know that I had been messing around in her things. I had never shown any transvestite tendencies, but the need to wear women's clothes might be easier to explain than how I had given some of her stuff to Anne Hutchinson, or that I had entertained a female guest for two weeks while she was gone.

I was now reasonably sure that this wasn't some ingenious hoax that Dave Hedman had cooked up with Emily, but I was equally certain, too, that if I told anyone that a woman nearly four hundred years old had moved in and slept with me while Emily was in Europe, it wouldn't be long before I was incarcerated in some mental hospital.

I assured Anne that she didn't have to make a dress. Tomorrow, although it was still snowing heavily, we were in for a spring thaw. The streets would be quickly cleared. I'd take her shopping, and buy her several dresses and whatever other things she needed. In the meantime she didn't have to worry. No friends were going to arrive today. For the next twenty-four hours we were as snug as two bugs in a rug.

I had no sooner said the words than the telephone rang. Anne jumped out of her chair and clung to me as I answered it. "More voices by electricity,"

I assured her and let her listen.

"Are you talking to me?" a female voice accosted me over the phone. It was Liz Johnson, a friend of ours. The Johnsons lived in Braintree, a few miles away. Chuck had told me, after I had spoken at the First Parish Church, that he could trace his ancestry back to a Johnson family who were among the first to arrive in the Massachusetts Bay Colony and that he had always been interested in his colonial past. I was tempted to tell Liz that a former Puritan was listening to her but I resisted the impulse.

"Sorry," I told her. "Since Emily left I've been talking to myself." I smiled quizzically at Anne hoping that there wasn't more truth than poetry in my words.

"Chuck and I want you to come to dinner Saturday night," Liz said. "Dave Hedman and Barbara Zoltan, a woman friend of his, are coming. I told Emily that we wouldn't take no for an answer."

I was in no mood to spend an evening playing bridge or explaining how I was spending my time while Emily was gone. Although Saturday was a few days away, I was wondering how I could leave Anne, assuming that she was still here. I protested and told Liz that I was sorry and I cited the snow and the impossible driving. "You don't have to worry," I told her, "I have plenty to eat."

"I know the real reason that you can't come," Liz said. "You're having an affair with Anne Hutchinson." I could hear her laughing hilariously, and I knew that Emily must have reported my conversation to her. "Chuck won't mind," Liz said chuckling. "You can bring her along."

Smiling at Anne as we were listening, an insane idea, complete with a covering excuse, jumped into my brain. "As a matter of fact, I might just do that," I said. "A lady who calls herself Anne Hutchinson telephoned me yesterday and told me that she knows a great deal about the real Anne Hutchinson. I told her that I would meet her in Boston on Saturday and take her to dinner."

"Does Emily know this woman?" Liz suddenly didn't sound so cordial.

"No," I said cheerfully. "I told you that Mrs. Hutchinson just phoned yesterday. Somehow she heard about my 'sermon.'" As I spoke to Liz, it occurred to me that this would be a good time to flush Dave Hedman out. "Actually, I think Dave will be fascinated. He told me that he was interested in the phenomenon of past-life regression under hypnosis. Maybe he'll try it on Anne. It will be a learning experience for all of us."

A little reluctantly, Liz agreed that I could bring my new woman friend. I was watching Anne's face as I mentioned Dave's name but there was no reaction whatever. She obviously had never heard the name before. Either she was an excellent actress or I had to give up the idea that she might be one of Dave's patients.

Anne was more startled by the telephone than anything she had seen thus far. "With electricity, thou canst talk to all thy friends without seeing them," she said in awe. "But thou cannot see their faces to tell what they may be thinking."

Anne asked me to telephone another friend so that she could hear them and was very disappointed when I told her that unlike her I didn't have many friends or relatives in Boston. A little testily I showed her the Boston telephone directory and told her that she could call up her relatives. She quickly grasped that the directory listed telephone numbers and that she could telephone anyone by electricity. To my surprise, without glasses, she could read the fine print in the telephone book. She slowly flipped her way to the H's and was counting the Hutchinsons.

"They're probably all relatives of yours," I told her. "You and Will were a population explosion all by yourself." She counted sixty-two Hutchinsons and was delighted to discover that there were only twenty Winthrops and only a few Welds. "Try Wilson," I told her. She did and shrieked in dismay. There was a solid page of Wilson phone listings, but only about fifteen Cottons. "No matter what their religion," I told her, "theologically, the Wilsons still outnumber you."

I still couldn't believe that at fifty-two she could read the phone book without glasses. "Will had spectacles," she shrugged, "but I needed them not. My eyes were strong from much reading." Then, in very feminine fashion, she changed the subject. "Thou tellest me thou loves me, but methinks thou art not proud of me. Thou said to your friend that I am a woman who thinks I am Anne Hutchinson, but thou dost not believe it."

"Jesus Christ," I yelled at her, "whether I believe you or not, I'm in awe of you."

"You take the Lord's name in vain," she said and her eyes were big and solemn. "His spirit is not within you."

"I'm sorry," I said, and hugged her. "Before you leave I may even become a born-again Christian. But right now, I'm not introducing you as a resurrected woman to my friends." I smiled at her weakly. "And keep something else in mind. I'm married. We're breaking the Seventh Commandment. Committing adultery."

She laughed. "Poor Robert. You forgot. Will is dead. Thou art committing adultery. I am not. I can even get married again."

"Not to me," I assured her. "I may have Muslim ideas, but two wives is still against the law in the Massachusetts Bay Colony."

5

Wondering how we were going to spend the day, I told her that for the next few hours I needed to gather my wits. To do so, like she had done when she was on trial, I needed to write it all down. I showed her a pile of books. "They're all about you," I told her, deciding that any new information she might acquire about Anne Hutchinson was already in her head. "It's really too bad you didn't keep a diary; you could have saved all this speculation about yourself."

"Perchance that is why I am here," she said with a doubtful laugh. "My beloved Jesus Christ is giving me a second chance." Turning the books over, she read the titles with sudden interest: *The Life of Anne Hutchinson* by George Ellis; *Anne Hutchinson, the American Jezebel* by Helen Augur; *Unafraid, A Life of Anne Hutchinson* by Winifred King Rugg; *Scarlet Anne* by Theda Kenyon; *A Woman Misunderstood* by Reginald Bolton, and *Divine Rebel* by Selma Williams, which, so far as I knew, was the only one in print and had been written by a woman who admired her as much as I did.

"There's more," I said, piling books in her lap. "Here's *Saints and Sectaries* by Emery Battis. It's all about you." I laughed. "But Emery was quite sure that you were no saint. Here's a play, *Goodly Creatures*, by William Gibson. You're the star. Gibson kind of likes you. And here are two novels, *Witness* by Mary Heidish and *Covenant of Grace* by Jane Rushmore. They were written just a few years ago. If that's not enough, here are Winthrop's *Journals*, which he kept until he died. He didn't like you very much. And here's *The Antinomian Controversy* by Charles Adams. He was so intrigued by you that he collected the transcript of your trials, plus a book that Winthrop wrote about you after the trials and a sermon by John Cotton that mentions the problems he had with you. Adams collected them for scholars to offer whatever evidence that might still be available, so that they could figure out what you were up to and what kind of person you really were. Your name and the fact that you were banished for your religious beliefs fascinates millions of people. Your name is in all the history books."

"Methinks I am a famous person," Anne said quite coolly. "But I understandeth not why. All I desired was that men and women find God within them."

38

"Don't worry," I told her. "Fame is fleeting. Most of these books are out of print. Today very few people know your name or have read about you. If by some chance you were on the 'Good Morning America' show tomorrow, and told millions of people that you were resurrected, two hundred million Americans would ask: 'Who the Hell is Anne Hutchinson?'"

She listened to me wide-eyed, not fully comprehending. "You have to understand," I said, knowing that I couldn't possibly bring her up-to-date, "today people don't worry much about the Holy Ghost or God. Some people even think God is dead. But I think that you're unique—not because you believe in Jesus but because you talked back to men at a time when women kept their mouths shut. Even today, many men try to convince women that they alone sit at the right hand of God."

I shrugged, and continued. "I suppose I should bring you up-to-date. Up until about seventy years ago, men managed to stay almost completely in power. Then women were finally permitted to vote for the man running for governor or president who pleased them best. Long before that, you talked back. I know that you told men and women that God loved them and that they were all under a Covenant of Grace, no matter what they did. They called you a daughter of Satan then, but you'd be a heroine now. For a hundred years after you died, you were bad news. No one wrote a biography of you until 1845, nearly two hundred years later. Forty years after that, Charles Adams 'discovered' you. But another fifty years went by, until the 1930s, and then a few women, who weren't afraid of men, became aware that you were the first fly in the ointment. Helen Augur, Winifred King Rugg, and one man, Reginald Bolton, wrote those biographies you see there, but they couldn't figure out what motivated you. Another thirty years went by. Then in 1962 Battis decided you deserved a new interpretation, a psychological study."

I laughed. "I am sure you don't know what *psychological* means but don't let it go to your head. Battis' book is out of print, and very few Americans ever read it anyway. The truth is that last night, if you had knocked on any other door and told whoever answered it that you were Anne Hutchinson, they probably would have called the police."

"Police?"

"The constable."

She smiled. "Will was a constable some of the time. Thou dost not have to call the constable. I will leave."

"Where will you go?"

"I know not." Tears were running down her cheeks. "I will pray to my beloved Jesus to put me back where I came from."

I hugged her. "Forget it. Whatever happens I won't banish you." I grinned at her. "If I really brought you back to life, then—like it or not—I'm stuck with you."

I was determined, if nothing else, to hide behind the typewriter and try to determine whether this woman was really only a weird catalytic reaction that didn't exist at all. But if she did exist, what was I going to do with her? Before I started writing, I showed her an example of another electric miracle. She was awed by the plastic typewriter case, which I told her was a new kind of material stronger than wood. She quickly grasped the typewriter keyboard and spelled her name, "Anne Hutchinson," and then slowly, using one finger, she typed "is fearful. Robert doth not believe she is really Anne. Doth Anne believe? No. Anne still doth not believe that she liveth. Anne is in New Netherlands. Her children are dead. Soon the Mohegans will murder her. They are firing the faggots——." She stopped picking out the letters and stared at what she had typed and burst into tears. "I cannot think straight," she said. "Maybe I am dreaming. Perchance I will soon wake up."

She sobbed into my shoulder. "Don't cry," I told her, "I am unnerved enough. Maybe, like your friend Mr. Shakespeare said, "We are all such stuff as dreams are made of.'" I shrugged. "Maybe there is a God out there who loves you. Maybe He is dreaming both of us. Let's pray that He never stops."

Another thought crossed my mind. I had often been amused by the idea of a time warp. Was science fiction nonsense? Suddenly I was wondering if a massacre in 1643, in what is now known as New York, was somehow occurring simultaneously with the "reality" of the world three and a half centuries later. Was time as we knew it an illusion? Were men and women living in centuries past and centuries future coexisting in the same time frame?

"Thou art certain that I am dead," Anne said, breaking into my thoughts.

"Not after last night," I assured her. "I am quite sure that if I prick thee—thou wilt bleed." I didn't tell her that not only was I convinced she was quite real and that I was not hallucinating, but also I was sure all this would end when the men in the white coats arrived and solicitously took their "Anne" back to whatever asylum she had escaped from.

The truth was that I didn't want to believe that either. While the concept of resurrection had never interested me very much, for many years I had accepted the idea of an impersonal kind of reincarnation. Based on our twentieth-century knowledge of the universe, no energy ever disappears. I never believed that I could personally walk the earth again in a future era but I had often had strange dreams of past lives. After I had had a few drinks, to startle my friends, I would tell them that I was sure that I had been a student of Socrates and that I had tried to convince Socrates not to be a martyr. It was better to live than drink the hemlock and be remembered forever. Or I might have facetiously told them that I was sure that I had been a calvary officer in Napoleon's army and tried to dissuade Napoleon from seeking more fame by invading Russia. Having had a long-time love affair with butterflies, I was closest to my real beliefs when I told them I was quite sure that somewhere along the line, I had joined a more realistic kind of reincarnation, a never-ending circle. In previous lives, I had crawled the earth as a caterpillar and later flying as a beautiful butterfly, Monarch of all I surveyed, I had kept the cycle in motion until I finally came back as a man.

But reincarnation is an Oriental idea. The early Christians came up with a more saleable proposition. "By man came death but also came the resurrection of the dead." One dies as the Adam-man and comes back in one's own image as the Christ-man. Being reincarnated, of course, doesn't restore one's body and one's soul. The soul, or the energy of the spirit, may survive, but it is unlikely that one will remember who one was, and the chances are that in successive rebirths a man or woman won't resemble his or her present self. On the other hand, to rise from the grave and recognize all one's old friends and have a reunion in Heaven—that is really something to look forward to! Especially if you come back in reasonably good health.

So far as we know, no resurrection of any sort has happened yet. But nothing disappears from the earth. Scientists agree that when we die the energy that comprised our bodies simply assumes a different form. So isn't it possible that a chance concatenation of atomic impulses could reassemble the body and mind of one long dead? And let him—her in this case—continue to live out life hundreds of years later? If anyone had suggested such an idea to me a week ago, I would have laughed and said, "Why not?" Put enough software into a computer, feed in the right kind of plot you want, and the computer will write a story better than I or anyone else could dream up. But I wouldn't have believed it. Now, watching Anne as she turned the pages of books about herself, I wasn't so sure. I suppose I should have been frightened. Maybe I was slowly going crazy? Perhaps I was just hallucinating. Maybe, like those stories of *Topper* or *Donna Flor and Her Two Husbands,* I had created my own ghost who talked to me, but whom no one else could see.

As I was thinking these thoughts, the front doorbell rang. I realized that it was the newspaper boy collecting. I gave Anne two dollars and told her who he was. She should open the front door and pay him. Smiling and asking me whether dollars were wampum, she greeted the boy. It was obvious that she wasn't a ghost. He could see her. He squirmed a little uncomfortably when she told him, "Thou remindeth me of my second William—poor William, he was only twelve. He was murdered by the Indians, too." She asked the boy if he had ever seen any Indians and he shook his head, and told her, "Just in the movies."

Back on the window-walled porch where I was typing, Anne curled up in a chair next to the fireplace that I had lit. For a moment she ignored the pile of books I had given her and stared at the wind-driven snow splattering question marks on the windows. Then she said quietly, "They banished me because I believed in miracles and because the miracles in the Scriptures were not the end of miracles. I told them that miracles could still happen." She smiled lovingly at me. "I know not why I, or thee, have been chosen or whether, like the magistrates and ministers in the Colony, thou willst reject me, but I am not, as thou may thinketh, a mad woman. I know what Isaiah said: 'Thy dead shall live, my dead shall rise.' And Paul told the Thessalonians: 'If we believe that Jesus died and rose again so God will bring Him those who sleep in Jesus . . . and the dead in Christ will rise first.' And to the Corinthians Paul said: 'If there were no resurrection of the dead . . . We of all men are most to be pitied . . . for all is vain. Let us eat and drink for tomorrow we die!'"

She sighed, "In truth, dear Robert, I believed that much of this was poetry written to reassure those who were afraid to lose their bodies. I was not afraid to lose mine because I knew that Christ Jesus is continuously resurrected and there is no death for those who discover that love is an indwelling Spirit within them. When that happens, a man or woman becomes Jesus."

"That's another reason why you were banished," I said. "John Winthrop and Thomas Dudley and most of the ministers and magistrates expected that come the millennium they would rise from the grave and greet each other as long lost friends." I laughed. "You can stop worrying about one thing. The world hasn't changed that much. Millions of people we now call Christian fundamentalists, Seventh-Day Adventists, Jehovah's Witnesses, and others believe that the soul survives and will go to Heaven and have a spiritual body that is recognizable. I don't know what happens to the babies who die young, or in childbirth," I said a little sarcastically, "but if they are resurrected, no one will know to whom they belong. Maybe there's an adoption agency in Heaven."

Anne was listening to me with a faraway expression on her face. Finally she said, "'And I saw the souls of those who had been beheaded for their witness to Jesus and the word of God . . . and they lived and reigned with Christ a thousand years . . . But the rest of the dead did not live again until the thousand years were finished.'" She was quoting from Revelation. She smiled at me a little uncertainly. "I never really believed the revelations in the Scriptures. But perchance this is the first resurrection."

I shrugged. "That's the problem. Neither you nor anyone else, then or now, could convince most sane people that you really have returned from the dead. Your four Johns may have believed in a Second Coming, but God help the person who insists today that he or she is one of the saints that is marching in." I held her hand. "You have to understand, I don't believe in miracles—past, present or future. Anyway, you're too sexy and earthy and lustful to arrive at the First Coming. I'm sure that Jesus would have made you wait another thousand years. When God opens the Book of Life, he'll get around to dealing with the rest of us."

She smiled at my teasing. "I am not lustful—just loving. But even if I were a whore, it doth not matter. God hath given us a covenant of grace. If you believe that the Holy Ghost abides within you, nothing else matters. You will be saved."

"But what if I don't believe that?"

"It is impossible to live and not believe that God is within you."

"That's one more reason why you were banished," I told her. "You were living in an utopian theocracy. You told everybody that it didn't matter what they did in life—whether they worked hard, prayed to God, went to church, or drank booze, chased women or did or didn't build a good estate in this life. Nothing mattered. Your friend, Captain John Underhill, got caught with his pants down in the cooper's wife's house behind locked doors. He was your disciple. He told John Winthrop that they were getting religion together. Winthrop didn't belief him. Underhill was stripped of his rank as head of the militia and kicked out of the Colony. Do you think John Underhill will be saved?"

"Poor Robert," she sighed. "Thou still dost not believe. When thou dost, thou wilt know that God doesn't condemn men and women because they love one another."

"God may not, but men and women do," I said. "You've never met my wife but I don't think she will love you." I shrugged. "But I agree with you. What you are saying is really a democratic point of view. In a very real sense you were one of the first revolutionaries in America. You were writing a Declaration of Independence and a First Amendment to the Constitution a hundred years before your time. You were undermining the Calvinistic work ethic. Do you understand what I am saying? Do you know what democracy really means? Even today, most people don't know know how to function in a democracy, and they don't like rebels any more or people with revolutionary ideas. The only revolution Americans respect is their own revolution. They give lip service to democracy, but they elect men like Winthrop and Dudley, who take charge and crack the whip and get things done."

"I had much conversation with Harry Vane and John Cotton about democracy," she said. "John-Luv did not believe in democracy. He told me, 'I do not conceive that God did ordain democracy as a fit government for either church or commonwealth. If the people be governors, who shall be governed?'" Anne had curled her legs partially under her. She knew that her bathrobe wasn't covering her crotch, and she intercepted my interested glance with a smile. "At the moment, what I did or did not do is not the problem. For some reason, both my soul and body are here. Unless thou desirest my body again, you may continue to push the buttons on your machine, and I will read about myself. Perchance in these books I may find some reason why I am here."

Once again it crossed my mind that it might be a mistake to let her "learn" about her life from other sources. A clever woman—which Anne obviously was—could absorb enough from these biograpies to make the reality of her all the more believable. But in spite of myself I was begining to accept the idea that this woman was really Anne Hutchinson.

If I couldn't swallow personal resurrection, there had to be some answer. Death and renewal had been built into the religions and mythologies of the world since the beginning of man. Lesser forms of life die and they are reborn. Many living forms survive through parthogenesis. In the twentieth-century organ transplants—hearts, livers, bone marrow and eventually brains from otherwise dead bodies—have become a partial resurrection from death. Frozen sperm and ova and carefully frozen fetuses donated by men and women in the prime of their sexual life makes a resurrection of their genes centuries from now completely possible. Ultimately, cryogenic specialists may replicate biblical resurrection by freezing bodies for many centuries and restoring them to life in another era.

Perhaps if men and women dared to think about the miracle of their own lives, the miracle of an occasional bodily resurrection was not beyond belief. Either Anne was revived by pure chance—or else someone "up there" had listened to my plea to adopt an ancestor. Whatever the case and like it or not, for the moment, I was both the father-protector and lover of a child bride, aged fifty-two.

6

By late afternoon the day was beginning to assume overtones of marital domesticity. Sitting at the typewriter I was doing more thinking than writing, and I was wondering in particular how I would introduce Anne to other twentieth-century marvels such as organ transplants, genetic engineering, the automobile, airplane, television, and—even more mind-boggling—how to give her a three-hundred-and-fifty-year capsule history of a world that in one way, at least, she had helped to create.

Around one o'clock I made her a ham sandwich and opened a bottle of beer, which she ate and drank with appreciated "umms" and "thank thees" but now she was totally engrossed and didn't stop reading or turning the pages of more than ten books about her that I had accumulated. But then, as the day grew shorter, I noticed her staring into space and her eyes were wet with tears.

"Does reliving your past make you morose?" I asked.

"No. I am angry." She pointed a finger at the pile of books. "I have skimmed them, but mostly what they wrote about me is all inside out—especially that Master Battis." She picked up the book *Saints and Strangers* and read: "John Winthrop had a keen and appreciative eye for a pretty face, even those women he disliked. When he had dealings with a pretty woman he took good care to note her comeliness on the pages of his journal . . . but neither he nor his contemporaries thought Anne Hutchinson sufficiently beautiful to be worthy of comment. He seems to have reserved the word 'fierce' to describe the New England weather and the temper of Anne Hutchinson.'"

"I may not be beautiful," Anne continued, her nostrils flaring delightfully. "But I am certain that Master Winthrop would have liked to subdue me with a whip and his prick instead of words. Hast thou read all his *Journals*?" She pointed at the two volumes. "I shall read them much more carefully but from what I have seen, Master Winthrop was more interested in reporting adultery and sin and describing the birth of monsters than he was in anything else. Poor Margaret. She was too weak. Master Winthrop needed a witch to make him fly right."

She sighed. "I am older now, but I was only forty-two when I arrived in

Boston on the *Griffin*. I think I was pretty and I had nice clothes that I had made myself. Master Symmes, the preacher, followed me around the ship like a dog in heat. And John-Luv was very happy to see me when I arrived. Dost thou think I am ugly?"

I laughed. "With your wide-apart green eyes practically swallowing any man who looks at you, your full lips pouting, and your high cheekbones and square jaw and a strange kind of glow to your skin, with your chin stuck out ready to challenge any man, you are not only pretty but you are provocative and erotic. When you challenged poor Master Symmes the way you presumably did, quoting Jesus and telling him that you could tell him things that he could not bear to hear—then for him, at least, you probably turned into the kind of woman that some men would like to turn over their knee and spank before they fuck them."

"Art thou that kind of man?"

"I don't want to spank you," I chuckled. "But I'm sure that you're aware that you are a woman who can make a man erotic and ready for action without realizing it and whether he's ready or not."

"I understand not *erotic,*" she smiled. "But thou dost sound like Will sometimes. Dost thou desire to fuck?"

I grinned at her. "Eventually—but right now I am going to have a cocktail." I explained that the word didn't really mean a "cock's tail," but that after drinking one some men thought they were the only rooster in the barnyard. That restored her sense of humor.

She told me that she rarely drank anything but a little wine—or sometimes a rum flip but she would try a cocktail. She tasted my scotch but didn't like it. "Strong water," she said. "Will called it *usky beathea,* the Scottish words for water of life." She laughed. "Thou hadst ought be careful. Too much of it takes away the life between a man's legs."

I poured a couple of jiggers of vodka into cranberry juice and told her that it was called a Cape Codder, which amused her. She remembered that the Separatists lived on Cape Cod. But the Puritans in Boston never liked them. She drank it enthusiastically and asked for another. By the time she was sipping the second one, her tongue was really loose and an idea occurred to me.

I could not only introduce her to televison but I could videotape her at the same time. No matter what happened, if I had a tape of her I could prove at least that she existed. Watching me set up my television camera on a tripod, she was totally intrigued. I placed her on the living-room couch with a small flood lighting her area. But when I turned on the television and the tape recorder and she saw herself appear as a cloudy image on the screen, she screamed and held her face. "It's like a mirror," I told her as she finally peeked at herself cautiously.

But for some reason I couldn't get a clear image of her on the tube.

Thinking I had too much light, I aimed the flood light at the dark wood ceiling and finally turned it off. With just the room lights, her face was a little clearer but it was still suffused with a hazy glow that made her unrecognizable. Strangely, my bathrobe which she was wearing, as well as the couch and room background, were sharply clear and delineated on the screen.

"Is that my soul?" she asked, pointing at the screen.

"No," I assured her, crossing my fingers and hoping that it wasn't. "That's still invisible. Your skin and clothing reflect billions of little rays of light. Ordinarily the camera would reassemble them into a picture of you."

"Methinks it sees the light of God dwelling within me." She smiled and, gaining confidence, she evidently decided to give the camera one more test. She stood up and opened her bathrobe and stared at her ghostly naked image on the screen while I tried unsuccessfully to sharpen the picture. She was obviously feeling the vodka. "I wish that Master Winthrop could see me now," she chuckled. "I would'na be afraid of him this time."

Before she sat down she turned, bent over, lifted the bathrobe again, and peered back at her hazy behind. "Be that my bum? I never saw it like that," she marveled.

I checked the tape recording and discovered that even though her image was cloudy I was capturing her throaty voice. Deciding that there must be something wrong with my television camera, but hoping it might clear, I let the camera and tape run. "I never thought you were afraid of Mr. Winthrop," I said, remembering how she talked back to him at her trial.

"I was so sick in my bowels and so frightened that I had a hard time controlling myself. My papa had told me long ago to read Proverbs: 'the fear of man is a snare.' I told Will that, afraid or not, I wasn't going to let Master Winthrop know it. I know that he told Will to try and shut me up." She grinned. "I just read in his *Journal* that he said that my Will was 'a man of very mild temper and weak parts, wholly guided by his wife.' That is not true!" she said indignantly. "Will was a gentle man. He did what he desired. Unlike Master Winthrop and Master Dudley, he wished not to be king of New England."

Anne kept staring at the television set, fascinated like me by the strange phenomenon of a nearly faceless woman. She paused and then shrugging, perhaps thinking this was normal, she continued. "John Wheelwright told me, 'The Hutchinson family is not much inclined to subtleties' and that was right. Will did not mince words. When John Oliver followed us to Connecticut, and tried to make him repent, Will told Master Oliver, 'If I had to choose between the church and Anne, I'd take Anne'—and that I was a saint. He told Master Oliver that he could tell John Cotton the same thing, and John Cotton had better think about that."

Anne suppressed a little sob. "As much as I loved John-Luv, Will was more a saint than John-Luv or myself. Will understood that the spirit of love dwelleth in a person, if he but recognize it."

"You still haven't told me how you were involved with John Cotton," I said, wondering, as I had ever since I had adopted Anne Hutchinson, what it was over and above her religious identification that had impelled her to break up her home and come to New England.

"I loved him very, very much," she answered softly. "I have not read all those books that thou gavest me, but methinks that John-Luv kept our secret." She smiled. "I fancy this woman Helen Augur, even though, like Reverend Buckley, she called me an American Jezebel."

"They weren't the only people who called you that," I said. "Your friend Reverend Thomas Weld, in the preface of the book that he and Winthrop wrote about you and Wheelwright, insisted that you were a Jezebel."

Anne scowled. "Master Weld was no friend of mine. Poor Jezebel. She worshipped Baal. Papa told me that the tribes in Israel were very primitive people. Baal was one of their first gods. Unlike the god of the Jews and the Puritans, he was a forgiving god. Not until Jesus, did the Gentiles understand what God was really like and that he had given them a covenant of grace—forgiveness and love. But this Master Battis, who wrote about me, is wrong. He thinketh that I married Will because I could not dominate Papa. He saith that I loved Papa but I was afraid of him. He saith that I was 'the hapless victim of personal insecurity' and that that was my nemesis. He thinketh I needed to prove that I was right, but that is silly and very wrong."

"Last night you told me a little about your father. It's obvious that he wasn't really a Puritan."

Anne laughed. "He certainly was not. He enjoyed the ritual of the church, but he believed not in all the hokus pokus. He thought it was a solace for the people. My papa was a very great man who wanted people to learn and be happy. He was not like the Puritans. He loved London and the King. We celebrated Christmas and New Year's, May Day and the Twelfth Day, Plough Monday and Shrovetide, Easter and Whitsuntide, Candlemas Day and All Hallow's Eve, and every holiday, and while Papa played no cards nor chess nor silly games, because he was so busy learning, he objected not to them. He did not think that being happy and playing games stopped the people from knowing God. He even took me and Momma to the bookstalls at St. Paul's to see the gallants parading through the Cathedral in all their frippery.

"Sometimes Momma was convinced that he was letting me read too much. She kept telling him that I was nearly twenty and I had no marriage prospects. No man wanted a woman who talked back or who was too opinionated." Anne smiled lovingly at me. "But I was not insecure. And Will minded not. He fancied a woman he could wrastle with—mentally and physically. He loved to tumble in bed—but not with the Gospel. Will was a slow reader, and he was not a Puritan. He liked to sing and dance and play cards and go to the tavern and to the fairs, and once in a while he got drunk and maybe even diddled some lady's arse, but he was not a wencher. Mostly he was too busy buying and selling cloth, to worry whether Adam had sinned or not. Will loved me because I liked nice things to wear and very soon I knew almost as much about the cloth as he did. There was wool from Yorkshire, and cotton and coatings from Manchester, and people had moved to England from France and Holland who could make baize and serges and bombazines. From Coventry there were blue woolens, and in London, Will bought bengals and calicoes from the Orient and camlet made of silk and wool or camel's hair, dimity and rougher cloth like fustion and canvas, as well as durant, tammy for petticoats, tiffany and linen, sleazy, and prunella for the ministers' gowns and for women's shoes, and paudusoy for suits and petticoats, and kersey for stockings."

She stopped and came up for air and looked at me with a big grin. "Dear Robert, I was never naked like this for so long in my whole life. Will had a shop filled with more kinds of cloth than I can remember. Me and all my girls had many pretty gowns, and were none too happy with the 'sad colors,' the dull browns and reds and greens of the Puritans." She laughed. "But neither were most of the Puritan ladies, rich or poor. It got so, until Master Winthrop and the magistrates made it a new law and made people dress according to their income, you could not tell a servant from a free man. But no one really paid any attention to such male silliness except John-Luv, and he and I argued about that many times."

Giving up on the television camera, I sadly turned it off. Whether she was *the* Anne Hutchinson or not I wasn't going to be able to prove it with a videotape. "Love of clothing hasn't changed very much," I told her. "And you can't tell who is rich or poor by their clothing today either. But don't worry. I'm probably not as rich as Will was, and as much as I enjoy having you naked and readily available, I'll take you shopping tomorrow."

Delighted, Anne gave me an affectionate, unghostly hug. "I loved to traipse with Will to the shops in Old Boston and London," she grinned. "Or even without him, and to see all the cloth and fancy dresses. All these books that you gave me give the impression that I led Will around by the nose and that only because of me did we come to the Colony. That is not true. I most certainly wanted to see John-Luv for a lot of reasons beyond his preaching. But I wanted to see my Edward too. Will had planned for more than a year that we would go to America. I told you that his brother and our son Edward had gone to America on the same boat as John-Lov and his Sarah. It was a long year before we were reunited, but I knew that we would eventually join them. During that time, Will sold everything in Alford and set up a trading business in London. He knew that he could make even more money selling cloth to the colonists than he did just trading in Old Boston, London, and Alford, and he was very excited about the journey."

Anne smiled reminiscently. "In 1610 and 1611, when I was living in

London, Will kept coming down to the city by horse, followed by his wagons filled with cloth. The journey took two entire days, and he would stay overnight at places like Ely and St. Ives. Will finally owned a shop in London. Then, after we were married, he took me with him to London twice a year, or more when I was not carrying a child. He knew how much I fancied the city. But Momma did not like Will. And she was very angry the day Papa took Will and me, dressed as a boy, to see Thomas Dekker's play called *The Honest Whore*. Listening to the characters, I was learning to swear, and I kept saying things like 'Zounds,' and 'Od's Foot,' and 'Od's Blood,' and she wanted Papa to keep me in my room all day.

"When Papa died in 1611, and I was actually twenty, Momma decided that living in London was too dangerous for her family, especially her Anne, who was spending too much time in St. Paul's Churchyard reading new books that the Stationers put on sale and watching all the young male peacocks strutting about the city pursued by beggars and whores. What was worse I had discovered the Family of Love." Anne grinned at me. "Like thee, I fell in love with a dead person, Henry Nikales. He was born in 1502. I did not try to bring him back to life, but then he did not believe in bodily resurrection either. Another Dutchman, Christopher Vitell, who could write English, translated his writings from the Dutch. Many years later, when I was living in Alford, I discovered that Christopher's sister-in-law, Elizabeth Bancroft, was preaching in Ely. She was a Familist. When Will went to London I stayed in her house many times."

"That isn't what you said at your court trial," I said. "Hugh Peters insisted that you 'did exceedingly magnify the woman of Ely—a woman in a thousand,' but you claimed that you had never met her."

Anne smiled sadly. "I lied. John-Luv knew Elizabeth too, but he held his tongue. I was not completely honest about many things. If I had been, John-Luv and I would have been hung on the Common." Seeing my dubious expression, she got up and hugged me. "But I am not lying now—I am Anne Hutchinson, and I love thee."

She squirmed affectionately against me. Her bathrobe was dangling open and I clasped her behind and kissed her breasts. We were close to making love again, but I held back, determined to keep her talking.

Snuggling against me, occasionally sipping her third vodka and cranberry juice, she said, "I truly did not want to move back to Alford—or even to marry Will. I told him that I loved him as much as he loved me, but he could never live with me day in and day out. Like Chaucer's Clerke, I told Will, 'Of boke to rede, I me delyte.' I had divers things to learn, and I knew that Will was not a man to sit with his face in a book. But Will told me he did not mind if I read myself blind. He told me I could read to him to my heart's content. He loved to listen to my pretty 'red rag' as he called my tongue. He might fall asleep but he would still love me. But he warned me, if I became too rambunctious he might have to slap my arse." Anne laughed. "He never did. We had many things that make a good marriage. First, we loved to play see-saw."

"See-saw?" I asked, puzzled.

"Pully-hawly. Swive. Fuck. Like you, Will was 'my gentle knight, a pricking on the plain,'" she said, and I recognized the quote from Spenser's *Faerie Queene.* "We loved to dance. We loved children, and we liked nice things like good food and silk, and silver and pretty clothes. My tongue was not always pealing."

"Tell me about the Familists," I said. "That really surprises me. I had never heard of the religion until I started to read about you. Then I realized that the Puritans detested them and the Ranters—and especially the Quakers, who they thought were the anti-Christ."

"I know not about Quakers," she said, and I realized that was true. George Fox, the founder of the Quakers, was only about sixteen when Anne died. Anne's friend, Mary Dyer, became a Quaker and was actually hung in Boston Common because she wouldn't repudiate her beliefs, but she had lived to see the Quaker infiltration into Massachusetts. Not much was known about Anne's sister Katherine, who was fifteen years younger than Anne, but I had read that she had left Boston and had gone to Rhode Island with her husband. Katherine was evidently as fiery as Anne. She first became a Baptist and then a Quaker.

"The Ranters said that every man and woman was God, and no one needed to read the Scriptures or listen to ministers," Anne said.

"Isn't that essentially what you were saying?" I asked.

Anne shook her head. "I believe you are not God until you are at one with the Holy Spirit within you. Then, you can know God, but you cannot *be* God." She smiled. "Man alone cannot resurrect his soul, or his body."

"But you are convinced that you are resurrected?"

She shrugged. "Dost thou have any other explanation for me? In sooth, I am very uncertain. If I am me—and I am living again—then dear Jesus is bound to tell me why. I did agree with the Familists that there was no need for bodily resurrection. The resurrection of the dead is fulfilled in you and me. Dost thou understand that?"

"Not at all," I said. "I'm sure that you know that the Familists believed the millennium had already started. Jesus had returned to earth for a thousand years and they were the saints who were preparing for the ultimate kingdom of God."

She nodded. "Such thinking was heresy in England and in Old Boston and New Boston. John Cotton believed in the Second Coming. I tried to show him that he was saying the same thing as the Familists. But he denied it. I told him that his sermons sounded very much like Henry Nikales, who wrote in one of his books, *The Glass of Righteousness:* 'God is a living God, a perfect clear light and love itself. God reveals himself to humans and we may become Godded like Him when we are fully aware of His Spirit within us. Through Jesus Christ, we are renewed in the human spirit, and we are brought into a good-willing life, but only when we become incorporated into Christ as a loving person with Him. We must follow Christ even to his death on the cross in perfect obedience to his Holy Spirit of love.'"

She sighed. "Thou lookest as bewildered as Will used to. Dost thou not understand what I say?"

"Mostly," I laughed. "But like Will I was once a businessman. I really don't care whether I'm 'saved' or not."

"Work alone shalt not save thee," she said positively. "But belief in God's grace will. Master Nikales wrote: 'The true light is the everlasting life and has its origins and forthcoming out of the lovely being of the true mind of the eternal and living God. This light shows itself in the world through illuminated men and women or Godded men and women, and through persons, the most High is revealed.'" Anne stared at me thoughtfully for a moment. "That makes more sense to me than trying to prove whether God gave Abraham a new covenant. I told John-Luv that I did not care what all those Jewish prophets wrote in the Old Testament or whether Christ were related to Abraham. God sent his only son to tell us the truth. God, Jesus Christ, the Holy Spirit were all one. They are the light dwelling within thee and me."

"So you really were an antinomian before you arrived in New England?"

She laughed. "That is a silly word. I am opposed not to all the laws of the Scriptures or to the magistrates. But when I told John-Luv my thoughts, he was all apucker. He was sore afraid that I might talk too freely. 'If a pursuivant hears thee,' he told me, 'thou shalt end up in jail and thou might be publicly whipped.'"

She explained that *pursivant* was the name they had given to Archbishop Laud's spies, who reported all heretics to him. She shook her head reminiscently. "John-Luv told me that in some ways he agreed with me but that we must be careful about what we could say and could not say. Johnny, my brother-in-law, who married Will's sister, lost his church in Bilsby and could no longer preach. The last time I saw John-Luv before he left for America was five years later." She smiled. "That was in March 1633. Two days methinks I shall never forget. He had left his wife, Sarah, and his church in Old Boston and was in hiding." She paused, sifting her memories. "Poor John-Luv. I was a she-devil to him, a temptation he could not resist. He told me that every time he had met with me in the past five years that he had promised God he would reject me. But after Elizabeth, his first wife, died, and even after he had married Sarah to have the children he could not have with Elizabeth or me, he still could not banish me from his thoughts." She sighed. "Nor could I stop needing him. I knew it was going to happen. I wanted it to happen. I was five months pregnant when John-Luv left me."

She looked at me a little starry-eyed. "Thou callst this drink a Cape Codder. It maketh my tongue loose. There was a rock in Plymouth, which I never saw, on which it was said the Separatists stepped off their ship." She handed me her empty glass. "I do not need another. I need a Plymouth Rock to cling to. I fear I nearly told thee things that all these years no one else ever knew except me, Will, and John."

"Maybe that's why you are here," I said, fascinated and amazed that I was discovering the real reason that Anne had been so anxious to follow her teacher to America. "You can finally tell the world the truth. You were much more than a Puritan. You were a vibrant loving woman. I can't understand why Cotton ever deserted you."

She shrugged. "He had no choice—but in truth we deserted each other."

7

Certain that before the night was over Anne would tell me much more about her relationship with John-Luv, I asked her if she would help me make dinner. While we were broiling a steak and softening some broccoli in boiling water, I kept thinking how adaptable the human brain is. While I still didn't believe that this loving woman had returned from the grave, I was accepting the reality of her slicing tomatoes and asking me if they were poisonous. She claimed to have never eaten one. It occurred to me that without having any idea of how things work, or the centuries of trial and error that went into making electric lights, radio, the recording of the human voice and image, and the live transmission of sound and images, Anne was already as nearly comfortable with them as a young child.

But if she were a woman who had lived centuries ago, could she ever adjust to the complexity of this world—and a Boston ten thousand times bigger than any city she had known, or cities where practically all the inhabitants owned at least one horseless carriage, a creation in which more people self-destructed annually than the entire population of New England in the early seventeenth century?

But one thing at a time, I kept telling myself. I couldn't be dreaming. Assuming that she was Anne Hutchinson, I almost literally owned my pretty ancestor, and I wanted to learn much more about her past. A loving past, that, I was slowly beginning to realize, had not been confined to one man. With dinner I opened a bottle of Cabernet Sauvignon, and as we ate I got her back on track.

"When did you first meet John Cotton?" I asked. "History books don't tell too much about him except that he was probably the best educated and most respected Puritan preacher in all of England."

Sipping the wine, her eyes stared past me into another world. "After my daughter Mary was born," she said finally, and her eyes were dreamy, "I met John-Luv in April of 1628. I had been married for nigh onto sixteen years. The older children were able to take care of themselves, and my mother and Will's mother helped me with the babies. In the spring and summer when I weaned one baby, and I was not too far advanced with another, I would ride with Will to Old Boston, where he kept another shop. I went with him regularly in fine weather to the various fairs. Sometimes we rode together in the same wagon, or if some other man came along, I would lie on the bolts of cloth Will was carrying. Will was forever going either to Boston or to London. The road was exceedingly bumpy. I preferred horseback. Either way, if we left around six in the morning, we would arrive in Old Boston early in the afternoon, for it was about twenty-five miles distant from Alford. We had many a friend there and on many an occasion we would stay with them for several days."

"Did you ride pillion?" I knew that in the time of the Stuarts many of the more daring of the ladies of the court rode alone—sidesaddle. But pillion—sitting to the rear of the man with the lady's feet slipped into a separate leather contraption to keep her from sliding off—was the most popular method of transporting women.

I might have known that Anne was a lady of a different breed. "Faugh!" she said. "I hated to ride pillion. After we were married, I told Will that since we could own horses I wanted to learn to ride like a man. He thought it was a very good idea. If I could spread my legs around him, why could not I spread them around a horse?" She laughed. "It would keep me in good shape for see-sawing with him. Whenever I was not too big with a baby, or he did not have to bring back cloth we each rode a horse to Old Boston. I wore breeches, and carried my good gowns in a saddlebag. Sometimes we made the trip in a wee bit over five hours."

"When did you first meet John Cotton?"

"The first time I rode to Old Boston with Will I heard tell of John-Luv, but I had never met him. I knew he had studied his books at Trinity College at Cambridge until he was twenty-seven. Then, in 1610, when I was still residing in London, he was made Vicar of St. Botolph's. He preached there until 1632, about six months before he left for America. I had heard about his honey voice and his defiance of the popery in the church, but after I married Will I was too busy having babies and learning how to have them and care for them to go with Will to the fairs. I went to church at St. Wilfrid's in Alford. It did not even bother me that the minister was a silly man who should have been a Catholic priest rather than preaching in the Church of England. When I was young I told Papa that I wanted to be a minister like him, but after I married Will I decided I would prefer to be a physician, even a chirguen. Will told me that I should remember that I was a woman and be happy to be a midwife and not try to fly to the moon." She laughed. "Imagine—there's no woman on the moon, only the man in the moon. Will had to keep reminding me that ladies were put on the earth for the comfort of men.

"When Mary was born, we had ten children and even Will had to admit that I had organized our family like a captain in the militia. I told Will that if he could go to the fairs and sing and dance and booze a little—and I was sure, knowing Will, feel a few ladies' arses—I needed a few holidays too. He agreed. The first time was the May Sheep Fair. Thousands of sheep were sold every day, and the merchants in Boston shipped wool to the Dutchmen. We visited two days with the Gortons. Many years later Sam Gorton, who had a nice home in Old Boston, moved his family to the Massachusetts Bay Colony, but he detested the Puritans, particularly Master Winthrop, and he did not reside in Boston or Plymouth long. He was living in Plymouth near the Island when I was exiled there. He raised a bigger rumpus than Roger Williams ever did. Sam liked me and told Will that I was a lady who some day would jostle the world." She laughed bitterly. "I wonder what he thought when he discovered that the Indians had set me on fire.

"I was a fighter but I could be a lady too. The first time I saw John-Luv I was all gussied up in a blue silk farthingale that made my titties pop out and squeezed my stomach so tight that I could scarcely draw breath. Wearing a ruffle and a lace cap, I sat in the first row and stared in ecstasy into John-Luv's face and listened for two hours to his honey-filled voice.

She sighed, "I was enamoured of John Cotton the first time I saw and heard him. He was talking of many things that I had thought. I had read the Scriptures from cover to cover right often, but for seventeen years, since Papa died—with the exception of Johnny Wheelwright, who only came around once in a while—I had no one to talk to or ask the thousand questions that were seething in my poor head. I knew that somehow I must dare to talk with this man. Alas, all the ladies wanted to talk with him alone, too. But I soon learned that John Cotton not only preached every day, but almost every morning and afternoon he gave an hour or more as a personal teacher to those who needed him. For a few days every month in the spring and summer and fall, while Will did his trading at the fairs or mingled with his friends pitching the bar, tilting the ring, or playing shuffleboard or other games, I was in St. Botolph's to hear John."

Anne smiled. "On our third trip to Old Boston—it was in July 1628—I finally baited the bear in his study at St. Botolph's. He wasn't a fierce bear. He was a couthy bear, and it was all I could do not to hug him. He wasn't like Will, who was tall and wiry and hard as oak. John-Luv was a softer-looking man. He had golden hair that hung down to his shoulders. He cut it shorter when he came to the Colony but he was never a roundhead. He had big brown eyes and a face so full of love and affection that I knew for certain that more than one lady wanted to snuggle in his arms. But I soon learned that sometimes he was a sad bear too.

"That first day, when I told him who I was, I was surprised to learn that he had met Papa, and knew that Momma was a Dryden. He had heard about Will and knew that Will was a prosperous merchant in Alford. Later, when he knew more about Will and me, I told him that I was lonely for someone to talk to and think with. But he always told me that I should be proud of Will: 'Ministers and scholars,' he said, 'eat the bread of idleness. No calling more wasteth and grieveth a man than the ministry. The ploughman's work is a pastime compared to theirs. His labor strengthens his body but a preacher's life wasteth body and spirit.'"

Anne floated for a moment on her memories. "The next day after his sermon John asked me if I would like to see Boston from the church tower of St. Botolph's. He told me that the cathedral was built in the fourteenth century. In the seventh century the city was named Botolf's Town, after a Saxon monk. It was finally pronounced Boston. We walked up the winding cathedral staircase—three hundred and sixty-five steps to the tower, one for each day of the year with seven doors for the days in the week and fifty-two windows for the weeks. We were alone on the parapet. Looking down and out to sea I felt so close to God I was overwhelmed, and I sobbed my joy to John-Luv, and clung to him for a moment."

Anne smiled tremulously. "I could not help myself. I loved God and John-Luv all at the same time. He pushed me not away but held me soothingly in his arms for a long time and he could prevent himself neither. I could feel him grow big against me."

She sighed. "I never met anyone who knew so much as John Cotton. He not only read Latin and Hebrew but he also spoke both languages. I think, at first, he was a wee bit shocked that I could quote the Scriptures as well as he could, but methinks I did not understand them so well. He was also surprised that I had learned to speak French and read that bonny language when I was in London. He thought the French were a very frivolous people. I told him that he and John Wheelwright were the only Puritan ministers who knew that John Calvin had not understood the New Testament. Men and women were not eternally damned or made sinful by Adam's fall, and being of the elect, or obeying the laws of the Scriptures would not assure anyone of salvation. I told him that God knew that men and women are weak and would sin by reason of their flesh—so that while the law doth not change, man can repent. Repentance freeth him and he shall no more be wholly under the law but under grace."

Anne smiled. "John-Luv told me that I was partially right. That I needed to understand much more. God had freely promised Christ his benefits and only asks of men and women that they, by faith, receive Christ into them and repent of their sins. I agreed with him, but he was not too certain that men and women could achieve salvation in spite of their sinful natures, or that they are accounted just in God's eyes. I told him that men and women are justified and their sins are remitted, because Christ's righteousness is now a part of them. John-Luv thought that they must achieve justification before sanctification by a lifetime of strengthening their beliefs and living righteously." Anne grinned reminiscently. "We discussed these ideas for quite a long time."

I couldn't help laughing. "The problem was that Cotton and all the Puritans—including you, so far as I've been able to figure out—believed that those who are both justified and sanctified automatically become saints in Heaven and would achieve glorification whether they sinned or not." I patted her hand. "From your standpoint the rest of us are reprobates. Obviously, sinner or not, the reason that you're here is that you were one of the elect."

"I believe that not!" Anne snorted. "And I believe not that grace releases anyone from obeying the law of the magistrates. I told John what Henry Nikales said: 'Those who think that Law is abolished have not the Love of Christ formed in them. The Law is not abolished; it is fulfilled in Love. He that loveth doeth the will. No one ever transcends righteousness, for the entire work of God toward salvation has been making for the fruits of righteousness. . . .The Lord received me into the grace of His Love, and made me one with Christ and those who discover that will all become saints, and enjoy His heavenly riches.'"

She shrugged. "I talked with John-Luv on four separate days for several hours in his study in the church that first summer. He kept warning me of the dangers of Familism, and he was sore provoked when I told him that he was a Familist himself. He still believed that Familists thought they were beyond the law, and if each man and woman received a free gift of grace, without works, then there would be no law of any kind. John knew, as I did, that some Familists lived communally and they believed so much in loving one another that they did not think it a sin to love another person's wife or husband. John thought that was quite despicable, but I sensed as he held my hand and tried to warn me against such insanity that he was taking a fancy to my body as well as my soul.

"I was thirty-six years old and he was forty-four. His wife Elizabeth had given him no children. I saw him again in the spring of 1629, after my Katherine was born, and I was in love with him." Anne smiled. "Like all of us, he was two persons—a church person, who never revealed his private fears and worries." She laughed, "and a Hamlet person. He told me that when he was with me he was able 'to be and not to be' at the same time. Only then could he stop worrying about 'not being.'

"I told him that Will and I always found time for mirth and laughter. But John-Luv told me, 'I'm not certain that men should make an occupation or recreation as stage players or musicians, but sports and playing cards and singing and dancing are all right if they interfereth not with providing for oneself and family.' I called him my sweet Puritan." Anne sighed. "When he lived in England he was a sweet person. But when he came to the Colony Master Winthrop and Master Wilson made him sour. I was the only person, except his wife Elizabeth and later Sarah, who knew that he had been to the Globe Theater and had read many plays by Master Shakespeare.

"John-Luv and I talked together many times but I told him not that I loved him until the summer of 1629. When I did, he only smiled and said: 'It is a spiritual love we have for each other, dear Anne. Our souls are one soul engrafted in Christ Jesus.'"

Anne laughed. "But I knew that he always made time to see me. That fall, in September, he invited Will and myself to his home to meet his wife, Elizabeth. Elizabeth was a dainty woman. She weighed only about one hundred pounds. She had narrow hips and talked much with me about her miscarriages. She asked me if I could tell her how to keep a child in her womb and I told her that I did not believe that medicines would do her any good.

"'John needs a strong woman like thee,' she told me. "I am certain John likes thee—thou art the only woman he has invited to share his board.'"

Anne shook her head sadly. "I loved Elizabeth. She played the lute and virginal and sang so beautifully. But after that one meeting, we never saw her again. In March of 1630, just as spring was coming and I was looking forward to returning to Boston, John was stricken with tertian ague. Some people said it was the plague, some said the mosquitoes from the fens brought it. Unable to preach, he and Elizabeth went for their nursing to the estate of the Earl of Lincoln, a wealthy Puritan friend of theirs. John survived but poor Elizabeth died in July."

Anne stared mournfully at me. In the candlelight, tears sparkled at the corners of her eyes. "Oh, dear God, it was a terrible year. My loving, sweet Susanna, my second-born, only sixteen years old—she died of the fever in September. The plague was upon all of us. Then the Lord took my Elizabeth, and she was only nine and then dear little Will, only seven. My own Will was near death, too, but somehow I and all the other children escaped the awful sickness."

"What medicines did you use?" I asked, trying to comfort her but well aware that no one in the seventeenth century was much more advanced in the arts of curing human sickness than alchemists like Paracelsus, or the followers of Galen, who favored the lance over chemical concoctions. The thought crossed my mind that if this really were a resurrected woman, scientists, biologists, and twentieth-century medical practitioners would be pounding on the door to examine her flesh and blood, bones, genes, and every part of her anatomy, were they to hear of her.

"Medicine, pooh!" She scowled at me. "Before we arrived in Boston, the best doctor, Samuel Fuller, lived in Plymouth. John Endicott begged him to come to Salem to save his wife, who was dying of the fever. He came and later he lived in Mattapan for awhile. He was a blood-spiller. Like most of the others who claimed to be doctors, he was sure that no matter what ailed thee, blood-letting or cupping would cure thee. He would visit twenty sick people or more a day. Master Endicott's wife died, anyway, and a few years later so did Dr. Fuller, both of the fever." Anne shrugged. "I believe in Ecclesiastes' warning: 'He that sinneth before his Maker, let him fall into the hands of a physician.' Most of the doctors were not any better than my friend, Goody Hawkins. Some people thought she was a witch, but she adored me in a dimwitted way. She gave all the young women who could not conceive a mandrake root and told them to eat it."

Anne giggled. "Mandrake roots are twisted like the prickle of the Devil himself and taste worse. For a woman who was having a pregnancy sickness, Goody recommended that she bleed a cat's ear into the milk of a woman suckling a male child and drink it. Or to ease childbirth, she should take some hair from a virgin's head, cut it up fine and mix it with twelve ant's eggs, and milk from a red cow, or strong ale. But Goody was not any crazier than some of the doctors, who told you that the best cure for belly flux was powder made of wolves' guts and borewood stirred in the oil of wormwood. For loose bowels and other ailments many women preferred beaver's cod."

"Beaver's cod?"

Anne grinned. "The prickle of a dead beaver ground up instead of a wolf's guts. They fed it to their husbands to make them more active in bed."

"Did you believe in such cures?"

"No. But some herbs and flowers make good medicine. Basil helpeth a woman in travail. Opium from a poppy is good for toothaches. Fennel helpeth milk to flow in nursing women and helpeth to get rid of urine. Horehound cleaneth your lungs and maketh your breath taste nice. So does mint. I told Elizabeth Cotton that the only way to prevent a miscarriage was to stay in bed and smell tansie but too sure of the tansie, I am not. Valerian is supposed to make you lustful." She laughed. "I tried it with Will and we wore ourselves out one night. I never liked tobacco or the smell of it burning, but if thou mix it with malt, elder root, and honey, and boil it all together it helps heal sores. Wild carrot seeds are good for kidney stones, and strong beer and honey will help a sprain. Will did not believe that prevention was better than any cure. Perhaps he was right. In the winter, two or three times a week, he would make us and the older children a rum flip before we went to bed."

"How did you make those?"

"For two people, you need a pint of dark rum, nearly as much strong beer, then sweeten it with molasses or sugar, and plunge a hot iron in the mug, and sprinkle it with nutmeg." She laughed. "Will said that would prevent most any sickness. We often went to bed a little fuddled but we never had runny noses or phlegm. Dost thou have any rum or beer?"

I nodded. "There's a poker near the fireplace. You can wash it and heat it while I mix up a batch."

8

Ten minutes later, with steaming mugs, we were sitting in front of the fireplace and I finally got Anne back to John Cotton.

"A whole year passed before I saw John-Luv again. And I was pregnant yet once again." She smiled. "But it was spring, 1631. I was only ten weeks along with my new baby, who turned out to be a boy. We named him William after Will and his dead brother. It was not an easy thing to convince Will, but I told him that I wanted to ride with him to the first fair. He was afeard that I might dislodge the baby, but I told him I had never lost a baby yet—before or during birth. All I had to do was squat at the right time and take a few deep breaths and my little darlings slowly slid out into my hands. But in truth, this time I would not have cared if I did miscarry. It was my thirteenth child. Will agreed with me. I was nearly forty. He was forty-seven. We had done God's work. Fortunately, Will was calming down a little. He liked to snuggle on my titties, but he did not need to fill me with his prickle so often.

"John-Luv was very happy to see me alive and back in the front benches at St. Botolph's. The first day his sermon was like a love poem that he had written just for me. John wrote beautiful verses. He concluded his sermon speaking to God and thanking Him for the many friends who loved him in his late travail. Later, in his study, he read me a new poem he had written when he was thinking of me:

> Oft have I seen thee look with mercy's face
> And through thy Christ have felt thy saving grace
> This is Heaven on Earth if any be
> For this and all my soul doth worship thee."

Anne smiled at me through tear-flooded eyes. "That afternoon he walked with me to his lonely house, and I told him again that in my times of trouble, though he knew it not, he had been a great solace to me. His spirit was constantly at my side encouraging me that I should not despair. And I had revelations that made me aware that we both had work to do. A whole world to bring to Jesus and our Lord."

Once again Anne was staring reflectively into the mug of rum flip. "I told thee that I often had strange foresights. I knew this day that John-Luv needed my body and my soul together. Inside his house, I fell into his arms." She smiled at me bashfully. "It is not nice for a woman to tell her husband or her lover about another lover——"

I kissed her cheek. "Believe me—I'll not love you less."

"We had the entire afternoon together. John had not been with a woman for eight months. I told him not to fear. I could not get pregnant, and I was certain that he would not disturb the baby already in my womb.

"'God forgive me,' he sighed, as he helped me out of my farthingale and petticoats, and I finally stood naked before him. 'Worshipping dear Anne's body, I am worshipping Thee.'"

Anne smiled. "For three hours I was, for him, the Shulamite woman in the Song of Solomon, and he, for me, the adoring prince. But afterwards, even though he had no wife, he was very remorseful. He told me that we must never again give in to our fleshy needs. We had broken the Law of God—the Seventh and Tenth Commandments."

"But you didn't feel like a sinner?"

Anne laughed. "Women are more honest with God than men. I did not believe that God would be angry with me, then or now. I loved Will and I loved John Cotton—both of them with all my heart and soul. God gave us the light of His love for Him and for all His creatures."

"Did you ever tell Will?"

"Not then. Not until I was pregnant again, and he knew that it could not be his child."

I stared at her astonished. "Are you telling me that Susanna was John Cotton's child?" At last, I could understand why Anne Hutchinson had been so insistent that she must follow her teacher to New England.

She nodded. "John-Luv did not believe it, but 'tis true. After William was born in September of 1631, I told Will that I was weary of child-bearing. I knew that it was too soon. I was only thirty-nine, but I told him that if we could be careful for a few years, then we could fuck to our heart's content." She grinned. "I must have believed that I was already beyond conception. John-Luv had met Sarah Hawkridge Story, a widow with a young daughter. 'I love thee, Anne,' he told me. 'But I must resist thee. Sarah is only thirty. With her, I can have children.'"

"Were you jealous?"

Anne shook her head. "If you really love a man, you want what is best for him. I had met Sarah, and she was a pretty thing. I knew that she could never challenge John's mind, but she would be a comfort to him. John got his wish. When they sailed for America on July 1, 1633, Sarah was pregnant and we both prayed that she would arrive in Boston before the baby was born. Poor thing. I did not learn about it until much later. Edward wrote me a letter that Sarah had given birth at sea on board the *Griffin*. John's first child was born August 12, 1633, and later he was baptized Seaborn Cotton."

She laughed. "Was not that a nice name?" She looked at me with a loving expression. It was eight o'clock. I had kept her talking right through dinner. Although she had drunk two glasses of wine on top of the vodka earlier, and she was still nursing her rum flip, she didn't seem "fuddled." It had stopped snowing. The night sky was scudded with thin white clouds and blinking stars. I didn't want to turn on the television set and thrust her into the insanities of the twentieth century—not yet. We had nowhere to go except to bed. I told her that first I wanted her to finish her John-Luv story before she seduced Robert-Luv again.

She laughed. "The story doesn't end in England," she said. "Art thou not weary of my tongue flapping? We must wash the dishes."

I told her that would be easy. Water and electricity would do the job too. "But I am a little mixed up with your story. Not much was ever written about John Cotton's life." I grinned. "On the other hand, after reading some of his sermons, I would never want to adopt him for an ancestor. He was too autocratic for me, and his sermons were long and boring. How could you forgive him? He was very nasty to you, especially when you were on trial in your church."

"I never minded how long John's sermons were," Anne said. "I knew that sometimes he was a little confused himself, but he made my brain whirl with ideas. Will had talked about going to New England for several years, but I would never have gone with him, if John had stayed in Old Boston. But the poor man could not remain there. Archbishop Laud demanded that he come to London to answer charges in a High Court against him. John knew that he would end up in prison. So, less than six months after he married Sarah, he went into hiding and she did not see him for nearly a year until the *Griffin* was ready to sail for New England. John was sure that the archbishop knew that he and John Winthrop had been friends. Two years before, in 1630, John had traveled all the way from Old Boston to Southampton to bless the *Arbella* and the first Massachusetts Bay colonists, who had received a charter from King Charles."

Anne sighed. "Little did I think then that I would be leaving my beautiful home and moving to the Colony. John-Luv let me read the sermon he had given. He bade them Godspeed with a verse from Second Samuel. 'Moreover, I will appoint a place for my people in Israel, and I will plant them that they may dwell in a place of their own, and move no more.'

"Archbishop Laud wanted to make sure that John did not escape to America," Anne continued. "Everyone knew that John was not conforming to the Thirty-nine Articles of faith that Laud had published. John's congregation did not have to kneel at the taking of the Eucharist: the cross on top of the King's Arms, which was carried by the Mayor of Old Boston, had disappeared, and John refused to wear all the approved ecclesiastical vestments. He even performed marriages without a wedding ring." She shrugged. "John-Luv was a heretic before I was. If the archbishop could have found him, even though he was the most respected Puritan preacher in all of England, he would have had him hanged.

"Then Will found out that John was hiding near London, almost under the archbishop's nose. Will had opened a shop in London a few years before, and he had long talks with John Humfrey, Increase Nowell, and others who expected to get a patent from King Charles. Will was sure that the colonists would provide a great market for cloth." Anne smiled. "Happily, I had not become pregnant for nearly two years. So in February of 1633, I persuaded Will to let me come to London with him and our Edward, and Will's brother, Edward, and his wife, Sarah. We all knew that the *Griffin* was being put in condition for another trip to the Colony. The rumor was that John Cotton and his wife, Sarah, were leaving on it—but not from Southampton. From some other port to elude the pursuivants."

Anne laughed. "The archbishop couldn't find John, but I did. Sarah told me where he was. We stopped at Boston on our three-day trip to London. Sarah was so happy to see me. She had just missed her monthly bleeding and she wanted me to tell her everything I knew about having babies. Even though she had a daughter by her first husband, she was very nervous. To make things worse, John told her that she must stay in Boston until the last minute to make the pursuivants believe that he would be returning to St. Botolph's. Sarah gave me a letter she had written to him. John-Luv was living in Kent at Ramsgate, in a country estate of a friend. Two days later in the early afternoon, we arrived at Ramsgate and stayed overnight. All of us had a long talk with John. Edward and Sarah decided then, along with our Edward, that they would sail to America with John when the *Griffin* was ready. They expected to leave in June. John wanted us to come along too, but Will said that he couldn't leave England for another year. It would take him that long to sell our house and his shops."

"So you stayed in Ramsgate," I said, knowing that must have been when she went to bed with John. "How did you arrange that?"

"It was not an easy thing," she said, and her eyes were crinkly with suppressed laughter. "Will knew that I enjoyed London and I wanted to see some plays at Blackfriars, but I told him that I had also missed John-Luv and needed someone to talk to about many things in the Scriptures that had been bothering me. I knew that Will was going to be in London for at least five days. I told him I would miss him, but I needed time to think and read. He could buy me some printed plays at the Stationers in St. Paul's and later we could read them together. I told him that when he returned with his full wagons I would be waiting for him to go back to Alford."

She shrugged. "We had rented a very nice room in the Tavern. Will kissed me goodbye, and told me not to forget that he loved me, too. I hugged him and splattered him with tears, and told him that I was his wife and lover, first and foremost." Anne shook her head. "Perhaps I am a daughter of Satan, but I cannot believe that loving is bad. John was very frightened when he discovered that I was still at the Tavern. I was a woman without her husband for five days, and he had not been with a woman for five months. The nights in Ramsgate we embraced in an almost continuous fog and chill. Disguised in seaman's clothes, John arrived every night muttering, 'The Devil himself is encouraging us.' But nevertheless we made love and slept together until morning."

Anne sighed. "Poor John-Luv. Sometimes he was so sad and needed to repent for his sins and mine that afterwards he would break out in tears. But he could not help himself. Each night he returned and he asked God to forgive him for his need for dear Anne's flesh and her wonderful pixieish mind."

For a few moments Anne was lost in her thoughts; then she continued, "I had lived nearly forty years. I should have known that after months of no seeding, my womb was lonesome and needed to replenish itself. This time with a daughter fair. John-Luv's second child was born November 15, 1633. I called her Susanna. It means 'graceful lily that never dies.' John did not see her until nearly a year later when we arrived in the Colony in August of 1634. Poor Susanna, the Indians murdered her."

"No, they didn't," I told her. "For some reason she was spared. The Indians took her captive, but they had taught her to speak their language. A few years later she was finally ransomed by the Dutch settlers but by then she didn't want to leave her new Indian friends. Presumably, she always liked them very much. Colonial records reveal that she returned to Boston and married a John Cole on December 31, 1651, in Rhode Island and hopefully lived happily ever afterwards."

Anne listened to me open-mouthed. "Oh, dear God, of all my children, why did you save her?" Sobbing, she hugged me, her face buried in my shoulder. "Did John-Luv know that she survived?"

"I would think that he did," I said. "He lived another nine years, until 1652."

"So Susanna moved back to Boston and married John Cole," Anne sighed. "Johnny was just a baby—only a few years older than she. Sam Cole owned a tavern and inn next door to our house. Johnny must have decided the Island was a better place to live than Boston. Life is very strange. John-Luv lived not far from our house, up on Cotton Hill." She shook her head sadly. "The last time I saw Susanna she was beginning to look greatly like her father. I wonder if he ever spoke to his daughter."

My bathrobe had slipped down off her shoulder, and I caressed her back and tried to soothe her. Finally, she whispered. "Thank thee, dear Robert.

My beloved Jesus must have forgiven me a little to have brought me here."
She pointed out the window to the backyard, which I had floodlighted. "It is
no longer snowing. If this really be Mt. Wolleystone, could we walk together
in the snow? I did that many times with Will on moonlit nights. I desire to
see it again."

9

Anne's request to go for a walk in the snow jelled an idea that had been flitting in the back of my mind for the past few hours. Obviously she couldn't go out walking in a bathrobe, and before Saturday arrived I most certainly had to get her dressed, if I were going to take her to dinner at the Johnson's house. God—or someone out there—had provided me with a fifty-two-year-old naked child whom I couldn't leave on someone else's doorstep. But how could I take her to a woman's store wearing just a bathrobe? And if I got her dressed in Emily's clothes and Emily's shoes, none of which would fit her, I knew that would require some explanation to a curious saleslady, especially if Anne hinted that she had just arrived from another century and was speaking her melodious English with its *thees* and *thous*.

Then I had a bright idea. Tomorrow, I would take her to Boston to Lord & Taylor in the Prudential Plaza wearing a ski suit. Tonight on the dark streets of Merrymount, which is only a half mile from Mt. Wollaston, I could test the ski suit and see how she looked in it. I hoped that a combination of Emily's ski jacket and my ski pants and ski boots, with a few extra pairs of wool socks to make them fit, would create an outfit that wouldn't attract too much attention. Why we would arrive at Lord & Taylor dressed for winter sports to buy a complete wardrobe was a question I didn't intend to answer tonight.

Once again I was overwhelmed with the thought that this couldn't be happening. I was dreaming it. Carrying an armful of ski clothes, I led Anne to the bedroom and asked her bluntly: "You're not really Anne Hutchinson, are you? You can drop the act. Stop playing the game—I like you anyway. You're obviously a smart cookie."

She stared at me with a puzzled expression. "I am not a cookie. All my brain doth tell me that I am Anne Hutchinson. I told thee everything. Why I am here, I know not. All I can tell thee, if so many years have passed, then I must be the living body and soul of my former self." She brushed tears from her eyes. "I told thee, although John-Luv tried to make me say things that I did not believe, I never believed that this could happen to me or that the corruptible body of anyone could return to earth." She shook her head sadly.

"Perchance, this is my punishment."

"Punishment?"

"Living again, without friends or family, in a strange world filled with mysterious things I do not understand is a terrible punishment. It maketh me all a mort." She smiled. "I expected to be saved and to be in Heaven, but perhaps this is really Hell."

"You don't have to worry," I said. "I'm only a half-ass devil." I couldn't help laughing but I was determined to give her one more test. "You said during your trial that an oath is the end of all controversy. Do you still believe it?"

"Of course I do," she answered without hesitation.

"Wait a minute." I returned to the bedroom with a King James Bible. "Okay, swear on it!"

Tears in her eyes, she put her hand on the Bible. "May God make me vanish and return to dust if I lie. I do swear that I am Anne Hutchinson."

Either God wasn't listening or she really was Anne. I hugged her.

"To Hell with doubts," I said. "I love you. You have one friend. I don't care whether you are my dream, a ghost from the past, or a soul with a body. Just stick around for awhile."

"Stick around?" She laughed. "Thou saith such strange things. I am thy child and lover. Thou art stuck with me."

Dressing Anne for a winter walk proved more erotic than I had anticipated. Shedding her bathrobe, she watched me poking in the dresser for underwear. I produced boxer shorts and a T-shirt and she held them up astonished.

"In the winter I wore woollen stockings and many petticoats," she said. "But nothing like this. The only time I wore men's clothing was when Papa took me to Blackfriars."

"Don't worry," I told her. "John Winthrop was sure that you wore the pants in the Hutchinson home. Today, women not only control most of the wealth of the country, but many of them dress like men. Some especially love men's shirts and jockey shorts."

Giggling, she wiggled into the T-shirt. Her full breasts and nipples, confined under cloth and pointing provocatively at me, were more challenging than ever. Her expression, as she examined herself in the mirror, still naked from the waist down, was girlish and innocent. I couldn't help myself. I cupped her face and kissed her tenderly. Laughing she pulled me back on the bed on top of her, and kissed me enthusiastically. "I hope thou art not disappointed with me," she said, enveloping me with a wide-eyed look.

"Why should I be?"

"I am not so good a wife as thou mayest have thought."

I laughed. "I think you were a very good wife. You can't help yourself. You're a love bug." I kissed my way past her belly to her bush. "Before we go shopping tomorrow, I'm going to trim you up." I told her. "Your pubic hair is so lush it will show under your dress. Ladies don't wear petticoats anymore, and I refuse to buy you pantyhose. You'll have to shave your legs and under your arms too."

"I do not think I would like to do that," she said. "With no hair I would look like Venus."

My face was between her legs and my tongue had found her clitoris.

"Oh, dear Jesus," she moaned. "Thou must not do that."

"Don't you like it?"

"Aye, I do! I do! But I must smell of piss."

"More like newmown hay," I chuckled. "Didn't Will or John-Luv ever kiss your pussy?" I asked as I continued my labial explorations.

"Oh, dear Robert, it pleaseth me. Only one man ever kissed me on my cony." She sighed. "Oh, please! Dear one, please stop or I will explode."

Laughing, I stood up. "We won't eat the whole cake now," I said. "We'll save it until we come back from our walk."

She patted my erect cock. "It has more patience than I."

"Who was the other man who kissed your genitals?" I asked, suddenly remembering her admission.

"He was much younger than I. Poor Harry. He thought he loved me more than any woman, but in truth, his problem was that he lived in the Colony for nearly three years and all that time he had no wife."

I shook my head in amazement. "I presume you mean Harry Vane. He was governor of the Colony. Did you go to bed with him too?"

She smiled. "Not always to bed exactly." She was examing the ski jacket, looking for buttons. "I'll tell you about it later. What is this?" she demanded.

"It's called a zipper." I held out the jacket and she slipped into it, and to her delight I zipped it up. She was more amazed with it than with electricity and kept moving it up and down. "All those little teeth," she marvelled. "They snuggle into each other like a young man and woman, and never let go."

Wearing the T-shirt and my shorts, she slid into the nylon ski pants and marvelled at the smoothness and lightness of the cloth. She couldn't believe that with a woolen sweater under the jacket she would be warm enough.

Knowing that she would see automobiles on the plowed roads for the first time, I decided to introduce her to oil. "Man has learned how to control fire and burn other fuels beside wood," I told her. "Were you aware of coal?"

She nodded. "In England we had some coal and peat, but not in New England. All we had was wood and there was never enough of that in Boston."

"When the earth was formed, God, or whoever was in charge, not only filled it with coal, but in a time-span of a million years decaying vegetation and fossils were compressed and produced oils."

"Whale oil?"

"No. This oil is buried deep in the earth but it burns. People were aware of it for thousands of years but only in the past hundred years have men learned what to do with it. Now the entire world is dependent on it. Oil has made it possible for millions of people to live in a cold climate. If there were only wood to burn to keep warm, Boston would have no more people living here than there were three centuries ago."

Talking to her, I led her down into the cellar and opened the door of the oil burner and showed her the churning hot flame.

She screamed and clung to me. "The Lord hath given thee a piece of the sun," she whispered in awe.

"What the Lord giveth he can take away too," I said. Knowing that she couldn't possibly comprehend, I told her there wasn't enough oil left in the earth to last another century. "Unless men and women stop believing in miracles and find new sources of energy, the oil supply will be pretty well exhausted before you've lived out your second life on earth.

Still talking to her, I led her back upstairs to the garage. "When you've thought about it, perhaps you can tell me why God has given the anti-Christ so much power in the world. But first I want to show you an invention that has helped Satan pursue his evil ways more than anything else on earth." I opened the garage door, and pointed at two Cadillacs—one, the latest model, was Emily's. "From oil man learned how to crack off gasoline and run an engine with fire instead of steam produced from coal." I knew she had no idea of steam engines either, but she was examining the cars from all sides and was particularly interested in the tires.

"They have wheels," she said, and she tried to dig her fingers into them. "Thy wife and thou both have thine own coaches? Thou must be rich. Where dost thou hitch the horses?" She ran her finger over the sides of my car, a ten-year-old monster built when no one worried about engines that consumed gasoline like a thirsty animal. "Be this iron?" she demanded. "Or what thou callest plastic?"

"A little bit of both," I told her. "The horses are an engine—and that is under the hood. A transmission—and a lot of gears—transform the energy to the wheels and make it go. It is called an automobile."

"*Auto* means self," she said. "Does it go by itself?"

"Not quite. It needs a driver. In the United States there are more than a hundred million of these contraptions on the roads. Without horses to pull them they go ten times as fast as a horse can travel in an hour. If you get in their way and the driver doesn't see you, he or she can kill you. Every year automobiles kill more people than lived in the Bay Colony for the first hundred years."

I opened the door to my car so she could get in.

"It's almost as big as a wigwam," she said. "The poor people in Boston could have lived in them." She examined the white leather seats and shook her head. "'Tis leather, I am sure. People now sit on leather?" She slid into the front seat and lay down. "'Tis nearly big enough to sleep on." She laughed. "I remember that Ben Jonson wrote 'Every pettifogger's wife has a coach so that he may marry. Then he marries that he may be made a cuckold in it.' This coach is almost big enough to seesaw in but it hath no curtains."

Laughing, I opened the garage door and was happy to see that the twenty-four-hour accumulation of snow was not so deep as I had feared. The driveway could be shoveled out clear to the street in a few minutes.

"Tonight," I told her, "you will see many of these automobiles out on the road." Sitting behind the wheel I told her that tomorrow we would drive the car to Boston. "Right now, I just want you to hear the sound of the engine. It's going to make a big noise."

I turned the key and the engine roared to life. She screamed, clutched my arm, and buried her face in my shoulder. "It growleth like a yowling cat," she said. "And now it purrs. I do not trust it. Methinks, dear Robert, I cannot live long in your world."

"Of course, you can," I told her. "Think about the Indians. Think how they must have felt when the English arrived in the colonies, and the Indians saw guns and ploughs and swords and shovels and axes for the first time." I turned off the engine and led her into the street. Suddenly happy again, she waded through a snowdrift tossing snow around her and exclaiming, "I really love the winter. Will filled the cellar with smoked meat, salted fish, potatoes, turnips, pumpkins, squashes. I spun cloth and taught the young children how to read and went to church on Sundays and Lecture Day, and I read the Scriptures. Many nights a few of our close friends read plays like *Bartholomew Fair,* and *Eastward Ho,* and new plays by Master Shakespeare which Harry Vane had brought with him from England."

She laughed. "Harry loved to pretend he was an actor. He read various parts with Will and me and Mary and John Coggeshall and the Aspinwalls. Unlike most of the Puritans we felt certain that we could love God and laugh too."

We were walking toward the beach and the shoreline of Quincy Bay, which was less than a half mile away. Anne noticed the suburban homes on eight-thousand-foot lots that we were passing. "Electricity," she said pointing to the soft glow of lights in the windows. "There are so many homes here," she said. "Many of them are much bigger than they were in Boston. You said that you live near Mt. Wolleystone, but all around Will and me was a forest with a meadow and swamps running down to the Bay." She clung to my arm. "Oh, dear Robert, I am afraid. Tell me why I have come back here."

I had no answers. "Except for the Blue Hills, which you called the Chevy Hills, the forests are all gone," I told her. "The farms that replaced them are gone too. This place is called Merrymount. It's known as suburbia. People live here and in hundreds of places like this all over the United States. Every day they drive their automobiles to Boston and other cities that are even bigger."

"What kind of work do they do?"

I shook my head, puzzled as to how to explain a service society and insurance companies and banks and cities filled with lawyers and financial geniuses and theaters and hotels—cities with no factories to speak of at all. How could I describe factories to her—factories where cloth was spun and food prepared and appliances and automobiles were built? Factories which were once family-run and family-owned she might have understood, but not only had these been eliminated but most of her work as a wife and mother had disappeared too. How could I tell her that the concept of man as a provider for the family and his children, with all of them working together to provide food, clothing, and shelter had practically disappeared from the Western world? Three hundred and fifty years later, even the farms to feed the people were big business and no longer dependent on the industry of one man and his wife and children. We had achieved freedom from want by a division of labor, but we hadn't yet learned that the family, like it or not, must become a new kind of world family with no room for internecine warfare.

But somehow I was sure that with her religious beliefs in God's grace, and her belief in the indwelling Holy Spirit within each one of us, Anne would be delighted in men's and women's new freedom. She would probably be sure that our interdependency was all part of God's larger plan to make us aware of our need to love one another.

"I'll tell you about work and war and what's happened in the world later on," I told her. "Right now we are walking a few hundred yards from where Thomas Morton hung his britches from a maypole. He wanted to make sure that everyone could find their way to Mare-mount, the mountain by the sea where he proclaimed himself "mine host." Did you know about Morton?"

She chuckled. "Sam Maverick told me all about him and Captain Myles Standish, the Separatist who captured him, and sent Morton back to England." She laughed. "For a few years the Puritans were very afraid of Morton. When he got back to England he contacted Sir Fernando Gorges, who was very close to King Charles, and they nearly convinced the King to revoke the patent that Charles had given the colonists. Later, when Morton came back to New England, Master Withrop sent John Endicott to Mt. Wolleystone. They set Morton's plantation afire and put him in jail."

I was a little surprised that she obviously knew Samuel Maverick so well. Maverick was a name that had entered the English vocabulary because, much later, a descendant of his who lived in Texas had refused to brand his cattle. Not much was known about Sam Maverick except that he had arrived in Massachusetts Bay a few years before Winthrop and had taken possession of

Noddle's Island. Sam's island had nearly as much acreage as nearby Shawmut Island, which later became Boston. Noddle's Island is now known as East Boston, and the mud flats extending into the harbor have become Logan Airport. In Anne's time it was a lonely island isolated from the peninsula of Boston. Maverick had fortified it for himself and ran his own ferry service for his friends.

"Sam told Will and me that Morton arrived about 1626," Anne said. "He settled in Mt. Wolleystone to trade with the Indians for beaver, otter, bear, sable, fox—all manner of fur. Everybody in England wanted fur coats and fur hats. Will was buying and selling fur, but he never made as much money as Morton. Beaver was selling for ten shillings a pound in London. Sam told us that Morton earned thousands of pounds trading with the Indians for beaver skins alone."

I whistled. "A thousand pounds in those days would be worth twenty thousand pounds today."

She shrugged. "Most poor people and apprentices would work for a few shillings a day. A man who was worth a thousand pounds was very rich. That is why the Puritans were so eager to come to New England. They never fooled me. Worshiping God their own way—without the Papists—was only the milk in New Canaan. The cream was that they could get rich at the same time. They were more interested in salvation through works and wealth than being one with the Lord."

"But everyone believes that you were a Puritan, too."

"How couldst they? Master John Wilson called me a leper and a heathen and even more terrible things when they excommunicated me from the church. When I walked out of the First Church in Boston, all of them—many who had sworn they were my friends—said not a word. They silently watched. None of them who had come to my house, month after month, dared to stand up and support me. I told Jesus that I would never go into any church again—He was my church—and I never did."

Anne smiled sadly. "But perchance my friends were right. I was too honest. I never could abide hypocrites. People like Master Winthrop and Master Dudley, who professed to love God, could not believe that the poor Indians were God's creatures too. Even when they managed to convert the Indians to Christianity, they were still second-rate creatures." She sighed. "In truth, John-Luv was a hypocrite too. I told him that I loved him because he believed in God's infinite grace but he did not believe that God's grace was for everyone—especially not the savages."

Before I could ask her more about the Indians, I saw the headlights of an automobile behind us cutting a swath of light on the dark snow-covered street and revealing the snow piled high by city plows.

"Oh, Jesus!" Anne screamed. "'Tis a dragon breathing fire." Before I could grab her she plunged into a snowdrift. Pulling her to her feet as the car went by us, I told her that it was only an automobile, no different from the one she had just sat in. But she was still trembling. "It frighteneth me." She watched its taillight disappearing. "It's like those monsters in King Arthur's day."

"You must have read Malory's *Mort D'Arthur*," I said and hugged her. "We have something in common. I grew up reading fairy stories."

"King Arthur was no fairy story," she replied. She was still trembling. "It was history. Poor, poor Isolde. I loved her very much and Tristan too. Momma was afraid that I thought I was Isolde of the fair hair."

"But you were really Anne Hutchinson."

"Thou made me take an oath," she reminded me. And then she noticed a street sign on a lamp post that we were passing. She spelled out the letters *N.A.R.R.A.G.A.N.S.E.T.T.* It readeth Narragansett," she said, quite amazed. "Their sachem, Miantonomo, was a friend of mine."

I laughed. "He would be surprised to know that Narragansett Road is next to Chickatobut and Pontiac Road—Indians I'm sure he never heard of. About sixty years ago this land was still the forest that you remember. Then it was sold to a realty development company. When they laid out the streets, they named them after Indian tribes and they sold the land to build homes."

We were approaching the shoreline of Quincy Bay. A little to the west we could see a larger hill than the one we were walking on. A black shadow, it was pinpointed with lights against the clear sky. "That's Mt. Wollaston." I pointed it out for her. "To the north you can see the skyline of Boston and insurance buildings and bank buildings that rise more than a thousand feet in the sky with fifty or more floors one on top of the other." I pointed to the boulevard that curved around the bay. Those flashing lights that you see are your dragons. Inside each of them are Protestants, Catholics, and Jews. John Winthrop tried to keep the foreigners out, and he succeeded for about a hundred years, but now there are more former Irishmen, Italians, Puerto Ricans, Chinese, Poles, and Swedes in Boston—not to mention Germans, Frenchmen, Dutch, Japanese, and Spanish—than there were original colonists. The Massachusetts Bay Colony became what is known as a state in the United States, and it is still called Massachusetts. Rhode Island, Connecticut, Maine, and New Hampshire, along with forty-seven other states, extending beyond and into the Pacific Ocean are now called the United States of America." I shrugged. "We all call ourselves Americans, but so far as I know none of us has ever lived before."

We were walking along the cove of Merrymount beach. My last words were out of my mouth before I realized their implication. When she clung silently to me, I could feel her shivering. "Now I am the alien," she said softly. "I fear people will not welcome one who has returned from the grave." She stared at the waves pounding on the shore. "The ocean looks angry and cold. I know thou willst tell me that there are no lobsters, no cod out there. They are probably gone like the forest, along with its bears and lynx."

"There are a few lobsters left," I told her, "and cod. But no bears and big cats."

We were now only a few feet from the water. The tide was full and still roiled by the storm. Huge black waves with frothy angry white tips were washing up on the shore. Suddenly, before I realized what she was going to do, Anne said, "Methinks I should return to oblivion."

Before I could stop her, she had dropped my arm and run toward the water. Within a few inches from the angry sea she tripped and fell to her knees and sprawled on the stony beach. When I reached her, her fingers were being licked by the waves. I rolled her over and dragged her a few feet up on the beach.

"What the Hell were you trying to do?" I yelled at her. Pulling her to her feet, I realized that she was staring at me and beyond me—wide-eyed in a trance.

I shook her like a rag doll. "Anne, sweetheart, for God's sake, speak to me! What's the matter with you?"

Sobbing, she finally answered. "I cannot run well in thy shoes. I am sorry that thou art stuck with me but perhaps not for long."

"For Christ's sake, don't do that again!" I told her angrily. "If you're going to disappear, just go up in smoke. Don't leave me with a corpse." Then I hugged her. "Honey, I am not stuck with you. I love you. I didn't fall in love with you because you're a quitter, but because you dared to live and be you."

She squeezed my hand. "Thou mayst lose my body but thou willst never lose my mind."

"What does that mean?"

She shrugged. "For what seemed an eternity just now, a voice kept speaking to me and telling me: 'Death and resurrection are continuous. Thou must tell all my creatures that the only sin against me is killing one another. Thou hast not much time.'"

"Are you telling me you had a revelation?" I asked skeptically.

She nodded. "A voice told me that I have much to do."

"What in particular? Whose voice was it?"

She smiled. "It was my own voice speaking to me through Jesus."

"You mean you saw Jesus?" I tried to hide my incredulity.

"No. Dear Robert, thou must try to understand. My indwelling spirit—or thine—is a light. Sometimes 'tis bright, sometimes scarcely to be seen."

"What did it say to you?"

"Before I tell thee, I must think on it, and I must know more about thy world, which methinks is close to destruction."

"By whom?" I demanded. "You mean God is going to wipe us out?"

"No," she shook her head sadly and kissed my cheek. "God is going to let

His creatures wipe themselves out." She still was speaking in a faraway voice. "I know not yet what I must do, but I learned who thou surely art and why thou lovest me." I looked at her startled.

"Who am I?"

She laughed. "Thou knowest so much about me. Methinks thou should be able to answer that."

10

Later, in bed, still very much subdued, Anne lay naked in my arms. Like long-time friends, rather than young lovers, which we most certainly were not, we held hands making contact through each other's fingers, unable to evoke in words that we liked each other despite the crazy throw of cosmic dice that had brought us together.

"Dost thou ever pray?" she finally asked, her soft words almost escaping me, as if she knew the answer in advance.

I shook my head. "I never believed in a personal God who was interested in any man's or woman's prayers. Most prayers are take-care-of-me-first-prayers or don't-let-me-die-prayers. If God could grant them, we'd all be gods. I squeezed her hand. "But I'm not a very good example," I said. "Millions of Americans are still Puritans at heart. They may give lip service to God—call themselves Christians—but they are taking no chances. They keep trying to pass laws making prayer in public schools compulsory. The President and many of the governors of various states want to force a Christian God on the country." I laughed. "Some of them should pray that God will help them get out of the messes that they have created."

"I understand you not. We had schools in Boston. Will contributed more than six pounds to building the house for Master Daniel Maud so that he could have a place to teach the children of the freemen. He led the children in prayer and taught them religion and how to read their slates. Every day our sons Samuel and Francis went to Master Philemon Permort's Latin School. It was beside our house on Sentry Lane. The General Court passed a law: it was the responsibility of all parents to teach their children 'in learning and labor and other employments that might be profitable to the common-wealth.'"

"Boston is no longer the tight little island it was then," I said. "Now it's a melting pot. Puritans would be sure there are more anti-Christs than anyone else living here, and that includes Papists and Jews. The Jews have the Torah and Haftorah, which includes some of your Scriptures, but they're quite sure that Jesus was not the Messiah. Many Protestants don't believe that Jesus was really the son of God. The problem is that most of them believe that they are not praying to the same God."

Anne smiled. "I believeth not that Jesus cares how thou prayest, or whether thou thinkest God is different and not really his Father. He only hopes that thou wilt discover the Holy Spirit—the light of God that is within thee. Once thou dost, thou canst not deny it, and thou wilt be saved."

"Saved for what," I challenged her. "I don't want to live in Heaven. It would be too bland and dull."

"Oh, Robert, thou teaseth me. I believe not in a Puritan Heaven. Heaven is not a place. 'Tis a state of being. That is why I am here. I am slowly discovering that if you love God, you never stop being. I did not die when Uncas torched my pyre, but for a long time I ceased to be conscious. My being was in a blank space."

"Who made you conscious again?"

"Jesus—because I loved him. And thou, because thou loved me."

I stared at her. "I'm beginning to think that you are trying to convert me. Your problem is that I am not a Puritan. I was indoctrinated in a graduate business school of Harvard." I laughed. "The same college that your Puritans started. It's main purpose is to teach men and women how to live higher off the hog than their fellow citizens and the Devil take the hindmost."

Anne was impressed that Harvard College was still in existence. She knew that the Reverend John Harvard had given his library and eight hundred pounds to the seminary in New Town, and in 1636 the General Court had named the college Harvard in his honor and renamed New Town, Cambridge because John Harvard was a graduate of Cambridge University.

"The seminary students were much like their fathers," Anne grimaced. "Good Puritans. They believed they were among the elect who would be resurrected when Jesus came again. They thought they were the saints and that Christ was pleased with them because they spent most of their time getting rich—building their good estates and dividing all the land in the Colony for themselves—and cheating the Indians. They were certain that God and Jesus only loved the freemen. Only freemen and their wives could become members of the church."

"Your husband was a freeman," I said. I was aware that in the early days of the Colony only male freemen could vote or hold office or become magistrates. To be recognized as a freeman you had to be an inhabitant of the Colony, who owned property or who had arrived with some wealth or connection to wealth, and you had to be admitted to a fellowship in the church as a believer in the Puritan God, and His Scriptures. In other words, wealth and property, coupled with a discreet silence about one's most intimate beliefs—whatever they may have been—assured church membership.

"Will and I were never unequivocally accepted by the wealthy colonists," Anne said. "Will was a deal earthy, and his parents had never been wealthy. The General Court permitted him to buy six hundred acres in Mt. Wolleystone because they felt certain that he must be worth a few thousand pounds. But although Will was appointed surveyor for a time, he never took control of thousands of acres of land as did Master Winthrop or Master Dudley or some of the other original signers of the charter. Will was a freeman and, in truth, a deputy magistrate, but he was never invited into the inner sanctum. Master Winthrop was not exceedingly happy when Will expanded the house that Edward had built for us before we arrived." She laughed. "Methinks it riled him that our house was nearly as big as the governor's house."

"Most people think that Winthrop was not even aware of you—not until you tried to take over the church." I said. "He probably thought you wanted his job as well as John Wilson's."

"That is abundantly foolish!" Anne grinned at me. She knew that I was teasing her. "When we arrived in 1634 there were only two hundred and sixty-five members of the church, and scarcely four hundred other people—servants and apprentices and children in the whole miserable town of Boston. No one was fond of Master Wilson. He thundered and yelled and sounded like Jehovah gone mad. Methinks I could have preached more thoughtful and interesting sermons than he did. Maybe even better than John-Luv." She laughed. "Most everyone was delighted when, a few weeks after we arrived, Master Wilson went back to England for a whole year to try and convince his wife to come to the Colony. While he was away John-Luv took charge and became the preacher. As for Master Winthrop, methinks he would have wanted to spank me because I had the impertinence to talk back to him. He told his wife, Margeret, that I was an insolent hussy."

"But you wanted to be rich and famous, too, didn't you?" I demanded, egging her on.

"Damn thee!" She clapped my bare behind resoundingly. "That is not true. I said not a word to anyone nor complained about Master Wilson except to Will. That first year we were all not a little diligent trying to survive. I did not waste my time gossiping with any of the women. In truth I watched and listened. I was fascinated by the Indians. Those in the Bay Colony were very poor and sickly. They had lost many of their people to the plague and pox, which they felt certain the white man had brought from England. But they knew that an abundant number of us had died from it likewise. Squanto and Massasoit, sachems of their tribes, had been in great measure benevolent to the Separatists. They taught them how to plant corn and fertilize it and grind it. But slowly the Indians learned the truth. The ministers tried to convince everybody that the Indians were the lost tribes of Israel, that they had been abandoned by God and now were Satan's devils.

"John-Luv agreed with Master Winthrop, who said it was our duty to convert the Indians to Christianity. We must stop their powwows, which led to rioting, and show them that their medicine men were teaching them the Devil's work. Poor John-Luv. He was particularly out of countenance that the Indians were polygamous and frequently exchanged wives." She giggled. "I told him that he was a man who did not let his left hand know what his right hand was doing. When he complained about the Indians' lack of virtue, he was holding my cony with his left hand."

Anne sighed. "I remember it, because happy with him I was not. We lay on bearskins that he had purchased from the Indians. It was November of the first year. There was a fire in his study fireplace. We had broken the Commandment three times since I had arrived." She shook her head. "I truly did not feel sinful. I loved him with my soul. But John-Luv was not so generous with *his* soul. The Colony had given John a big house, which was built on Trimontaine. Trimontaine had three peaks, West Hill, Cotton Hill, and Beacon Hill. Beacon Hill was the tallest. On top of it was a thirty-foot-high pole with a large bucket filled with tar. On foggy nights it was lighted to guide ships into the harbor."

"You were telling me about making love to John Cotton in his study," I reminded her. "Where was Sarah? Wasn't she suspicious?"

Anne shrugged. "Sarah never disturbed us. But making love right under her nose made me all apucker, especially because, while John and I both delighted in each other's flesh, we were slowly discovering we were not enchanted about what was churning around in each other's minds. I told him that he need not vex himself—I would never tell anyone that dear Susanna was his child."

Anne sighed. "But what vexed him beyond compare was my 'too quick tongue.' He kept warning me that I should keep my feelings about grace and the Indians to myself." She paused, drifting for a moment on her memories. "John kept telling me that the time for revelations and prophecy was over. But I told him, 'I am not like thee, John-Luv. I believeth not that I am one of the elect. I care not whether I am resurrected in this flesh.' I told him that I was not like Master John Eliot either, who had only learned enough of the Indian language to try and convince them that the English were the chosen people. Master Eliot thought he was a Fifth Monarchist, and a future Apostle, and would be received directly into Heaven by Jesus because of his good works. I cared not, if the Indians had thirty-seven different gods. I told John that I agreed with Roger Williams. Roger sent John a letter which made him very angry. 'We had not our land by patent from the King,' he wrote. 'The natives are the true owners of it. We ought to repent of such a receiving of it and give the patent back to the King.'"

Anne shook her head reminiscently. "That was our first disagreement. John-Luv was very patient with me. He insisted that we had not cheated the Indians of their land. 'Roger Williams is wrong,' he told me. 'It was not the King's intention to take possession of this country by murder of the natives or robbery. Where there is a vacant place, by the law of nature (*vacuum domicilium cedit*) there is liberty for the son of Noah and Adam to come in and inhabit it, though they neither buy it, or ask their leaves.'" Anne shrugged. "According to John-Luv, 'In vacant places he that taketh possession of it and besoweth culture and husbandry upon it has a right to it.'"

"That's always been the conqueror's justification," I said. "The Puritans in particular, quoting Scriptures to suit themselves, were convinced they were accomplishing God's work. A hundred years later Cotton Mather, John's grandson, preached that the 'Devil decoyed these miserable savages to New England in the hopes that the Gospel of the Lord Jesus Christ would never come here to destroy the Devil's absolute empire over them.'"

I shrugged and continued. "Three hundred years later the same superrace mentality produced a man named Adolf Hitler. Instead of the Indians, he killed six million Jews and millions of other people. The truth is that without a sense of manifest destiny or a Christian belief in works as their salvation, the Indians had no need to accumulate wealth. Unlike the Europeans, their total population was very small. The land was lush with food. Indians escaped boredom by changing their residence. They were nomadic, but for a very good reason. When they abandoned a particular hunting or planting ground for a season or two they gave God time to replenish the land. The land wasn't 'vacant.' They needed for survival the land that the Puritans took from them or forced them to sell."

I purposely inferred that God personally replenished the land. After two days with Anne I was beginning to wonder if perhaps all of us were the product of divine tampering with our destinies.

"That is what I told Will!" She clapped her hands enthusiastically. "God gave us the land. We must use it wisely. There was enough for all of us. We must share it with the Indians. They were God's children too. But John-Luv thought we must Christianize all of them. He was especially upset with Roger Williams. Roger told him, 'Christening maketh not Christians. I could maketh all the natives in Rhode Island observe the Sabbath,' he said. 'Plausible persuasions are the result of powerful forces or armies. But only God can turn a soul from its idols both of heart and worship and conversation, before it is capable of worship to the true living God.'"

Anne continued, "I told John-Luv that Roger understood the Indians and loved them better than did Master Eliot. What difference did it make if they had many different gods? They knew there was a Devil. They called him Hobomok. But they had one great Spirit—Kautanowwit. The Indians thought that when they died they went somewhere to the southwest. That was their Heaven. Miantonomo told me that he had been to the Southwest. The Indians who lived there were also aware of the same great Spirit. They called him Wahkontah."

Anne shrugged. "The Indians knew not the words, but they understood that the Holy Spirit was in them likewise. I told John-Luv that we were destroying their traditions. If an Indian became a Christian, he would no longer pay tribute to his sachem, and he disobeyed his leaders. But he could never become a church member. So the Indian knew not whether he was afoot or on horseback. And he knew that the English truly hated his people. The magistrates kept passing laws against them. An Indian could have only one wife; they must observe the Lord's Day; they must not pick lice off themselves and eat them; they must not grease themselves; they must not let their hair grow long; they must not abuse themselves with strong liquors; they must not commit adultery; and they must not howl when they were in mourning." Anne laughed. "The Indians were supposed to behave better than many of the Englishmen in the Colony."

She was silent for a long time and then, leaning on her elbow, she stared quizzically at me. "Dost thou wish to make love, or go to sleep?"

"I *am* making love," I told her. "Hold my cock and tell me what you are thinking."

She grasped it affectionately and smiled as it grew strong between her fingers. "I told John-Luv that God might perchance forgive him and me for our love of each other's flesh, but he would never forgive the colonists for what they did to the Pequods." Again she was silent and stared at the ceiling for a long time, but she still held onto me. I kissed her breasts, admiring the soft glow of her flesh, and asked her what she was thinking.

"The Spirit said, 'Behold I will come quickly,'" she sighed. "Why do men, who say they believe in God, hate each other? Why do they murder each other? The only sin against God is killing another person. Papa told me that so far as he could figure, men had been at war with one another more than half the time since God created the world. I never believed that men and women must suffer because Adam and Eve disobeyed God."

"Not all Christians believe in Genesis, or in creationism, as it is called today," I told her. "About a hundred and fifty years ago, a man named Charles Darwin pretty well established that men and women evolved from a missing tribe of great apes."

Anne looked at me wide-eyed. And then she laughed. "I never did believe the world started with Adam—but I must think on that."

"Monkeys or men," I said, "your father was right. War is never ending. God must enjoy watching his creatures destroy each other. About thirty years after Uncas torched you and you disappeared from the earth, the Puritans engaged in an all-out war with the Indians. It was called King Philip's War. Metacomet, a Wamponoag, who was the son of Massasoit, presumably started it to wipe out the English. No doubt he had good cause. But he gave the Colonists the excuse they needed. Before the war was over in 1676, nearly one-third of the entire 30,000 population of New England—some 6,000 Indians and 3,000 white men—had been brutally killed. Percentagewise, the death toll exceeded any war since. I know nothing of the circumstances, but your son, Edward, who was a captain, was killed in King Philip's War in

August of 1675.

"Oh, dear God!" Sobbing, Anne covered her face with her hands. "I should hate the Indians too," she moaned. "But I never did. They were the hangmen, but Master Winthrop and Master Dudley tied the noose."

11

It was eleven o'clock. I asked Anne if she were sleepy. Smiling, she shook her head. "How can I sleep? My mind is as excited as my cony. Canst thou come inside me and still talk?"

With her long legs clasping me gently, she stared up at me wordlessly for a few minutes. Her thoughts were far away and her eyes were not focusing on me. "What are you thinking about?" I asked.

"My soul and thine are blended," she answered. "I was thinking if a man and woman are truly aware of each other's spirit, then together they can experience Christ's second coming."

I laughed. "You mean the millennium? According to Scriptures God was angry at the Israelites for disobeying Him. He let the Gentiles take over for awhile until the Jews stopped sinning against Him. But He never set the date that He would rebuild the Tabernacle of David. For the most part, the Christians and Jews have stopped fighting each other. But there's a new anti-Christ in the world—the Soviets, who don't believe in God or Jesus Christ."

Enjoying her vagina gently nurturing me and floating on her flesh, I rambled on trying to bring her up to date. "I don't believe God is personally interested in what is happening," I said. "Maybe He believes His creatures can only learn to love by suffering. Freedom to believe in whatever God—or conception of God—one has gradually became a way of life in the late eighteenth century. It created the environment to question whether the kings and emperors and bishops and priests and ministers and rabbis—and finally the magistrates and deputies too—believed in the same God that the people did. Kings continued to wage war on kings, and peasants fought their battles and each other. Occasionally they rebelled and assassinated their kings and their leaders. The names change but the process goes on. Men and women have died by the billions to achieve freedom to believe in their own notion of God. In the New World our motto became 'In God we trust,' but we still didn't believe in each other's God.

"A few years before you were born, England destroyed the Spanish Armada and the Spanish Catholic dream that it was their destiny to make their God the only God in the world. While you were alive, and until you

84

died, I'm sure you must have been aware that the Protestants and Catholics, backed by Pope Urban the VIII, were in continuous war all over Europe for thirty years."

Anne shuddered. "I remember. On my fortieth birthday I heard that Count Tilly with thirty thousand Catholics finally captured Magdeburg and butchered and raped and murdered more than twenty thousand men, women, and children. The mercenary soldiers even turned cannibals and ate some of their victims."

"About fifty years after you died," I told her, "the Americans fought the French and Indian War and finally, because King James was horrified by the rumors coming back about the intolerance of the Puritans, he revoked the Massachusetts Bay Colony charter. The Indian massacres not only continued under royal governors, but the seeds were planted for a Revolutionary War, which took place some seventy years later. Your great-great-grandchildren finally got their complete independence from England and the king, and the thirteen colonies became thirteen United States with a Constitution that finally gave each person the freedom to worship God the way he or she wished."

I continued. "Many Englishmen actually died to achieve the same kind of freedom in America that they had denied the Indians. But back in England the British weren't too happy with us either. A few years later when they were at war with France, we kept trading with the French because they helped us win our Revolutionary War. So another skirmish, called the War of 1812, took place. After that, although most of the rest of the world was at war, America had a relatively peaceful fifty years. Then the Northern states fought the Southern states."

I explained to her that not only had the enslavement of black men become a way of life for the Southern colonists, but they too were seeking freedom to establish their own nation. "The Northern states won the Civil War," I said. "Presumably the black men were free men, but more than a hundred years later most of them are still poor and very few white people marry them and they live in segregated parts of our cities."

"Can they vote and be deputies and governors?" Anne asked.

I nodded affirmatively, aware of what she was thinking. "But for a long time, women, black or white, couldn't vote. Like you, they were not 'free' women. That took another fifty years. Women can vote now and hold political office. You could be governor of Massachusetts." I grinned at her. "You're just the right age and you have wonderful credentials. It's time that Massachusetts had another Hutchinson for governor."

Anne still couldn't absorb the new status of women. "Women no longer have to obey the Fifth Commandment?" she asked. "Women are equal to men?"

"Better than men." I nuzzled her breasts. "Women can nurture men and they have brains too. But most men won't agree with me. Anyway, before you can become governor, you've got a lot of catching up to do, especially about the male pastime of waging war. I'll skip the Spanish-American War, which was short and ridiculous."

Anne's fingers were kneading my behind, but at the same time she was listening to me intently. "Fifty-two years after the Civil War," I told her, "we sent several million Americans to France to fight the German king, who was called a *Kaiser*. He wanted to take over France and every other country in Europe. We told ourselves we were fighting in Europe to make the world safe for democracy. We and the English and the French won the war. But several billion people in the world were not ready. Even today most men and women don't want the kind of freedom that you were fighting for," I shrugged. "I'm not even sure that you believe in complete religious freedom. Perhaps you really want everyone to think the way you thought."

"That is not true."

"You insisted that all ministers except Cotton and Wheelwright were not 'sealed' because they preached an Old Testament religion and because they believed that the only way to achieve salvation was through hard work and piety. If you had had your way, would you have let John Wilson and Hugh Peters preach?"

"Thou confuseth me. I did not say that 'works' was wrong. I simply said that men and women should not depend on works to achieve sainthood. It was the ministers who were intolerant, not I. People should think for themselves."

"That's hard work and most people avoid it," I said. "Anyway, I still have to bring you up-to-date on man's inhumanity to man. Twenty-one years later, after we had supposedly won the First World War, we discovered that we hadn't. Once again the Germans were overrunning Europe, and this time they had a whipping boy, the Jews, on whom they blamed all their troubles. Like the English with the Indians, the Germans thought they were the super-race. At the same time, the Japanese had decided that the Chinese, who owned much more land than they did, were an inferior people, and they marched into China and overran it. Pretty soon the entire world was at war again on one side or the other. In those days, our president was a man named Franklin Delano Roosevelt. He offered a new reason why we were fighting, but it was really the same reason. We were fighting for basic human freedoms: freedom from fear, freedom from want, freedom of speech, and freedom of religion. Millions of men and women died in that war, and Americans invented a new kind of weapon, a nuclear bomb, that would make your Puritan muskets and carbines look like popguns."

"Methinks the world hath forgotten God," Anne said solemnly.

"Or you might say that God has finally given us the means to destroy the world He created and is sitting back waiting to see if we are going to do it. Keep in mind I've only scratched the surface of wars that have been fought all over the world for the past 350 years and are still being fought. Since World War II, in a weird kind of gentlemen's agreement, nations may continue to fight each other but not use the ultimate weapons, atom and hydrogen bombs, as they are called. So Americans have continued to fight in other people's wars, in faraway places like Korea, Vietnam, and Central America, because we fear a new style of anti-Christ which we call Communism. And now we have a relatively new nation in the world—the Union of Soviet Socialist Republics, or the Soviets or Russians, as they are called. Their leaders tell their people that democracy is dead, and most people cannot be trusted to elect responsible magistrates. Millions of them presumably don't believe in God or Jesus. The State itself is omnipotent. But this is only temporary. Eventually, they tell their people, the state will wither away, and everybody will live in a Communist heaven. The Soviet leaders are terrified that we're going to try and convert their people to Christianity or Judaism and make religious beliefs more important than their laws."

I grinned at her. "Their former leaders, Marx and Lenin, had something in common with your Mr. Winthrop and Mr. Dudley. Like them, these Marxists had their own version of a better world—Utopia. If necessary, Utopians will murder millions of men and women to make their Utopias come true. But when you, Anne, told everybody that even sinful people could experience God's grace, you were challenging the colonial state. Utopians can't tolerate freedom of thought *or* religion," I laughed. "The big question that you should ask God is to tell you why He brought you back to life. Even as we lie here, our leaders, or the Soviet leaders, could decide to push a few buttons and destroy all of us for our own good. The world is filled with self-righteous men. Whether they believe in God or not, they're convinced that their beliefs are best for everybody. Unlike the American Indians, the self-appointed leaders of the Massachusetts Bay Colony had a sense of destiny. They refused to live and let live. They believed it was their mission to save mankind."

"Thou dost not believe that this is Satan's work?"

"Blaming it on Satan is an excuse for stupidity," I said. "Why not blame it on God? If He is so all-powerful, he could put a stop to it. Either that or He enjoys the game."

"Thou dost not understand. God gives us a choice. His Son was like us, a man of flesh. Jesus died to save us and to show us the way. All God asks is that we become aware that all of us share His Spirit together." She snuggled her face against mine. "Methinks that thou art aware of God within thee. Thou art God."

"No, thou art," I said and hugged her. "I prefer a female God. She may be the only hope for the world. Even though some courageous females fight back, women are still enslaved by male delusions of grandeur. Whether man descended from Adam and Eve or monkeys, man becomes the aggressor.

With a big stick, or rock, he quickly learns that he can dominate other men and take the women he wants. Thousands of years later he has improved his weapons, but not his brain. When he finally mastered a bow and arrow, a stone axe, a mace, a musket, a machine or bombs, he knew that he could go one step further. He had power in his hands. He could become a leader. Slowly the smartest men of the tribe figured an easy way to retain that power. They invented the sun god and the earth gods and gave them huge cocks to show how powerful they were, and they appointed as ministers the medicine men of the tribe to tell their people that only the leaders knew what the gods were saying. If anyone questioned the leaders' heavenly connections, they were bopped on the head with a rock or pushed off a cliff, and the people were told that the angry gods had done it. All over the world these smart men of the tribe convinced their people that they had an inside track. Divine Rights. The only problem was that they were mortal. They grew old. They died. So they always had to pass the crown to their children.

"But gradually other self-appointed deities usually appeared, younger men who figured out the system. They wanted their piece of the pie too. Today, many of our medicine men believe that symbolically a young man must destroy his father. The son resents the father because the latter has sole access to the mother's vagina." I laughed. "You can see that it shakes down to a question of penis power. Men forced women and their children to worship a little piece of flesh that could grow big and impregnate a woman—whether she liked it or not."

Scowling at me, Anne revived my penis, which had left her nest during this long diatribe. "Sometimes, dear Robert, methinks thou art flouting me," she said. "I am not afraid of thy weapon, or of any cock. What good are they without a woman to succor them?" She sighed. "I do not understand half of what thou telleth me—all these wars, or that men are monkeys—but I do know that most of the Puritans hated the Indians. Master Wilson called them 'the most sordid and contemptible part of the human species,' and Master Hooker said 'they were the veriest ruins of mankind on the face of the earth.'"

"The beat goes on," I said. "The Anglo-Saxons and before them the Germans and the Romans told themselves that the rest of the world was filled with the dregs of the earth: barbarians, blasphemers, anti-Christs, wogs, kikes, and African savages who were not even a part of the human species." I hugged her. "Almost as bad as those, were people like yourself, who don't agree with them. The Puritans were what we call the conservatives, the Rightists. You and Roger Williams and all the people who fled to Rhode Island to pursue your own version of religious freedom would be called political activists today. You were against the regime. You were the radical Left. You were as great a threat to the Puritan leaders and their style of government as the Indians were."

Anne shrugged. "That is not true. Thou soundeth like John-Luv. He continued to tell me that I was a lover of anarchy, that I wanted no government or laws of men. I told him that many laws of the Scriptures and the laws of the magistrates were written by men who did not understand salvation, and that many of the laws of the Old Testament were written by men who believed in a wrathful god, not the loving, caring laws of Jesus." She sighed. "Neither the Jews nor most of the Puritans could understand that."

"You should have kept a diary or a journal," I told her. "Winthrop did, and he wrote many letters. So did your John-Luv. Their sermons and letters and writings slanted the history books their way. You were the troublemaker and libertine—another Thomas Morton. Today everyone believes that the Puritans were in danger of being wiped out by the Indians. Supposedly, there were only a few of them in the midst of thousands of wild savages who would just as soon scalp them as look at them. Winthrop and Wilson were certain that the Pequods would take advantage of the dissension you were causing and murder everyone in the Colony. You and John Wheelwright were telling everybody that even sinners could experience God's grace and be saved."

Anne scowled at me. "That did not mean they could break the law and not be punished. As for Master Morton, I care not that he could evidently hold his nose and sleep with the Indian women who drenched themselves in moose oil." She laughed. "The Scriptures never said the men could live without women. That's a Papist dream. Sam Maverick told me that Morton was not the only Englishman who traded with the Indians—rum and strong liquors for furs—or slept with their women. But Morton did not cheat them and he never harmed them. The Separatists were not truthful. Morton never traded guns with them or gave them guns. Neither the Massasoits, the Wampanoags, the Narragansetts—not even the Pequods—had any muskets or carbines when we arrived in Boston. That was nearly fifteen years after the Plymouth Colony was founded. All the Indians had were bows and arrows and tomahawks. They rarely were able to kill a man with an arrow unless they ambushed him."

Listening to Anne, it occurred to me that she would be very much in demand on the college circuit as a lecturer, with her revision of history, or as a guest on a television talk show. An indefinable glow seemed to light her face. The combination of her warm mellow voice and sea-green eyes mesmerized me. Staring directly at me as she spoke, she searched my face as if she were looking for a way into my brain. Combining a believable childlike innocence with an underlying sense of loving laughter, she could make me believe—or as I discoverd later, almost anyone believe—that she was not only telling the truth, but that she was sharing her soul, or perhaps even the Holy Spirit with me.

To even think the word *soul* made me chuckle. I was sure that Anne was composed of flesh, blood, and bones. Despite her charisma, I was still pragmatic. Her resurrection was a miracle that only her lover could believe. But I was fully aware of her hypnotic potential and her faith that she had returned to earth for some purpose and that her mission in her second life would slowly become apparent to her.

Now she was telling me that a few months after she had arrived in Boston on August 12, 1634, the Pequod sachem, Sassacus, and his secondary chiefs had been invited by Harry Vane to Boston from Connecticut, where they lived, to arrange a new trading agreement with the colonists. The Pequods had also asked the governor to help them settle the feuds that had developed between them and the Narragansetts. The old sagamore of the Narragansetts, Canonicus, had passed the reins to his nephew, Miantonomo, and presumably Canonicus was responsible for the intermittent raids on the Pequods.

The magistrates, led by Dudley and Winthrop, demanded four fathoms of wampum—intricate, impossible to duplicate, hand-made, Indian shell beads being used by the colonists for money—plus forty beaver skins and thirty otter skins to underwrite the treaty.

"Will thought the price was outrageous," Anne said. "The Pequods refused the deal with them and left Boston very unhappy with us. But later the Pequods offered all their rights to Connecticut, if we would start a new plantation there. 'So as to be at peace,' Master Winthrop told the magistrates, 'and as friends to trade with them and to defend them against the Narragansetts.'"

Anne also explained that during the next two years the Puritans decided to form the Saybrook Company to colonize Connecticut. They built a fort at the mouth of the Connecticut River. But later in 1636, Uncas, the sachem of the Mohegans, who lived in the New Netherlands, convinced Winthrop that the Pequods were plotting against them.

"Supposedly, Uncas told him, 'Out of desperate madness the Pequods do threaten shortly to set upon the Narragansetts and thee jointly.'" Anne smiled. "But Harry Vane had arrived from England the year before, in October of 1635. Because he was royalty and had close connections to the King, Masters Winthrop and Dudley were always palavering him. They convinced the freemen of the Colony to elect Harry governor."

Anne shrugged. "Poor Harry, he was only twenty-four. All the magistrates were older and much shrewder than he was. Harry and I had become exceedingly good friends, so I knew what was happening in the Colony. Harry invited Miantonomo to Boston from Rhode Island, along with the Massachusetts Bay sachem, Cutsahanoquin. The chiefs were met in Roxbury by an honor guard of twenty musketeers, who escorted them to the meeting-house in Boston. Harry had been living in John-Luv's house, which I told you was only a few yards up the hill from my home. Harry invited Miantonomo and the other chiefs to dine with him at Sam Cole's Tavern, which was next door to my house. So Sam's wife, Anne, and I and several other women helped serve the meal. The Indians ate their own food, but Harry did what no other governor did before him. He broke bread in the same room with the Indians. Harry introduced me to Miantonomo. 'Fine woman,' he told Miantonomo, 'she liketh Indians.' Harry concluded a treaty with them, and they agreed not to make a separate peace with the Pequods until the Pequods stopped harassing the Connecticut plantation."

Anne shook her head. "Who was harassing whom was the question and Harry knew it, but then the Pequods murdered Captain Walter Norton, Captain John Stone, and several other men who, according to the Connecticut colonists, were sailing peacefully along the Niantic shore. But the Pequods did not believe they were on a peaceful mission, especially after they captured one of their sachems and demanded bushels of wampum for his release.

"Then Master Winthrop told Harry that he trusted not Miantonomo. Even though he and John-Luv had been responsible for banishing Roger Williams from the Colony, Master Winthrop knew that Roger was friendly with the Narragansetts. He asked Roger if he could work out an alliance with Miantonomo against the Pequods. Harry knew that the magistrates were trying to play off one tribe against the other, but there was nothing he could do about it. Later, Roger told Harry that he was very sorry for his part in the treaty. It ended with five hundred Narragansetts and about fifty Mohegans helping a small company of Englishmen massacre the Pequods. Their horrible agreement was that the English would spare the Indian women and children, and the Narragansetts could adopt them."

Anne shuddered. "Even now, it makes me ill to talk about it. Master Winslow had arrived from Plymouth in Boston, but the Separatists refused to send any of their men to Connecticut to help fight the Pequods because we had never helped them. Jack Underhill told me what happened at Mystic Fort. About one hundred of our militiamen marched to Connecticut along with Master Wilson, who had returned from England and had been appointed chaplain. Together with the Narragansetts and the Mohegans, who had been loaned muskets for the occasion and taught how to use them, they burned the Pequod fort and wigwams and murdered more than four hundred Pequods, including many women and children. The poor Indians who survived fled into the swamps to escape death. Later Jack claimed that he repented his part in the slaughter, but when Will asked him, 'Why should we be so furious? Should not Christians have more mercy and compassion?' Jack told him, 'I would refer you to Scriptures and David's war. When people have grown to such a height of blood and sin against God and man, they deserve the most terrible death that may be. Sometimes the Scriptures declare it. In such cases, women and children must perish with their parents or husbands.'"

"God was on the Puritan side," I told her sarcastically.

"The Puritan God was not my God," Anne said vehemently. "The Narragansetts were so shocked by the slaughter that, even though they hated the Pequods they told Jack, '*Mach* it! *Mach* it!' meaning 'It was all for naught.' The English were much too furious and had slain too many men. Harry could not abide the magistrates either. He was very angry when he discovered they sold the Indians they had captured to English colonists in Bermuda for slaves. Instead of letting the Narragansetts adopt the women and children, Master Winthrop told Uncas the Mohegans could have them."

Anne frowned. "They knew that the women would end up as second and third wives and would be slaves for their Mohegan masters, who could fuck as many women as they wished and not pay any attention to Master Winthrop's laws about adultery. When it was all over, Miantonomo no longer trusted the English, particularly Masters Winthrop and Dudley. And he was right."

"Do you know what happened to Miantonomo?"

Anne nodded. "A few years after Will died, I left Rhode Island and went into Dutch territory. I was sure that the Bay Colony magistrates would take over the Island, and Roger Williams would never get a Colony patent from the King. Then poor Miantonomo was captured in a raid by Uncas. In September of 1643, Randall Holden, who had just returned to the Island from Boston, told me that the General Court had met with Uncas and informed him if he wanted to stay at peace with the English, he must 'take away the life of Miantonomo because of his mindless and treacherous disposition against Uncas, and because Miantonomo was a disturber of a common peace of the whole country.'"

Anne snuggled against me. "Please, Robert, hold me tight. I am afraid to think about it. Even though they banished me and excommunicated me, the magistrates were convinced that I too was a disturber of the common peace. I was Satan's daughter. Two days after Uncas stabbed Miantonomo to death, he and a hundred or more of his tribe did what Masters Winthrop, and Dudley, and Wilson dared not do. They murdered me and my dear children."

"Do you really think that Winthrop told Uncas to kill you?"

"Not in actual words. That was not like Master Winthrop. All he had to tell Uncas was that I was dangerous—a witch—and that I was casting a spell on Uncas, and trying to kill him because I was angry that he had murdered Miantonomo."

"You've bewitched me," I yawned. "I've been inside you for nearly an hour and I'm still erect."

She kissed me tenderly. "Your poor pillicock needs to be rocked to sleep." With her legs around me, her heels digging into my buttocks and smiling confidently, she whispered, "Rock-a-bye, Robert. It won't take long." And it didn't for either of us.

Finally, burrowing sleepily into my arms, she said softly, "'Behold I am coming,' Jesus said. 'Blessed is he who watches.'"

12

I awoke with Anne kissing me. "'Tis morning," she whispered into my lips. "Six o'clock. Thou fell asleep asking me why Jesus had deserted me. Thou asked why did not God strike down Uncas and save me from the flames. I fear that thou dost not understand resurrection. Jesus told us in two Gospels, Matthew and Mark, 'He that loseth his life for my sake shall find it.'"

Anne smiled. "That means there is no death. If thou art fully aware of thine inner light, thou may lose your conscious being for a time. But if thou believeth, and a person living on earth believeth and loveth thee, thou mayest live again and again in thine earthly body. You must understand this, dear Robert. If perchance I become formless again, I have not died. Before I ceased being in my previous existence, I knew that Jesus wanted no churches or temples or cathedrals built for him. No priests, ministers, or rabbis, no crosses with His body nailed to it, no saints with graven images, no Eucharist blood of the lamb, or bread and wine. Rather, He wants all of us to be His prophets. Like Peter and Paul, we are all sons and daughters of God. I am His prophet, too, and so canst thou be.

"The holy inner light of the Spirit is within each of us. We show our love for God and our inner light by loving each other. In the process we become immortal."

I looked at her a little sleepily. "Did Jesus tell you this personally?" I asked a little sarcastically.

"Sometimes thou soundeth like Master Dudley at my trial," she said blithely. "Jesus never spake to me as thou and I art talking to each other now. He reveals Himself to me suddenly in a flash. I know that He is there and He careth for me. It was He who came to me last night on the beach."

"What does He look like?"

"He hath no features, no body—just a warm loving light that floodeth my heart and brain and suddenly makes everything clear. His spirit always comes to me in times of desperation. He knew last night that I was ready to drown myself. He was with me that awful day in March when Master Wilson called me a leper, and He walked out of the meetinghouse with me and Mary Dyer, who was the only person who dared take my hand. A week later at our farm at Mt. Wolleystone, I told Edward that I would not wait for Will to come back to Boston to get us. Even though we had no horses, we would go to him. Two days later, we got lost in a spring snowstorm—like the storm yesterday. We knew not where we were, and I felt certain that we should all freeze. But Jesus was with us. Suddenly Miantonomo and twenty more of his Narragansetts appeared in the forest. Miantonomo looked like a demon god. He was very tall, and his face was dyed with fierce-looking red and black slashes. But he remembered me and he smiled and bowed his head and said: 'Cummanitoo. Cummanitoo.'"

"What does that mean?"

"He meant that my soul, every soul is God. God filleth all places and things and all good is in God." She smiled. "Dost thou understand? The Indians knew not the words, but they were aware of the Holy Spirit. Miantonomo probably saved our lives. 'Me watch over you. You friend,' he told me. They stayed with us that night, and during the next two days they led us to the Island." She smiled at me. "That was another time that I saw the light of Jesus, and I knew that I would live in that light forever."

"But you died, and certainly not with the light of love."

She shook her head like a patient child explaining the truth to an adult. "I ceased being for a moment in time, but there was no pain. Before the flames of Hell washed over me I fainted. I woke up in the arms of Manitoo," she smiled. "That is the Indian word for a man who is a god."

I laughed. "I tell my wife occasionally that I'm God, but she doesn't believe me. But assuming that our idea of time is relative, and the time in 1643 when you ceased to be is occurring simultaneously with all other time, why were *you* chosen to leap across the centuries?"

"How dost thou know that I am the only one? Perchance there are other souls who have crossed over, or are about to appear again. Perchance thou hast died sometime in the past and now liveth again."

"Not likely. I have my birth certificate, and I'm still living a normal life." I grinned at her. "You haven't answered my question."

"I believe that I am here once again, a conscious being because the time is coming for a new understanding of God's Holy Spirit. How long I will continue to live my life in this century, or when I will remerge with the Holy Spirit, I know not. Perchance, for reasons that I do not know yet, I am needed here."

Listening to her, I wasn't too sure that Anne could make the transition whether she was needed or not. Nagging at the back of my mind for the past forty-eight hours was how I could ever orient her brain or guide her into the final years of the twentieth century. In adopting an ancestor, I had never assumed that she would arrive on my doorstep or become a lover. Could she, or I, or any of the greatest men who had ever lived, cope with the disappearance of the world as we had known it? This wasn't the relatively slow

future shock that living people have to encompass but a frightening accumulation of ten generations in which men had transformed every mechanical
aspect of the world they knew and along with it the human brain's response.

In some areas, especially religion and philosophy, change has been slow
and minute. In the arts of music and painting and even in storytelling, it
might be possible to absorb such a change. Making money and the upward
mobility of the world's people of "mean condition," all seeking to share a
larger piece of the economic pie, was comprehensible. Psychology as a semi-
science did not exist in Anne's day, but human behavior wasn't essentially
different. Three centuries later people like the Winthrops, the Dudleys, the
Saltonstalls, and the Cottons could be found in public life. It was still a world
filled with two kinds of people, one group who believed that human progress
was moving in a straight upward line and were doing their best to aid and
abet it. But the large majority, like the Indians we had displaced, were still
content to fill their bellies, keep warm and comfortable, fuck regularly, and
expect their children to take care of them in their old age.

Despite her belief in God's grace and forgiveness, I still believed that
Anne was essentially a Calvinist. If she had read the sermon that Winthrop
had given aboard the *Arbella* when he and the first colonists were en route to
America, she no doubt would have agreed with him. "We shall be a city
upon a hill," he said, paraphrasing the Scriptural words. "We must be knit
together," he preached, "as one man . . . and . . . delight in each other, make
other's conditions our own, rejoice together, mourn together, labor and suffer
together, always having our eyes on commission and community in work."

But Anne's religious beliefs, whether she realized it or not, had undermined Winthrop's sometimes communitarian, sometimes aristocratic ideal,
and laid the foundation for individual freedom—not only of worship but also
of a pursuit of happiness via works and material things that I was sure would
horrify her. She was alive now in a world where, despite the odds, millions of
people cared more for megabucks and winning the lottery than for God's
grace. She had yet to discover via magazines, newspaper, and television that
men and women spent as much time escaping work as working. Play was no
longer a vehicle to catch the conscience of the king. Play was the aim of
millions of Americans and Europeans. We had recast the work and thrift
ethic into a new kind of spend-to-play ethic on which the whole economic
system was based.

The only need for a forgiving God of grace was someone to pray to.
Although they hated to admit it, most people were afraid that the new God
of Consumption might be a wrathful god. Someday he might turn on them
and tell them coldly, "The house has gone broke. It's too late to cash in
your chips."

I kept these thoughts to myself, but I did tell Anne that we should keep
her resurrection a secret. I had no idea how many people had read about her

in history books, but those who had admired her might not be too happy to discover that once again she was walking the earth amongst us.

"In the seventeenth century," I told her, "many men and women believed that your friend, Henry Nikales, and many others could talk to God. Nikales claimed he had direct revelations. The Catholic church also created many saints before and after you lived, who were presumably in direct communication with the Heavenly Father. But not any more. Today people are not only more cautious about revelations and prophecy than the Puritans were, but they are more cynical. If you insist that you have returned to earth, because it was part of Jesus's plan, I'm afraid you would be put under psychiatric observation." As I spoke, I was conscious that Saturday night I was going to have to tell the Johnsons and Dave Hedman who she was, but I felt sure that they wouldn't be anxious to publicize her.

"I told Master Winthrop that 'the fear of man is a snare.'" Anne was gently and quite voluptuously trickling her fingers over the length of my body. She kissed my eyes and nose and mouth. "I am who I am." She giggled, "And right now I am a woman who needs thee inside me."

Once again, for nearly an hour, we took each other totally out of this world. Orgasm for both of us was a momentary death followed by a laughing resurrection. Still panting, she lay on top of me. "For a moment I died and thy soul was joined with mine. Oh, dear Robert, the Lord must be happy in my need for thee, because it is my need for Him too."

"Whatever the Lord may be thinking," I told her, "we've got to get back to reality. After two days, you can no longer be the perfect wife—barefoot, if not pregnant." I laughed. "Today we are going shopping. You must have clothes." I ruffled her pubic hair. "But first I'm going to trim you."

"Dost thou wish to cut my hair?" she asked when I produced scissors.

I chuckled. "Not the hair on your head. We'll find a hair dresser for that who will fix it so you won't have to cut it. When you wear your hair up you should look like a queen. When you let it down for your lover you should look like a seductive Eve."

I told her to stretch out on her back with her arms over head. She watched me quizzically while I cut the hair under her arms, collecting it in a handkerchief, and trimmed her pubic hair.

"When I gave my children their first haircut, I saved their hair," she said. "But I understand not why thou art saving mine," she said as I knotted the hair that I had cut into a handkerchief. "Proper women never cut their hair under their arms—or down there. Why didst thou do this to me?"

"Women never stop tinkering with their bodies to make them exciting to men," I said. "I'm sure Cleopatra discoverd that men want women to look like Venus. It's an exciting contrast to their own hairiness."

"Why didst thou not cut off all the hair on my belly?"

"Because a woman's pubic hair in a neat triangle is very exciting for a man," I laughed. "It prickles them in just the right places. I suppose if you wore petticoats or pantyhose, I wouldn't have to trim you. But a woman who has such a nice behind as yours shouldn't constrain it. Pantyhose aren't very sexy. You shouldn't wear them. Women should be happy when men enjoy their feminine attributes—and vice-versa," I hastily added. I led her into the bathroom and gave her a razor. "When you get in the tub I'll soap you up, and you can finish by shaving your legs."

"The Puritans did not like women to tempt them," she said, as she slid under the warm water I had drawn. "They would put them in stocks or whip them. Do all women in America tease men now?"

"You'll soon discover that young women are sex objects and for sexual teasing. But not for gratification. We still have a leftover Puritan way of life. Like your Mr. Winthrop, millions of American males can't stop thinking of sex. Winthrop wrote a lot of sexy stuff in his *Journals*. Anything that was a little lascivious he gave as much space to as his political problems. You skimmed his *Journals* yesterday. He was lucky they weren't published when he was alive."

Anne frowned. "I must read more of his words. Thou saith young women are sex objects. But I understand that not."

I shrugged."Three centuries later, many women think that men still don't care about their brains—only their breasts, vaginas, and buttocks. And they are right—most men only care about that until the women are about thirty-five years old. After that, most women become latter-day Puritans. They let their bodies grow fat, and they think they have nothing left to attract men except the hair on their head." I laughed. "You'll discover that while most women are very careful never to reveal any other hair on their bodies, they spend millions of dollars annually arranging the hair on their heads."

Anne shook her head. "Methinks I need to talk to a woman. It is very confusing. Thou tellest me that thou dost not wish me to wear petticoats but thou also dost not wish anyone to see the hair on my cony."

I laughed. "As you will discover, today ladies do not cover their legs in public. That is probably why they shave them. Today dresses are very thin, but ladies still do not want men to see the shadow of their cunts. They think that is much too tempting for men."

"Do ladies wear woolen stockings like men?"

"They wear nylon. You'll love it. It's better than silk."

Anne was shaving her legs with remarkable efficiency. "How doth a woman hold her stockings up?"

I grimaced. "Pantyhose. A lady's stockings and underwear are now all one piece."

Anne grinned at me. "It seemeth to me, dear Robert, that thou must be accustomed to pantyhose. I saw many of them in your wife's drawers. But alas they fit me not."

I had decided on Lord & Taylor's as the best place to get Anne complete-ly outfitted because it provided easy access to the Prudential Building and the Sky Walk, from which I could show her Boston, but it was also a few minutes drive from the State House and from School Street, where I knew she had lived. Knowing full well that even in one lifetime you can't go home again, I wondered how she would cope with the distance of five lifetimes.

It occurred to me that it would be interesting to take her to the present site of the First Church, which was now a Unitarian Universalist Church and known as the First and Second Church. It had been rebuilt on the corner of Marlboro and Berkley Streets several centuries after Anne died. Back in 1907, when it was still flying a Congregational banner, relatives of John Cot-ton had spent many thousands of dollars to build a memorial to him inside the church. The monument incorporated a stone pendant from the east portal of St. Botolph's Church in Old Boston, and at the base of it was a life-size statue of Cotton lying on top of what seemed to be his tomb. With one hand holding a Bible against his chest, the stone John was staring straight up to Heaven.

I showed Anne a photograph of the memorial and told her that the statue had been destroyed in 1968 in a fire that gutted the First Church. I didn't tell her that John must have felt uneasy lying in state in a church that no longer believed in the divinity of Jesus.

Shaking her head disbelievingly, she stared at the picture for a long time. "Poor John-Luv. They tried to make him a saint," she said. "He looks like an archbishop laid out in Westminster Abbey." She smiled. "Methinks they did not understand what John preached. He would have asked God to destroy such an idol." There were tears in her eyes and I knew she was feeling melancholy, but she snapped back and smiled fleetingly. "Anyway, I can assure thee that John was much more handsome than this cold stone effigy."

By ten o'clock I had shoveled out the driveway and was ready to drive to Boston. A touch of spring was in the air. Most of the snow would be gone by nightfall. It was too warm to dress Anne in a ski suit. Wearing my T-shirt and jockey shorts, she tried on my trenchcoat. It was much too big. Emily's spring coat looked fine, but Anne's legs in my woollen stockings and ski boots looked a little incongruous. But there was no choice. I told her that our only problem would be to get from the Prudential Underground Garage into Lord & Taylor's before someone thought she was a female flasher. She couldn't comprehend a garage, but she was fascinated when I explained to her what a flasher did.

13

Huddled beside me in the automobile, fastened in with a seat belt, Anne clutched my arm and cringed when she saw cars coming at us from the opposite direction. Red and green and yellow traffic lights fascinated her. But when she saw trucks thundering past us, she slid down on the seat and hid her face in her hands. I explained to her that trucks were big wagons with motors and that in the twentieth century meats and vegetables, beer and liquor, and all the products made by men and women got moved across the country in them.

"Trains are no longer used," I told her. "Except to transport heavy stuff like iron and coal." As soon as I said it, I realized that trains meant nothing to her nor factories either, for that matter.

"I am frightened," she said. "I fear I may piss. Why do people need to go so fast? Methinks the Devil himself is driving them to Hell."

"Three centuries ago it took three hours to get to Boston from your Mt. Wolleystone," I told her. "Now you can drive there in twenty minutes."

I decided not to tell her that some people spent two hours or more a day getting back and forth to work, or that our hurried lives are more harried than hers had been. She'd find that out soon enough. We were approaching the hill at Wollaston. "This is where your farm was," I said, and pointed to a train hurtling under a bridge near the Mt. Wollaston stop on the Quincy Red Line transit system. "That's a train. It moves people from one place to another," I told her. "If you didn't wish to drive to Boston, you could walk over there to the station and someone else will drive you on a train to the city."

Bewildered, Anne was staring at the solid masses of houses near the road and the ugly one-story buildings, butted one against the other. "There's still a sky," she said a little plaintively. "But now there are no trees and earth. Everywhere I look I see signs shouting at people to come here or go there or buy this. Dost thou read them all? Dost thou think they are pretty?"

"Pretty awful," I said. "But this is like Babylon. No one cares any longer."

Next to a gasoline station and a firehouse, I stopped the car and pointed to a historic sign so that she could read it: "In William Hutchinson's House

99

near this spot, his wife Anne tarried on her way to Rhode Island, exiled by the General Court in April 1638."

Anne read it silently, a few tears starting down her cheeks. Shaking her head, she buried her face in my shoulder. "Will, dear Will, hold me tight," she murmured. "I am dreaming a terrible dream." Then she smiled forlornly at me and wiped her face in a handkerchief I gave her. "Sometimes I forget. I think thou art Will. I am dreaming this, Robert, am I not? If I am not truly resurrected, but if, as thou told me, all time is happening at once, then help me get back to my real world."

"I don't want to lose you," I told her. "But I would help you if I could. Unfortunately, I don't know how. You may never be able to go home again. This may be your real world until you die again. Hopefully not for many years, though."

Then her mood suddenly changed. She smiled at me. "I'm grieved to make you sad," she said. "I love thee, but be not surprised if I must go home again. Neither I nor thou know the way of the Lord."

I was dimly aware that Anne understood her resurrection better than I ever would. Home for her was neither then nor now, but forever. I continued to drive toward Boston and tried to explain to her that time had left very little trace or memory of the Shawmut peninsula that the Puritans had inhabited and renamed Boston.

"When you lived here," I told her, "there was only one narrow dirt road out of Boston by way of Roxbury."

She nodded. "I was kept prisoner in Joseph Weld's house in Roxbury. It took Will two hours to get there by horseback. Boston was surrounded by water. The Great Cove was on one side, and the Charles River and the Back Bay on the other."

"Now there is an expressway that connects the North and the Shores with bridges and roads built over marshes. You can drive directly to Plymouth or Provincetown or Newport, Rhode Island, where you lived after you left Boston."

Preparing her for the city, I told her that of the hills which she called Trimountaine, comprising Cotton's Hill, Beacon Hill, and West Hill (or Mount Vernon Hill), only a much smaller Beacon Hill remained. "In your time it was one hundred and ten feet higher than it is now. About one hundred and twenty-five years ago Boston was so crowded that the city planners decided to go all out and fill in what you called the Back Bay. They did it by reclaiming the land from the top of Beacon Hill and filling in the marshes. The process had begun before the Civil War, and by 1856 they went at it in earnest. Thirty years later, they had practically filled in Back Bay."

I pointed to the Prudential and John Hancock skyscrapers that we could see dominating the western horizon. "Those buildings are on the edge of Back Bay. In the 1900s the filled land became Commonwealth Avenue and many other intersecting streets. Wealthy Bostonians lived there. Boston was a most prestigious city. Some people called it the Athens of America because so many writers and philosophers lived here." I shrugged. "But two generations later most people do not remember that Boston either."

"Papa told me that a Greek philosopher, Heraclitus, believed that everything changes and nothing remains the same. Out of conflict cometh harmony. But too much harmony engenderth conflict. Life is a circle." She sighed. "It is not a very happy philosophy. Methinks things should always get better until we have a Utopia. Not like Master Winthrop's but more like what Sir Thomas More wrote about. I wish thou couldst have seen Boston when I lived here. We lived on Sentry Lane next to High Street. Across the street was Master Winthrop's house and just below that was the meetinghouse and Master Wilson's home. But it was not a very pretty place either. The streets were often deep in mud and stank of people's slop."

"There's no mud in Boston now, only litter," I said. "But your house is gone. It was burned to the ground in the great Boston Fire of 1711, along with Mr. Winthrop's home." I told her that Winthrop's home had been sold to her brother-in-law, Richard, in 1650.

She couldn't believe it. "Art thou telling me that Will's brother, Richard, bought Master Winthrop's home? He must have grown exceedingly wealthy. Please tell me about him."

"Winthrop died in 1649—six years after you," I told her. "Evidently Richard was more pragmatic than you and Will. He stayed in Boston where the money was."

"I never asked my family to believe as I believed," Anne said. "Edward returned to Boston too. Francis was more like me."

While I knew that she couldn't comprehend it, I told her that there were no Puritan homes left in Boston. The only remaining colonial house in Boston was Paul Revere's, and I knew that his name would mean nothing to her. "But the streets are still there," I said. "And after we have bought you some clothes and had lunch, I'll take you downtown and show you where your home was."

We were on Boylston Street opposite the Prudential Center, and Anne was watching with wide-eyed amazement the hundreds of people milling along the sidewalks and crossing streets between the creeping automobiles.

"Art they not afraid that thou willst hit them?" she gasped as one man escaped by inches.

"This is a city of jaybirds," I laughed. "You left your mark on Boston. Bostonians still do not obey laws that they don't approve of."

"I like all the confusion," she said happily. "And the people buzzing around like bees. It reminds me of London and Cheapside. I told Papa that I wanted to go to the Mermaid Tavern on Bread Street, but he said it was a place for dissolute actors and whores."

Anne was especially astonished by the women. "They show their legs and walk upon stilts. Methinks I would topple over in such shoes."

I parked the car in the Prudential Garage under Lord & Taylor and led my bewildered lady, who believed that only the Devil could live so deep in the earth, to the elevators. When I pushed the button and a flying box arrived, Anne leaped back, startled. She leaned against me in the elevator. I was almost as nervous as she was—especially when the door opened on a floor filled with women's clothing. I pushed her into the fray and tried to ignore the frowns and giggles as I ushered my hippily dressed ancestor in search of more appropriate body covering. This was a sanctuary of females in which no man entered without exciting suspicion.

I realized that I was about to spend a small fortune on a wardrobe for a woman who, resurrected or not, loving her husband or not, was a woman Emily probably would not approve of. I was greeted by a middle-aged saleswoman with a supercilious what-the-hell-are-you-doing-here expression on her face. "May I help you?" she condescended to say to Anne.

Momentarily, I was at a loss for word. Then to my shock and before I could answer, Anne filled the vacuum.

"I am Anne Hutchinson," she said coolly, as if the whole world would know her name. "My friend and I desire to speak to Master Lord or Master Taylor."

By this time several grinning customers were watching and listening. They had caught sight of Anne's woollen-clad legs and ski boots. "I'm sorry," the woman answered with a slight sneer. "Unless you are acquainted with God and know your way around Heaven, I'm afraid that neither Mr. Lord nor Mr. Taylor are available." I wondered if she were thinking of calling a store detective to evict us.

"I'd like to speak to the floor manager," I said, recovering my tongue before Anne might respond that she did indeed have a direct line to God. "This woman has just arrived in Boston, after suffering near death at the hands of the enemies of the State. She was ruthlessly stripped of her clothing and tortured. Fortunately, I was able to save her life. Right now, I want to provide her with a complete wardrobe. Three or four dresses, necessary underwear, stockings, shoes, and a new cloth coat. In addition, I think she needs a more modern hairdo. If you're not interested, we'll go elsewhere."

By this time we were the center of attention of a dozen or more women, who were listening and staring curiously at us. One of them, hearing what I had said, put her arm around Anne and was asking, "You poor dear, who did this awful thing to you?"

"The Indians," Anne murmured, obviously enraptured by my James Bond version of her assassins. Fortunately, a crisp young woman arrived in time to prevent further exploration of Anne's "problems."

"I'm Miss Green, floor manager," she said. "I'm sure that we can help you." She stared at Anne a little dubiously, but made no comment.

I asked her if she could take us to a fitting salon where we could talk privately, and I told her that I was prepared to purchase whatever clothing my friend would need for the next few months.

After a quick conference with the saleslady and with me dragging a reluctant Anne, who was staring in astonishment at racks of ready-made dresses and sleek female dummies, Miss Green led us to an attractive mirrored room.

"Now," she smiled at me, "If you can supply me with credentials and tell how much you wish to spend, I'm sure that we can transform your friend."

It was obvious that the clerk had told her who Anne thought she was. I handed her my Visa card. "Please understand, Miss Green, no matter what my friend may tell you, neither of us want any publicity."

Evidently feeling a bit warm in the store, Anne had unbuttoned Emily's coat, revealing my boxer shorts and T-shirt.

"Good God," Miss Green gasped, unable to suppress her astonishment. "Where did you get that outfit?"

"Not from God," I assured her. "But the fewer questions, the better."

Miss Green shrugged at Anne. "Mrs. Mahoney heard you say that you were Anne Hutchinson. Not *the* Anne Hutchinson, of course."

I gave Anne a warning glance, hoping that she would deny it and keep her mouth shut, but I soon discovered that Anne was much too sociable for that. "My friend feareth that you will think that I am a madwoman. But if I am not me, who am I? My brain knoweth nothing else."

Anne's answer left open the question of schizophrenia, but the floor manager evidently decided not to pursue it, and I suddenly realized why. Anne was engulfing her with a hypnotic, almost childlike expression of love and naiveté that seemed to come from a purer, trouble-free world.

Almost reluctantly Miss Green shook off her momentary enchantment. "Well, Mrs. Hutchinson, the important thing right now is to enhance your beauty and bring you into the twentieth century." She smiled at me. "She is a very striking woman. How much do you wish to spend?"

"Let's try to keep it under two thousand dollars."

"Dollars?" Anne asked, puzzled. "I understand not."

"It's roughly two thousand pounds," I said.

She gasped. "That's an exceedingly great lot of money."

"Not so much as it was in your time," I shrugged. "Don't worry about it."

"But I cannot pay thee back? What will thy wife say?"

That was a good question. I knew the Lord & Taylor employee was listening to us with a great interest. "If you don't keep your mouth shut," I told Anne a little sarcastically, "someone is going to offer you much more than that for your life story. Your picture will be on the cover of *People* magazine," I told her. I knew that she was bewildered and that she didn't even know what a magazine was. But little did I know that within the next ten days she would accomplish what Winthrop and Dudley had prevented her from doing. "Anyway," I said, remembering her nonmonogamous life, "What did you say when Will spent a lot of money on some dream or other?"

Anne grinned. "Thou art teasing me. I am not a dream, and Will never spent money on another woman."

"You're not just another woman," I shrugged. "Anyway, let's cross each bridge as we come to it."

"You mentioned that Mrs. Hutchinson should have a hairdresser," Miss Green interrupted us. "I agree with you. I can arrange that right here at Lord & Taylor's. Do you wish to help her pick out her clothing?"

"No, thanks, I'm sure that she knows more about women's clothing than I do, but I do think that with her patrician face she should have a breezy, sexy, sophisticated look—right out of *Town & Country*. Anne should have the image of a wealthy Back Bay lady who appears to be not much over forty."

"I am fifty-two," Anne said. "I understand not what is meant by Back Bay." She turned to me. "Thou toldst me that the mud and marshes are no longer there. Are they filled with ladies?"

"Not quite." Miss Green laughed and looked at her watch. "It's eleven. We'll need three hours. Can you come back around two?"

I told Miss Green to make it one-thirty. I decided that I could walk over to the Boston Public Library, which was just across the street. When she was ready, I wanted to take Anne to the top of the Prudential Building and show her the Boston to which she had returned.

But Anne flung herself in my arms. "Please, dear Robert, I am perplexed. I know nothing about how women dress today."

"One thing you have to understand," I told Miss Green, who obviously didn't believe a word she was listening to in what she thought was some joke or charade, "in Anne's world, the males had passed what is known as sumptary laws, defining in particular how women must dress. Clothing had to be very plain and not seductive. Although they knew how to make brilliant dyes in England, in the colonies the colors were 'sad colors,' dull reds, greens, greys, and blacks. Laces and ruffles were out. No garments could have silk, silver, or gold thread on them. Wools and coarse cottons, and linens for the rich, were a way of life. Women wore bonnets out of doors, and many ministers felt they should wear veils, especially in church."

Anne agreed. "Neither men nor women could wear slash sleeves, or gold and silver girdles, immoderate breeches, double ruffs, capes, shoulder bands, beaver hats, nor roses on their shoes." Anne was still clinging to me. "My husband, Will, sold ready-made clothes for men. Breeches and gloves and hats and things like that, but women bought cloth and made their own clothing, or even spun wool and flax and made their own woollens or linens.

Walking through your shop, I saw so many dresses. They were all sewn and stitched. How do you know you can fit them to me?"

Miss Green laughed. "From what I've seen, Mrs. Hutchinson, you have a shape that many younger women would envy. You have nothing to fear. We'll fit you like a glove. You'll love our new spring line. Along with several of our best salesladies, I'll personally help you select your clothes. Your friend can stay with us, if he wishes, but I'm sure that you'll be more comfortable trying on things without him."

Anne reluctantly agreed. "Come back to my office on the top floor," Miss Green told me as I was leaving. "We'll have a new Anne waiting for you."

Anne's last words, which raised Miss Green's eyebrows, were "Shouldst I tell her that thou dost not like pantyhose?"

14

In the reading room of the library I tried to read Nikales' *Revelatio Dei* that the staff had located for me, but I couldn't concentrate. It was obvious that Anne had been influenced by Nikales and his Family of Love philosophy, as well as his belief that, in the mid-1550s, the millennium had already arrived and God was talking directly to the saints, who would be running things for the next thousand years. Whether Anne believed that or not, I didn't know, but if she did, only five hundred years had passed since Nikales had prophesied. Obviously, there were still another five hundred years to go. And I was worried that Anne, with her Jesus-style openness and naiveté, telling strangers who she was and how she had arrived here, would inevitably attract morbid—I use the word advisedly—curiosity.

Despite what anyone said or wrote about death and dying, no healthy person wants to leave this world. The reason that Christianity has captured the imagination of a large part of the world is the belief in a hereafter and a resurrection. Leaving aside a cynical majority who would be sure that Anne was some kind of a mental case, she would still attract millions of believers who would literally want a piece of her flesh, or to touch her at least, in the belief that her miracle was transferable. Or—and I shuddered at the thought, since resurrection disturbed the order of things as much as a belief in a covenant of grace did three centuries ago—she might very well reenact, in some modern form, her original fate.

I was well aware that over and above all these fears was the fear of losing her. No matter how impossible and impractical it might be, I wanted to shield her from the twentieth century. At the very least, I wanted us to discover, alone and together, why she had returned to earth. But even beyond this, I was aware of an even more dangerous truth: I was playing Pygmalion. I found her naked on my doorstep. If it weren't for me, despite her origins, she might well have frozen to death. She was my Galatea, my creation. I loved her and I didn't want anyone else to have her.

How impossible that daydream was I quickly discovered when I hurried back to Lord & Taylor. A smiling secretary, who introduced herself as Maggie Austin and whose desk guarded the entrance to Miss Green's office, informed me that Mrs. Hutchinson was still in the beauty salon.

I noticed a seedy-looking young man, wearing blue jeans, a 35mm camera slung over one shoulder, sprawled in a reception-room chair. Flipping through a fashion magazine, he watched me and Miss Austin with a wary expression.

"You'll love her new clothes," Maggie was telling me. "She's so pretty. No one believes that she's fifty-two. She told us that Lord & Taylor reminded her of London in the seventeenth century."

I knew that the young man was absorbing this conversation. "Is the lady a historian?" he asked with a sly grin.

Trying to avoid conversation with him, I shrugged. "She's well read."

Maggie smiled at me. "Mr. Rimmer, this is Mr. Dremler. He's a senior at Boston University. He's waiting to see Mrs. Hutchinson."

"Saul's the first name." The young man didn't stand up. "I help pay my way through school by doing freelance stories for the *Globe Herald* or the *Phoenix,*" he said. "Your name is familiar. You're a writer, too, aren't you? I hope that we're not competitors. This story is a lulu."

"Goddamn it!" I yelled at Maggie. "I told Miss Green we didn't want any publicity."

"Don't blame her," Saul said coolly. "My girlfriend was shopping downstairs when you and Mrs. Hutchinson arrived. She knew that I was majoring in history and government. She telephoned me. Whether your lady friend is a little balmy or not, it will make a good story." He laughed. "I understand that Mrs. Hutchinson is a lot sexier looking than the statue of her in front of the State House. I'm hoping that I can get her to pose next to it."

"There's going to be no story and no pictures," I growled at him. "Do us a favor and get the Hell out of here."

"Are you her keeper?" Saul asked sourly. "Can't she speak for herself?"

I could visualize his headline: *Puritan Lady Returns from the Grave.* "Whether she can or not," I said, "let's say that she's having identity problems, and I'm not going to let anyone exploit her. You can take your camera and leave."

I had scarcely said the words when we both saw Anne step out of the elevator. Open-mouthed, I gasped. Wearing a white nutria fur coat, her hair swept back behind her ears, fluffy and wind-blown on the sides, it hung in a soft blonde knot on her long neck. She was breathtakingly beautiful. Her only makeup was a slight touch of eye shadow and a soft blush on her cheeks. Her face lit with love and joy when she saw me. I was aware that Saul was snapping pictures of her, but how could I stop him?

"Oh, dear Robert," she sighed and pulled away from Miss Green, who was supporting her on high heels. She ran into my arms, nearly falling as I caught her. "I cannot believe it," she said. "A man named Michael fixed my hair. He did not believe me when I told him that when I had lived in Boston, if a strange man touched a lady's hair, he would be put in the stocks on Lecture Day."

She giggled, "Dost thou like me? I must learn how to walk on these foolish shoes. But I have a more sensible pair, so do not worry." She rubbed the fur collar against my cheek. "Fear not, I did not buy this coat. Miss Green wanted to show you how a Puritan looked in twentieth-century beaver. I told her no Puritan lady dared wear a beaver coat." She laughed. "But the Indian ladies did—with nothing much under them." She slid out of the coat and handed it to the floor manager. "Thank you. I really feel more comfortable in the camel-hair coat that we chose." I was still staring at her open-mouthed. "Dost thou not fancy my dress?"

She was wearing a black knit dress with a white collar and cuffs that buttoned down the front with gold buttons. A gold chain around her waist and gold loop earrings made her look both sophisticated and virginal.

"You're absolutely stunning," I said, as Miss Green handed her a wide-brimmed white hat with a black sash that she had been carrying.

"Your lady is now ready for church or lunch at the Ritz," Miss Green said. "The rest of her clothes will be waiting for you downstairs. Mrs. Hutchinson has been very frugal with your money. In addition to this dress, she selected a lovely sapphire-blue spring suit in Italian spun rayon, which only cost $250, and three other less-expensive dresses in the $100 range. She told us all about her husband, Will, who was a cloth merchant. She was fascinated with how much finer are the threads in our cottons, wools, linens, and synthetic fabrics. She picked out several blouses and sweaters to go with three different skirts. She also has a handbag into which we have put handkerchiefs, combs, and a few cosmetics. Her complexion is so good, I agreed with our beautician. She needs very little makeup."

"And I have little tiny things to wear around my bum that they call panties," Anne laughed, holding up her breasts. "My diddies feel as if they were floating. They are held up in what Miss Green calls a bra. Petticoats are so thin that they call them slips, and you only wear one. Methinks, I may freeze. And when thou seeth my underalls that are both panties and stockings, thou may not be very pleased. But they slide down very easy." She started to lift her dress to show me, but suddenly she was aware of Saul grinning at her.

"What is that thing you are pointing at me?" she demanded.

"It's a camera, Mrs. Hutchinson." Saul was obviously as surprised at Anne's modern appearance as I was. And it occurred to me that even if he had pictures, I doubt that he could convince anyone that a woman who looked like Anne and looked as though she had just stepped out of *Vogue* magazine was really a resurrected Puritan.

"I'm Saul Dremler," he said. "A reporter. I'd like to do a story about you—with pictures—for the newspapers. I can't believe that you've never seen a camera."

Anne shook her head. "I understand not reporter, newspapers, nor camera. I am not a story—nor picture. How do you do a story? That is make-believe."

Saul shrugged. "You told people that you are Anne Hutchinson. If you believe that, that's a story!"

"But you believe it not?" Anne's wide-apart green eyes were deep wells. For a moment, Saul was confused by her look, as if she were silently probing his brain.

"It's not easy to believe," he said uneasily. "Maybe it's an Easter joke."

"Easter is a Papist holiday." Anne frowned. "Are you a Catholic? Both Miss Green and Maggie burst into laughter.

"I'm a Jew, obviously," Saul said.

"It's not obvious to me. Saul of Tarsus was a Jew who became the first Christian."

Saul grinned at her. "He wasn't a believer either—at first."

"You are right. Neither he, nor the Apostles, were sealed until they really understood the meaning of *Pascha.*"

"You mean the Exodus of the Hebrews from Egypt?"

"No, I mean Jesus Christ's deeper understanding. The Passover of the spirit of God and his substitution of the Eucharist, the bread and the wine, for the sacrifice of the Pascha lamb. Both, of course, are elementish church ceremonies that may show the way but do not reveal that the spirit of God dwells within you." She stared at Saul. "You are the first Jew whom I have met. Methinks I would like to talk with you."

"Please, Anne," I scowled at her, knowing that she was getting out of hand. "This man wants to exploit you. He already has pictures of you. That's what his camera does. It captures your soul."

"Only God can capture another person's soul," Anne said. "Why art thou afraid of this young man, dear Robert?"

Giving up temporarily, I told Saul to meet us downstairs at the first-floor elevators. Miss Green had collected the various charges, and she gave me the total. "It comes to $1,646," she said. "Of course, Mrs. Hutchinson is only equipped for spring and has no evening clothes. We tried to convince her that she should have some summer things, shorts, polo shirts, two-piece cotton knits, sun and swim separates, and a bathing suit or two. She was a little shocked that women show themselves to strange men almost as naked as Eve." She smiled at Anne. "You really don't have to worry. Your body is in very good shape, and your skin almost glows. But we couldn't convince her to buy any summer clothes. Mrs. Hutchinson tells us that she isn't sure that she'll be around for summer." Miss Green looked at me quizzically.

"What do you mean by that?" I asked Anne. "Where are you going?"

"Not where—but when, dear Robert," Anne smiled fleetingly at me. "And when, I know not."

Once again I realized that Anne wasn't telling me what her revelation last night had been, but now was not the time to pursue it.

Miss Green was saying goodbye. "We enjoyed having you with us, Mrs. Hutchinson," she said and squeezed her hand. "Please come back soon. I enjoyed the little song you sang for us, 'Pined Am I and Like to Die.'" Miss Green smiled at me. "Mrs. Hutchinson has a warm, sultry voice. You should take her to the Bay Tower Room to hear the Sons of the Virgin."

"Sons of the Virgin?" Anne burst out laughing. "Who are they?"

"They're a soft-rock group, who play music for dancing, but in between entertain with music from the sixteenth and seventeenth century, complete with lutes, guitars, and even a virginal. Their name is in honor of Elizabeth, the Virgin Queen."

The manager agreed to have Anne's clothes carried down to my car in the garage. I had decided that after I locked them in the trunk and Anne had changed her shoes to a more practical, low-heeled pair, we would have lunch in the restaurant at the top of the Prudential.

It would have been possible to bypass Saul in the elevators. I told Anne that I not only wanted her to see the city once again, but I had hoped to have her continue her story about John-Luv and Harry Vane, and what happened in Boston before and during her trials and after her banishment.

"There will be time tonight and tomorrow night," she told me. "Today is Thursday. Thou told me that thy wife would not return until a week from next Tuesday. I have much to learn about thee and the world and only a little time to learn it. Methinks this boy Saul liketh me and will not harm us. With his big blue eyes and tousled hair he remindeth me of Harry Vane." She sighed. "Like Harry, he is a boy that any mother would like to hug."

"You mean that any woman would like to hug," I said a little peevishly. I wondered if Anne in her reincarnation was as happily polyandrous as she had been in her previous life. "What's this song you sang, 'Pined Am I and Like To Die'?"

"It's about a young girl who would like to make love but does not dare." Anne giggled, mischief dancing in her eyes. "I'll sing it for you tonight. Art thou jealous? she asked, and looked at me so lovingly that I was ready to reserve a room at the Sheraton Hotel and ask her before we made love to pose for me naked in her new hat. It was a picture of her that even now I would like to have had.

"Of course I'm jealous of you." I grinned at her. "Jesus, as the spirit of God, may be dwelling in your soul, but you are a very attractive woman. I am sure that even Jesus, as a man, would have had to pray to God to help Him resist you."

15

Waiting for the elevator to take us to the Sky Walk at the top of the Prudential Building, I asked Saul what he knew about Anne Hutchinson.

"I read her trials," he said. And the way he spoke he made it obvious that he wasn't convinced that my Anne was *the* Anne. "I'm planning to go to Harvard Law School in the fall. One of my professors told me to read the trials because they were quite fascinating. Mrs. Hutchinson acted as her own defense attorney. She really confounded the witnesses against her who were acting both as judge and jury. Later Winthrop was so embarrassed about the trial that he wrote a book decrying the Antinomians and tried to justify himself."

Saul shrugged. "To tell you the truth, I didn't understand all that covenant of grace and covenant of works stuff, but I liked the way Mrs. Hutchinson talked back to those holier-than-thou Puritans. After my girlfriend called, just to refresh my memory, I looked Anne up in the *Encyclopedia Britannica.*" He chuckled. "Too bad she didn't keep records of her weekly gatherings of women. She evidently questioned whether the ministers knew what they were talking about. That makes her the first woman in America to take on the male establishment. She should be made honorary chairman of the National Organization of Women. Along with Roger Williams, she also helped lay the groundwork for the First Amendment." He grinned at me. "That's all I know about her, except that she was scalped by the Indians."

"I understand not the *Encyclopedia Britannica* nor the First Amendment," Anne said, ignoring that Saul was obviously talking about Mrs. Hutchinson as if she were some other person.

"I'll tell you about them later," I told her. I was determined not to let Saul probe into details of Anne's arrival on my doorstep or learn that she had been sleeping with me for two nights. Sleeping with a spirit passed the boundaries of credulity. "I think you should accept the fact that this woman believes that she's Anne Hutchinson," I told him. "She has convinced me that she is, and that she lived here in the seventeenth century. Until we have a clearer understanding of why this resurrection has occurred—if it has occurred—we should accept her on her own terms, at least until she has had

111

time to assimilate the world she is now living in. I don't want anyone to try and discredit her, or make a fool of her. It could be dangerous to her survival. In simple words, Saul, if it weren't for Anne, who is a much more trusting person than I am, you wouldn't be here. I think you should tell her who you are and whether you agree. Basically, I'm asking, for her sake, that you trust her. Pretend that you are the Saul who became Paul. Making a joke out of her would destroy her."

"Do you think I am a joke?" Anne asked Saul.

A little chastened, Saul shook his head. "I really don't know what to think. It is obvious that you can't prove who you are." He gestured at the people waiting for the elevator to take us to the top. Many of them were staring at Anne in open admiration of her beauty and an indefinable presence that I hesitate to call a halo. Let's say it was a glow that spiritualized her.

Saul was aware of it too. "They can't keep their eyes off of you," he said. "But if you told them that you were a reborn Puritan, they'd think you were daffy. You look more like the Queen of Bosnovia or some mythical kingdom." He shrugged at me. "Anyway, fair's fair. If you trust me, I'll trust you. There's no story, unless she convinces me." He grinned at Anne. "In that case I'll most certainly be your disciple. As for me, I'm a Jewish kid from a middle-class family in Brookline who hopes to go to Harvard Law School in the fall, after which I will become a wealthy lawyer and defend the Mrs. Hutchinsons of the world." He grinned. "After all, as a Puritan she's practically Jewish. The Puritans thought they had arrived in New Canaan and that they were the chosen people."

"Who knows?" I said faintly sarcastic. "You may become her apostle." We finally entered the elevator, and I cautioned Anne, who clung to my arm, to keep swallowing as we shot up toward Heaven.

As I paid our admission to the Sky Walk Saul asked Anne why she called me *thee* and *thou* but himself only *you*. Anne bussed his cheek. "You will become *thee* when you are aware of the spirit of love in you, as Robert is aware."

I grinned at Saul. "Watch out. She's trying to convert you."

We walked into the enclosed observation area, and Anne gasped as she looked down. "You are standing closer to Heaven than you were on Beacon Hill." I pointed out the gold dome of the State House. "That's the top of Beacon Hill, now. As I told you, about a hundred and fifty years ago they cut it down to fill in the Back Bay. Boston is now the capital city of Massachusetts. The governor and the state representatives and the senators work over there in the State House and pass laws and transact state business." I smiled at her rapt attention. "You can't see the statue of yourself from here, but you are standing outside the governor's window warning him to keep the state out of church affairs."

Saul chuckled, but Anne was too startled by the panoramic view to respond. "Now, I know how God must feel," she said in awe, as she surveyed the earth below her. "But if this be Boston, it is not my Boston."

"Yes, it is," I told her. "But you must have patience to rediscover it. Boston has a soul unlike any other city on earth. The American heritage is here, and man has not destroyed that. If you look closely and ignore the skyscrapers and eliminate a few bridges and highways and let the water slip back over some of the buildings, you'll see your Boston again." I pointed out Boston Common and showed her how it was bounded by Commonwealth Avenue and Beacon Street.

"Where is Muddy River?" she asked. "I walked through the marshes many times with John-Luv to see his farm."

Surprised, Saul pointed out the Fenway and the edge of Brookline. "There's a river flowing through there called Muddy River. Who is John-Luv?"

"John Cotton," I said, hoping he wouldn't pursue it.

"I remember," Saul said as he continued taking pictures of her. "Mrs. Hutchinson said in her trials that she had come to Boston because he was her mentor."

Looking at the eastern side of Boston, Anne recognized the harbor islands in the distance. I pointed out East Boston. "You called it Noddle Island. Sam Maverick owned it. Now it is connected to Boston by a tunnel. Just beyond Noddle Island, the land is filled in and we have an airport called Logan." As I said it, Anne pointed excitedly to the sky. "It's a huge bird, a huge bird," she yelled.

"It's not a bird," I told her. "It's an airplane. Men and women are inside it. About one hundred years ago, man learned how to fly."

"God must have taught him," Anne murmured, and I noticed that she was trembling. "But where doth he fly to?"

"Around the world," Saul said. "To Europe, to England. You can fly there in six hours. Come on, be honest. You know that you've seen an airplane before."

"Damn it," I grabbed his arm. "Stop challenging her. Anne hasn't seen a supermarket, a shopping plaza, or watched television yet. She saw her first automobile less than twenty-four hours ago."

"I'm sorry," Saul said. But I knew he still doubted me. "I guess I should've asked you the big question. Where in Hell did you find her? When did she arrive from Heaven?"

Before I could answer, Anne held her hand out to him. "I came to Robert's house two days ago. Where I was before, I know not. Like Moses told Jethro, 'I am a stranger in a foreign land.' Many years ago, when I came to Boston, it took us not six hours but sixty-eight days to get here." She sighed and her eyes were wet with tears. "I cannot believe that man flies. I wonder, myself, why I am here?" She smiled at Saul sadly. "How can I make you believe?"

"The best way to believe," I told Saul, "is to listen to her. At lunch, she can tell us both what it was like to cross the Atlantic in 1637." There was a method in my madness. Temporarily, at least, Saul was diverted from asking what Anne and I had been doing the past two days.

In the dining room on the floor below, I asked the head waiter for a table near a window overlooking the Charles River. It hadn't occurred to me that Saul, wearing worn blue jeans and a wool shirt, wasn't dressed for the occasion.

"He's our son," I told the waiter. "Just came home from college without his suit."

Nodding sympathetically, the waiter returned with a jacket and a tie. As happened frequently, Anne's melancholy suddenly washed away, and she was bubbling with laughter. "Dear Robert," she said, "I am so happy that we have adopted Saul. Methinks he is a nicer person than he pretends." As she followed the waiter to the table, Anne whispered to me, "I cannot believe mine own eyes. All this silver and the white linen tablecloths. This must be a very expensive ordinary."

"What's an ordinary?" Saul asked.

"An eating place where mostly men ate and played cards or dice," Anne said. "The taverns did not usually serve food. In London, the twelve-penny ordinaries were for the rich, or those who pretended to be. The three-penny ordinaries were not so social, and the lower-class ordinaries were filled with cony-catchers, cutpurses, and punks. Some of them were just stews."

Laughing, Saul said, "I don't understand you. Please translate."

"Cutpurses were pickpockets," I interjected. "In Anne's days the men wore their purses sewn on their britches. A cutpurse could slice one off without the wearer knowing it."

"Punks were prostitutes," Anne said. "The stews were supposed to be baths, but all a man ever bathed in them was his pizzle." She laughed. "Cony-catchers were men who waited to dupe farmers, like Will, when they arrived in the city, and cheat them out of their money. Will told me all about the seamy side of London." She smiled at me. "Thou still hast not told me what kind of an ordinary this is?"

I laughed. "Actually, other than its being a restaurant on top of a building, it's an ordinary ordinary. You will soon discover that many Americans don't eat at home anymore. This is a restaurant. There are hundreds of thousands of them in the country." I pointed westward up the Charles River. "In the distance you can see New Town. It is called Cambridge now. That's where the General Court of Massachusetts tried you. You can also see the tops of the buildings of Harvard College."

Our waiter brought us a menu and when Saul saw the prices, he was suddenly embarrassed. "I don't mean to sponge on you, but I don't have enough money to eat up here. If you want me as a guest, I'll promise to listen and try to believe." He grinned at Anne. "What was the *Mayflower* like? I know that wasn't the name of the ship you came over on, but I've seen that one."

"There's a replica of the *Mayflower* in Plymouth," I told Anne. "Not the original ship."

"We sailed to New England on the *Griffin*," Anne said, "on July 10, 1634. We arrived in Boston on September 18th. There were five Separatists aboard, but they went to Plymouth. The Separatists would have nothing to do with the Church of England. In Boston we did not renounce the Church of England, but we abandoned Popery. The *Griffin* was the same ship that brought my son and John-Luv to Boston the year before. Including the crew of thirty men, there were one hundred and four passengers, twenty-five cattle, and as many sheep. Will said the ship weighed three hundred and fifty tons, and was one hundred and ten feet long. There were sixteen of us in our family. Will and me, all our children, my sister Katherine, two maiden aunts, and two men who were apprenticed to Will. Will paid seven pounds apiece for each of us except Susanna, who was only eight months old. He paid an additional sum for a tiny cabin for us and for Susanna and Katherine, who was only four, and William, who was only three. My sister Katherine, my aunts, and the older girls, Faith, Bridgit, Anne, and Mary, slept on mattresses in the women's quarters below deck. And the boys, Richard, Francis, and Samuel, slept in the men's quarters."

"The trip wasn't cheap," I said. "A pound in that era would be worth close to $20 today."

"We sold our house in Alford," Anne said. "Will had made a will. We estimated that his estate was close to 4,000 pounds."

"Did you bring your own food?" Saul asked.

"We brought food for the first year in New England, but the owners of the ship provided food for the trip." Anne smiled. "Will always said that I had a good head for figures. I remember he told me that the ship's provisions included twenty hogshead of salted beef, 15,000 pounds of hard bread, fifty bushels of peas, fifteen firkens of butter, 1,200 pounds of cheese. To drink, we had six tons of beer, five tons of water, thirty gallons of brandy, and thirty gallons of madeira and canary wine."

"You mean you had more beer than water?" Saul was obviously impressed.

Anne laughed. "No one in England drank water if they could help it. A little beer or wine made you forget how crowded we were, or how bad it smelled if you stayed below. The owners also brought many hundred pounds of half-cooked bacon, haberdyne—dried codfish—and smoked herring. I brought cabbages and onions, turnips and parsnips, and lemons and enough eggs for two weeks."

"What else did you bring? Saul was obviously fascinated by Anne's details. But I knew that he was searching for some anachronism, some detail out of historical context.

"Before he died, Master Higginson, who was a minister in Salem and arrived in New England just before Master Winthrop had obtained the Massachusetts Bay Charter, wrote John-Luv a letter. He told him, 'Before you come, be careful to be strongly advised in what things are fittest to bring with you, for a comfortable passage at sea. Remember that once you passed England and when you come to land, there are neither markets nor fairs to buy what you want.'" Anne smiled at the waiter who was pouring white wine I had ordered. "In addition to many bolts of cloth we brought nearly a half ton of other things. I remember not all, but Edward, my son, told us to bring at least two hundred and fifty bushels of meal, fifty bushels of peas, fifty bushels of oatmeal, twenty-five gallons of aqua vitae, ten gallons of brandy, five gallons of salad oil and vinegars, and cheeses, sugar, pepper, and many spices." She laughed. "We would not grow fat, but it was enough to keep the family alive the first year. Our food was all stored below, along with iron pots, kettles, frying pans, wooden dishes, spoons, knives, and trenchers. Will also brought bellows, pails, shovels, hoes, saws, nails, hammers, augers, axes, a wheelbarrow, a cart, spades, chisels, pitchforks, three ploughshares, and a little wood boat."

"What was the boat for?" Saul asked.

"To catch fish," Anne laughed. "That first fall and spring I caught plenty of fish in the town cove to feed us."

"What was it like being on a ship for nearly three months," I asked. "Where did you cook?"

"On deck, we had an open hearth fire. We used charcoal. It was very warm some days. For the most part we did not bother to cook. Will ate in the roundhouse cabin with the men a few times, but in good weather we usually ate on deck. I was constantly worried because the sailors were teaching Richard, Francis, and Samuel how to set the sails, and every time I looked one, or all of them, were climbing the rigging." She shook her head reminiscently. "The worst part of the trip was that we were all too much together. Sometimes I like a lot of people, but sometimes I like to be alone and think. Every time that Will was busy with the men, Master Zachariah Symmes, a minister who was leaving England because Archbishop Laud's spies were after him, kept fawning all over me. He told me that I seemed to know more about the Scriptures than many ministers. He asked me if I really understood the meaning of Solomon's song, but he pretended to be shocked when I told him that it was exactly what it seemed to be, a poem written to a beloved human peison. He told me that as soon as he got his ministry in Charles Town he would welcome me to his meetinghouse. I never told him what I was thinking—that he was a wormy man with bad breath. Instead I finally said, 'I have much to tell you, but you could not bear to hear it.'"

"That wasn't the way it sounded at your trial," Saul said.

"I may have been quoting Jesus, but what I meant was that I would not get into his bed if he were the last man on earth!" Anne laughed. "Next to Mr. Symmes were the horrors of three dreadful storms. Some days we could not eat at all. The boat was tossing like a chip, the mariners were slipping and sliding and pulling ropes up and down. And the ship would climb to the top of the wave and then crash down to the other side. Will was sure that we were on our way straight down to Hell. But I knew that we would get to Boston."

"How did you know that?" Saul demanded.

Anne smiled at me. "I told dear Robert. No great thing has ever happened to me but that it was revealed to me beforehand."

"Ah," Saul said, evidently thinking she might betray herself. "Then you know what is going to happen to you right now."

Lost in thought, Anne sipped her wine. Finally, she said, "I knew not who Robert was, but I knew that he was waiting for me." She stared at Saul. "I know not who you are, but I knew last night I would meet a young man and he would believe."

Saul frowned at her, but he was obviously entranced. "Believe what?"

Anne smiled. "You will know when it happens."

"Tell me more about the trip," I said, trying to divert her from any revelations to Saul. "Did you get seasick?"

Anne laughed. "Mr. Symmes did, but none of my family was sick or had scurvy. I told Mr. Symmes that I would give him some of my wormwood or burnt wine. They are very good for nausea. But he would not take them. I brought many herbal medicines with me, plus conserve of rose, clove, gilliflowers, green ginger, and, of course, prunes and raisins to free one's bowels. Many times the ship was rolling so much it was not easy to shit or wipe one's arse." She grinned at me. "Ladies on that trip could not have worn pantyhose."

"Where was the toilet?" Saul asked.

Anne looked puzzled. "There was no toilette."

"He means the place where you relieved yourself. Stools or chamber pots."

"Oh—jordans," she said, using what I guessed was a slang expression. "There were seats in the bow—the head. When the ship rolled, the water washed through the scuppers and the slop went overboard, but mostly you held your nose." She smiled a little anxiously. "Speaking of these necessities, where doth a woman piss in this ordinary?"

16

Anne was surprised that there were separate accommodations for men and women, and she was hesitant to enter the ladies' room alone. I assured her that I couldn't go in with her, but she need not worry—water would flush and carry everything away, even this high in the air. After showing her the door I told her that I'd meet her back at the table.

Saul grinned at me when I returned. "The big problem is that Mrs. Hutchinson is not only prettier and looks sexier than most mortal women her age, but she has mortal functions. I never heard of spirits from the other world who had to piss."

I could have added "or who were so loving in bed," but I didn't. "At the moment," I told him coolly, "You're the barnacle on the ship. I have no need to prove that she is resurrected."

"But I think she does," Saul said. We saw her returning to the table watched with admiration by many of the diners, who were obviously wondering who this beautiful woman was. Before she could hear him, Saul continued, "and if she is really Anne Hutchinson, she's a lady who speaks her mind, come Hell or high water."

To my surprise, when I suggested we could all have a lobster, Anne said she had never eaten one. "Massachusets Bay was filled with them," she said, "but many of us believed Leviticus: 'Whatever in the water doth not have a fin or scales shall be an abomination to you.'" She smiled. "I think, dear Robert, that I will have flounder."

Saul eagerly agreed to the lobster. "Whoever you are," he told her grinning happily, "you're a better Jew than I am. So far as I'm concerned most of the biblical laws were written for another time."

"I agree with you," Anne said. "The Puritans argued over what day was Sabbath Day, Saturday or Sunday, but I believed that if one loved God, every day is the Sabbath. I agreed with Will that a body did not have to freeze to death or die of the heat all day long in the meetinghouse. One sermon on the Sabbath was more than enough—especially if Master Wilson and most of the ministers in the Colony preached for two hours." She sighed. "In England, Will and I and the children looked forward to Sunday. In the spring and summer, we played outdoors. In the winter our family read and played games together. But in Boston everyone was very grim. If you were one of the elect—members of the church—you were expected to be there early Sabbath morning and all afternoon, as well as Lecture Day on Thursdays."

"But you believed in the Old Testament, didn't you?" Saul asked.

Anne shook her head. "Not everything. Papa told me he was certain that the earth began long before the year 4,004 B.C., nor did the Lord have a seven-thousand-year-plan," she smiled. "If that be correct, then the time must have come for Him to take over and establish His Kingdom. But medoubts that has happened. Robert told me that men and women came from monkeys. I believe not that." She shrugged. "Neither do I believe that Adam and Eve sinned against God and that we must pay for their sins."

"But you believe in the Ten Commandments, don't you?" Saul asked. He obviously knew that under John Winthrop the Puritans had tried to establish a Bible theocracy based on the Decalogue.

Anne shook her head. "Not all of them—not when the minsters and magistrates interpreted them to suit themselves. Honor thy father and mother does not mean that one must honor the State as thy father and mother. Men make up the State—and many of them are not worth honoring. I do not believe that God is a jealous God. He is a loving God. When we become aware of His Spirit within us, we will want no other gods before Him." She smiled archly. "Moses wrote God's words himself to frighten his people because they were sinning against themselves."

"What about murder, stealing, adultery, coveting thy neighbor's wife?" Saul asked.

"God has given us Christ—His being. His Holy Spirit. His being is within all of us. Christ lived eternally and He died eternally."

"There are a lot of sinners in the world who don't give a damn about the Holy Spirit," I pointed out.

"Those who sin against themselves, loveth not and discover not the light of God within them. Methinks they will be vanquished."

"You mean because Jesus will return and destroy them?" I asked a little sarcastically.

"No. Because those who loveth their fellowmen will no longer obey the laws made by those who sin against the Holy Spirit."

"You mean that the meek will inherit the earth?" Saul asked.

"Not the meek," Anne said coolly. "The earth beongs to the strong who will, if necessary, meet fire with fire."

"What about Christ?" Saul asked. "Is he a white person, a black, or even a woman? There's a statue of Christ in New York, carved by a woman. It's called Christa. Her uplifted arms form her body into a female cross."

Anne smiled. "Ah, thou dost not understand. These are graven images.

Papa told me—and I think he was right—many men and women need graven images. They need something definite to pray to because they have not totally experienced Jesus within them. When you do, you will know that the spirit is neither male or female, nor black nor white. It is simply God's endless love."

She patted Saul's arm affectionately, "Saul, who became Paul, wrote a great love poem about it. It's in Corinthians. You should read it."

"I read it," Saul chuckled. "I'm a Jew who is happy that a Jew showed Christians the way. But I am surprised that you swallow St. Paul hook, line, and sinker. He thought women were inferior people."

Anne smiled. "Paul was no saint. He was a man who loved Jesus, and the Holy Spirit. I know not much about the world today, but I thinketh men still fear women. Even I am a bewilderment to Robert."

I laughed. "I'm sure of one thing—neither Winthrop nor Dudley thought you were a saint. I've only known you a few days, but I can't help wondering how you survived in the Bay Colony without getting your head put in the pillory, or why you weren't publicly whipped on Lecture Day. You must have been aware that the civil laws of England and the Colony were based on biblical laws. Thou shall not murder, or steal." I couldn't help grinning at her. "Or commit adultery."

The waiter brought our dinners and Anne gasped in surprise at the lobsters and her flounder. "Each hath its own dish," she marveled. "There are no trenchers." She picked up a fork. "I am not very graceful with this tool," she said, "but I will learn." Then after a happy mouthful, she answered my question. "You were born without sin. All children are born without sin. There is no original sin. Adam and Eve, as perfect people who fell from God's grace, is a Hebrew myth. Men and women who do not love will harm their fellowmen. When they do, they sin against God. Children who do not grow up loving God and recognizing the Holy Spirit within them are the children of parents who are unaware of the indwelling Christ. They will sin against their fellowmen. For those, we must have the laws of men. But the only valid laws are those that are similar to God's laws. It is not God's law to kill a fellowman. He who doth not keep the Golden Rule sins against God. Murder and war are direct sins against God." Anne smiled at me dreamily. "As for adultery, if it denies love and caring and is an exclusive substitution of eros—love for another person—and denies the original marriage, then adultery is wrong and negates the indwelling spirit of love. Such adultery creates a Hell in one's heart and conscience."

"Obviously, you were one of the Protestant radicals," Saul said. "I read about them. In essence they laid the groundwork for the Reformation and got King Charles beheaded."

Anne gasped in surprise. "I knew not what happened to King Charles. Master Winthrop must have jumped for joy. But he was no better. The real anti-Christs are those who think they can rule men by man-made laws."

"Winthrop didn't know that Charles was beheaded either," I said. "He was dead when Oliver Cromwell took over and King Charles lost his head. Saul is right. Political rebellion was underwritten by people like yourself who challenged their leaders and realized that they were no better than they themselves were."

"Papa told me that Martin Luther started people thinking for themselves," Anne said. "And then Calvin. They both hated the Papists." She smiled sadly at Saul. "But Luther also hated the Jews. He thought they were the anti-Christ, sinning against God too, and he wanted to exterminate them."

"Have you heard about Hitler?" Saul asked her.

"A little," Anne nodded. "Robert told me about the last big war, but I would like to learn more. Some think Christ will return in a time of total warfare. 'We shall not all sleep, but we shall all be changed . . . in the moment, at the twinkling of an eye, at the last trumpet.' So it says in Revelation. But methinks, like Paul, if you believe that Christ has not risen already, your faith is futile. He reigns now, and must reign till he has put all enemies under his feet."

"Don't tell me you believe in the millennium?" Saul asked scornfully. "So when did it start?"

"I know not. No one knoweth the Lord's timetable. 'He cometh as a thief in the night,'" she smiled. "But if He findeth me naked, the way he made me, I will not be ashamed."

To steer Saul away from a Second Coming, which obviously was crazier to a Jew than was an immortal Anne, I said, "You have to understand, Saul, that when Anne lived the printed Bible was their television. Instead of movies, soap operas, and news, families read the Scriptures. The potential of resurrection, the last judgment, and the millennium provided suspense in their lives, and the stories of God's anger with the Jews were easy to equate with their own problems. After centuries of Catholic domination, thousands of people decided that the priests and monks didn't understand the Scriptures any better then they did themselves. Hundreds of self-appointed religious leaders suddenly had their own revelations. There were all kinds of religious gatherings. Brownists, Separatists, Arians, Arminians, Socinians, Ranters, Anabaptists, Familists, and the Quakers. Anne doesn't realize it, but I think her beliefs are very similar to the Quakers. Quakers like George Fox reflected much of Henry Nikale's beliefs and his Family of Love. Many of them, including Nikale's followers, believed they had direct revelations from God." I didn't add—"and so does Anne." I was unhappily afraid that Anne would tell him herself. But she took off on a different tack.

"My sister, Katherine, was as much a rebel as I was," Anne said. "When I was excommunicated and we moved to Pocasset, I gave up the formal church, as did many of the Islanders. We had home conventicles without the need for preachers. Katherine became an Anabaptist." She laughed. "She even convinced Roger Williams to be dipped naked all over again, when he was forty."

"Did you believe in baptism?" Saul asked.

Anne shrugged, "The Puritans assumed that baptism was the equivalent for Gentiles of circumcision. They did not think circumcision was necessary. Robert is not circumcised, art thou?"

Saul nodded and stared at me, obviously wondering how Anne would know whether I had a foreskin or not.

Ignoring his silent question, I told Anne that today, while it wasn't compulsory, most Gentile males born in the past fifty years had been circumcised. "Presumably because circumcision permits the male to be more sanitary," I said. "On the other hand, today we have plenty of soap and water."

Saul laughed. "The real reason for circumcision is that a penis without its foreskin looks as if it was more erect and ready for business. Women prefer it that way."

"That is silly," Anne said smiling at him. "Women care not whether or not a man be circumcised. Nor doth the Lord. Circumcision and baptism were dreamed up by the priests and rabbis. I believe not in baptism, particularly baptizing an innocent baby. No one should be baptized until he or she has consciously experienced Christ within him. Then by baptism he announces that he is truly resurrected, here and now, and is living his life in the Kingdom of God." She smiled. "But you must understand that I did not always believe this. One must grow in understanding. When Zuriel was born, here in Boston, John-Luv insisted that he must be baptized." She grinned conspiratorially at me. "For many reasons I made not a public issue of it. When I lived on the Island, there were both Dippers and Sprinklers. As a ritual, acknowledging the indwelling spirit, I told Roger that baptism was harmless enough, and it might even do some good. Quite a few young men and women were dipped in the river stark naked. I remember that Sir Thomas More in *Utopia* and Francis Bacon in the *New Atlantis* thought that young men and women should have the opportunity to see each other naked before they were married. Thus, before they got married they would know what they were getting."

Saul shook his head bewildered. "You mean you actually read those books?"

"Papa had many books, and then when Harry Vane returned to England he gave me sixty-three books he had brought with him to the Colony." She smiled. "Will said that I had more books than Master Winthrop, but most of them were not Puritan books."

Saul laughed. "I know you're not Jewish, but if you believe Paul who wrote to the Romans, 'For they are not all who are of Israel,' then since you are a Gentile believer in the most of the Pentatauch, I guess we are cousins."

Anne smiled. "According to ministers in the Bay Colony, the Puritans in particular were adopted by God into the family of Israel. They were holding the fort until Christ redeemed the Jews in the Second Coming."

Saul laughed, "You really do sound Jewish. Do you believe in Easter?"

"Easter is a pagan holiday." Anne smiled at Saul, and it was obvious that she enjoyed lay preaching. "The Papists invented it. Papa was fascinated by Christ's resurrection. I have thought much about it since I was young woman. There is nothing about the forty days of Lent in the Scriptures. We did not celebrate Easter nor Christmas in the Colony. But methinks that was a mistake. We should not be ashamed to remember that these were part of the mysteries of ancient holidays that were celebrated long before Christ died on the cross. To convert people to Catholic Christianity, the Church Fathers purposely and very gradually changed the meaning of these celebrations and observances, which were related to the fertility and sun gods. It took many centuries because there were no books. There were no written words to remind people that Christmas was originally a heathen holiday and that nobody knew when Christ was born."

"But you believe that he was the son of God?" Saul asked.

Anne smiled, "We are all sons and daughters of God. But as it has been in the world since the beginning, and even since Jesus made us aware of the indwelling spirit within us, most people live and die without experiencing the deep joy of communion with God's infinite love and creativity. When I was young—only twelve—and we were living in Alford, England, before Papa was given back his ministry and a church in London—St. Martin's—I knew that he spent much of his time reading Greek and Latin. He told Momma that he was reading about the early Greek and Roman mystery religions, and he was sure that the Puritans were making a great mistake by taking all the mystery and magic out of religion. Papa enjoyed Christmas and Easter and Latin masses, and words that people didn't fully understand, and the power of the cross, and the exorcism of devils, and holy water, and the rings and pieces of magic paper, and bread and wine that became transformed and were supposed to be the blood and body of Christ. 'All these are ways of dealing with human misery and repentance by a forgiving God,' he told me. 'They give people something to live and hope for.'

"Papa believed that the Puritans were too influenced by John Calvin's God. 'They think God gave Abraham a deal,' he told us. 'All Abraham had to do is to believe in the coming of Christ or the Messiah, and God would forgive his children.'" She smiled at Saul who was listening to her intently. "This got rid of some of the problems that Adam had caused by eating the Apple of Knowledge. Now there was a way to escape the original sin and achieve salvation, but like Calvin, the Puritans played at being God. They insisted that God knew exactly who would be saved and who would go to Hell. Although God had given us a covenant of grace, it would only work for the elect. They believed because they had given their consent to God and worked for His glory and theirs at the same time that they were the elect." She shrugged. "If you had not been born in the right family, you might work all your life, but you could never become one of the visible saints."

Anne responded to our happy grins and appreciation of her by wrinkling her nose. "Momma told Papa that even though she would never become a saint, she was sure that she would get to Heaven. But she was not too sure of Papa. Especially, when he told her—when I was listening—that since the beginning, before God gave us Jesus, he had made man aware that death and resurrection was the nature of the Holy Spirit. He told Momma that man became religious when the first realized that the earth was the wife-mother, and that she must be seeded by a god who dies but who will rise again. The seed of the harvest lives again and produces a new harvest over and over again."

Enjoying our attention Anne continued. "Papa told us about many of these early religions where men and women worshipped the sexual organs of their gods. On the Day of the Blood, a day in March similar to Good Friday, the Roman god of fertility, Attis, was fastened in an effigy to a tree and pierced with swords by the priests. They supplied their own blood so that Attis might bleed to death, like our Jesus bled on the cross. Then they buried Attis in the earth, which was called Cybele. Soon Attis came to life, and his seed provided new crops and a new harvest.

"The Egyptians believed that in the beginning the goddess Isis was married to Osiris, who was murdered by the god of darkness, Set." Anne chuckled. "Set cut off Osiris' testicles, which supplied the seed to the earth, and the earth became barren. But Isis finally found his pizzle and balls and they were reattached to him, and Osiris came back to life. Finally, like Jesus, Horus was born to Isis and Osiris. Papa told us many other similar stories." She shrugged. "But he never dared preach about them."

"What you're telling us," I said, "is that most religious people, even today, refuse to believe that the story of Jesus' crucifixion was actually a revision of early pagan stories. It was a way of putting new wine in old bottles."

"I just read a new book called the *Sexuality of Christ*," Saul said, obviously fascinated by the discussion. "It's by a Jew, of course, Leo Steinberg. Steinberg reveals that in the Renaissance artists were fascinated with Christ's genitals, both as an infant and as a man. In several paintings it is obvious that his loincloth conceals that Christ had an erection."

Anne's eyes were twinkling. "Methinks that is true. The soul doth not lust but it loveth. Many women love Christ both as God and as a man. The Puritans rejected all images of Christ. Even the Papists were afraid that men and women might identify him with their own fleshly needs. But men and woman seeking Christ and his fertility in the merger of their bodies discover that the ultimate mystery is God Himself, whom we shall never know. But God wants us to know His great love for us, so he gave us His son, a man, a human being just like you and me. He did not give us Christ at the beginning of creation, because He knew that man was not yet perfect and not ready for Jesus. But the Holy Spirit was dwelling within Adam and His first creatures."

Anne grinned at me. "Even if they be monkeys. Men and women in the beginning were like infant children. To a child everything is mysterious. A baby wants love, but he knows not how to give it. After many thousands of years, believing that many of us could finally experience His love directly, God gave us Jesus. Jesus tried to teach us that God is not just in Heaven. He is not out there somewhere in the sky. He dwelleth within each of us and every living thing. But even now, after nearly two thousand years, methinks most men and women still have not learned how to love. They think those who love are weak. They are embarrassed to talk about the wonder and mystery and joy of their flesh and blood responding to each other, or that our mating is God's reason why we are here in the first place." She smiled. "When I lived before, I was already resurrected, because I knew that the spirit that was dwelling within me was the resurrection and the life."

All the time that she had been speaking, Saul had been snapping pictures of her. "It sounds like a great philosophy of life," he said. "But I don't think you'll convince many Jews—or Catholics for that matter. What about Passover? From what I read, the Puritans juggled with Passover."

"So did Paul." Anne said. "I finally agreed with Papa. People need magic and mystery in their lives. Most of my friends—especially the women—believed in astrology and witches and the Devil. Even Will believed that I was like I am because I was born under the sign of Leo. I thought on this a long time. I have only been alive again for three days, but methinks with all your inventions there is still much more that man doth not understand than that which he does."

She grinned at me. "I know I am wagging my tongue too much. Forgive me, but my head is full of things I have not said for a long time. I like the mystery of Passover. When I lived here, our year began in March or Nisan, the same as the Jewish year, when Moses lead the Hebrews out of Egypt. The Puritans believed in Exodus as the truth. I did not. I believed most of it was written by a great storyteller. Methinks that Egypt is really the symbol for sin. God told Moses that His people must be punished for their wicked ways and because they did not believe, He would not lead them to the promised land. The Feast days of God—which are Passover, the Seven Days of the Unleavened Bread, Pentecost, the Feast of the Trumpets, the Day of Atonement, the Feast of the Tabernacles, and the Last Great Day—are similar to the pagan holidays, with one exception. Man had learned that there is only one God. But he misunderstood God. The prophets like Moses and Leviticus thought God was a vindictive God and that He must be propitiated with the slaughter of two goats for Israel's sins."

She smiled. "Methinks the priest, or rabbi, who brought the goat's blood within the veil and sprinkles it on the mercy seat, or the throne of Heaven, is similar to Christ returning to the Kingdom, where he is supposed to remain until the millennium. The first goat died for our sins. The second goat, Azazel, the scapegoat, was sent into the wilderness. When he returns, he becomes Christ who dies for our sins."

"Do you really believe all that garbage?" Saul demanded. "Christians have been trying to merge the resurrection myth of Christ with the predictions of a coming Messiah for two thousand years."

Anne shook her head. "The resurrection of Jesus is not garbage. Jesus Christ is the ancient myth become reality. Jesus realized that the bread and wine on Passover was a more acceptable symbol than the Passover lamb for those who did not believe in Hebrew law. Robert told me that most people, today, believe that men and women descended from monkeys. However we may have got here, or how long it has taken, we are no longer like monkeys." She laughed. "I do not think monkeys have long conversations like this, or think about life and death very much. But perchance they come closer to God because all they know is life. We are aware that we will die, but we know not when. We must understand that the nature of life and death is a recurring cycle." She smiled. "Methinks that is why I am here. Perchance, I was here before, and perchance I will be here again."

"I don't know what it is about you," Saul said, shaking his head. "But I hope that I may call you Anne. You set my brain whirling. You can probably convert more Jews to your kind of thinking-man's Jesus than anyone else." He shrugged. "I really hope that you're for real."

Anne held up her last spoonful of chocolate ice cream. "Robert thinks that he is dreaming me. Methinks that I am dreaming this delicious cream that is frozen and yet is not frozen. Perchance God is dreaming all of us." She smiled at Saul. "Forget not that Paul, the first Christian, was a Jew."

"If God is dreaming, let's hope that he doesn't wake up," I said. I looked at my watch. It was two-thirty. "Whoever is dreaming whom, I want Anne to see herself as others see her. The quickest way is to leave my car where it is."

"Wilt thou come with us?" Anne asked Saul.

"When you ask me like that, what choice do I have?" Saul asked, and the enraptured expression on his face made him look like a schoolboy who has fallen in love with his teacher.

17

Going down the escalator to Boylston Street, we were surprised to discover that a southerly breeze was blowing. Spring was nibbling on Boston's doorstep. The snowfall, which had been much lighter than in Quincy, had disappeared, and the temperature had climbed to nearly sixty degrees. I hailed a taxi to take us to the State House. Anne sat between Saul and me, and told us that she had never seen such traffic or confusion since she was in her teens and living in London. The nobility lived in beautiful homes along the Strand, she said. Each family's coat of arms was carved over the door. Sloping down to the Thames were beautiful gardens and lawns. At night, young ladies wearing masks would wait for their gallants, who would take them for a ride on the river in silken-covered boats. Everyone traveled by river. Laughing, she sang us a little song. "Two pence to London Bridge, three pence to the Strand, four pence to Whitehall stairs, or else you go by land."

"The poor went by land," Saul laughed. "But they didn't wear silks and satins. Servants—those who paddled the boat—wore yellow livery. Workingmen wore russet homespun. The cloth was so heavy, you'd melt under it." Shrugging, he rubbed the legs of his worn blue jeans. "The world hasn't changed much. I wear the twentieth-century student's uniform."

Walking to the left of the main entrance, Anne held my hand and kept staring at the gold dome of the State House. "Thou tellest me that this is the top of Beacon Hill," she sighed. "But I cannot believe it."

I pointed to the windows, "Up there is where the governor of Massachusetts works. Now, instead of deputies, we have state representatives and senators elected by all the people."

We led her gingerly across the still damp lawn to the bronze statue that Cyrus H. Dallin had sculpted of her and which had been placed on the State House lawn June 2, 1922. With a stone balustrade behind her, Dallin's version of Anne was a wide-eyed, virtuous, God-fearing woman, in total command of herself. Weathered green, she was staring heavenward through the branches of an elm tree in some kind of mystic elation. One arm was round a female child of six or seven who, like her mother, was wearing a Puritan cap. She clasped her mother's lower gown, but she obviously was not seeing the same heavenly vision as her mother.

"She looks like a Papist saint," Anne said, "not like me." She chuckled. "Will would have laughed. No matter what he said, I was no saint."

"Maybe that's why you're here," I said. "God is giving you a second chance."

Anne smiled doubtfully, ignoring my sarcasm. She gestured at the Common and the traffic on Beacon Street. "From what thou hast told me, people hath not changed much. Medoubts that saints are any more welcome in Boston today."

"Maybe not welcome," Saul said, "but with the world on the brink of suicide, millions of people keep praying that there is some other way out. If you wish, you could be famous overnight. Instead of preaching to sixty women in your home, you could preach to a hundred million." Saul was standing back from the statue evidently trying to figure out how he could dramatically photograph a live woman against her own monument. "Who's the kid?" he asked.

Anne murmured, "John-Luv's."

Though I doubted that she cared, I was glad that Saul didn't hear her. I wondered if a saint or any woman—even three centuries later in a much more promiscuous age—could ever convince the male population that she could love two men, and maybe three, at once.

Lost in thought, Anne was staring at the statue of herelf created more than three hundred years after her death. She read aloud the inscription on the monument:

In Memory of
Anne Marbury Hutchinson
Baptized at Alford
Linconshire, England
20 July 1591
Killed by the Indians
At East Chester, New York 1643
A Courageous Exponent
of Civil Liberty
And Religious Toleration

Since Anne hadn't answered Saul, I told him, "It's probably Susanna. She was the only Hutchinson with Anne who survived the massacre."

Tears were trickling down Anne's check. "She survived because Uncas was told not to kill her." Anne said. "It proves what I told thee. Both Master Winthrop and John knew what was going to happen. John spared his own child."

Fortunately Saul didn't hear her, but I realized that whether he fully believed it or not, he was accepting Anne's resurrection as a reality. I still wasn't sure that I had convinced him that publicizing her would be the equivalent of feeding a Christian lady to the Roman lions. Biologists, medical men, psychiatrists, ministers, priests, rabbis, evangelists, theologians—not to mention politicians—would all join hands and deny her and probably ridicule her. It was one thing to preach an afterlife, but something else again to accept it as a fact of life. And what could this Anne tell them that would irrefutably prove her former existence on earth?

After a few days of national attention, her only believers would be religious crackpots. But even those who sincerely believed in a Second Coming would have difficulty accepting a female as Christ's emissary. When I voiced these thoughts and suggested that the thousand years during which Jesus Christ would supposedly run things before restoring the Kingdom of God had come and gone, Anne just smiled. "How dost thou know anything? Methinks that the Second Coming is continuous. It occurs for every man and woman when they finally understand the true words of Jesus and become aware of His spirit within them. It can happen now even to thee, dear Robert, or to Saul, or anyone." She smiled and squeezed my arm. "Thank thee for listening to me—even if thou doubtest. I am only certain of one thing. The true words of Jesus are not in Revelation. The John who wrote Revelation was not the Apostle John. The man who wrote it wanted to frighten the Hebrews, who were constantly fighting one other. He wanted to appease those who believed that the world was coming to a bloody end."

She shook her head. "It's very sad. Simple people all pray that their enemies will be wiped out but that they will survive because they are good, and hope that they will live forever in the Kingdom of God. I told John-Luv I thought that when Paul said, 'Let no man rob you—and do not be deceived by the cult of angels,' he was warning people not to accept pagan beliefs like the Apocalypse and Armageddon. Papa told me that the John of the Book of Revelation was a politician. He told me to read St. Augustine's *De Civitate Dei*. Augustine understood better what Jesus truly meant."

I stared at her more than a little astonished. "You mean you read a book by a Catholic saint?"

Anne shrugged. "John-Luv read Augustine too, but he and Master Winthrop still believed in a pagan Jesus—a man whose eyes were like flames of fire and whose robes were dipped in blood and out of whose mouth came a sharp sword. St. Augustine knew that the battle between God and Satan had already been fought, and that God had won. The battle that remained was between God's creatures who were aware of the indwelling light and love of the Holy Spirit, and those who blindly, with closed minds and ears, persist in their own self-destruction. Perchance that is why I am here—to help the blind to see and the deaf to hear."

Saul turned to me. "One thing is obvious. This time around, whether it worries you or not, Anne isn't going to hide her light under a bushel. You've got to accept her the way her husband Will did."

Anne squeezed my arm affectionately. "Methinks Robert is my husband Will!"

"Jesus save me!" I muttered. "That's all I need. You resurrected and me reincarnated!"

Saul chuckled. "It makes some kind of cosmic sense." He sounded as if he believed it. "If God has brought you back to life, why not restore your former husband too!"

"It solves the problem of adultery," Anne's eyes were twinkling. "And explains why Robert feels jealousy on my account."

So Will had been jealous of you, I thought, but I decided to explore that subject with her privately.

After Saul had exhausted the photographic potential of Anne's statue, I told them that now we could easily walk down Beacon Street to King's Chapel. As we passed the statues of Horace Mann and Daniel Webster, guarding the main entrance to the State House, and Joseph Hooker, a Civil War general on horseback, I tried to explain to Anne that these were famous Americans who had lived long after she had died, but who, in some ways, had invoked the same belief in freedom of thought and religion that she had.

"But the thing that will amaze you," I told her, "is that from all the several billions of Americans—male and female—who have lived and died in the past three centuries—only two woman are remembered in Massachusetts history and are immortalized with statues on the State House lawn. You— and a dear friend of yours." I pointed across the east lawn of the State House that we were now passing toward the sitting bronze statue of a beautiful young Puritan woman. "There's your friend, Mary Dyer."

We walked up to the statue and Anne read aloud the inscription in a momentary state of shock:

Mary Dyer
Quaker
Witness For Religious Freedom
Hanged on Boston Common 1660
"My Life not availeth me in Comparison
to the Liberty of Truth"

"Oh, dear God," Anne cried. "Poor Mary. She was like mine own child. I loved her truly and she loved me. Why was she hanged? What is a Quaker?"

"Very much like a Familist," I said trying to soothe her. "The first time that Mary arrived in Boston to fight those who were persecuting the Quakers, she was arrested, released, and told that if she ever came back she would be executed. But within a month she did come back. Endicott was the governor, and she brought linen with her to be used as grave cloths for his victims.

Naturally, Endicott wasn't happy with this idea or with her." I shrugged. "If you had lived into your seventies, you would probably have come back to Boston and been hung along with her."

Back on Beacon Street, guiding Anne, who was momentarily lost in her thoughts, we passed Pemberton Square. Pointing in the general direction, I mentioned that this was where Cotton's home had been located. Both his home and land disappeared long ago and were buried under the Court House and other tall buildings. We noted that Anne was trembling. Her mind was evidently flooded with ancient memories, but she smiled at us bravely.

"I remember not any street like this," she said as we walked down the hill. "But if this be the place, there was a lane. I could walk to John's house from mine in just a few minutes. John was the most important minister in the Colony," she told Saul. "We paid him ninety pounds a year, and the General Court gave him more than an acre of land. But John-Luv was not too happy with the location. His home overlooked the the homes of poorer people who lived below him on the hill and that made him nervous." She smiled fleetingly. "Most of them were not homes. Hovels and wigwams— many with a whore or two who took care of the poor sailors who sneaked ashore after dark. They were dangerous men, who had had no women for months on end."

"A hundred years later," I said, "at the beginning of the Revolutionary War, the whole area on the other side of Beacon Hill was called Mt. Hoardom. A Lt. Williams in His Majesty's army wrote in his journal: 'No such thing as a playhouse in Boston. They were too puritanical a set to admit of such diversions, but no town of its size could offer more whores than this one could.'"

I didn't bother to tell her, or Saul, who was too young to have known it, that Mt. Hoardom finally became Scollay Square, home of the Old Howard Burlesque—a sailor's paradise. The latter-day Puritans had finally eliminated that "Sodom" and replaced it with the Government Center, a forbidding place with no semblance of sin or anything to attract pleasure lovers at night, or at any other time. "Sex" had moved to lower Washington Street, and once again the new Boston Puritans—Irishmen and Italians this time—were trying to squeeze it into some other part of the city. Or, impossibly, eliminate nude strippers and adult bookstores altogether.

The thought crossed my mind that in three hundred and fifty years from now the skyscraper erections, which dominated the city—and which seemed to me to be sexual frustration manifested in stone and glass, that had created a new Boston in less than thirty years—would likewise have disappeared. Man's buildings and monuments to himself had greater longevity than their builders, but from a historical perspective, not much.

I knew that Anne had never seen King's Chapel, nor was aware what happened to the Church of England and Boston. "After the Colony lost its

Charter," I said, sounding to myself like a Freedom Trail Tour Guide, "a man named Sir Edmund Andros was appointed governor of the Colony. One of his first official acts was to have the Colony purchase a part of the old burying ground, which I'm sure that you will remember, and build a church that conducted Anglican services. The first Church of England services in the Colony were conducted in the original King's Chapel buildings in 1754. They were destroyed by fire, and the present stone temple was built in the late nineteenth century. But some of the old burying ground remains. Your friends, John Winthrop and John Cotton, are buried there.

As we entered the ancient cemetery, Anne read the inscription on the doorway. "Major Thomas Savage 1682." She sighed. "Tommy lived a long time." She said. "What about my daughter Faith?"

I told her I didn't know whether she had died before or after her husband.

"How old was John-Luv when he died?" she asked.

"Sixty-seven," I told her. It was part of the trivia I had accumulated, in spite of myself, as I had delved into her life. "He was preaching at Harvard and evidently caught the flu when he was being ferried back and forth to New Town." I grinned at Anne. "You would have enjoyed the text from his last sermon. It was based on John: 'And the word was made flesh and dwelt among us, Grace be with us all.'"

A few feet from the entrance we located Winthrop's tomb, and next to it the slate slab marking John Cotton's last resting place. Bending over, Anne read the worn marking. "Here Lyes Entombed the Bodye of the Famous Reverend and Learned Pastor of the First Church of Christian Boston. Mr. John Cotton, sixty-seven, December 23rd." She shook her head and said sadly, "Poor John-Luv. If he knew that he had been buried so close to Papist priests wearing surplices, repeating set prayers, and carrying crosses, he would have been exceedingly uneasy in his grave."

I laughed. "Two centuries later, he would have been even more uneasy. The church is now a Unitarian Universalist Church, and so is your first meetinghouse, which was finally located on what was called Back Bay."

"Unitarian Universalist, I know not." She looked at me puzzled. "What doth that mean?"

"Did you ever hear of Socinius?"

She nodded. "He believed that God could not have a human son. My good friend Thomas Pynchon, who moved out of the Colony to Springfield, believed that Jesus obeyed God's will, as we all should, and that Jesus's ministry and beliefs were more important than his death and suffering for our sins. Methinks that is most likely." She shrugged. "But I never did say it aloud before this."

"Unitarians don't believe in the Trinity." I said. "The Puritans became known as Congregationalists, and today, as members of the United Church of Christ, there are several million of them. They still believe in the Trinity, but many Unitarians are like you. They believe they can talk directly to God and make their own arrangements with Him. And most of them probably believe that God's Spirit dwells within them, but they're embarrassed to talk about it."

"Thou art teasing me." Anne sat on Winthrop's tomb for a moment and was staring pensively at the many slabs in the cemetery. She brushed away the tears gathering in her eyes. "If I dug down there, I wonder if I could find John-Luv's bones and his skull." She shrugged. "I feel like Master Shakespeare's Hamlet: 'Alas poor Yorick.'" Her green eyes, catching fragments of the setting sun, were focused on a world that I could never see. "It's strange," she said finally. "I am here in my corruptible body, the body I insisted could not return from the grave, and John-Luv, who was so sure he was one of the chosen and believed that he would return along with Jesus in his mortal body—where is he now?" Her words dropped like tears on his grave.

It was a question neither Saul nor I could answer. I noticed that Saul was shooting his second roll of film.

"Where did you live in Boston?" Saul asked.

Anne pointed at the old City Hall. "In that direction—if this be the place." She smiled at diners in the Maison Robert restaurant who were watching us from their table windows. "All these great buildings confuse me." Back on School Street she pointed to the Parker House. "Master Portman's School was on Century Lane. If that street you call Tremont Street leadeth back to the Common, then up there is Tremontaine—the three hills. Then this School Street must be Sentry Lane. It was not a street, then—just a path." She pointed across the street to the Boston Five Cents Savings Bank. "Mr. Atherton Hough lived over there, and Mary and John Coggeshall next to him, and across the lane from us."

At the corner of Washington Street we looked in the windows of the Globe Book Store, a colonial red-brick building that had been preserved as a historical site.

"In the eighteenth century that was the old Corner Book Store," I told her and Saul. "It was built in 1711 after the big fire that must have destroyed Anne's home. For a hundred years it was a hangout of many famous New England authors." Looking in the windows of the store, I told her. "Your home was located here on what is now the corner of School and Washington Streets."

Looking at the building from the park on the opposite side of the street, Anne shrugged. "I loved my home, but I mourneth it not. Will worked so hard to make it better than our home in Alford, but it never was. We did not stay long enough here. Even before I was murdered, I had lost it. Edward, who returned to Boston, sold it to Will's brother Richard." She smiled sadly. "My favorite preacher is Ecclesiastes. 'One generation passes away, another comes . . . There is no remembrance of things to come by those who come after.'"

"Supposedly, you can't go home again," I said trying to cheer her up. "But you're proving that gloomy old prophet was wrong."

"How much land did you have?" Saul asked.

"A half acre." Anne stared dubiously up School Street. "I could see all the way up to the burying ground. I had a big garden on the west side of the house." As she spoke, I knew that she was conscious of the street noise and the tooting of automobile horns. She held her hands to her ears, and then she laughed. As often happened when she shifted moods, her whole bearing became girlish and made me want to hug her. "Zounds!" she said. "This Boston is a noiser place than London ever was. If thou art in the right place," she said pointing at Washington Street, "that was a muddy road called High Street. North of us down the road a little was Sam Cole's Tavern. Sam Cole was a merry old soul." She sang the words. "He sold you his pipe and sold you his bowl. Full of beer or rum. He was a member of the church, but his ordinary was always filled with boozers. He made Master Winthrop abundantly unhappy."

Anne pointed in the direction of State Street. "The Market Place was over there behind those awful buildings." Trying to get a sense of direction, she looked southward down Washington Street, and saw the old South Church. "That church I know not," she said. "But it is on Master Winthrop's land. His home was near there overlooking the marshy road along the waterfront. Just opposite our house on the other side of High Road was the meetinghouse and the first church. Master Wilson's house was next door." She grinned. "This was a pleasing location, the best part of town. The Governor and Master Wilson could watch each other, and they both could watch me, but they never came to my meetings."

"If you had had room for a Jew," Saul said, "I'd have been there." It was obvious that Anne had captured his imagination. Ever since we had left the State House, even while he was taking pictures, he had been totally absorbed in her words.

"Jesus was a Jew," Anne said and kissed his cheek.

Saul grinned at her with moist eyes. "It's nearly five o'clock. I must go back to school," he said. "Whatever happens, I am privileged to know you. You can trust me. I am a believer." He shrugged. "But if you're in the vanguard of a Second Coming, you'll have to perform miracles to prove it."

Anne smiled. "Methinks thou art a miracle. Is that not enough?"

Saul told us that he was writing a term paper on what would happen if the United States had a libertarian government. "It's a subject I would like to discuss with you," he told Anne. "I'll have the pictures I've taken of you printed tonight. Where can I see you tomorrow? Where are you going from here?"

"It's up to Anne," I said. "I thought we might walk down Washington Street to State Street and then over to the Fanueil Hall area. It's approximately where the first marketplace was. Later we'll take a taxi back to the Pru and get my car." I smiled at Anne. "You must be pooped."

Anne grinned. "Pooped sounds naughty. Tired I am not. I am so awake, methinks I could fly."

I gave Saul a card with my address and phone number. I wasn't too happy to have him involved or underfoot, but I was aware that like it or not, Anne wasn't my private property. Even if I were Will reincarnated, I couldn't contain her any more than he could. Will told Robert Keyane when he questioned him in Rhode Island that his wife was a saint. I grinned, thinking, if the saints were marching in, I suppose I might as well be among that number.

I told Saul to telephone me around noon. "Keep in mind," I warned him. "You've had twenty-two years to assimilate the past three and a half centuries. Anne has only had three days. When she discovers that Satan rather than God is still running things, she's going to need more than one disciple."

"Maybe she's the true Messiah," Saul said with a grin, "the sin-bearing servant."

"What did he mean by that?" I asked Anne as he walked away.

Anne chuckled. "Dear Robert, in truth thou doth not know thy Scriptures as well as Will did. Saul, as a Jew, prefers Isaiah's vision of Christ, rather than John's 'Behold my servant shall deal prudently. He shall be exalted and extolled very high.' God told Isaiah: 'Just as many were astonished by you, so His visage was marred more than any man, and His form more than the sons of men. Kings shall shut their mouths at Him. For what hath not been told them, they shall see, and what they had not heard, they shall consider.'"

Oblivious of the people watching, she snuggled her face against mine. "That is the Jesus I know."

18

Six hours later I was lying in bed with Anne at the Parker House. A little exasperated, I told her that she still hadn't learned to keep her mouth shut. Three centuries ago at her trial she had backed Winthrop and Dudley into a corner, and had them baffled. But, alas, she couldn't stop talking. Now she was about to do it again—blow the top off of Boston. If she ever appeared on a radio or television show, she'd not only lose her former saintly, history-book status as a high-minded, church-going, Jesus-loving wife and mother, but she'd have a million Bostonians arguing whether she was a clever promotional fraud cooked up by some record company.

"This time," I said as she lay naked on top of me and swallowed me with her eyes, a sorrowful expression on her face, "instead of few thousand people and a governor who would have personally liked to whip your bum, there are millions of people out there who will insist that you have committed the impossible no-no. Worse than insisting that even the wicked are saved by the Lord's covenant of grace, you are putting yourself in the position of encouraging people to say that you have pretended to be Jesus Christ Himself and mixed sex and religion. Not only leftover Puritans but Boston Irishmen, Italians, and maybe even the Archbishop will denounce you. What's worse, I'm sure you don't understand people like TV talk-show hosts. Their passion is taking charlatans apart and letting them squirm while the people watch."

Grinning at me provocatively, Anne wiggled around until she had captured my pizzle. "Only worms and snakes squirm," she said happily, "and lovers when they are happy." Her haunches in the air, she snuggled into my shoulder. "Sorry, but I am not squirming. God is love. I never loved like that Prudence person who told me how bad it was. That kind of loving maketh a woman a dried-up old raisin. Ashamed I am not. I am sure that Jesus was a loving man. He suffered and died for one human sin that covers all the rest, and that was the sin of not loving." Her eyes twinkling, she kissed me enthusiastically. "Singing happy songs about a man and woman's need to love one another is not wicked. Only Satan is happy when we denieth love."

Thinking about it objectively and not worrying about consequences, I had to admit that Anne's sudden but not unexpected notoriety and her ability

136

to capture an audience had been amusing and proved that I was not alone in being fascinated by this woman.

After Saul had left, we wandered through Fanueil Hall until about six o'clock. Wide-eyed, chattering incessantly, amazed at the choices of food to eat and cooking specialties from every country in the world, admiring the clothing and gadgets and books and games and crafts, Anne kept wishing that Will could see all this. "'Tis the biggest fair, I ever saw, dear Robert," she said. "Thank thee for taking me to see it." Then impulsively, to my embarrassment right in the middle of the crowd, she hugged me and kissed me. "And Will is seeing this too, is he not? Thou art Will—and Robert too."

Beginning to wonder who in Hell I really was and whether I was dreaming all this, I asked Anne if she wanted to drive back to Quincy and relax after an arduous day.

She looked at me demurely. "Wouldst thou consider a strange request?"

"Sure. Why not?"

"I would relish sleeping with thee tonight on Sentry Lane. Methinks that there must be a tavern nearby."

There was: the Parker House. I exacted a promise from her that she wouldn't announce at the registration desk that she was *the* Anne Hutchinson— it was suspicious enough to be arriving with no luggage. I told the clerk that our baggage was at the airport. We were between flights, and my wife wanted to stay in Boston where early American history had begun. In particular we'd like a room overlooking King's Chapel.

While Anne was hanging out the window trying to eliminte old City Hall and a collection of buildings from her mind, and at the same time tell me what Boston had looked like when she lived here, I ordered hors d'oeuvres and drinks. Scotch for me and a pina colada for Anne, which she enjoyed so much she wondered if she could have another. "'Tis rum as I never tasted it." She stared at me dreamily. "Dost thou need to hug me as much as I needeth to hug thee?" she asked.

There was no question about that. For more than two hours we floated on each other's flesh in a never-never land where we intermittently explored each other's mind, as well as each other's body, and we wished that we could stay that way forever. Finally, she asked me the conundrum question. "If thou art also Will, art thou angry that I am in love with Robert too?"

Before I could answer that I probably would be, she added, "Wouldst thy wife, Emily, be angry if she could see us now?"

I laughed. "You can bet on it. No woman shares her husband willingly. She's afraid of losing him."

"But I desire not to take you away from her. Perchance, if she had a John-Luv in her life she might feel the same way as I did. I never loved Will less. I really believeth that thou art Will. Art thou jealous?"

I shrugged. "I don't know if I could cope with a woman who wants her cake and eats it too."

"Then thou art not Will." She grinned at me. "I loved Will because he was Will and not John-Luv."

"What about Harry?"

Before she could answer, Anne kissed me enthusiastically. "Like Saul, Harry was a boy. I was forty-two. He was twenty-three. We liked each other very much."

"You were his loving mum?"

"I will tell thee later about Harry," she said, changing the subject. "Doth Boston have a watchman?"

"A watchman?"

"Men who watch for fires and clank through the town telling the hour and making people go home to bed, if it be after nine. We had six of them." She gestured toward the window. "And we had our own militia—soldiers up there on the hill with a beacon to sound the alarm for Indians, and the French or Spanish. Jack Underhill was in charge. One night he awoke everyone with bugles blowing and a loud clatter." She laughed. "Oh, dear Robert, it was greatly amusing. I saw Master Winthrop stumbling around in his nightgown. Everywhere men and women were bumping into each other in a panic, running here and there, shouting and swearing. Jack told Master Winthrop it was a test, 'to see how we would behave.' Master Dudley was furious. But in truth no one knew what he was doing."

"There're no soldiers on the hill now," I told her. "But we still have hundreds of constables riding around in cruising cars, and we have a curfew of sorts. Restaurants and bars close by one o'clock—and it's not safe to walk the dark streets all alone."

As I spoke, I remembered the Bay Tower Room, on the thirty-third floor at One State Street. The building was on the general site of the First Meeting House, and the restaurant at the top is an expensive supper club that overlooks Boston Harbor. We hadn't eaten since two o'clock, and it was now eight-thirty. It didn't occur to me until we took a taxi for the short ride, that Miss Green had mentioned a trio, who played soft rock music for dancing, switched hats during the evening, and entertained with songs and music from the Elizabethan era. Nor did I realize that the Sons of the Virgin would charm Anne more than the view.

A half hour later, we were sitting near a window overlooking the waterfront far below us. Anne was still wearing her new black knit dress and picture hat, and her face was ethereal in the dim light. People sitting next to us in a crowded cocktail lounge were obviously aware of her, but she was like a child savoring a fairyland. "I'm closer to Heaven," she said staring at the waterfront, "than any Puritans ever were. Boston is alive with electricity," she said in hushed voice as she sipped a rum collins that I had ordered for her. "But I know not this city."

I pointed down to the Fanueil Hall area where we had been earlier. "Four thousand weeks ago you were buying corn down there. The water flowed up to the edge of where that granite building is. It was called the Town Cove. Will invested in a dock in that area. I think it was called Bendall's Dock."

"I remember! I remember!" Anne said excitedly. "Will got fourteen men together, including John Coggeshall and Edward and Tommy, who married Faith. They raised a hundred pounds to build a wharf." She smiled affectionately, and I thought a little tipsily at me. "If thou art not Will, how dost thou know about that? Thou must be Will." She peered into the night. "But where is the Town Cove gone? I see it not."

"It was filled in several hundred years ago," I said, aware once again that in the dimly lit room Anne was truly radiant. Some kind of inner light gave her features an almost otherworldly soft focus. It resembled an effect film-makers try to achieve with vaseline-coated lens when they close in on a leading lady's face at the moment of surrender. I wasn't the only one who noticed it. People passing our table stared at her, and when the waiter led us into the dining area close to the dance floor, Anne stopped conversation. Who was she? A Hollywood star? No. As Saul had pointed out, Anne had the indefinable quality of royalty.

Blithely unaware of the attention she was getting, she told me to order whatever I thought she should eat and drink. "Thou art my master," she said in a suppliant tone that would make anyone believe—for the moment, anyway—that she meant it. "I trust thee."

I thought we had both had enough to drink, but I ordered a bottle of Cabernet Sauvignon to go with our filet mignons. Entranced, Anne was watching several couple swaying together and listening to a group of three young men playing a medley of romantic Neil Diamond songs.

"There was one thing I hated about Boston," she said. "That was that we could no longer dance. It was against the law. In England in summer and winter, Will and I danced outdoors at fairs and festivals. We would do the galliard, and Will loved the volta. The Puritans even hated morris dancing and the branle." She explained that the branle was a go-around dance where, with your partner, you pretended that you were acting whatever the title of the song might be. "The Puritans preached that dancing and sounds of pipes and drums and lutes made men too lascivious. All we could sing were Psalms." She chuckled. "It was in truth moaning, not singing. But they thought the volta was the Devil's work."

I told her that I knew very little about Elizabethan music or dancing. "What was the volta?"

"An Italian dance. The man embraces the woman, turns her in a two-step, and lifts her high in the air. It is danced in very fast time. As he turns, a woman's petticoats fly around her knees. You could sometimes see her con, and the man dancing with her could feel her heart beating against his face." She grinned at me. "Will was very good at it. When I was too big with a child, he would dance the volta with all the young maids who adored him."

Waiting for our dinner to arrive, I led Anne onto the dance floor. The trio was now playing modern and less syrupy versions of old songs. Anne clung to me and quickly learned, on a crowded floor, to follow me to the sad sensual music of *Smoke Gets in Your Eyes*. I whispered the words in her ears. "Now laughing friends deride, tears I cannot hide. When your heart's on fire, smoke gets in your eyes."

By the time we finished eating, we were both feeling warmly expansive. I should have realized that Anne, even without the stimulus of liquor, was a totally social person. Now with several rums and a half bottle of wine flowing in her blood, she loved everybody. Her happy smile embraced people at surrounding tables who couldn't stop staring at her.

Then the trio, which had stopped to rest, returned to their platform, and one of them, a tall six-footer with blonde hair, stepped up to the microphone.

"I'm Tom Smeaton," he said with a slight Cockney accent, and he waved at the other two men. "These are my brothers, Dick and Harry. In England, for awhile, we called ourselves Tom, Dick, and Harry. But the truth is that we are related to Queen Anne. I hope you remember Queen Anne." He whipped his hand across his throat. "She was one of the wives of Henry the Eighth. Henry divorced Catherine, his old wife, because she couldn't produce a male heir, and he married Anne. But when Anne rewarded his efforts with a daughter, Elizabeth, Henry wasn't very happy with her either. Especially so because he thought she might have been playing tiddlywinks with Mark Smeaton. Smeaton was a court musician, who played the lute and was very good on the organ and virginal."

Tom spoke the words so that the sexual overtones were apparent, and Anne along with everyone else burst into laughter. "Taking no chances," Tom continued, "Henry sent Anne to the chopping block. He took a lot of other wives, but—Smeaton or not—Elizabeth survived. Henry's other daughter, Mary, wasn't very well-liked because she burnt a lot of Protestants at the stake. Ten years after Henry died, Elizabeth finally became queen. Henry had never actually denied that she was his child. As you probably know, she became known as the Virgin Queen. So obviously, we're not really her great, great—add a few more greats—grandsons, but we do feel a kinship with Elizabeth. While she was queen, London was a swinging place. Of course there were killjoys called Puritans who thought the end of the world was coming, but the wicked people didn't worry about that. Like all of you here this evening, they knew they were going to Hell anyway—so why not live it up?

"In between providing smaltzy dance music so that you can fall into each other's arms, high in the sky overlooking Boston, we also provide a nine o'clock interlude—an Elizabethan change of pace. Dick pipes the flute. Harry plays the virginal—he's good with virgins—and I play the lute. As you shall hear, we all sing and we hope that we may transport you to another era where your ancestors spent their hard-earned money just as you are dining with wine, women, and song.

"Our first song is based on a poem by Robert Herrick that was set to music by William Lawes in 1630. It's called 'Gather Ye Rosebuds While Ye May.'"

Listening to him open-mouthed, Anne kept murmuring. "Oh dear Jesus— I am so happy. Like me, these dear boys are from England. I love them."

The Sons followed their first song with one called "The Owl" which had a chorus: "Nose, nose, nose/and who gave thee that jolly red nose?/Cinnamon, ginger and nutmeg and cloves/That's what gave me this jolly red nose."

Then Tom Smeaton said, "As you can see, the Elizabethans didn't like to call a spade a spade, especially when they were singing sexy songs, which they adored. If you don't understand the innuendoes, see me after the show, and I'll fill you in. Now we'll sing you a sexy one about the Bellman—a man who knew the right bell to ring.

"Maids to bed and cover the coal/Let the mouse out of the hole/cricket in the chimney sing/whilst the bell doth ring/If fast asleep, who can tell/when the clapper hits the bell?"

After bringing the house down with more verses of that one, the group sang "Watkin's Ale": "There was a maid this other day/and she would needs go forth to play/and when that be heard a lad/what talk this maiden had/ therefore he was full glad/and did not spare For I will/without fail give you Watkin's Ale./As she walked she sighed and said/I'm afraid to die a maid/To say fair maid, I say—wither you go to play?/Good sir, then did she say. What do you care?/Watkin's Ale, good sir, quoth she, what is that, pray tell me?"

Whispering to me and telling me that she hoped I understood what clapper in the bell and Watkin's Ale meant, Anne was bubbling with laughter. Then I made the mistake of challenging her. "Too bad the group hasn't got a virgin daughter," I said. "She could sing the song that you sang at Lord & Taylor's, 'Pained Am I and Like to Die.'"

"Dear Robert," Anne chuckled. "I will ask them. Perchance they will let me sing it for you."

Aghast, not knowing whether to grab her and pull her back to the table, or just strangle her, I watched her walk toward the trio. I could see her speaking rapidly to Tom Smeaton, and he was nodding enthusiastically. Then, while she took the lute from him and stood beaming at a cheering audience of more than two hundred people who could both see and hear her, Tom announced:

"Tonight, we are privileged to have a woman with us who claims that she knows more Elizabethan songs than we do—particularly the more bawdy ones, which seem to delight you one and all. Not only that but she can accompany herself on the lute. I give you a lady from another world. She says that she is English and that her name is Anne Hutchinson, and she lived here in Boston more than three hundred years ago." Tom smirked. "She doesn't look like any Puritan to me, but how can you not believe her? Perhaps she really is Anne Hutchinson, who as I remember from my history books once wrestled with the governor of Massachusetts and nearly won."

Dumbfounded, I watched Anne smile appreciatively at the applause. She gave the lute a quick testing string pluck. "I wish not to take too much of your time," she said.

"Many years ago the only songs they sang in Boston were Psalms. A good friend of mine, Joseph Cotton, helped a poet, Francis Quarles, with a new translation of the Psalms, and these were printed in a book by Stephen Day in 1640. It was called the *The Bay Psalm Book*. Whenever you met a Puritan singing, you could be sure that he or she was singing a Psalm. The poetry was terrible. To make the Twenty-third Psalm rhyme, it was sung, 'The Lord to me a shepherd is. Want therefore shall not I. He in the folds of tender grass doth cause me down to lie.'"

Anne beamed at the laughter she had generated.

"In truth, we dared not sing anything else in public. But some of us relished singing songs about love and the everlasting mystery of men and women wanting one another. A few moments ago my dear friend and protector asked me if I would sing a little song about a young lady who lived in England many centuries ago. While I am a stranger here myself, from your laughter, I can see that some things hath not changed exceedingly much. Methinks that many young ladies, before they are married, still have the same problem—whether to do it or not?"

Singing and playing a plaintive tune on the lute, I realized that her audience was as bewitched by Anne's warm caressing voice as I had been. "Pained am I and like to die/and all for lack of that which I/do every day refuse/I musing sit or stand/Someone puts it daily in my hand." She grinned slyly, making it obvious what was put in her hand. "To interrupt my muse/ The same thing I seek and fly/ And want—which none would deny/ In my bed, when I should rest/it breeds such trouble in my breast/That seems my eyes will close/If I sleep, it seems to be/Oft playing in bed with me/But waked, away it goes/'Tis some spirit sure I ween/ And yet it may be felt and seen/ Would I had the heart and wit/ To make it stand and conjure it/That haunts me thus with fear/Doubtless, 'tis some harmless sprite/ For it by day as well as night/ Is ready to appear/ Be it friend or be it foe/ Ere long. I'll try what it will do."

Smiling happily at the enthusiastic applause and the cries of "More! more!" Anne sang "Up I Arose," a song about a young lady who lay with "a quidam clericus" (which she translated as a priest) who got her pregnant. She followed that one with "Thinkest Thou to Seduce Me Then" and topped them all by explaining that she could see that her protector was becoming fidgety, so she would only sing one more song which was in French. "But I will sing it slowly and tell you first it is called 'La doleur de Mon Con, Perè.' This song is about a sad little virgin maid who is feeling frisky in her privy parts. She asketh her father what she should do, and he tells her to try a piece of warm coal. Coal did not help, so she asketh her mother, and her mother telleth her to try an eel or a sausage. But eels are uncomfortable and sausages are messy, so she asketh her brother what to do, and he recommendeth that she try *d'y mettre l'outil de mon compagnon,* which meaneth his friend's utensil. She did and now she burns not anymore. By the grace of our Lady she is cured."

Despite the enthusiasm of the crowd to have her continue and Tom Smeaton's announcement that she was welcome to join the Sons and sing with them every night, I decided that the time had come to usher my lady back to her table. I scarcely had expostulated that now she really *was* in trouble, when a bejeweled, white-haired woman appeared at our table. She had a wrathful expression on her face.

"You obviously are a sick woman," she said through pursed lips. "Trading on the reputation of our dear Anne Hutchinson, using her name so that you can sell your filthy songs is disgusting. Insinuating that Mrs. Hutchinson was a sex-crazed woman is cheap and repulsive. I shall complain to the management to stop such vulgarity." Her diamond rings flashed her anger toward Anne's eyes.

"Who are you?" Anne demanded, not at all frightened by this latter-day saint.

"I am Prudence Mercy Awkley, president of the Boston Historical Society," the woman said. "I can trace my ancestry back to the Massachusetts Bay Colony. I know all about Anne Hutchinson. My relatives signed a petition supporting her against Governor Winthrop. Anne Hutchinson was a moral woman who believed in Jesus. She never would have made a public spectacle of herself singing nasty songs."

"Whether you like it or not," Anne said, "I am Anne Hutchinson. And I bore fifteen children. I can assure you that I enjoyed making babies as much as my husband did."

Momentarily speechless, Prudence gaped at her.

"Methinks God doth not worry when his creatures love one another or sing about loving," Anne said, smiling coolly at her. "But he may not be happy with squirrel-brained women like you who bedawb themselves with jewels and gold and probably no longer enjoy the parts that God gave them to enjoy."

Prudence stomped off muttering, "You're a foul-mouthed woman."

Then, to my shock, I saw Sally Lane, waving to friends and admirers as she passed, heading for our table. Without being asked, Sally sat down in an empty chair. "I remember you," she said to me. "You were on 'People Passion' with me about a year ago. You had a new book out on porno films." She grinned at Anne. "You better watch out. Your protector is a sexy senior citizen. He has good taste in women. You're not only very pretty, you can sing. Are you a friend of the Smeatons? What's this line about you being Anne Hutchinson?"

"Look, Sally," I said hoping that I could forestall the inevitable. "Anne will tell you that she is Anne Hutchinson. But whether she is or not we're not anxious to prove it. We want no publicity."

Sally wasn't listening to me. "You mean that she really believes that she has been reincarnated?" Sally's eyes were wide open, savoring in advance how she could run with this one on her noon-time television show.

"Resurrected is the right word," I said impatiently. "Just look at her and you can see how impossible that is."

"Nothing is impossible to the Lord," Anne said with a mischievous smile.

"Are you one of those Jehovah's Witnesses?" Sally asked dubiously, and it was obvious that she didn't want to tangle with their beliefs that Jesus was about to return with a sword in his hand.

"I know nothing of witnesses to Jehovah," Anne said. "But I have no doubt that I have lived before."

That was all that Sally needed. Flinging question after question at Anne, she tried to undermine her conviction and get her to admit that this was really a pretty slick promotional gimmick. But Anne ignored my continuous warning that I thought it was time we should leave. She was obviously enjoying herself. I was sure she didn't understand everything that Sally asked her, but she parried Sally's questions so skillfully that she would have convinced a doubting Thomas. Doubting or not, Sally no longer cared. A woman like this who claimed that she had returned from the grave and could describe the manners, morals, and environment of Puritan Boston in minute detail was a show stopper.

She laid it on the line. "I like you, Anne. I want you on 'People Passion' next week. I have a cancellation Tuesday. That gives my program directors four days to do the research for me and get some feedback from people on the show." She smiled at me. "I don't want to explore your relationship with Bob right now, or how you discovered each other, but I hope that he'll come on the show with you. All I need to know is how to get in touch with you."

"We're not going to be on any television show," I said emphatically, and I shook my head vigorously at Anne, who was nodding agreement. "You don't know what you're getting into," I told her. "Sally will make mincemeat out of you. She'll take you apart while a million people watch, delighted to see you get your comeuppance. It's ridiculous. You're going to be on television, and you've never even watched television. You don't know what the Hell it's all about."

"That's great!" Sally told her enthusiastically. "You don't have to worry, Anne. All you have to do is be natural and confident just like you are right now."

"You mean naive?" I asked gloomily.

Anne patted my arm. "Thou saith thou fancieth women who talk back to men. What can Sally do? Banish me from Boston again?"

"No way," Sally assured her. "I'm going to pay you seven hundred and fifty dollars just for being you." She smiled at a man who had come up to the table and was impatiently waiting for her. "This is Steve Carlson," she said. She introduced him as her television producer. "It's all set, Steve. If this is the blockbuster I think it will be, you can take Anne national." She asked me if I still lived in Quincy. When I responded that I was flying to Israel with Anne tomorrow and show her Calvary, Sally just grinned and said, "I've got your phone number on file. We'll be in touch with you Monday morning."

19

I awoke the next morning at the Parker House with Anne kissing me with a hundred little kisses. Groaning, I complained that it was only seven o'clock—much too early to be awake. Wasn't she exhausted after such a hectic night? Then, hugging her, I told her I no longer had any qualms about making love to what might be her soul rather than a corruptible body but I was beginning to believe that the resurrected were stronger than the living.

"Thou art a sleepyhead," she grinned at me as she played idly with my pizzle. "I've been awake an hour. When I lived across the road from this inn, I awoke every morning at six."

"But you and Will didn't play seesaw three times a day," I said, well aware that part of me was joining the living, even if my brain was still asleep.

"If thou desire not to be inside me," she said after I had already disappeared into her vagina, "thou dost not need to."

Whether I needed to or not was beside the question. Later, smiling contentedly at me, she said, "I like this Parker House inn, but I am weary of ordinaries. Canst I make breakfast for thee in Quincy? I desire to learn how to use electricity."

As we drove toward Quincy, she suddenly began to worry—or pretended that she did—that I was angry with her for singing last night with "those nice boys," and she kept promising not to make any commitments unless she consulted with me first.

"Canst thou send an electric message to Mistress Sally Lane and tell her that my mind was not right?" she asked, surprising me that she had so quickly grasped the potential of voice transmission. "But thou must not forget that I canst sleep not in thy bed when thy wife returns, and thou canst not continue to give me money. This Sally friend of yours may pay me so much I can build my own cottage." She smiled sadly at me. "I would miss you, but I fear not being on my own. I was without Will after he died."

I assured her that Sally was no friend of mine, and Sally wasn't going to support her, but little did I realize, then, how fast money could flow to a person who believed that Jesus might be here on earth with us right now and who also believed that she had been chosen as emissary of a beneficent

146

millennium which was already in progress.

"As much as I care about you," I told her, "I also believe in women's liberation. It would be a sad irony if you returned to earth and some man like me tried to control you. You are you—Anne Hutchinson. You are a symbol of women's equality." I grinned at her. "Anyway, I told you that I'm attracted to women with strong minds who also enjoy loving surrender—especially women like you who enjoy seducing a man as much as he enjoys seducing her." I told her that my only complaint was that I was afraid of surprises. "You've proved that you're not a sanctimonious woman who spent all of her spare time reading the Scriptures and communing with Jesus and the Holy Spirit. Before you tell the world what you are really like, I think it's time that you told me what happened during the three years you lived in Boston. Did you sing bawdy songs at your lecture meetings? And what about Harry Vane? I know that you think that I'm a reincarnation of Will, but if Saul is a reincarnation of Harry, I'm not at all sure that I'm willing to share you with a young lover." I laughed at Anne's pixie grin. She was fully aware that I was teasing her. "One John-Luv and a husband should be enough for any woman."

"Oh, I do loveth the way thou speaketh to me." Anne squeezed close to me in the car, and I had to warn her not to be too friendly or I couldn't concentrate and we'd end up in a ditch.

"I told you that I arrived with my family in Boston September 18, 1634. Edward had been living in John-Luv's house on the hill. By the time we arrived, he and Will's brother had dug the cellar and framed in our house on the corner of High Street. Before winter, with the help of John Bigby and of Edward Dennis, a tailor—both were apprenticed to Will—we were completely closed in, and our fireroom was as big as Master Winthrop's.

"Will was given the hand of fellowship and accepted as a member of the church immediately, but Master Symmes convinced Master Dudley that I believed in personal revelations." Anne shrugged. "The Puritans were convinced that neither God nor Jesus spoke directly to people any more. John-Luv allayed their fears and convinced Master Wilson that Satan's daughter I was not."

She laughed. "Not then anyway. But John told me privately that I frightened him more than a little. He refused to believe that Susanna was his child, although with her blonde hair and brown eyes, she was looking more like him every day. He told me that I must abandon my Familist thinking—and especially my notion that my revelations about future events were as infallible as the Scriptures. 'But,' I told him, 'if I said that to Master Symmes I meant it with a sense of humor. Many prophecies in the Scriptures were dreamed up by the prophets to resolve the problems of the times. They were not infallible either.'

"John-Luv admitted that I leavened his thinking. Only with me did he ever reveal his own uncertainties, or laugh at people like Master Dudley, who put all their faith in works and building a good estate as necessary for their salvation.

"I told him that I could not believe that the most famous preacher in England had to bow and scrape to Master Wilson. I knew that he was as bored with Master Wilson's Hell-and-damnation sermons as I was, but John-Luv kept trying to assure me that being appointed teacher for the First Church was a great honor. There was no doubt, he told me, that the meetinghouse was a leaky mud hut and could not be compared with the cathedral he had preached in for twenty years in Old Boston, but I must remember that as Gentiles we were building a future here for a new religious state, and we were realizing God's covenant with the Israelites to restore the Kingdom of God."

Anne shook her head. "The trouble was that John never took arms against his sea of troubles. He was a pacifier. I told him that I was Socrates' gadfly, who was not afraid to sting the lazy horse and get him off his arse. Fortunately, I did not have to sting Master Wilson's arse right away. In October he returned to England, to try once again to persuade his wife, Elizabeth, to come to the Colony and suffer with the rest of us. For a whole year while he was gone, at last John-Luv was on his own and in full charge of the First Church."

She smiled reminiscently. "For the next twelve months, until Master Wilson returned in October of 1636, John dared to preach what he truly believed. He said it, not in so many words, but he made it apparent that a hypocrite could have Adam's righteousness and still perish unless he came into union with Christ.

"It was a good year. Will and I worked very hard, and I was very happy. Often we had no bread, but we had plenty of fish and turkey. Prices on corn and wheat were exceedingly high. I learned how many good things to eat could be made from pumpkin and squash. We had good supplies of rum and cider and madeira, and Will sold all the cloth he could get delivered to Boston. A few months after we arrived, Edward sailed back to England to marry his sweetheart, Katherine Hamby, and they both returned to Boston the same year. Faith found a nice boy—Thomas Savage, a tailor. She was seventeen when they married. Bridget was being courted by John Sanford, son of a wealthy man who came to the Colony to make cannons and gunpowder. John-Luv married them in June after Zuriel was born. Bridget was two years younger than Faith, but she got herself a richer man." Anne laughed. "None of my daughers were like me. I did not marry until I was twenty-one. All Faith and Bridget thought about from the time they were twelve was being the wife of some good man." She shrugged. "Most women take the path of least resistance. It is easier to be protected than be a protector."

"I told you about my sister Kate. She was a fiery one. She married Richard Scott. They both detested Masters Winthrop and Dudley and could not bear to listen to Master Wilson. But unlike me, Kate knew that the better part of valor in Boston was to keep one's mouth shut and agree with the saints.

"So did I—for the first year. Janey Hawkins and Mary Dyer and I helped many women give birth, and I nursed many others and quite a few men through terrible sicknesses that winter." Anne grimaced. "Poor Janey— Master Winthrop was certain that she was a witch, and John thought I should not have her for a friend. She was a little daft on her remedies. I told her that she particularly liked mandrake root for just about everything because it looked like a man. But Janey was a good midwife.

"That fall and winter I worked from dawn to dark preserving food, spinning cloth, and helping Will fill the cellar with food. When the first snow fell, we were prepared. The winter was fierce. I never saw so much snow before. It hugged Boston like an overcoat, but we were warm inside. In the evening, my family were all snug together, and we read Scriptures and sang songs, and I played my lute and Will played cards with Edward and Dennis and his brother. We invited only friends like Mary and John Coggeshall, whom we could trust, to join us. But Annie and Frances, my old-maid cousins, were terrified that Master Winthrop might have a spy peering through the cracks and report back to him how happy we were.

"For the most part I remained at home. But I calculated how to see John-Luv once a week and talk with him in his study."

Anne yelled and hid her face in her hands as a car passed us and almost hit an oncoming car. "Methinks this is a very dangerous business," she gasped. "What would happen if another automobile hit us?"

I shrugged, but later my answer would return to me. "I don't know about you, but I'm sure that I wouldn't be picked out for resurrection. Anyway," I chuckled, "it seems to me that you were involved in a very dangerous business, too. From what you have told me, I presume that you and John-Luv did a lot more than just talk in his study. How did you know that Sarah wasn't listening at the door or peeking through the keyhole?"

"Sarah would have never done that!" Anne said. "I was her friend too. Whenever I said goodbye to John-Luv, I always spent an hour or two with her. Methinks she knew that I loved John as much as she did, but she was not jealous of me. She knew that I was one of the few persons that John dared to speak honestly with. In April, before she told John, she told me— she was pregnant again, and she prayed that I would be with her when she had her second child in December."

Anne stared at the early northbound traffic moving toward Boston on the Expressway and sighed. "I wish that Will could see this. It took us three hours by wagon to get to Mt. Wolleystone from Boston. In late April, although the nights were still cold, Will would often camp there for a few days with his brother and the servants. While Will was plowing the fields, they were building our plantation house.

"By May I had planted a house garden in Boston, and I had much time to myself. Annie and Frances and my daughters Bridget and Frances took care of the younger children, Sam, Anne, Mary, Katherine, William, and Susanna. Will was very busy. He was angry with Henry Beggs, who built our fireplace. He charged twice as much as he should have. Will finally sued him in August for charging excessive wages. I knew that twice a week John-Luv walked through the woods by himself to Muddy River, where his plantation was. He wanted to make certain that the men he had hired were doing the plowing and planting. John was very methodical. I could set a clock by him. Whenever I had finished my chores on Tuesdays or Fridays, I would wait for him by a huge chestnut tree in a lonely part of the forest three miles from our house. He would greet me with a big frown on his face. 'Thou shouldst not be out here alone. There are Indians and bears,' he said.

"'I am not afraid of bears,' I told him. 'I came here to hug one.'"

Anne chuckled. "We had found a place in the deep marsh grass where no one could see us. On hot days it was soft and cool on our bums. During that spring and summer we were together many times. Sarah was fragile, and she never walked very far, as she was afraid of losing her child. I would bring a basket with bread and melons and some rum." Anne giggled. "Sometimes we would get tipsy and frolic naked like characters in Master Shakespeare's *Midsummer Night's Dream*. Then, all covered with seed and pulp and love juices, we would wash in the Charles River.

"After we made love, John-Luv would worry and tell me how wicked we were, and how I was especially in trouble, because some women had reported to Master Wilson—and of course Master Winthrop knew about it—that I thought I was too good to go to their prayer meetings.

"'They saith that thou believeth thou art already sanctified by Christ,' John told me. 'And have no need for prayer. They thinketh that I am in thy power because I do not admonish thee.'

"'Thou canst not admonish me,' I teased him. 'If thou tells them thou loves their sister,' I kissed his pizzle, 'with the pure love of Jesus, of course.'"

I was driving along Wollaston Boulevard with Quincy Bay on our left when Anne suddenly became aware that automobiles came in many different shapes and sizes. "Why do they make so many different kinds?" she demanded, forgetting John Cotton for a moment.

"You're living in a world where man builds things that are only supposed to last about ten years. Cars not only wear out quicker than they should, but the manufacturers keep making them different so people will think their car has gone out of style, and they must have a new one. Every year there are new models, and everyone spends many years of their lives earning money to have the latest model. The same thing applies to clothing and practically everything else you can buy."

"Dost thou mean that my new dresses will quickly fall apart?"

"No. But in a year or two they will be out of style. Everyone who sees you will think you are too poor to afford the new style." I laughed. "You can't leave your clothing in your will to relatives, like many Puritans did."

I knew that I was trying to explain our throwaway society to a woman who must have cherished her meager possessions.

"It is just as well," she sighed. "I have no relatives."

Before I could get her back to John Cotton, she saw a man and woman jogging along the beach sidewalk. She grasped my arm excitedly. "Why are so many people running? Why is everyone in such a hurry to get somewhere?"

"Those two aren't going anywhere," I told her. "They're exercising—keeping in shape."

"I understandeth not those words."

"You've returned to a world where millions of people earn their living sitting on their asses," I said. "After which they fill themselves up with too much food and get too fat. Then they have to pay money to people who tell them that if they want to live longer they should stop eating so much, lose weight, and maybe even jog—run—a few miles a day."

Shaking her head in wonder, Anne laughed. "Methinks I have much to learn. Every day I jogged from early morning to night—but not to keep from growing fat!"

"But you did," I chuckled. "You kept in shape. That's probably one reason why your John-Luv couldn't keep his hands off your body. You obviously provided some spice to his life."

Anne shrugged. "He told me his bowels yearned for me, but I knew that often his mind listened not to his cock." She grinned. "There were many times when John was a contented man and was well-nigh certain that God was not angry with him for loving me, and he worried not that we were sinning or breaking the law. But, of course, he never stopped preaching—not even when he was lying in my arms and his cock was deep inside me."

"I upset him when I told him that men and women should never stop seeking answers. God and Jesus wanted us to be seekers—only by seeking would we discover that the Holy Spirit was within us. 'Christ after the flesh, and the literal blood of Christ doth not save us,' I told him. 'Wordy preaching with no spiritual understanding is empty and worthless. It is not Christ crucified but Christ formed in us—the Deity united to our humanity, realized with premeditation—that maketh a man or woman able to enter the Kingdom of God.

"'The reason I do not attend prayer meetings,' I told him, 'is that I believe not that God listens to those who pray to Him to forgive them for their sins.' Christians are not bound to pray constantly at set times but only as the Holy Spirit moves them to pray. I told him that I believed that God would raise up other apostolic men and women for our times who would preach the true gospel."

Anne shrugged. "In truth, my words drew a knife between us—especially when I told him that he should become the Apostle John, the Second, and I would be his minister."

From the corner of my eye, I could see Anne smiling sadly. "On top of that, while he was telling me that these were dangerous errors, and I must never say such things to any other person, including Will and my children, I told him that I was pregnant again.

"'It is thy child in my womb,' I told him. 'Will and I made love this winter, but I always had my monthly flow afterward. Most of April and May Will has been at the farm.'" Anne grinned at me. "I told John-Luv that when Will and I slept together—how do you say it—Will was too pooped. John-Luv never believed me, but it was true. The baby was born in March of 1636, and I named him Zuriel, which means in Hebrew 'My rock is God.' Zuriel in the Old Testament was the son of Abihaal, a Levite. I reminded John that the Levites were in charge of maintaining the Tabernacle in the wilderness, just the same as he was in the Colony."

When I turned into my driveway on Narragansett Road, I noticed that Anne's eyes were beginning to fill with tears. "My poor baby, Zuriel, was only seven when the Indians killed him. He was my second love child. I told John-Luv that I blamed him not. As soon as I knew that I was pregnant, I teased Will into playing seesaw again. Babies are not predictable, I told John. They could arrive sooner than expected."

Anne clung to me for a moment, "Dear Robert, thou art the only person to whom I ever told the truth about me. Zuriel was my last baby, but I became pregnant once more in March 1638, in John-Luv's house—during my excommunication from the church." She sighed. "Even when he was praying for me, John couldn't resist Satan's daughter."

20

Back in the house, Anne unwrapped her new clothes and proudly displayed them to me. Finally choosing a skirt and blouse, she took off her black knit suit. "Thank thee, dear Robert," she said and hugged me, "for all these pretty clothes, and thank thee for taking me to Boston. I was very happy, but I am even happier to be alone again. Sometimes, I relish quantities of people and sometimes I grow weary of them and wish to be with only one person."

Cracking eggs, dropping bacon into a frying pan, she told me that she was happier here than eating in an ordinary. Now I could pat her arse—as I was doing—and teach her about electricity. I told her that all I really knew about electricity was how to turn on switches and put in plugs. Eating with a spoon, because the sunnyside-up egg was too drippy to maneuver with a fork, she continued to tell me about her life in Boston.

"Harry Vane," she said between mouthfuls, "arrived in Boston early in October of 1636. He was on the same boat with Master Wilson, who finally returned with his wife. On his first Sunday Master Wilson shook my hand and stuttered how happy he was to see me and how pleased he was to be reunited with his church in Boston. He introduced me to a boozy-looking, red-faced minister who had come to Boston on the same boat with him. It was Master Hugh Peters, who looked like a monkey in heat. I fancy we took an instant dislike to one another. I was glad when he was finally sent to a church in Salem, but I had not seen the last of him.

"No one could deny that Harry Vane was the most handsome young man who had come to the Colony. I soon learned from the gossips that Harry's father, Sir Henry Vane, had been made a knight by King James when he was only seventeen. Harry was born when Sir Henry was only twenty. Harry grew up in Raby Castle. I saw it once. It looked as if a king were living there, and one had—more than six hundred years before—King Canute. The castle had terraces half a mile long with an entrance hall supported by six pillars. The Presence Chamber where Sir Henry entertained could accommodate seven hundred knights at one time.

"After spending his boyhood amidst all those riches, with tutors to teach him the arts, sciences, and languages, Harry had gone to Magdalen Hall at

153

Oxford and later studied at the Westminster School. When he graduated he traveled in Europe for three years. He lived in Paris, Vienna, Geneva, and Rome. I felt certain he must be the spoiled brat of a royal family. Margaret Winthrop told some of the women whom she met at the town spring that Harry's father was in great measure advisor to King James, as well as being treasurer of the Royal Household.

"A week after Harry's arrival, because Will had been appointed a deputy magistrate with the General Court, we were invited to a reception at Master Winthrop's house, and I met Harry for the first time. He had wavy brown hair, which hung down to his shoulders—the hair length that Master Endicott and Dudley detested. With flashing brown eyes, he was a good head taller than I. I spoke naught but a few words to him, but he held my hand an extra measure and whispered to me, 'It is truly a bonny evening. I would prefer to be walking by the ocean with you.' I was certain that he was just flirting with me—a woman old enough to be his mother. It is obvious that he was bored with people like Master Bellingham and the ministers, who were fawning all over him as if he had been sent to the Colony by the King himself.

"I was five months pregnant with Zuriel. Although I finally talked with Harry a few times at John-Luv's house, where he was living while a big addition to the house was being built for him, in truth I did not know a great deal about Harry until after Zuriel was born. I knew that he was very rich. Before the first snowfall, he had paid carpenters to build a big fireroom addition to John's house, where he could entertain. It also had a bedroom with a separate fireplace."

Anne smiled at me mischievously. "Harry had the biggest feather mattress you ever saw. Two people could disappear in it." She laughed. "We did, but that was much later. During the winter months Harry spent much of his time traveling by horseback around the Colony and visiting the various towns and forts. He even went to Connecticut with Master Winthrop's son, John Junior. John had received a commission from the King, sent over with Harry, to begin a new plantation there and to be governor of it."

"According to your biographers," I said, "by this time you were doing a little bit of preaching yourself to gatherings of as many as eighty people who came to your house twice a week. Was Harry among your admirers?"

Anne frowned at me. "It is not true. I never preached. In January of 1636, I was seven months pregnant and I was too big to get around very much. To break up the long winter nights, Will and I invited some of our close friends—the Coggeshalls, Mary and John, the Coddingtons, Mary and Will, the Aspinwalls, Elizabeth and Will—to our house. All of the men had been elected to the General Court, and they liked to talk with each other. Unlike most of the Puritans, they enjoyed a little card playing. We were careful that no Puritans could peek in the windows, and sometimes the ladies even played cards with the men.

"I soon discovered that, like me, the women enjoyed John-Luv's preaching more than Master Wilson's. Because I seemed to know more about Scriptures than they did, they kept asking me to explain the difference between them.

"I explained that John was teaching that the Holy Ghost dwelleth within a person—just as if you were already in Heaven. I told them that every man and every women is justified even before he believes. Faith is no cause for justification." Anne shrugged. "I knew that I was putting some words in John's mouth that he never spoke, but I had always tried to convince him that he should stop dilly-dallying. He should admit that the words of the Scripture, especially in the New Testament, prove that a covenant of grace was given to all of us by the Lord." She smiled. "Maybe I exaggerated a little bit, but I told the ladies that the Spirit came to us through our inheritance of Abraham's carnal seed. They liked that."

"Did you continue seeing John while you were pregnant?"

"Why not?" Anne demanded. "I was carrying his child, and his wife Sarah needed my help. Her baby girl was born September 15th—a month before Harry Vane arrived. I was with Sarah during the birth. I stayed with her for three nights. After that, for several weeks, I came every day, and we took Seaborn, who was only two years old, back to our house. They named the new baby Sarah after her mother." Anne smiled. "I was only three months pregnant with Zuriel, and Sarah was not of a condition for a man yet.

"John-Luv was wary of me, but we could never talk long together without touching one another. It was like making a hole in a dam. Once the trickle started, the dam quickly broke and the waters of love gushed through. But in October, after Harry arrived and was living in John's house, we were both afraid that Harry would guess that when I was in the study, we were doing more than merely chatting.

"Then the harvest came at John's farm and at ours at Mt. Wolleystone. It was too cold to meet John-Luv and to romp about naked outdoors, and I was too big with child anyway." Anne grinned. "Methinks the Lord contrived to keep our secret. After Zuriel was born, John-Luv still wanted me but he was sore afraid that I was talking too much and telling people that he was the only minister who understood the Scriptures. He told me that if I did not stop that, they would surely put two and two together. But worse than that, he was jealous."

"Jealous?"

"Of Harry. In late March, when Zuriel was only a few weeks old, I was aware that every Sunday and Lecture Day, Harry, who sat with the men on the men's side of the meetinghouse, was watching me. I was sitting with Mary Dyer and Mary Coggeshall. Master Eliot was the guest preacher one Sunday afternoon. Zuriel was asleep in my lap, and I was taking notes on the sermon. After the services, Harry immediately came up to Will and John

Coggeshall and asked what they thought of Master Eliot's sermon.

"'I have nothing to say,' Will told him, 'but I'm sure that my wife will be happy to tell you what she thinks.' It was only four in the afternoon, and Will invited Harry back to our house. The days had grown longer. It was still light, and Will had some work to do in his shop at the back of the house. The children and Annie and Frances were upstairs. I sat near the fire. Zuriel was fidgeting and I knew that he was hungry and could not wait. So I undid my gown and nursed him. Harry watched me with tears in his eyes.

"'Never have I seen such a beautiful mamma with her baby,' he said. He told me that I reminded him of a Madonna painting by Jean Fouquet, which he had seen in Antwerp, except that my face and breasts were more beautiful.

"'I wish I were your child,' he said. Zuriel had stopped nursing and had fallen asleep. 'I would trade Heaven to take his place at thy nipples.' Laughing, I told him that he had scarcely left the Heaven of his own mother's titties. 'But I am certain that many young women would be happy to take thee on their breasts.'"

"'Wouldst thou?' he asked softly.

"Methinks I blushed. I knew that he had more in mind than suckling a woman. He was twenty-four—a man who, according to my reckoning, had not been with a woman for seven months or longer."

Anne grinned at me. "As thou knoweth, Robert, I am a greatly impulsive woman. In truth, without knowing then how brilliant a mind he had, I could not resist the boy." She sighed. "In a moment of happy insanity I told him that I had more than enough milk for two babies and that if he wanted to suck—though it scarcely tasted so good as cow's milk—he could help himself. I put Zuriel in his cradle."

"'Oh, dear Anne, thank thee,' he said as he fell trembling to his knees in front of my chair. He exposed both of my breasts and held them gently in his hands, and he kissed them reverently and took a little suck from each of them as I caressed his beautiful brown hair.

"'Thy milk is very sweet,' he said, and before I could turn away he kissed me fervently on the mouth. 'But not so sweet as thy lips and mouth.' Then once again he was kissing my titties and telling me: 'I am not only a son of God but thou maketh me son of a goddess.'

"That remark was an invitation to discussion," Anne said. "I tried to divert him from my breasts by asking what he thought about Master Eliot's emphasis on works to achieve salvation." She grinned at me. "I was well aware that offering my new suitor such delicacies in my fireroom, when the children or Will might come prancing in was not a happy idea."

"'I obviously needeth a woman,' Harry said. He grinned down at the bulge between his legs and shifted his codpiece as he stood up.

"'But not a mother,' I said, refastening my gown. 'I'm forty-four. Thou couldst be my oldest son.'

"Harry laughed. 'Thank God that I am not,' he said. 'Without thou knowing it, I have talked about thee to John Cotton. I have been in love with your mind and the sight of thee for more than a month.'

"'I know that thou watcheth me at the meetinghouse,' I told him. 'But the real me—and my mind—thou knowest not.'

"'Ah, but methinks that I do,' he said. 'I have had long talks about thy beliefs with John, and with your friends, John Coggenshall and Will Coddington. They much admire thee. They telleth me that once or twice a week they come to thine house, and they saith that thou art the most learned woman in the Colony.' Harry stared at me with a stern expression on his face. 'They telleth me that thou art not really a Puritan. If Master Dudley truly knew what goes on here, next Lecture Day, right in front of everyone, thou wouldst get thy bare arse whipped.' Harry scowled at me. 'And if they knew what I really thought about them, they would all stop kissing mine.'"

As she sipped her second cup of coffee, I could see from her expression that Anne's mind was adrift in another century. "That night," she said finally, "I felt guilty about Harry. I knew that when the time was right he would want to make love with me, and I knew that I would not stop him. Dost thou understand, Robert? Women grasp at their youth as much as men do. I could scarcely believe that such a virile young man would want an old lady like me."

"The Lord must love you—he preserved you so well," I said. "I can't believe that you were more beautiful at forty-four than you are right now at fifty-two."

"Nor can I," she replied. "All these centuries have passed, but I have been reprieved from old age. I am only eight years older than I was."

"You've got a good twenty years ahead of you," I told her. "I'm sure that you will be beautiful long after I'm gone."

"I understand you not."

"I'm quite a bit older than you are right now. I doubt if I will make ninety."

"Thou willst not die," she said emphatically. "Like me, thou may disappear for a time, but then thou willst return. That is Jesus' gift to those who believe."

"I love you," I said and embraced her. "And I have no doubt that you are Anne Hutchinson, but I don't believe in miracles for myself. Anyway, I'm fascinated with Harry. According to his biographer, he spent three years in Europe studying theology. His father was so shocked to learn that he had been influenced by Calvin's beliefs and that Harry was practically a Puritan that he threatened to disown Harry, especially because Harry would have nothing to do with the Church of England. Presumably Harry told his father that the reason he wanted to go to New England was to live the kind of religious life he had come to believe in. I'm sure that had he been a poor man, Archbishop Laud would have had him hung. Laud tried to make him an Anglican, but after a long discussion Laud gave up and told Harry's father that it was better for Harry to go to New England and cool off for awhile. His father agreed, but Harry was supposed to return in three years or he would lose his inheritance."

Anne shook her head. "The kind of Puritan history that thou hast been telling me about is not always correct. During April and May in 1636, before Harry was elected governor of the Colony, I shared many hours with him. Harry was no follower of Calvin. He told me that Calvin's belief in pre-destination, that God had chosen the elect—those who would inherit the Kingdom of God—was an exceedingly dangerous philosophy. So far as he was concerned, the Puritans were proving it right here in Boston. They were creating a society on earth and postulating one in Heaven in which the common man had no place. The only purpose in life for ordinary folk was to live to work, and die for those chosen by God who would inherit the Kingdom of Heaven. Harry was certain that one day soon both Calvin's daydream and Queen Elizabeth's merry England were coming to a violent end.

"'Men create their own millenniums' he told me. 'They don't listen to God or they would know that the things of men are not forever. Everything changeth, even the belief in kings and popes, who are supposedly chosen by God to survive because they convinced the people that they were nominated by God Himself. But in France, Germany, and England, people were finally reading the Scriptures themselves and they were learning that their rulers were just men and women who ate and drank, shit and pissed like everyone else.'"

As she had seen me do, Anne opened the dishwasher and stacked the dishes in it. "Do we push the electric button now?" she asked.

I shook my head. "Bostonians still don't like to waste water. Not for just a few dishes with cups and saucers. Just stack them in—we'll push the magic button later." I laughed. "Tell me more about Harry."

"At first, Harry was careful not to challenge Master Winthrop and all the believers in a covenant of works, but Harry soon understood that even the ministers did not practice what they preached. He was shocked to learn that more than a thousand people were expected to attend church, including a few Indians, but few of them could ever be given the hand of fellowship or accepted as members of the church—or even as freemen. The workers in the Colony knew the truth. No matter how hard they worked—unless of course, they piled up a lot of money—they would never be judged justified or sanctified. In plain words, Heaven was not waiting for them. Satan was."

"Did you know that Harry was finally knighted in 1640?"

Anne nodded. "I wrote and asked him to come back to Rhode Island, but he wrote me that Will and I should return to England. He had more faith that people in England would learn how to live together democratically than they ever would in the Colonies."

"Harry died trying to prove it," I said. "He was beheaded by Charles II on the 14th of June 1662 for refusing to renounce his beliefs."

Anne gasped. "Oh dear God—poor Harry! I knew it would happen. I told him a few months before he returned to England that I knew we would both die before our time, at the hands of people who were afraid of losing their power over others."

"Did Harry believe in your revelations?"

She shook her head sadly. "No more than thou believeth. But one day thou willst believe."

21

By noon, wondering when Saul would telephone or if he had convinced himself that the Anne Hutchinson story was too incredible to bother with, I was still learning that when it came to loving, Anne was a risk-taker equal to any twentieth-century lady.

"About the middle of May," she told me as she sipped a preluncheon glass of white wine while we waited for Saul, "Harry told me that Sam Maverick had invited him to dinner at Noddle Island and to bring along his friends, the Hutchinsons. Sam was rich and well able to spend a day away from work, but most of the people in the Colony, especially Will, even resented the time they lost on Lecture Day. It was spring, and Will was spending every day he could at Mt. Wolleystone getting the land ready for planting. But he told me that he had no objection if I went with Harry, but not to advertise.

"Will knew that Master Winthrop had decided that Harry should be elected governor of the Colony. Master Winthrop was certain that Harry's father, Sir Henry, had great influence with King James, and we needed friends in the royal palace. Rumors persisted that the King was going to revoke the Colony's charter and turn all the land over to Sir Fernando Gorges, who was preparing a fleet and an army to make the Puritans surrender."

"'But Dudley thinks the boy is wet behind the ears,' Will told me and laughed. 'If Harry told Thomas Dudley that he thinks thou art a saint, that would finish him with Dudley and Master Winthrop, whether he has any influence at Court or not. As for me,' Will told me, 'I like the lad and I know that thee and he have many things to talk about.'

"By this time Harry had moved into the addition he had built on John-Luv's home, and he was being invited by one family or another to share their meals with them. Harry invited John to come with us to Noddle Island, but he refused because he was exceedingly busy working on various changes in the Colony laws. Harry knew it not, but John-Luv was not very happy with me either.

"'Methinks, Anne, that thou art too friendly with young Vane,' John had told me.

"I responded a little angrily since he had been distant and aloof with me ever since I told him that Zuriel was his child. He had baptized Zuriel, but he had never once kissed the poor little tyke, who, I assured him, had a big head and ears just like his and plenty of brown flecks in his green eyes. 'You may be sure, John-Luv,' I told him, 'my friendship with Harry is not a belly-to-belly friendship like ours was.'

"'I knowest thou art angry with me,' he answered. 'I want thee as much as I ever did. But thy continuous conventicles worry me. I know that thou praiseth my sermons, but I beg you not to criticize Master Wilson so vehemently or the other ministers. There is much talk about the many people who are gathering in your home once or twice a week. Master Winthrop is fearful that these discussions in your house are not to clarify Scriptural questions, but that you and Master Coddington and many others are not happy with the way the Colony is being run.'

"'I have begged you many times to join us,' I told him. 'There is not only talk but also music. Harry plays the flute. He also knows many lovely songs with words by English poets, like Thomas Campion and John Dowland.' I told John that he reminded me of a song I liked very much. It is called 'His Golden Locks Time Hath to Silver Turned.'" Anne grinned at me and sang a verse: "His helmet now shall make a hive for bees, and love sonnets turn to holy Psalms." She chuckled, "but John-Luv laughed not when I sang it, nor did he get the message and give me a hug."

"So, despite John, you spent the day with Harry on Noddle Island?"

"And the night, too," Anne giggled. "We did not plan it that way. Last night when thou took me to the Bay Tower Room, you pointed to East Boston and mentioned that it was now connected to Boston with a tunnel and a bridge. The only way to get there when I went with Harry was by ferry. My friend Thomas Marshall ran the ferry, which was really a pinnace rowed by two boys. The wharf was only a few minutes walk from my house. I met Harry there at nine in the morning. He had visited the Island before, and he liked Sam Maverick. No one in Boston knew much about Sam. He was a loner. He had come to New England two years before Master Winthrop—in 1628. He told us that he took possession of Noddle Island rather than Shawmut, which became Boston, because there was much more wood on Noddle. Actually it was 600 acres. It was nearly as big as Boston, which had only 780 acres and a lot of that marshy. Sam lived on the Island with four Negro slaves from Barbados. He employed three apprentice handymen and their wives. There were also two other women in the main house, which was more grand than Master Winthrop's. Methinks they slept with him."

"Both at once?" I grinned at her.

"I know not," Anne laughed. "Methinks they took turns. Sam told us that evening, although he did not advertise it, that he was Anabaptist. Like the Anabaptists in Germany, he believed that in the right circumstances and with the right women bigamy was not such a bad idea for the woman—or the man.

"In addition to the fireroom there were three bedrooms in the main house, and another one in an addition to the house. That is where I slept, and where later Harry crawled in with me. Beyond the mansion there were stables with eight horses, a piggery, and a millhouse to make barrel staves and clapboards. Sam was completely independent. He had cleared several acres and grew more crops than he needed. In addition to selling wood to England, he sold corn and other vegetables in Boston.

"Sam sent a wagon to meet us at his dock. It was a beautiful morning, but Tom Marshall told us when we were crossing over to Noddle in his boat that he had a bone feeling that it was too warm for May. By afternoon there would be a shift in the wind and we would have heavy winds from the north. And, in truth, he was right. Around four in the afternoon, when we were ready to be rowed back to Boston, the sky turned black and the waves in the harbor were several feet high."

Anne's eyes twinkled. "We could not sail back to Boston, or even row. The waves would have swamped the boat. Harry was certain that the Lord was smiling on us and had arranged things so that we could stay overnight. Sam was delighted. 'I haven't seen a great deal of you two all day,' he told us, 'but now the Lord hath given me company for the night.'"

"What did you do all day?" I grinned at her, guessing her answer. "And what about Zuriel? He was only a few months old. Weren't you nursing him?"

Anne shook her head. "Thou art worst than a pursuivant. Methinks if you had been Will, thou wouldst have spanked my arse."

"Maybe he should have. You still haven't told me how he reacted to having two kids who weren't his." I laughed. "Most people would think that he was the saint and not you."

"Before we left England, I told Will that I loved John, and that we had slept together when I stayed in Kent. But even though I was pregnant, I told Will I did not love him less. Will sighed and there were tears in his eyes. 'I never liked John much,' he told me, 'but I am happy to learn that he does not always practice what he preaches.' Will hugged me. 'But if John loves you,' he said, 'then he and I do have something in common.'"

Anne smiled. "Will knew that I knew that he had roamed from our bed once or twice. But we both knew that we two were the only pieces in a puzzle that fit together for life. He did not get angry with John until many years later. He knew that John tried to defend me when I was on trial before the General Court, but when Will heard what happened six months later in March 1637, when I was excommunicated from the church, Will was furious with him." Anne shrugged. "But by then we were no longer living in Boston, and we never saw John-Luv again. And I never told Will why John did what he did."

"You mean why he threw you to the lions?"

Anne nodded. "I will tell thee about that later. I told thee I made certain that Will would think that Zuriel was his child." She smiled reminiscently. "But maybe he did not believe me. He laughed very hard when I read him from Master Shakespeare, 'It is a wise father that knows his own child.'"

"What about Zuriel? Who took care of him when you went to Noddle Island with Harry?"

"Goody Hawkins was wet nursing. Will thought that Goody might be a witch. But I told him not to worry. A change of diet for a day would not hurt Zuriel." Anne laughed. "But Harry got his fill of mother's milk that day—milking me.

"Sam was disappointed that Will had not come with us, but like Will he was supervising his spring planting. 'Harry hath told me much about thee,' Sam said when he was showing us his stables. 'I know that Will has a farm at Mt. Wolleystone, not far from where my friend Thomas Morton once called himself 'mine host of Merry Mount.'

"Sam laughed. 'While I am more careful to stay out of trouble than Thomas did, this is a merrier place than Merry Mount ever was. I know that thou hast spent much time in Paris,' Sam said to Harry. 'Hast thou read the work of Doctor Francis Rabelais and his record of the deeds of Gargantua and Pantagruel?'

"Harry laughed and told him that he had not only read Rabelais, but he had brought a folio of the good doctor's work to the Colony. Sam was delighted. Unlike Harry, who had read Rabelais in French, Sam had a complete English translation of the book. Although it had been written a hundred years before the Puritans arrived in the Colony, Harry thought it should be read by every Puritan so that they could learn to laugh at their follies.

"Later that night, before we went to bed, Sam and Harry read some of Doctor Rabelais's book to me and Berthe and Martha—Sam's two ladies." Anne chuckled. "I remember one story. It was about Panurge, who was in love with a lady of Paris. Panurge had decorated his codpiece with little pink embroideries and was about to bring his lure to the attention of one of the greatest ladies. 'Madame,' he said to her, 'it would be for the greatest benefit to the Commonwealth and delightful to you, honorable to your progeny and necessary for me that I cover you for propagating the race.'

"The lady told him: 'You mischievous fool, is it for you to talk thus to me? Begone before I would have your arms and legs cut off.'

"That didn't stop Panurge. He told the lady from Paris that she could have both his arms and legs if she would play the brangle-buttock game, and he showed her his pizzle. 'Master John Thursday,' he called it. 'We'll play you such an antic, you will feel it to the marrow of your bones. We will find all the corners, cracks, and ingrained inmates of your carnal trap.'

"The lady told him, 'Go, villain. If you speak one more such word to me I will cry out and make you to be knocked down with blows.'

"But Panurge answered. 'They say indeed that hardly a man ever sees fair woman that is not also stubborn. How happy shall that man be to whom you will grant the favor to embrace you and kiss you and rub his bacon against yours. So thrust out your gamons.'

"Panurge would have embraced her, but she leaned out the window to yell for help. The next day at church, he tried again. 'Madame,' he told her, 'I am so amorous of you, I can neither pisser nor dung for love. It is said, that he, *a beau car le vit morte*—or to a fair quynte the priest mounts. Pray to God to give you my Master John Goodfellow that thy heart really desires.'"

Like any good storyteller Anne was laughing heartily at her own story. "This Panurge was exceedingly persistent, but the lady never surrendered to him. For revenge, he scattered some kind of dung on her gown and plaits of her sleeve and told her, 'I suffer for love for you. Pray to God to give me patience in my misery.' He had no sooner spoke than all the dogs in the church came running up to the lady and cocked their legs and pissed on her and all the way home thousands of dogs followed her and they made such a stream of urine that a duck might have swam in it. Rabelais said, 'Today it is the same stream that runs at St. Victor and so may God help you, a mill would have ground corn with it.'

"I'll say one thing for Doctor Rabelais," Anne smiled at my enjoyment of Rabelais's tall story. "Will never liked to read much, but he finished that book. Sam told us that, like Rabelais, his home was the Abbey of Theleme. 'Do what you will. The Island is yours to explore. If you wish, you may have horses.' Sam grinned at me and said, 'Harry told me that you can ride better than most Puritan ladies.' I knew that he was punning, but I agreed with him and told him that in Boston I dared not straddle a horse.

"'The woods are blooming,' he told us. 'There's a good trail around the Island. On the easterly side there's a small sandy beach that looks down the harbor. Come back to the house by three, and we'll feast together and talk.' Sam watched me climb on a gentle mare and laughed when I told him that I was happy that I had worn drawers today. He reminded Harry that it was spring. 'And by my troth,' he said, 'this lady would appeal to any man's fancy, young or old. The gowans are gay, lad,' he sang, and he was happily surprised when I responded with another verse of the song."

"What are gowans?" I asked.

"Daisies, methinks—any flowers floating on the breeze." Anne's smile was faraway. "But I told Harry as we rode off, 'Alas, the flower you have plucked today is going to seed.' But Harry did not care. He was like a young boy with his first maid. For a day and a night I forgot that I was an old lady.

"As we rode, Harry told me that I reminded him of a poem, 'The Good Morrow' by Master Donne, a poet and a minister who was the rector of St. Paul's when he died in 1631. Harry changed the words slightly and quoted

Reverend Donne's poem to me: 'I wonder what I did, till we lov'd. Was I not weaned until then? But suck'd on country pleasures childishly? Or snorted I in the Seven Sleeper's Den? 'Twas so. But this all pleasure's fancies bee. If ever any beauty I did see, which I desired and got, 'twas but a dream of thee.'"

Anne smiled with shining eyes. "My favorite poem by Donne was:

> Goe and catche a falling starre
>   Get with child a mandrake roote,
> Tell me, where all past yeares are,
>   Or who cleft the Divel's foot."

She shrugged. "Harry gave me a book of his poems and another book of essays called *Devotions Upon Emergent Occasions*."

"Then you know for whom the bell tolls," I said with a little grin.

"For me," she sighed, quoting Donne. 'And when these bells toll, they tell me that now one and now another is buried. Must I not acknowledge that I have a correction due to me and pay the debt that I owe?'"

Anne shook her head reminiscently. "Harry told me that Reverend Donne was an Anglican and not so sure of himself as most of the Puritans were. 'Master Donne was a laughing man,' Harry said. 'And he wrote that a really wise man is known by much laughing.'" Anne chuckled. "We were really laughing that day. Harry and I rode to the east side of the Island and discovered a beach in a shady little cove where you could pick lobsters out of the sea. Two beavers and many birds were watching us as we spread our saddle blankets on the beach.

"Trembling, Harry spoke to me in French: *'Tu es très belle. Tu es Dieu. Le spirite demeure en toi. Il rougit ta peau. Chére, Anne, je veux faire l'amour avec toi. Je suis très heureux que tu parles français. C'est très superieur á l'anglais. Le français a plus mots pour exprimer l'amour.'"* Anne smiled. "How could I reject him? I knew he needed a woman. I let him undress me and I lay down on the blanket, and he stared at my naked body in awe and sucked from my breasts which were oozing just a bit. Soon he was kissing my con and telling me, *'Tu as le plus joli con du monde.'* And I told him. *'Toi, tu bandes merveilleusement. S'il te plait, mets ton bâton dans mon con.'* and he did." Anne stared pensively at me. "Like thee, Harry was a very gentle man. He was embarrassed that he could not contain his first erection, but we had hours and he quickly proved that a young man is a match for any woman.

"Swimming naked together in the cove, I told him, *'J'ai bu avec toi á la coupe du plaisir.'* Later in bed we recited together all the French words we knew for queynte and cock." Anne laughed. "There are hundreds of them. And I told him, 'Thou art still big inside of me. *Tu es un homme avec une très grande force vitale.'* Thou hast spent more time inside me than outside me."

And he answered, "As long as I liveth, a part of me will be inside thee."

22

I saw Saul turn into the driveway just as Anne was telling me that two weeks later, on May 25, the day after Harry was elected governor of the Colony, her brother-in-law, "dear Johnny," arrived from England with his second wife, Mary, and Will's sixty-year-old mother, Susannah. "I will tell thee about Johnny later," Anne said excitedly, waving through the window at Saul as he got out of a battered Volkswagon.

"Are there any more surprises?" I asked.

She grimaced. "I am fearful to tell thee. A year later I got pregnant again. But no matter what some people in England thought, it was not Harry's seed. Some people were certain that I had slept with Satan himself."

I opened the door for Saul. She hugged him enthusiastically, and kissed his cheek. I was beginning to realize that one reason Anne had drawn so many people to her was her overflowing affectionate warmth. She must have been in sharp contrast to the dour, reserved, British style of most of the colonists, who bore their suffering and love in silence.

"You'd better be careful," I grinned at Saul. "Anne thinks you may be either Harry Vane or St. Paul returned to earth."

Saul looked puzzled, but I didn't enlighten him. "I thought you were going to telephone before you drove out here," I said.

"I was but something very strange has happened. I couldn't explain it over the phone. Actually I'd have been here an hour ago, but I was so shook up, I lost my way."

Saul collapsed on the couch and stared grimly at Anne. "I couldn't concentrate on the paper I was suppose to write. You kept crawling though my brain, and I stayed awake most of the night reading everything that I could find about you in the Boston University Library. Then, this morning, when I picked up the pictures I had taken of you, I really thought that you had put the whammy on me. I thought that I had been so absorbed by what you were saying that I had messed up the lens setting. But then I realized that was impossible. I took forty-eight pictures of you yesterday with brand-new Kodak 35 millimeter color film." Saul was fumbling in a camera bag he had brought in with him. He pulled out a packet of prints and handed them to

166

me. "When you're in the picture," he said to me. "You're sharp and clear. The foregrounds and the backgrounds are perfect. Anne's dress and hat are sharp, but look at her face and hands. Wherever her skin shows it looks as if I had shot directly into the sunlight, or overexposed."

Anne was looking over my shoulder as I shuffled through the prints. I felt a shiver run down my spine as I remembered my own experience with the television camera. In all the pictures, Anne's face and features were blended in a pale glow that made her skin appear softly incandescent. Her lovely face was muted. It was obvious that she was a female, but it was impossible to recognize her. Where Saul had photographed her hands or legs, the same hazy glow appeared.

"It's as if you were photographing some kind of strange ghostly object," I said and I stared at Anne wonderingly.

She smiled back at me—a vibrant woman, very much alive. She took the pictures and flipped through them, recognizing her dress and hat. "How doth one take such a picture?" she demanded. "This seems to be a miracle that did not happen. Never mind," she patted Saul's cheek. "If thou wants a picture of me, thou canst have one drawn. Master Winthrop, John-Luv, and Harry all had their pictures painted." Her eyes were twinkling with laughter. "But no one ever wanted a picture of me."

"I do," Saul assured her. He tried to tell her how a camera exposed a light through the lens onto film and captured the image of a person. Then he touched her cheek and peered closely at her skin. "It beats the Hell out of me. Your skin feels like human skin. But——," he paused and frowned, unable to say what he was thinking.

"But what?" Anne asked.

"Yesterday when I read all that stuff about you, you were always telling people about the Holy Spirit dwelling within you. You said you thought the soul was nothing but light."

Anne nodded. "I believe that."

Saul shrugged. "It's crazy as Hell—but if no one can photograph you, you have your proof."

"What proof?"

"You insisted at your church trial that what you called the corruptible or human body could not be resurrected. Maybe you've returned to earth in some other kind of body. A soul is a mirror image of your former body. I know it's unbelievable. The idea scares Hell out of me. It doesn't make sense. I know that you eat and go to the toilet." Saul grinned at me. "It's obvious that Anne has lived here a few days, and that she's seen you naked. What about her? Did you make love? What's she like in bed?"

I scowled at him. "It's none of your goddamn business. Anne doesn't have to prove anything. To Hell with the pictures."

But Anne wasn't angry with Saul, and I gaped at her answer. "Jesus hath found Will again for me. I know not whether I am soul or flesh but methinks, whatever else I may be, that Robert is Will and I am his loving wife."

Saul shrugged. "You know more about resurrection than I do. Your friend Paul in the New Testament keeps insisting that people will come back from the grave, but he never does explain what makes them tick. Do they bleed?"

"Cut me and see." Anne held out her hand to him.

"This is ridiculous," I yelled. "If for some reason Anne can't be photographed, so far as I'm concerned, that's great. We don't have to dissect her to find out. It will put an end to her appearance on Sally Lane's show." To Saul's increasing dismay, I quickly reviewed Anne's starring role at the Bay Tower Room last night.

"You both let me down," he said bitterly. "Yesterday you agreed that I'd get first crack at the story. If Anne appears on 'People Passion,' that will kill any story I can write about her. It will be on the wire services and television news by Tuesday night."

"Sally won't want her," I said, little realizing that millions of people had a crying need to believe in a life hereafter. "How can you interview a ghost on television?" I told Saul that I had had a similar experience when I tried to tape Anne with my television camera, but I had blamed it on my own stupidity with mechanical gadgets.

"Did you lose her voice?" Saul asked.

"No."

"Then you can be sure of it, Sally Lane will love the idea. It proves that Anne is really Anne—a spirit from another world. All the crazies in the world will gobble her up."

"I do not like this conversation," Anne said, and her eyes were filled with tears. "Thou both speaketh of me as if I were dead."

Saul and I looked at each other and burst our laughing.

"To Hell with the story," Saul said and hugged her. "But to satisfy my own curiosity, I'd like to take some more pictures of you. Preferably naked. I've brought several kinds of film, including black and white and color, as well as negative film. I also borrowed a camera with better lenses and faster shutter speeds. If you pose naked for me," he told Anne, "we can find out if your entire body radiates. If you're going public, I'm sure that someone will try to find out."

"Pose—I do not understand," Anne said. "I am not ashamed of being naked. But being naked when everyone else is dressed maketh me nervous."

"Anne's not posing naked for you," I said angrily. "She doesn't have to prove anything. Supposing you do get naked pictures of her, what are you going to do with them? Sell them to *Playboy*?"

"Maybe I'll sell them to the Catholic Church," Saul said sarcastically. "To go with the Shroud of Turin."

I explained to Anne that the Shroud was a cloth people claimed had covered Jesus when he was in the sepulchre after his crucifixion. "There's an imprint of a man's face on it. Some people think it's a mysterious photographic-like transference of Jesus's face. It might have some bearing on our inability to photograph you."

"What doth it matter?" she asked. "What Jesus looked like is not important. There are no pictures of Jesus except by men who never saw him. Whatever happens, when I leave I would not wish to be worshiped as a picture or a plaster saint." She smiled tenuously at me. "I am certain that God hath brought me back to earth to tell people that His Kingdom is not up there in Heaven somewhere. It is right here where love is."

I frowned at her. "You keep saying *when you leave.* That frightens me more than not being able to photograph you. Where are you going? You're immortal. You can't die. Tell me the truth. You told me when you tried to drown yourself that you had a revelation. What was it?"

"Methinks I am here to try to save God's creatures from self-destruction." She sighed. "How I am to do it I know not. But it has something to do with my former life. I keep asking myself what did I do before that I have been chosen."

"I'll take a guess," Saul said, sounding almost prophetic. "But please don't tell anybody that I said it because half the time I think I'm dreaming this. In the sevententh century you tried to convince people that their ministers weren't telling them the truth. You nearly succeeded. Half the people in Boston were on your side. They believed in your covenant of grace. They were ready to tell the ministers to go to Hell, because they didn't know what they were preaching about. But when the chips were down, and Winthrop brought out the militia, they quickly backed down. Today, the numbers have changed. There're billions of people now instead of a few million, but the leaders in the United States and Russia and everywhere else are still the same. They trample on people like us and grind them to bits while they are shouting 'Glory be to God.'" Saul shrugged, "Like you, I'm an anarchist. Unfortunately, most people distrust anarchists as much as they fear their leaders. The state will never wither away."

Trying to shake the uneasy feeling I had that Saul might lead Anne into a greater mess than she was capable of handling, and the sense of contingency that Anne had put on our relationship, I said, "My feeling, Anne, is that you're here for the rest of your life. That being the case—you've got a good twenty or thirty years ahead of you. When you discover what kind of world you have returned to, you may think that Satan is calling the shots and God doesn't give a damn."

Then I remembered my plans for the day. It was nearly two o'clock, but we still had time to take Anne to a supermarket and a shopping plaza and get her acquainted with the great American religion and pastime of spending hard-earned money for many things one could live without.

"Tomorrow," I told Saul, "I'm taking Anne to dinner with a friend, who happens to be a psychiatrist. I'm sure that he will try to find out whether we should both be confined to a mental institution. But before that happens, I think she should see what man has accomplished in three centuries by tinkering with food and creating gadgets that she has never seen before in her life. Do you want to come along?"

Saul was delighted to come with us. "I have to be back in Boston by six." He explained to Anne that he had a girlfriend, Susan Weiss. "We're not married, yet," he explained to her as we drove toward a Super Stop & Shop. "But we sleep together and if we still like each other after a few years we will probably get married. Susan is a female whizz at math, and she loves astrophysics. She'll tell you all about how God created the cosmos with a big bang, and that cosmic radiation—hey, maybe that's your inner light!—does exist and permeates every living and material thing in the universe."

Anne was fascinated that many women no longer rushed into marriage and could support themselves and be independent of men, but she was practical, too. "What if thy Susan becomes pregnant?"

Saul laughed and gave her an extended review of condoms, diaphragms, and the pill. When I told him that Will had practiced coitus interruptus unsuccessfully, he was intrigued. "I have done that with Sue, too," he said, "when she lays off the pill for awhile." He told Anne about the fear of cancer from extended pill usage and was trying to explain cancer to Anne as we arrived at the supermarket parking lot.

"Methinks that was the sickness that killed Will's mother," she said. "Many old people wasted away." She smiled at me. "But if thou art really Will, then thou willst die in my arms very quickly."

"I'm already older than Will was when he died." I shivered, wondering if Will had had a heart attack or had died in the saddle. Grinning to myself, and thinking it could happen again, I decided not to ask.

As we walked together into the supermarket, a forty-year-old memory flashed through my mind. During World War II I was stationed in India. In those days, instead of worrying whether they might outproduce us, we were fighting the Japanese in Burma and Western China. I hired a Hindu bearer, Jagu, for thirty rupees a month—about nine dollars—to shine my shoes and polish my army brass and do odd jobs. In those days, as I teased Jagu about the Hindu belief in continuous rebirths until one achieved Nirvana, I was happy that I had not been reincarnated as one of the millions of Indians who were popping out of female vaginas at a rate equal to Anne's fertility. Jagu had also made me aware, as he fondled a Sears Roebuck catalog that I had given him, how the Western standard of living, really less than three centuries in the making, had not only freed women from their never-ending birth-slavery, but had reversed the death rate for females. Few Puritan women survived child-bearing as often as Anne had, and only rarely did they get a second chance at marriage, as Puritan men did. The day I finally received orders to go home, Jagu arrived with his next to last son, a bubbly two-year-old. 'Take him, Sahib,' he said. 'He is yours. Take him where Lord Krishna lives in America. Take him to Sears Roebuck. Here he will have nothing, and like me he will be dead when he is forty.'"

Like Jagu with the Sears catalog, Anne was fascinated and bewildered by thousands of things she had never seen before. We guided her through the aisles of packaged foods, from cookies to soup, from peanut butter to pickles, from cheese and butter to milk and ice cream, from canned tuna fish to canned peas, from toothpaste to mouthwashes, from shampoos to hair conditioners, from pills to cure headaches to creams to soften skin tissues, from soap powders to paper handkerchiefs and paper napkins and towels, from frozen dinners to showcases filled with every kind of meat, fish, and chicken she could think of.

Entranced, spellbound, afraid to touch the packages we put in her hands, she let us lead her in a trance through the market. When she read on a can that it was chicken soup, she was in awe, wondering who made it and how it got inside. And a dinner for one in a frozen package was beyond her comprehension. "All you have to do is let it melt and heat it up," we told her. And I bought a few packages to take home to show her.

When she saw the array of vegetables and fruits, she gasped. Touching each in amazement, she said their names aloud, "Oranges, apples, grapes, bananas, melons, carrots, tomatoes, cabbages, strawberries, potatoes. Oh, dear Robert, I really hope that thou art Will. He would be so happy to see this. The Lord hath taught men how to grow these things all winter long. Thy kingdom hath really come."

Saul tried to explain to her that many of the things she was seeing had been preserved over long periods and in cool places, or had been shipped by boat and plane from California or warmer countries.

"From Barbados?" she asked. "But that takes months by ship. Why do they not rot?"

"Boats go faster now, and we have airplanes," Saul said, and I knew that he was delighted with her childlike enthusiasm for everything she saw. Anne was giving both of us a new perspective. We were seeing our familiar and boring world with new insights and wonder through the eyes of a visitor from what was really another world. In the relatively short time-space of three hundred and fifty years—with many people still alive who had lived twenty percent of that time—man had achieved a materialistic control over his life and environment that would have astounded even the kings of the seventeenth century. It occurred to me that much of our dissatisfaction with modern life and our neuroses could be quickly cured by an outward-bound experience that reverted people to the kind of life their ancestors had lived.

"Methinks that everyone should be praising the Lord and every day be thanking him for such abundance," Anne said as we passed the checkout counter with a few delicacies I had picked up, such as lamb chops, salmon and shrimp, along with strawberry ice cream that Anne couldn't believe existed.

"Everyone must be very rich," she said as we drove toward the Braintree Shopping Plaza a few miles away.

"Not really," Saul said. "We live in a class society, and the percentages haven't changed much. About five percent of the people control fifty percent of all the wealth. About fifteen percent, some thirty-five million, are so poor that the government has to help feed them by giving them food stamps. In between, the large majority walk a razor's edge. They are called the middle-class, like you and Will probably were. Mostly, they die poor."

"But even the middle class and some of the poor have automobiles, television, radios, dish washers, and thousands of adults toys and gadgets," I said. "And so many calories to eat that even some of the poor overtax their hearts digesting it."

"I hope that all these people do not forget the Holy Spirit within them," Anne said, as we led her through the maze of the shopping mall.

"Look at their faces," Saul said gesturing at the crowds. "Most of them think this superabundance is a part of their inalienable right. You can be sure that they aren't thanking God. Most of them are trying to figure out whether they can afford to buy something they think they can't live without. If they haven't got the money, they can buy it on time and pay twenty percent more than it costs by paying for it in monthly installments."

"Doth no one build their own home, grow their own food, or make their own clothes?" Anne asked.

Stopping in front of a shoestore, while Anne gazed in awe at the choices, I tried to explain the division of labor to her. "In your days one or two men made a pair of shoes, or a single woman spun thread and wove cloth. Today there are no simple cobblers like your friend Nathaniel Ward. Instead there are factories where everything that is made is made by machine. One man or woman stamps out heels, another soles, another uppers, and another cuts leather and others stitch. So it goes with everything you see for sale, and today much of it is made from beginning to end by robots—machines that move faster than any man or woman could and do the job better."

"Nathaniel Ward was no friend of mine," Anne grimaced. "And Will insisted that his shoes were not well made. But methinks all these machines are very good. People do not have to work from dawn to dust. They have time to love God. This seems to be a better Utopia than Master More's." She turned to Saul. "I understandeth not what Robert hath told me about wars. Why do people still kill each other when God hath given them so much?"

"There are five billion people in the world," Saul said. "Most of them would be just as surprised at American luxury as you are. Their leaders know that they can never have all these things, so they offer them religions and gods who hate those who have material things. In some countries God is the State. In others, God is called Allah. To keep these societies functioning the leaders need an enemy. We are the enemy. Your Master Winthrop would understand that. To him you were the enemy. You were even more dangerous than the Indians. You told people that they could not sin because Christ had suffered for men's sins already. If men and women don't have devils, like you were to those Puritan theocrats, to fight, they might all stop working and start playing. Then the whole world would fall apart."

"I do not believe that. Thou art teasing me," Anne said as we left the plaza and a world of material things she couldn't possibly have encompassed. "I do not need Satan to make me work. I feel the spirit of life that is in the air—in things growing and dying and being reborn. In the tide coming in and going out, and the stars shining and the moon coming back after a month, and the birds singing. If thou but listen, a song of joy is murmuring in thy blood, singing in thy heart and brain. We must teach all these people who thou saith are bored that they have no holes in them. What I have seen maketh me happy for them and maketh me wish to sing."

Sitting between us in the car she did sing, explaining that the song was a poem by Thomas Campion: "To his sweet lute Apollo sung the motion of the spheres/ The wonderous order of the stars whose course divides the years/ And all the mysteries above/ But none of this could Midas move/ which purchasest him his asses's ears."

"Someone has got to tell you that the world isn't all shopping plazas and supermarkets," Saul said. "If there is a God, he's the ultimate gambler. The dice he is shooting are crime, murder, pollution, drugs, religious hatred, violence, terrorism with enough nuclear bombs in reserve to blow a billion or more of us all to Hell. Three billion or so may inherit the earth, but most of them will kill each other or they'll die of starvation as they grab for what is left. Even if someone dismantles all the nuclear bombs, there's an even bigger problem. If our leaders don't exterminate us in another hundred years, the nations that are poor will screw themselves and us to death. They will increase the population to six or seven billion people. Then billions will starve, and no amount of man's machinery or God's beneficence will feed them. The Africans are already starving by the millions."

Saul grinned at Anne. "I love you. I really believe that you are you. But I am a pessimist. What can *you* do? Why has God resurrected you? You may be a miracle, but it's a miracle that won't work. If many people start returning from the grave, we might as well quit. There isn't going to be room enough to stand up, let alone lie down and copulate."

All the time that he was speaking, Saul was smiling through his *souris* in a happy Jewish way at Anne's bewildered expression. He put his arm around her and bussed her cheek. "I really do love you, and so will Susan. But she is a feminist and believes in zero population growth, which means that all we have is the right to duplicate each other. Since you're on record as having had fifteen kids—a one woman population explosion—I'd like to know what you think about abortion."

I tried to protest that Anne couldn't answer that question. She had not had time to assimilate three centuries in three days. But, as usual, I underestimated Anne's curiosity and combativeness. Saul told her in some detail how woman could get terminate unwanted pregnancies without endangering their lives, and he told her that at least one nation, the Chinese, understood the dangers of uncontrolled population. In China a husband a wife were permitted to have only one child.

Anne quickly grasped Saul's challenge to her. "When I lived there were not so many people," she said. "Many children died at birth. Big families disappeared in less than half a century. We are God's creatures. We are not God. God gives the potential to become Him. But we must learn how by ourselves. God gives woman a short time to be fertile—maybe four hundred times to conceive, but he doth not wish her to bear four hundred children. He also gives man and the trees and the flowers many more seeds than they need. He doth not expect that they will all be fruitful. Thou asketh me if I think the Chinese people are sinning against God, or any woman who dispatches an child before it is born is sinning, and whether this abortion as thou callst it is a murder?" She shrugged. "Methinks God doth not want His children to starve, nor destroy His earth. God giveth each woman many opportunities to fertilize man's seed. Trees and flowers put forth many seeds that surviveth not. Men and women should have only such children as they can love and teach the love of God. A woman who doth not love the child within her should not bear it."

23

Back home Saul asked once again if Anne would pose for him naked. "You're taking Anne out tomorrow night, and I won't see her again until Sunday," he said. "I brought all this photographic stuff. We might just as well find out the truth before Sally Lane does."

Appealing to Anne, he reminded her that she had said in her trial that the Holy Spirit was light. "Light is a form of radiation," he told her. "But there are other kinds of invisible radiation. Radio waves, ultraviolet, infrared, gamma rays, x-rays. You may be exuding a form of energy that can't be seen, but you—your soul—," he shrugged, "some aspect of your reconstituted body may be emitting waves that will require entirely new imaging techniques to capture."

"All thy words confuse me," Anne said demurely. "But I will take off my clothes if thou and Robert also disrobe. In that way I will not be so conspicuous."

I protested but to no avail.

"Thou must believe the story of Adam and Eve," Anne grinned at me as she unzipped her skirt and let it drop to the floor. "I toldest thee I never believed that God grew angry because His creatures needed each other's bodies. He gave them love, too. If they chose lust, then they were not yet aware of His Spirit within them."

Saul enthusiastically agreed with her. Having no choice, I drew the curtains. A few moments later a naked Anne was being admired and photographed by her two naked acolytes.

Snapping pictures of her, switching from one kind of film to another, trying shots with full lighting and no lighting whatsoever, his penis bobbling and occasionally pointing at her when he grasped her and changed her position, Saul was more jittery than Anne was.

Laughing at both of us, she said, "Now I understand why men like soldiers' uniforms. Who would be afraid of them as God madeth them?"

She called Saul "our pretty boy" and kept telling me not to worry. She trusted him. "Thou art like my son Francis," she told Saul. "Thou art exceedingly outspoken, like me. Master Winthrop made Francis a freeman, and he received the right hand of fellowship and became a church member when he was only fifteen. But that was before Master Winthrop was so angry with me. But Francis never feared him, and he told Master Winthrop that I was right."

Listening to her, not knowing whether he was managing to capture her image on film or not, Saul was now fiddling with my television camera with no better results than I had had. No matter how he adjusted the lens, changed the lighting, or eliminated it all together, our naked lady appeared on the television tube as if she were from another world. She had even less definition than in the pictures he had taken of her yesterday. Without clothing, she was vaguely recognizable as a female, but the curves of her voluptuous body merged together in a soft haze, and her warm lilting voice seemed to be reaching us from outer space.

"The truth is," Saul said, as he got dressed and packed up his equipment, "whether any of these pictures I have taken of you come out, you are more awe-inspiring the way you are. If you were Catholic, the church would make you a saint and millions would come from all over the world to see you."

Still naked, totally unembarrassed, Anne was telling us that we made her feel like an angel, and she couldn't believe that the house could be warm enough in March so that one didn't have to wear clothes. She hugged Saul and kissed him goodbye enthusiastically. "Now I am not alone," she said. "I have two friends." Without asking me, she told Saul that when he returned Sunday he must bring Susan with him. "I know that I will love her, too."

"Two friends," she assured me when Saul had gone, and I was showing her how quickly frozen dinners could be prepared in a microwave oven, "but only one lover."

Deciding not to dress again, wearing only my terrycloth bathrobe, she happily recalled every detail of her afternoon at the supermarket and shopping plaza while we ate dinner.

It was six-thirty. "Aren't you tired?" I asked her when we finished the packaged veal cutlet and fettucine. "Last night we didn't get to bed until nearly two. You were awake at seven." I was still concerned that Anne would drown in the rush of centuries flooding through her brain.

But she assured me that she was wide awake and even ready for loving, if I wished. "But if thou art sleepy, I will read in those books thou hast about me and find out what was going on in Master Winthrop's head."

Carrying a second bottle of red wine into the living room, I had a better idea. "You might as well discover how most Americans escape the world and waste away their lives," I said, and I showed her how to turn on the television with remote controls and switch the channels around. I was yawning, but I was sure of one thing. Commercial television had never kept me awake. I could sleep through gunslingers, comedians with canned laughter, commercials by the dozens, and new commentators who rehashed the same stories with different characters night after night.

Anne stared at the screen totally entranced. I explained that the people she was watching did not live in the box. They were like the television pictures Saul and I had tried to take of her, but these pictures were transmitted on invisible waves from hundreds of miles away and by satellites around the world. "Anyone who owns a television set can turn it on and receive different pictures on different wavelengths," I told her. "This is what Sally Lane wants to do with you," I said as she watched a man interviewing a woman who was leading a protest against a waste-disposal plant that was going to be built in her community. "Hundreds of thousands of people will see you," I said, forgetting for the moment that they might only hear her.

I paused, waiting for her response, but she was totally involved with her new toy. Staring at one channel for a moment, she would flip the button and get a new one and murmur a startled "Oh my Lord! It's witchcraft."

As she changed channels, I tried to tell her that some channels specialized. This was a news channel, this a sports channel, a religious channel, this one a weather channel (predicting the weather fascinated her), this one a general-network channel, this one she had switched to was for regular movies, the next for sexy movies.

"What are movies?" she demanded.

"Plays—like Shakespeare wrote. They are acted out by men and women and recorded on film."

She stopped for a few minutes on C-Span and listened open-mouthed to several congressmen arguing for and against the federal bill to underwrite sewerage-disposal plants for towns and cities.

"What is sewerage?" she demanded.

I laughed. "Everybody's piss and shit. We spend billions getting ready to fight our enemies, if the need arises, but most of our cities are inundated in their own slop."

"Methinks I am in favor of sewerage disposal plants." She wrinkled her nose and switched again, this time to a news broadcast, which was interrupted every few minutes by commercials. The commentator mentioned that funeral services were being held for a local politician and that was followed by "Hey man, you need an American Express Card."

"It won't make you live longer," I responded to her puzzled expression.

Next was a shot of planes bombing some town in the Mideast. I explained to her that three hundred and fifty years later the Turks—or as we now say, the Arabs—thought Allah was better than the Jews' God, Yahweh—or God with no name. Now, instead of using spears and rocks, arrows and muskets they had bombs and tanks and machine guns to kill each other, as well as the woman and children who got in the way.

But she wasn't really listening to me. She was engrossed with the spiel of a highly mascaraed, blue-eye-shadowed young woman telling her that Oil of

Olay would keep her skin healthy, no matter what. That was followed by a news story from a courtroom, where a man was on trial for raping ten women. He claimed that he wasn't guilty. Before the words were out of his mouth, we were being told to "Come to Jamaica. Make your body feel cool—your spirits feel warm."

"Is that man going to Jamaica to make his spirit warm?" she asked, as a Gravy Train commercial kept repeating "Good gravy, that's what your dog deserves."

"No," I told her, "and the dog food has nothing to do with Jamaica." I yawned. It was only seven o'clock but I knew that I couldn't stay awake much longer. I handed her one of my blank lined notebooks. "You can make history," I told her. "I'm sure, from reading your trials, that you can take notes better than your friend Mr. Wilson did. Write down what you're thinking and what bewilders you. Some people think that television should be banished. Americans watch it six to eight hours a day and still don't know what is going on. The politicians use it to confuse them, the news commentators don't know or don't care what is news and what isn't news. All they want is for everyone to tune in to their program and look at the advertising, and if the people who make all the stuff they want you to buy didn't pay for the time the state would have to run the television stations. If that happens, people like Mr. Winthrop would become Big Brother and tell everybody what is best for them. We're between the Devil and the deep blue sea, and, frankly, TV bores me silly, but I understand how you'd be fascinated. By the way, even Outer Mongolians living in yurts now own sets and get color TV by satellite."

"News I understand not," Anne said. "Methinks it is not Jesus' 'Good News.'"

"There's only one way that intelligent people in America use television," I told her. "To watch a few films called documentaries shown on some channels. That will give you some perspective on what has happened during the past three hundred and fifty years. Or you can look at rented movies or cassettes produced by filmmakers. A few of them try to understand human interpersonal reactions and the problems of living and the fear of dying. All the rest—including the politicians running to be congressman, senators, governors, or President, and most of the so-called sports, baseball, football, hockey, basketball—is pure schlock. That's a Jewish expression. That means garbage that a few thousand, presumably intelligent, people turn out, round the clock, to entertain the vast middle class which doesn't read and doesn't think much, but believes in God and Hell and is easy prey for any kind of stupidity flashing before its eyes eight hours a day. I guess it makes people forget their day-to-day problems of survival." I laughed. "I'm sure that if you watch a small portion of the thousands of hours of syndicated crap that appears every day on television in America, you'll throw up—or decide that maybe

God has decided that His creatures are a failure and should wipe themselves out."

"Thou soundeth very pessimistic," Anne said. But I realized she wasn't paying too much attention to me. I decided not to keep interrupting her with my inanities. It occurred to me that if she would keep a diary of her feelings and emotions—*A Puritan Lady Tells All*—it would become a best-seller. She was scribbling away when I fell asleep.

I awoke, wondering for a moment if Emily had come home and why I was stretched out on the couch. My head was in Anne's lap. She had put a pillow under it, and her naked breasts were suspended above my face. The television was still going and she was watching a movie, totally engrossed. But I soon discovered that with one hand she was jotting in the notebook I had given her.

Anne felt the flicker of my eyelash against her skin, and she grinned down at my blurry awakening. "Now, I am certain that thou art my Will," she told me. "Many evenings in the winter, we would sit on our bench before the fire. When the children were in bed, he would snuggle up against me just as thou art doing. Thou wast snoring," she laughed. "I thought thy head might snap off so I pulled thee into my lap. Thou mumbled something about being pooped, and then thou fell asleep with my nipple in thy mouth."

Laughing, but not sitting up, I murmured my thanks. "Is this the tit that Harry Vane, governor of Massachusetts, suckled?" I asked taking another suck.

"I have no others," she said and shushed me. "I am seeing a story about a young woman who was angry with her father. She jumped off his big boat that hath no sails and is trying to get to New York on a big wagon filled with people and two men who are trying to go to bed with her. Look," she squealed happily, "he is hanging a blanket between their beds and calling it the Walls of Jericho!"

Grinning, I sat up and watched the late movie with her—*It Happened One Night*. She was delighted when Claudette Colbert hiked her skirt to hitch a ride and very pleased when Clark Gable finally married her. She still wasn't tired and probably would have watched the Late, Late Show. But I told her that it was one o'clock and we'd be out late tomorrow night too. "What did you write in your notebook?" I asked her.

"Many things." She picked it up. "I like all these people who tell me that I should buy things. There are many things that I would buy. I will read them to you. 'Toyota, the workhorse truck, five thousand nine hundred and ninety-eight dollars.' 'Oh, what a feeling!' the man said and jumped in the air just the way Will would if he had such a truck. 'Tuborg Beer. No jocks, no jokes, no cowboys—just great beer.' 'Almost Home peanut-butter cookies.' 'Speedy Mufflers—get ten dollars off!' What are they?" Anne didn't wait for an answer but kept reading the commercials enthusiastically. "Club Med. I want

to go there. The man says, 'You can do it all. Welcome to T.W.A.'" Anne
was bubbling with laughter. "An alphabet takes you to Europe for five
hundred and twenty-five dollars. I could go home to Alford. And I like
Jordache Jeans—they fit your arse like a glove—and Cottonelle bathroom
tissues. The woman says they feel soft on your bum, and Dry Idea to make
your sweat smell nice. And there was a garden weasel that breaks up the
topsoil, and a new improved Head and Shoulders so a man can put his head
on your shoulder and smell your hair, and there's Nu-Luv Diapers. I wish I
had had those. Lord, how much time for reading I would have had. But
methinks I am past having babies. If I do, thou knowest who the father is."
She grinned at me, breathless for a moment.

"I am certain the Puritans would banish television," she chuckled as we
walked toward the bedroom. "Not only because they can see a silly fat man
like Master Archie Bunker, whom I watched while you were sleeping, but
because people can learn things. Master Winthrop would be very shocked to
know that a woman, Mistress Thatcher, is prime minister in England and
seemeth to be more important than the Queen, who is another Elizabeth.
And there is some woman who wants to run the United States named Ger-
aldine Ferraro. She can talk faster than I can. I also saw a story about the
war you told me about, and I saw two presidents, Master Roosevelt and
Master Truman. And I know that there is a new president, and he hates war,
too." She shrugged. "But he feareth the Russians."

I wondered if she were mixing past and present in a weird Mulligan stew
in her mind. "The war you heard about happened nearly fifty years ago," I
told her. "Roosevelt and Truman are dead. For that matter so is Clark
Gable, the man you just saw in that movie. The pretty lady he married,
Claudette Colbert, is now a very old lady—nearly ninety."

Shedding her bathrobe and lying naked on the bed while I undressed,
she appeared to be trying to absorb that. "But they are not dead when I
watch them. I hear them speaking to me," she said. "They live again, and
their bodies are not corruptible."

"The big difference," I said, straddling her and kissing her in surprise
that I was once again renewed and ready, "is that they can only keep repeating what they said before. They can laugh, but only the same old laugh; talk,
but only the same old inanities; and cry, but only the same tears. They can't
talk back like you." I grinned at her as she arched to meet my cock. "And
they can't raise their bum to merge with a man like you're doing."

Anne's arms were around me, and I suddenly realized that she was close
to tears. "Perchance one day, like me, Master Roosevelt and Master Truman
and Master Gable will return. On, dear Robert, love me, for I am fearful. I
am swimming in deep water. I liketh this world so much I wish not to leave
it."

24

I fell asleep wondering how Anne's brain could ever process the overload that Saul and I had fed into it. Leaping across more than three centuries, with only the tiny historical background that I had provided her, was like expecting a computer to respond with insufficient memory built into the system. Neither the transistors nor the synapses in the human brain could sort out the bytes on a rational basis.

I awoke at seven in the morning, with one eye on the digital clock and was about to go back to sleep when I realized that Anne was not beside me. For a moment I wondered if my dream were over, and then I realized that she was puttering around the bathroom. Sitting up in bed, I could see her. She was staring at her naked body in the full-length bathroom mirror. I waited for her to return.

When she finally slid in beside me, she lay naked, staring at the ceiling. I realized that she was unusually subdued and that there were tears in her eyes.

"What's the matter?" I asked. "What are you thinking?"

Anne held up her hand. "I found one of thy wife's needles. I pricked myself in three places. I did not feel it. I did not bleed. Saul is right. I have not returned in my corruptible body. I am not a creature of this earth." She sobbed. "I fear thou willst think that I am an evil spirit."

I looked at her arm and noticed some indentations, but she hadn't punctured herself very deeply—or couldn't. "It doesn't matter," I told her. "Whether you are a ghost—or in fact as elemental as cosmic radiation—I love you." I hugged her. "Anyway, you feel real enough to me. You're a voluptuous woman. Yesterday when Saul was taking pictures of you, he was very much aware of you as a woman. He could scarcely concentrate on what he was doing."

Anne smiled. "I like Saul. He was so gentle and sweet with his pizzle pointing at me. I hope that last night Susan let him tuck it inside of her." She sighed. "But I do wonder about such things as invisible light. Maybe it is the Devil who hath taken over my body and is trying to harm thee."

"There may be God," I said. "But there is no Devil, except man denying himself and the inner light within him. Aren't those your sentiments?" That seems to be what you've been telling me."

Murmuring, "Oh dear friend, I thank thee for believing in me," Anne kissed me fervently.

"It's not difficult," I told her. "You are hypnotic. But I still want to know more about you. Before Saul came, you were about to tell me what happened when your brother-in-law, Johnny, arrived in Boston. Between May of 1636 and January 1637—for eight months—you and Wheelwright blew the top off Boston. You nearly started the Revolutionary War a hundred years ahead of time. Did Wheelwright attend your meetings? Were you sleeping with Harry and John Cotton at the same time?"

"I never slept with two men at the same time," Anne said primly. "I told thee John-Luv was growing wary of me. And being with Harry after he was elected governor was not easy for me. There was only a wall between his house and John's house." She grinned. "But we managed it quite a few times, and Jesus was watching over me. No matter what people said, I did not get pregnant until after Harry went back to England.

"Johnny had no place to live and no church, so he had no congregation to support him. Will and I agreed that he should move in with us. He had been very good to Will's mother, Susannah, taking good care of her, along with his wife, Mary, who was Will's sister. Johnny had three children by his first wife, Marie, who died in childbirth. We put his boys and girls into the separate bedrooms that we had upstairs for our children, and he and Will built a small bedroom addition on the house for himself and Mary. Grannie slept with Annie and Frances on the other side of the chimney, which was snug and warm in the winter. We knew that it would be temporary because soon one of the towns would need another minister. But I wanted Johnny to stay in Boston, and I asked John-Luv to help him because they were the only sound preachers in the Colony. If we rid ourselves of Master Wilson, Johnny and John-Luv could take over the church. Johnny could be his assistant." She laughed. "By my troth, I was certain that eventually they could convert the other ministers in the Colony to their ways of thinking.

"Harry liked Johnny and agreed with me. At first Johnny did not want to make any mischief. He was working at our farm at Mt. Wolleystone with Will, and he also earned money by helping unload ships when they arrived from England.

"But then, after Johnny heard Master Wilson preach for a month, he understood that I was right. Master Wilson did not truly understand the Scriptures, or understand that Jesus had already expiated for our sins. Johnny was cautious, but I was not. By August, more than sixty people were flocking to our house, once or twice a week. The Aspinwalls, the Coggeshalls, the Coddingtons, Atherton and Elizabeth Hough, Sam and Anne Cole; Thomas Oliver, the physician; the Colburns, William and Mary, who lived on Boston Neck; William and Mary Dyer; the Wardalls, Thomas and William and their wives, Elizabeth and Alice; William and Dorothy Brenton, Robert and Phillipa Harding. Many of them were quite wealthy, but they were not like John-Luv. They did not raise objections to poor people coming—like Tom Marshall, the ferryman, Ed Bendall, the dockman, Will Balston along with Sam Cole, an innkeeper, or Will Dyer, who was a milliner, or poor Janey Hawkins. And all my family, including Bridget and Faith with their husbands and Edward and his wife, were there." Anne laughed. "There were lots of others. At first the women came alone with only a few men. But men like Harry and Will Coddington enjoyed the women's gatherings as much as the men's."

"And they listened to you while you ripped apart Wilson's sermons and praised what Cotton had said," I said.

Anne shook her head with an emphatic, "No! No! I did not preach or hold the floor." She laughed. "Harry said that I was very parliamentary. Sometimes I started the discussion, showing how Master Wilson had misinterpreted the Scriptures, or I suggested that Johnny should become Second Teacher to the church because John was so busy interpreting church and state laws that he did not have time for all the problems of the members. Pretty soon all of the men and some of the women were expressing their thoughts too. It was like a Roman forum. We all knew that John-Luv's beliefs in a covenant of grace made more sense than Master Wilson's belief in salvation for only a few saints chosen by God. And the preacher's endless tirades about our sinful natures were boring and ridiculous. Most of the people who came to my house believed as Harry and I did—that there was a personal union between the Holy Ghost and a believer. Once a person understood this, he or she was sanctified. During the summer, I made it a point to go to other churches in the Colony—sometimes with Harry—and listen to other preachers, and I soon discovered that none of them were able ministers of the Gospel. Like the apostles before Jesus was crucified and resurrected, they were not true or strong believers. They were not sealed ministers, and they did not truly understand that Jesus meant for each of us to experience his crucifixion and his resurrection, and thus emulate him."

"Did you realize the implications of what you were doing?" I asked Anne who was sitting cross-legged, Indian fashion, on the bed, gesturing to me as she spoke, with her breasts swaying in sympathetic rhythm to her words.

"What dost thou mean?"

"That you were challenging the state as well as the ministry. The laws of the Commonwealth were based on a Calvinistic interpretation of the Scriptures. You were opening up the floodgates to democracy. You were implying that anyone could have revelations directly from God, and they didn't have to go to church to listen to ministers. All they had to do was have faith in their own inner light." I laughed. "If Harry and John Cotton had stuck by you, *you* might have started the Revolutionary War and got rid of the king of England a hundred years ahead of when it did happen."

Anne laughed. "'Twas not only I. Many people in the Colony, like Sam Gorton and William Pynchon, and many more in England believed that the king or queen had no divine right to tell people how they must worship God, or that the Pope is a direct descendent of Paul and Peter and speaks for God, or that Mary was impregnated by the Holy Ghost. One day people will learn that one believer alone or a small group of believers, is the only kind of church that Jesus established. Man needeth no ministers nor priest nor formal church. All he needs is to hear the God within him and listen to him.

"Everyone knew that Master Wilson seemed like a loving man in the daylight. But he was a hypocrite. Obadiah Holmes called him 'the bloody high priest of Boston, who would put to death anyone who would disagree with him on religion.' He accosted me one day in the market. 'We know what evil thoughts are transacted in your home, Mistress Hutchinson,' he said, leering at me. 'I fear the Devil has taken up lodging in thy beautiful body. Remember Jezebel. God appointed her for destruction.' He drew his hand across his throat as if he would be happy to be the Lord's executioner."

She shrugged. "That happened after he finally agreed with John-Luv, and they let Johnny preach a sermon one Sunday in late September. John let Johnny preach once again in October, because most everyone loved to hear Johnny. In truth, he was exceedingly handsome, and he spoke gently and never shouted like Master Wilson. But Masters Winthrop and Dudley and quite a few others could not believe their ears. Johnny denied John Calvin. He told them the truth. If there *was* any final judgment, those who believed in the indwelling spirit would be saved. God's only judgment was against those who loved Him not, and who loved not their fellow creatures. After that sermon, Will Coddington stood up and proposed that Johnny be appointed assistant teacher of the church. But Master Winthrop was not pleased. He wanted time to think about it—so no vote was taken.

"A week later, on October 25th, the General Court of Massachusetts was in session. Master Winthrop called in John-Luv and Johnny and told them the time had come to find out what they truly believed. Master Dudley proposed that I was the problem—the instigator of all the trouble, a dangerous woman—and said I should be called before the Court and be restrained. But Master Winthrop agreed with Harry that this was men's business, not women's. Most of the ministers were in town. I could have told them that neither John-Luv nor Johnny were in agreement as to personal union with the Holy Ghost but that the governor of the Colony, Harry Vane, and I were."

Anne laughed. "Though they listened for hours, most of the court understood not what John-Luv or Johnny were talking about. But rather than show their ignorance, they decided to put the matter over for further discussion.

"The following Sunday Harry and I and Will Coddington were certain the congregation would elect Johnny assistant teacher. We counted heads and were certain of nearly a hundred ayes. But when Master Wilson finished his sermon and Will Coddington called for the appointment of John Wheelwright as assistant teacher, Master Winthrop stood up indignantly.

"'I consent not,' he shouted. 'We have two ministers already whose spirits we know, and whose labors God hath blessed. We know not the spirit of Master Wheelwright. When I discussed his election with Master Cotton, he told me that although he thought reverently of Master Wheelwright's godliness, so as to be able to live under his ministry, yet seeing that he is a disputatious man, he could not consent to giving him a position in this church.'"

Frowning at her memory of that Sunday long ago, Anne slid back into my arms. "I was so angry with John-Luv that I very nearly stood up and asked him if he had truly said such a thing and why he was afraid of admitting what he thought in his heart. But Harry, sitting in the governor's seat on the pulpit, must have noticed that I was about to boil over. He saved my life. He stood up and pointed his finger angrily at Master Winthrop. 'Brother Winthrop,' he exploded, 'You are a man with two countenances. A few days ago at the General Court you admitted that Master Cotton and Master Wheelwright practically agreed with each other. Master Cotton told the Court that "the ultimate way to salvation is recognition of the Holy Spirit." Now you say that Master Wheelwright is a dangerous man. You call those who disagree with you opinionists. But I say that you are trying to sway this congregation to your opinions.'

"John-Luv immediately stood up and tried to pour oil on these troubled waters. 'No sanctification of the Holy Spirit can be evidence alone,' he said, 'without a concurrent sign of justification through one's work and adherence to the laws of the Scripture. Whether Master Wheelwright and I are in full agreement or not, methinks that a man of his ability should have his own church and not be beholden to senior ministers.

"At this point, Master Bellingham proposed, and it was quickly approved by Master Bradstreet, that rather than wasting time wondering how many angels could stand on the head of a pin that we should give Master Wheelwright his own church. The settlement at Mt. Wolleystone was growing and more than a hundred people lived there the year round. Master Bellingham pointed out that Masters Coddington and Howe had been trying to get a 'Chapel of Ease' at Mt. Wolleystone. It was not easy for the plantation owners or their workers and themselves to get to Boston for services, especially during the winter months.

"Talking about it later with Harry, he agreed with me. This was a way of getting rid of Johnny and hopefully silencing me, since Johnny would no longer be living in our house and feeding me with his beliefs. From that time, Master Wilson rarely spoke to me. But he told everyone to beware of me. Satan was using me to destroy the Colony. But my friends did not desert me. The following Sunday Will Aspinwall challenged Master Winthrop and told him that he was very offended by Master Winthrop's speech against Master Wheelwright.

"Master Winthrop denied that he had slandered Johnny. 'I admit that it was a failing,' he told the congregation, 'not to have dealt with Brother Wheelwright privately, at first, but I did not believe until hearing him later that he doth truly believe that there is a real union with the Holy Ghost that is entirely personal. In addition, he believeth that a person is more than a creature. In his views, a believer himself becomes God or Jesus Christ. Whether such doctrines are agreeable to the teaching of this church, I know not. I leave the church to judge. Especially, Master Cotton. But words and phrases are of human invention. In a true union, the words may remain the same but be something entirely different. In a union between husband and wife, for example, he is a man still and she is a woman (for the union is only in sympathy and relation)—yet a real or personal union it is not.'"

Grinning at me as she quoted Winthrop, Anne was trickling her fingers through my pubic hair. "Methinks that when Master Winthrop was in bed with either of his first two wives—both of whom died very young—or even with poor Margaret, he never had a real union with them either."

"Do you become the man you love?"

"Thou knowest that I do." She held my penis erect. "When thy cock is within me, thou becomest me and I thee."

Momentarily I tried to ignore her blithe invitation for a closer merger. I wanted to keep her on track. "Everything you told me happened in late 1636. You and Wheelwright didn't get thrown out of the Colony until nearly a year later. Why was Mr. Winthrop so patient with you?"

Anne laughed. "He was not patient. But he was not the governor; Harry was. Everybody liked Harry, and most of the wealthiest people in Boston believed that Harry and I were right. Then, in November, some members of the congregation at New Town, led on by their minister, Master Shepherd, met with us and asked us to submit a draft of our beliefs. They responded with their own listing of what they called our dangerous thinking. But we disagreed with them and told them in writing that the revelation of the Holy Spirit may come to anyone who believes in an absolute promise of free grace that persuades the soul of his interest in Christ and the infallible certain evidence of our justified estate.

"Poor Harry. He was so far out on a limb at this point that well nigh all the ministers in the Colony were against him, and John-Luv was being very careful what he said or did not say to both of us. Johnny told me that I should let things cool down. He had moved out to Mt. Wolleystone and dug a cellar for his new home. The General Court gave him two hundred and fifty acres of land. But until spring he had no church, and he preached in Will Coddington's farmhouse or ours—or sometimes even beneath a tree."

"Did he come back to preach in the Boston church?" I asked, knowing that he did.

"Not until January," Anne grinned. "I'll tell you about that later. In the meantime, a few days before the General Court reconvened in December, Will told me that he was going to resign as assistant magistrate. Harry had told Will privately that he was going to tell Masters Winthrop and Dudley that he must return to England because of pressing family matters concerning his inheritance. Will was sure that if Harry quit as governor, Master Winthrop would be reelected. He was scarcely speaking to Will anymore. He told Will that he must be a weak man because he could not shut a woman's mouth—meaning me.

"I felt certain that Harry was not telling the truth about his family problems in England. Anyway, he could not leave and sail the Atlantic in December. But I had no chance to be alone with him till after that Thursday night when he told the General Court that he must leave. Will was not at the opening session so when I heard what had happened I told Will that I must talk with Harry and find out what was bothering him. Snow was whipping across the hill as I walked up Sentry Lane to Harry's house. I prayed that John-Luv would not see me knocking on Harry's door.

"Harry greeted me as I were Jesus Himself come to save him. 'I should have told you,' he sobbed, as I held him in my arms. 'I love you, Anne, but it has been so difficult to be alone with you these past weeks. Truly, I have no stomach for Winthrop and his friends. They are making me forget that the Lord wants me to love them too. More often than not, I would prefer to run my sword through Winthrop and Dudley. But I have tried to be calm. I told the Court that I would have hazarded everything—even the danger of God's judgment upon me for my endless arguments over grace and work—I would have even shrugged at the scandalous things that they have been saying about you and me—as if we were the cause of all the problems in the Colony. But the truth was, I told them, that I must return to England to save my estate from ruin.'

"Harry finally smiled at me. 'It was not true, of course, but you have heard the rumors. Many people say that I continue agreeing with your belief in free grace because I am in love with you. Some of the men have even dared to ask me what it is like fucking a prophetess.' Harry sighed and told me, 'I fear not for myself, but for thee. Methinks that even John Cotton is jealous of thee, and he may have his spies watching us.'

"By this time Harry could no longer wait. His prickle was so deep inside me, and he felt so nice and hard that I exploded at the same time he did." Anne grinned shyly at me. "As thou knowest, sometimes I respond so completely that I nearly faint.

"When we caught our breath, Harry laughed. 'If I had had such release with thee a week ago, I would not have been so overwhelmed today at Court,' he said. 'After I told them that I must return to England, Master

Hough made such a long impassioned speech about why the Colony needed me and he raved on about the danger from the Indians and the peril of rising prices without me as leader that I broke into tears, and I confessed the truth. I did not have to leave immediately, but I must return to England soon and they should elect a new governor. The Court finally adjourned, after deciding that they should hold an election within the next few weeks.'"

Anne smiled reminiscently. "Harry kept kissing me and telling me that it was for the best. He did not wish to leave me. If he could have, he would ask me to come with him and be his wife. But he loved Will, too, and Will needed me. I told him that I loved both him and Will. But I was much too old. He needed a young wife, and I was afraid that if we were ever caught with our bare bums together, governor or not, we would be hung on the Common. But I told him, 'I pray thou willst stay and finish thy term as governor which continues until May.'"

Anne shrugged. "I knew the magistrates might not like Harry's religious beliefs, but they certainly would not want him quitting and going back to England and telling King James that the Puritans were at loggerheads with each other and were about to have a civil war."

25

Trying to decide what she would wear to dinner at the Johnsons' house tonight, examining her new clothes and, in very feminine fashion, modeling one outfit after another and asking me which I preferred, Anne blithely continued to tell me about Harry Vane.

"Harry's troubles were not over, and mine were only commencing," she said. "A week later, fifteen ministers arrived in Boston from every town in the Colony to give the General Court their interpretation of Scriptures and the covenant of works and grace. Then without any advance warning, about three in the afternoon on December 5th—I think it was—John-Luv sent a messenger to my house. I must come immediately. The ministers were assembled at his house and wanted to talk with me. I trudged up through the snow, and he greeted me at the front door. 'I tried to dissuade them,' he said, 'but they were going to tell the magistrates that they should investigate what you have been preaching at your symposiums.'"

Frowning, Anne shook her head. "The whole sniveling lot of them were waiting to pounce on me. Master Peters from Salem, Master Shepherd from New Town, Master Ward from Ipswich, Masters Weld and Eliot from Roxbury, Master Symmes from Charlestown, Master Phillips from Watertown, and of course Master Wilson. Pen in hand, he was sitting at a table waiting to take notes. He greeted me with words from Deuteronomy: 'If thy brother, son, daughter, or thy friends say unto thee, let us go and worship other Gods, thou shalt not consent unto them. But thou shall surely kill him. Thine hand shall be the first to put him to death.'

"'My God would never tell his creatures to kill one another, Master Wilson,' I told him. 'Even if one fails to find the Holy Spirit within one's self, as you have not, the Lord does not murder, He grieves.'"

"You obviously could outtalk and outthink Mr. Wilson," I smiled. "I've read that you told them bluntly that the fear of man bringeth a snare. But you trusted the Lord and were safe. Why did you tell them that they weren't sealed? That really made them angry. What did you mean?"

"I told them that a sealed minister had the full assurance of God's favor because he was fully aware of the Holy Spirit within himself and was not

189

merely parading empty words. John-Luv tried to convince them that he did not completely agree with me. But he did not completely disagree either." Anne smiled. "John told me later that Master Wilson had suggested that it was too bad they had not brought a brank from England for women like me."

"What's a brank?" I asked.

"A hinged iron hat with an opening for one's nose. They clamped it over the head of a woman who would not keep her tongue still. It fixed her tongue with an iron blade into her mouth. If she kept talking, it pricked her throat and tongue so that she bled. In some English towns they kept a brank in the vestry of the church." Anne shrugged. "We were a little more civilized in Boston—but not much." Quite a few women ended up in the marketplace wearing a cleft-stick on their tongues."

She laughed. "But as much as the ministers desired to gag me, they dared not. They knew I had many friends. They all argued and contended so much that it was difficult to hear myself think. Then, Master Weld, a very slippery man, with a voice that oozed with molasses but was really tar and vinegar, brought me over near the window and I knew he detested me. I answered every question he asked, and he wrote it all down in a notebook. But when I asked him to read back my answers, he refused. I told him that he was like Master Shepherd. He put love for an evidence."

"What did you mean by that?"

Anne grimaced. "I meant that professing love doth not necessarily mean that one loveth. The ministers called me Sister and said they loved me, but they made public all the things that I had told them in private. And they understood not, that unlike them, every day I was searching for answers and learning things that I knew not before. Most of the ministers had stopped learning anything new from the moment they were ordained.

"Finally, about six o'clock they departed John's house. They had not resolved anything, and John was disgusted with them. He had not invited any of them to lodge with him. Sarah gave us some porridge and left us to talk together in John-Luv's study.

"'I'm sorry, Anne,' he told me, 'that it has come to this. Thou mayst be right, but thou art too outspoken, and thou often misconstrues my words.' He sighed. 'And thou art in too much of a hurry. Thou doth not change the world over night.'

"'Some dare to try,' I told him. 'Some do not.'

"'I love thee, dear Anne, but thou must not speak for me.'

"'Thou professeth love,' I answered, 'but thou hath ignored me for months. I desire not to speak for you. I want thee to speak for thyself. I promise that whatever may happen, I will not betray our love, or let thee suffer because of it.'"

Anne sighed. "Poor John. He asked me if I loved Harry more than him. There were tears in his eyes. 'John-Luv,' I told him, 'not even Sarah loveth thee more than I do.'" Anne grinned at me. "It was inevitable. John-Luv opened my bodice and was kissing my breasts. Talking and loving each other were always one and the same with us. Soon we were playing seesaw on John's bearskin rug."

"Didn't it make you nervous that Harry lived only a wall away?"

Anne shook her head. "When I was with Will or Harry or John, I never pined for another. The man in my arms was my only man."

At breakfast, I read to Anne from John Winthrop's *Journal.* "According to Winthrop," I said, "five days after Harry nearly resigned as governor of the Colony, all the ministers arrived in Boston for the next meeting of the General Court. 'The Governor,' Winthrop wrote, referring to Harry Vane, 'expressed himself to be an obedient child of the church, and therefore not withstanding the license of the Court, yet without leave of the church he durst not go away.'"

Anne chuckled. "Harry was no obedient child of Master Winthrop's church," she said. "After Harry agreed to continue to act as governor, until the election in May, he made it very clear to Master Peters that he was very angry that the ministers had questioned John and me. And especially so, since he wasn't there, nor had he been invited." Anne smiled. "Harry should have known better than to tackle Master Peters in front of all his friends. I wasn't there, of course, but Harry told me later what happened.

"Master Peters rose up like an angry baboon. 'I'm very saddened to hear that you wouldst be so jealous of our ministerial meetings and attempt to constrain our liberties,' he told Harry. 'Especially when our efforts here are simply to pour oil on troubled waters and help the members of the Boston church to resolve their differences, which dissent, I am sad to tell you, is like a worm eating at the vitals of our country.'

"Harry knew that he was in trouble, and he quickly apologized, but Master Peters wasn't finished. 'Before you arrived here, Governor Vane, the churches were in peace. Methinks that you should consider your youth and short experience in the things of God and beware of peremptory conclusions derived from pride, idleness, and association and unfounded knowledge that you have derived from certain persons who thinketh God speaketh directly to them.'"

Anne's eyes were twinkling. "Harry knew that Master Peters was referring to me, and once again Harry spoke his mind. 'The Light of the Gospel bringeth a sword', he told Master Peters angrily, 'and the children of the bondswoman will persecute those of the free woman.'"

"Then Master Wilson started screaming at Harry, and he insisted before all the magistrates that if the alienation among the brethren did not cease, and if Master Cotton and Master Wheelwright did not speak firmly and deny that sanctification could be achieved without proper justification, and if his friend Mistress Hutchinson did not cease keeping her Devil-created symposiums, the Colony would be ripped asunder. He told the magistrates that only yesterday, Master Cotton had stated before the congregation, 'If a man were laid so flat upon the ground that he had no desires, but was only a bruised reed and awaked at the feet of Christ, nevertheless, if he had true desire for sanctification, he would be sanctified.' 'That is the kind of heresy Master Cotton is preaching,' Master Wilson told the magistrates.

"John-Luv was very angry with him. He told the Court that Master Wilson should apologize to him. But Master Wilson insisted that he had been called before the Court to speak freely and faithfully and to uncover the heresy being preached, not only in the Boston church, but in all the churches."

"The next day, John went to Master Wilson's house with Masters Oliver and Bellingham to receive his apology. But the ministers were on Master Wilson's side, and he would not relent. The ministers gave John a list of sixteen points of belief on which they demanded answers, and they told him point blank that he had too high an opinion of Mistress Hutchinson and too much familiarity with her. Then they voted to assemble again in March, at which time they would put off all lectures for three weeks so that they might convene a synod in Boston and resolve the problems of the church and correct all heretical beliefs in the Colony.

"Everyone in Boston agreed that Master Wilson had gone too far. But he insisted that although he spoke specifically, what he said applied not only to people in Boston but to all others throughout the Colony who were being misguided by false prophets."

"Meaning you," I said.

Anne nodded. "But the members of the church were very angry with Master Wilson. They demanded that John-Luv present a motion to censure him. The next Sunday, at the question period following Master Wilson's sermon, everybody was shouting at him at once. 'You are wrong,' they said. 'If the Holy Ghost dwelleth in a believer then he is already in Heaven. A man can be justified before he believes. Faith is no cause for justification.'"

Teasing her, I said, "But you weren't very nice, or ladylike either. History records that you and some of your women friends walked out of the church while Master Wilson was preaching."

Anne laughed. "Master Wilson often preached for two hours or more. What should a woman do who is having her monthly cramps or needeth to piss?"

I knew that what she was telling me was the relative calm before the storm, and I was continuing to probe about John Wheelwright when the telephone rang. It was Liz Johnson confirming that I was coming to dinner tonight. "Are you still bringing that woman with you?" she demanded.

I remembered that I had told Liz that my friend's name was Anne Hutchinson. Knowing that Anne couldn't possibly go through a whole evening pretending that she was someone else, I decided to drop my bomb before we arrived.

"You're all going to love her," I said. "And you might as well know the truth. The woman I am bringing is the original Anne Hutchinson. By some miracle, which I don't understand, she has returned from the grave."

There was a long silence and then Liz exploded in laughter. "Bob, you can't be serious!" she said. "Before Emily left, she was nervous about leaving you alone. She was afraid you might disappear into one of your never-never lands."

"This is no fantasy," I assured her. "You are going to meet a woman who lived three hundred and fifty years ago."

"That's not what you told me Wednesday," Liz said, a little too patiently. "You said the woman was a stranger. You said she was a woman who knew all about Anne Hutchinson. Are you sure that you're all right? Has Emily telephoned you? Does she know about this?" Liz sounded a little grim. "What cemetery has Dracula's wife been living in for the past three centuries?"

"I know it sounds crazy," I said. "But Anne is no vampire." I put my arm around Anne, who was leaning against me and listening to both sides of the conversation. "Actually, she has bitten me a couple of times," I told Liz laughing, "but not to draw blood. I just thought you should know about her before we arrive and you start quizzing us. Anne has been living here for the past four days. You don't have to worry about Emily. She told r ? that she'd call in exactly one week. That's next Tuesday. When I talk with her, I'll tell her about Anne and I'll tell her the truth."

"My God!" Liz gasped. "Emily is going to be pissed off at you. She always said that you were a patsy for any stray pussy. You better drop this one on some street corner before Emily comes home. Are you sleeping with her?"

Before I could answer, Anne took the phone from my hand. "I am Anne," she said. "Methinks Emily will not be jealous of me. I love dear Robert, too, but I do not want to take him away from Emily, and she need not be vexed. I shall be here for only a little while."

"Bob? Can you hear me?" Liz was shouting into the phone. "Don't trust her. She probably thinks that you're a good catch. Be here tonight. Cocktails are at six. And you can tell her that Barbara Zoltan, Dave's friend, and I will teach her the facts of life."

"What are the facts of life?" Anne demanded when I hung up.

"Everyone gives lip service to monogamy," I laughed, "but, like you, many men and women enjoy a reprieve from each other in someone else's arms."

Anne grinned at me. "Thy friend sounds like a Puritan. Methinks she is not an Anabaptist."

"What does that mean?"

"Many of the Anabaptists, especially in Münster, Germany, were bigamists." Anne's eyes crinkled with suppressed laughter. "The Puritans were sure that the Anabaptists, like the Turks, were anti-Christ. They hated men like John of Leyden."

"Who was he?"

"Many years before I was born, he convinced the Anabaptist women in Münster that a man could have two or even three wives—if he could afford them and take care of them in bed. The women agreed. They outnumbered the men after the Thirty Years War—three to one." She laughed. "It was better to have a little bit of something than nothing at all."

"Would you have shared Will?"

"Of course. But it was different in the Colony. There were not enough women to go around." Anne shrugged. "But men are not like women. They never share the wealth, if they can help it. Some men like Master Winthrop could not conceive that in certain circumstances doing one thing that might seem evil at the time is truly the best thing to do. It would have been better for the Pope to let Henry VIII have two wives or even three so that he could have gotten a male heir. It might have saved poor Anne Boleyn's neck."

I couldn't help laughing. "Do you think that my wife should let me marry you?"

Anne stared at me wistfully. "If thou wants to, why not? I am not her enemy. I know her not, but I love her too because she loveth thee." She shrugged. "John-Luv did not agree with such ideas, but Johnny thought that fasting for the sins of the Anabaptists, as the Puritans did, was silly."

"But Wheelwright preached a sermon on Fast Day, January 9, 1637," I said. "That was the first shot in the big war that got you both banished."

"But 'twas not because of bigamy," Anne said. "If anyone had asked Johnny, I'm sure he would have told him that Martin Luther was right. There are circumstances when bigamy can pour oil on troubled waters. Master Luther shocked many Protestants when he agreed that Phillip of Landgrave, a wealthy German king, could marry a second wife because he could no longer tolerate his first wife, who had lost her senses."

Before I could explore her easy-going extramarital beliefs any further, the telephone rang again. It was Saul Dremler. "How is she?" he asked.

"Happy, I think. Loving." I smiled at Anne. "And hoping that your friend Susan is being loving with you."

Saul laughed. "She is. We talked about Anne all night. Susan can't wait to meet her."

"Bring Susan tomorrow. What about the pictures?"

"That's why I called. They're just the same." Saul sounded both excited and subdued. "You can tell from the prints that it's a woman. She even seems to glow through the surrounding fog and haze, but her features are ghostly and indistinguishable." Saul paused, and I could hear him sigh. "You've got to face it. If no one can take her picture, Anne is a miracle exceeding any experience of the Catholic saints, or the Virgin Mary herself. I hope you know what you are getting into. If Anne appears on 'People Passion,' then the top is going to blow off." Saul sounded grim. "Your house on Narragansett Road may even become a shrine. Thousands of people will arrive with every incurable sickness you ever heard of. The house will be buried in bandages and crutches and wheelchairs. Anne won't have to do anything. Just her being there, smiling at the crowd, will cure them. She'll make Saint Anne de Beaupre and Bernadette of Lourdes look like small change."

I knew that Saul was right, and his confirmation of my own fears gave me the cold shivers. "But at least the Pope won't want to adopt her," I said lamely. "She's too much a Protestant, and, I might add, a small-p protestant as well—the best kind."

But Saul only laughed. "Don't count on the Pope's indifference," he said. "So far as I can figure out, Anne's mystical relationship with the Holy Ghost isn't too away from Catholic theological thinking."

While Anne and I cleaned up the kitchen and washed the dishes from breakfast, I kept wondering where and how I should continue the education of Anne Hutchinson into the mores and customs of the twentieth century. She was fascinated with my library of books and magazines piled high in one room after another. I explained to her that in addition to radio and television, we had daily newspapers and magazines of all kinds and I showed some of them to her. "Anyone who wants to know anything that is happening in the world can keep abreast of all the political and economic problems in every country in the world," I laughed grimly, "as well as decide who is to blame for the forty or more wars that are going on at the present time."

To her question, "How doth one have time in one life to know everything?" and "Why doth thou need to know all the man-made problems of the world?" I had no answer.

"Twentieth-century Americans are addicted to knowing what other people are doing," I told her, "especially in their bedrooms. Americans like to know all the petty details of the lives of famous people or celebrities," I shrugged. "And that's what you'll be when Sally Lane gets her teeth into you. She'll not only ask you what ate for breakfast, but whether your bowels are in good working order and how many orgasms you had last night."

"Orgasms? What are they?"

"Climaxes." I frowned at her bewilderment, not quite knowing how to explain what I meant. "How you feel when you are playing seesaw—when you can't stop, and you nearly faint." I laughed. "In plain words, no one knows whether Puritan ladies liked to fuck or not."

Anne was laughing heartily. "Some of us did. But we dared not talk about it."

"You better not talk about it now either," I said. "You're too trusting." Once again I tried to convince her that she shouldn't appear on the Sally Lane show. "She'll try to explore your sex life, and she really doesn't believe that you are resurrected. She'll try to prove that you're an imposter, a charlatan. Do you understand what I'm saying?"

"Thou dost truly sound like Will," Anne smiled. "I promise thee I will not tell this woman what thou and I do in bed."

"You'd better not tell her what you did with John-Luv or Harry Vane, either," I said. "I worry about you. At your trial when you got angry, you should have kept your mouth shut. Instead you put a curse on Winthrop and the magistrates and all their posterity, if they didn't believe you."

"I did not say believe me," Anne frowned at me. "I told them that if by their lives they put Jesus Christ from them, then the Lord would put a curse on them." She shrugged. "From what I've seen of thy world, things have not changed as much as thou thinketh. Men and women who loveth not each other still destroy each other. Is not that the Lord's curse? Methinks that is why I am here. Because God has restored me to life, people will know that their lives now and after they leave the earth are in His hands. If they wish salvation, there is only one way—by loving Him."

I was about to remind her that Jesus had said the same thing without too much long-term effect, when the telephone rang again. It was Sally Lane, and as usual Anne flattened herself against me so that she could hear this miracle of voices flying through the air.

"Just checking in," Sally bubbled. "My program director is making me an expert on Anne Hutchinson. But I've got to find a quick way, within the hour, to focus in on her life before we get into the truth or poetry of the situation. I've been trying to find copies of her trials but the only stuff I have is practically unreadable. I can't figure out all the nuances."

Anne slid the phone out of my hand. "This is Anne Hutchinson," she said. "I told the magistrates at my trials that I believed not in bodily resurrection. But the Lord has proved me wrong."

"That's it! That's great, Anne." Sally yelled enthusiastically. "Bob, do you have a copy of the trials that are easy to read?"

I was tempted to tell her to try the Boston Public Library but I knew that no one had transcribed the trials in their entirety into a meaningful drama. "I've re-created a modern version of them," I told Sally. "But you might as well know, Anne isn't going to appear on your program." I could see Anne scowling at me as I tried to explain to Sally that no one could photograph Anne or capture her face and features on video either.

"I don't believe you, Bob." Sally laughed. "You're spoofing me. I'm not worried. We've got the best television technicians in the city. They'll get her on video. If they don't I'll have Mel Robbins, or some artist, standing by who can draw her face. Right now, I'm sending a messenger to Quincy. I need to read those trials. I know you're not going to let me down. Let me speak to Anne."

Shrugging, I gave her the phone. "Anne, are you listening to me?" Sally asked. "Promise me that you'll be here Tuesday morning. Bob knows where to bring you. I need you here by ten-thirty. That will give us two hours before show time to get you acquainted."

Anne ignored my disgusted, shaking head. "Robert is not very happy about this," she said. "But he promises to bring me." Anne handed me the phone and I cradled it.

"Damn you," I said and slapped her ass. "I refuse to play Will."

She grinned at me. "But you cannot refuse. You are Will."

26

I had forgotten to tell Anne that the Johnsons' home was a woody, twentieth-century re-creation of what New England called a garrison colonial, with an overhanging second floor from which, presumably, a frightened seventeenth-century homeowner could shoot down at Indians who might be arriving for unfriendly business. Like many present-day New Englanders, feeling what may be a genetic longing for their past, Chuck and Liz had furnished the interior with many original antiques, including Revolutionary War muskets, as well as reproductions of furniture that might be called colonial, but actually spanned an Early American period of one hundred and fifty years. Anne had told me that her home on Sentry Lane had a long sloping roof typical of the first homes that the Puritans had built. I realized that when we walked up to the Johnsons' front door, which had a brass-eagle knocker on it that not only the style of the house but also the interior would be as foreign to her as my rambling ranch-style home had been.

Liz and Chuck greeted us at the door. Liz is a wiry, crisp woman with blonde-rinsed hair. In her early sixties, she thinks that she is very much abreast of the modern world and cannot be shocked by anything the younger generation can do. She even communicates with her grandchildren by listening to the latest popular music on Music Television, but it was obvious now from her quick, searching appraisal of Anne that she was sorry that Emily wasn't around to put a stop to whatever was going on.

Chuck beamed enthusiastically at Anne and to her surprise bussed her cheek. "My family is not so famous as the Hutchinsons," he said, "but I can trace my part of it back to colonial times, to Lady Johnson and her husband, Isaac, who arrived in Massachusetts Bay on the *Arbella* along with John Winthrop. The *Arbella* was named for Lady Johnson."

"Methinks I heard of them," Anne said. "Six months after they arrived, the poor souls died of the ague."

"Dave and Barbara are in the library sitting room," Liz said. "We have a wet bar in there. It's more cozy for conversation than the living room. But first, if Anne would like, I'll show her the rest of the house."

I knew that Liz was proud of her highly polished pine-floored living room. The wide planks, set with dowels, were partially covered with hand-some braided rugs. There was a vast clutter of ladder-back chairs, dry sinks, primitive benches and stools, pewter and brass pots and candlesticks, cup-boards filled with early American glass and china, and framed prints and hand-colored drawings dating back to the thirteen colonies.

"Chuck and I are escapists," she told Anne. "Like Miniver Cheevy we were born too late. But we really do enjoy the honest workmanship of the Pilgrims and the Puritans and the natural things of colonial times."

While Anne was obviously astonished at the clutter, she showed no sign of recognition. "Your home is not like any home I ever saw in Boston," she said, smiling innocently at Liz. "You have so many little things that you must love. It would take you many days to list them all in your will." She shrugged. "In my home we kept only things we used. At night you could smell fish-oil burning in the lanterns, or tar simmering in pine knots, or tallow candles streaming black smoke. You have electricity. You have ceilings and wainscot-ting. Only a few people like Will Coddington and Master Winthrop could af-ford to enclose their walls." She pointed at the fieldstone fireplace. "You have a fire going and a pretty iron pot hanging near it. But you do not have a fire to keep warm, and methinks, like Robert, you have a kitchen to cook in."

"Never mind," Chuck laughed. "We have a spinning wheel," he said, pointing at a polished reproduction of one.

Anne shrugged and, unknowingly perhaps, continued her putdown. "'Tis very pretty and exceedingly shiny, but where is the wool to spin?"

I was sure that by now Anne was well aware that no one spun wool or made any yarns or cloth in their home anymore, but her expression was to-tally naive. "My Will would agree with you," she said. "Why spin wool when you can buy cloth? Will could buy better cloth in Manchester than I could make. He could afford to buy it because he made a good profit selling it."

Within the first few minutes, it was apparent that Anne was imbued with a more capitalistic spirit than Liz, and she was destroying some of Liz's illusions about colonial times. The twentieth century might frighten Anne, but she was challenged by it. Liz and Chuck were more comfortable living in a world that never was.

Liz showed Anne a twenty-by-forty-foot patio enclosed with window walls that they had added onto the back of the house. It overlooked a swimming pool with a tall cedar fence in the background. "This area is more California colonial," Chuck told Anne. "Later I'll barbeque steaks out here." Before Chuck led us into the library and a well-stocked bar, I heard Liz tell Anne that the room we were passing was "the downstairs powder room," which Anne could use any time she wished.

"It's a toilet," I told a bewildered Anne, who had finally learned that word.

Grinning and not hearing Liz's answer, Chuck led me into the library where Dave introduced me to Barbara Zoltan, a pretty brown-eyed woman in her forties who wore her hair in a no-nonsense, brushed-back, boyish feather cut. She spoke with a too-perfect Harvard accent.

"What the Hell are you up to?" Dave demanded with a big grin. "We just got a fast glimpse of your new girlfriend. Barb told me that if she can look like that three hundred and fifty years from now, she's ready to die tomorrow. Be honest, where did you find her? I won't tell Emily. I know that, like me, you're true to women in your fashion, but your holiday isn't going to last much longer. What are you going to tell Emily when she gets home? I'd take Anne off your hands if I could, but Barb would probably be a little pissed if I did."

Barbara shrugged. "I know you well enough not to complain."

I grinned at Dave. I was sure that if Emily were aggravated with me, more than likely she would have run into his arms for a little hugging and solace, and he knew that I knew it. We had known Dave and his wife, Ruth, for twenty-five years. Since Dave had shown no interest in remarrying after Ruth died, I assumed, without asking, that Emily was occasionally making his bachelor life more tolerable. I had no objection, but it occurred to me to ask Dave that if Emily was consoling him in bed, what objection could she have to Anne? Hadn't Anne been trying to tell me, without exactly saying it, that the process of loving could easily lead to a progression? If you could love one person caringly, didn't it predispose you to love another?

"I didn't find Anne," I told Dave, skipping over my silent thoughts. "She found me." I quickly told him, while Barbara listened skeptically, how Anne had arrived on my doorstep. "What could I do? I asked. "Slam the door on her and let her freeze to death?" I am sure that by now Liz has told you that Anne is living with me. Sleeping with me too, and all that implies." I grinned at Barbara. "You don't have to worry, I don't think Anne would be any happier with Dave than she is with me."

Dave was watching Chuck pour me a Chivas on the rocks. Sipping his own drink, he said, "I told Emily, and I tell every woman I know, you can't really expect men to forsake all others. It's not in their genes. Especially, if a man manages to survive into his sixties. There are so many lonesome pussies furring their legs they can't help themselves if they pat a few now and then. But you'd better watch your step with this one, Bob." Dave was suddenly very serious and professional. He sounded as if I were already his patient. "I just hope that you aren't in so deep that you really believe that this woman has come back from the grave."

I shrugged. "When I was a kid, I believed in fairy tales. But Anne is no fairy story. Listen to her. You may change your mind. I thought you used past-life therapy at the Institute."

Dave nodded. "We suit the patient to whatever therapy works best. I'm Jungian in beliefs and so is Barb. She teaches at Simmons and is also on the staff at the Institute. I am sure that parts of our brains have assimilated ancient myths and memories. Some people are even able to recall an amazing amount of detail about previous lives they have lived." He laughed. "I haven't been able to personally discover that I've lived before, but I keep trying. If I have, I'm sure of one thing. I'm not living in the same body that I died in. Old skin and bones don't fade away. They rot."

He patted my shoulder philosphically. "A Jew may have managed to come back from the grave, but your friend is not Jewish. Anne Hutchinson died three centuries ago. No one knew what she looked like. And keep that in mind. That's important. It's something a problem patient would rely on. No one can identify her. Whoever this lady is, she's not walking around or making love to you in her former body. She's a twentieth-century woman. I'd guess that she's a classical case of hysterical neurosis of the dissociative type. It goes beyond simple amnesia and is called fugue. As in music, it is a complete departure from the main theme of one's life. Your friend has substituted for her present life that of a woman she had admired and read about in history books. But at any moment she could snap back into reality and experience a terrible shock when she realizes what she's been doing. Sleeping with a stranger, for example. You should bring her over to the Institute. Barb and I will be happy to evaluate her. I'm warning you, Bob. You should know who she really is. Maybe she has a husband and a family. When she realizes what she has been doing, she may become suicidal."

Dave stopped talking as Anne and Liz walked into the room, and Chuck asked them what they would like to drink. I had told Anne when we were driving to the Johnsons that Dave ran a hospital for people with mental problems, and since his wife's death, two years ago, many women had tried to inveigle him into matrimony. As yet, although he was in his middle sixties, he evidently preferred to love them and leave them, but at any rate not support them. Laughingly, I told her that possibly Dave was waiting for me to die so that he could marry Emily.

"Doth Emily love him?" she had asked.

"Although Dave is a big burly lovable bear, he's very intense and totally wrapped up in his profession." I shrugged. "But many women find him charming."

"Most women like doctors," Anne had laughed. "And most women can easily love two men, but they admit it not."

Now, after nodding primly at Barbara, to my surprise Anne proved it by bussing Dave's cheek enthusiastically. She blushed demurely when he didn't question her reality.

"Your husband may have thought you were a saint," Dave said, "but I'd call you a beautiful angel. It's obvious why you had fifteen kids. The poor man couldn't stay out of your bed."

Behind the bar, Chuck was taking drink orders. "Dave is already a little bombed on Chivas," he said. "Bob is catching up and Barbara is not far behind. What will you and Liz have?"

All of us were a little surprised when Anne answered, "Methinks I shall have a martini. Last night two of those made me feel as if I were two Annes. One of me was floating over my head watching the other me and telling me to keep my mouth shut." She laughed. "But I listened not."

"That's interesting," Dave said. "Some of my patients believe that they have an astral body. It's ectoplasmic, but it looks exactly like them. Some of them call it their soul. They claim that by careful meditation they can release their astral body from their temporal body. Even before they die, their astral body can move anywhere in the world at the speed of light. They think their astral body, or soul, never dies. Eventually it will inherit another temporal body."

Dave smiled at Anne. "Everyone hopes to live after death. The belief in another life is as old as religion itself. There are many words to express the idea. *Paligenesis,* from the Greek, means to return again. *Transmigration* means souls seeking new bodies. *Metempsychosis* is a bodily change of souls. But the Christians rejected these ideas from Eastern religions—especially continuous rebirth. It wasn't exclusive enough. According to Hindu beliefs, you are born again and again until you achieve Nirvana. But in some births you may return as an animal or even a fly." He laughed, "India is filled with bugs. It's against the Jain religion to kill them. But the Christian approach to the afterlife is really a stroke of genius. Christians believe that God creates them in His image and gives each of them a unique soul, which finally goes to either Heaven or Hell. If it goes to Hell, that's that. But those who have lived a good life and believed in the Trinity will survive judgment day and be resurrected."

Dave grinned at all of us. "I'm not sure exactly what you've been telling Bob," he said to Anne, "but according to what Liz has told us, either you've been resurrected ahead of time, or right now is judgment day, and you're on schedule because the end of the world is at hand. Or more believably, you were actually reborn some forty or fifty years ago and are now communing with your past life on earth."

Anne sipped her drink thoughtfully before replying. "I feareth that you are like the Puritans," she said quietly. "You do not understand resurrection. After my trials, when I lived in Portsmouth, I knew that no ministers could ever help me. I remembered that my father told me about Origen. He said that Origen was a Greek who had lived nearly two hundred years after Christ died. Origen believed that our souls, the inner light within each of us, lived from the beginning of creation, and he quoted Jesus. 'Ye shall see the Son of man ascend up where he was before,' Jesus said. And Jesus also said, 'I am the living bread which hath come down from heaven . . . Glorify thou me with thine own self and with the glory that I had with thee before the world was.' And Jesus made it apparent that he had been Elias and John the Baptist. He told his disciples, 'He hath come already, but they knew it not.'"

Anne paused for breath, but before anyone could respond, she continued to quietly quote Scriptures. "'There is no man or woman that followeth me,' Jesus said, 'but he shall receive a hundred fold, now in this time—houses, and brethren and sisters and mothers and children and lands, and persecutions.'" Anne emphasized the word *persecutions*. "'But in a world to come he shall receive eternal life. Many that are first shall be last and the last shall be first.'" She smiled, "Methinks, Jesus was saying over and over again that we live many lives. Whether it be in the same body or a new one matters not."

"But you believe that your body is the same body that you had," Barbara said. "How can you remember your previous body after so many years?"

Anne laughed. "I know that I do not have the same firm features I once had. My face is not so round, nor my titties so firm. But I have the same little skin spots below my left breast and beneath my bum that I had when I was twenty. Would you like to see them?"

"There's a better way to convince you," I said hurriedly before Anne could hike up her skirt in response to Dave's enthusiastic "Why not?" "Let Anne tell you what happened in Boston in 1637 before she and John Wheelwright were banished. I'm sure that you'll learn things from her that you never read in any history book."

27

Liz agreed that it was too early for dinner. While he was mixing more martinis and pouring scotch, Chuck told Anne that he had always wondered why John Wheelwright rode all the way to Boston from Wollaston to preach a Fast Day Sermon—especially since he had been given his own church at Mt. Wollaston.

"Johnny was given the land in October 1636, and a church was gathered," Anne said. "But there was no meetinghouse until the following spring. It mattered not. Johnny would preach anywhere, in a farm house or even under a tree. He came to Boston in January on Fast Day because Harry and I asked him to come."

"Harry was Sir Henry Vane, the governor of the Colony." I explained to them that Harry was only twenty-four at the time. But I didn't go into details of his and Anne's relationship.

"Harry had told the magistrates," Anne said, "that he could only continue as governor until the May elections. But Harry was afraid that unless we convinced the people in Boston that we were right, Master Winthrop would be reelected governor of the Colony. The tide was running with us, but if we sat on our bums and played Hamlet and took not arms against the sea of troubles, we would not pick the crop while it was ripe."

Anne grinned, possibly at her mixed metaphor. "Harry and I were determined that Will Coddington should be governor, and no one, not even John Cotton, was a better minister than Johnny. Harry was sure that when Master Winthrop finally realized that he was outnumbered, he would blow with the wind. I was sure that once Johnny tooted the horn strongly it would be heard in all directions, and John would join with us." Anne grimaced. "But when the cards were on the table, John-Luv still would not stick his neck out." She sighed. "And we underestimated Master Winthrop."

"Who was John-Luv?" Liz demanded.

"Are you telling us that you and Harry Vane, the governor, and John Wheelwright plotted against Winthrop?" Chuck was astonished. "There's nothing like that in any book I ever read."

"I care not what is in the history books," Anne smiled conspiratorally at me, "'tis all true. I told Robert that I loved John Cotton. I called him John-Luv in private. I loved him and I loved Harry too."

For the next half hour while Chuck refilled our glasses several times and Anne admitted that strong liquors loosened her tongue, she gave us a detailed running account of the civilian mutiny against Winthrop's dream of a Utopian community of brethren.

"We made sure that the meetinghouse was filled on Thursday, Lecture Day, the 19th of January 1637," she said. "Even before, at my house, we had counted noses. We knew that there were only a handful of church members who disagreed with us. John-Luv gave the first sermon that afternoon. It was so cold in the meetinghouse I thought my ankles had frozen. Snow was whipping against the building. John's sermon was based on Isaiah: 'Behold ye fast for strife and debate, and to smite with the fist of wickedness. Ye shall not fast, as ye do this day, to make your voice heard on high.'"

Anne smiled. "John knew not what Johnny was going to say, but he kept trying to convince us that our conflict over a covenant of works and a covenant of grace separated us not as much as we did think. Then Johnny took over the pulpit. 'How might we restore the Lord in our midst?' Johnny asked and replied, 'We must prepare ourselves for spiritual combat.'"

Quoting Wheelwright, Anne sounded as she were exhorting a congregation. "'The weapons of war are not carnal,' she said, 'but spiritual. We must prepare for battle. We must come out against the enemies of the Lord. If we do not strive, those under a covenant of works will prevail. We are not able to put forth one act of true saving spiritual wisdom, but we must put it forth from our Lord Jesus Christ with whom we are made one. We are not able to achieve any work of sanctification, or able to procure our justification, but it must be Jesus Christ Himself who applies Himself and His righteousness to us.'" Anne paused for a dramatic effect, "And then Johnny said, 'Brethren, I tell thee, those under a covenant of works, the more holy they are, the greater enemies they are to Christ! If we mean to keep the Lord Jesus Christ, we must be willing to suffer anything. If we will overcome, we must not love our lives, but be willing to be killed like sheep. It is impossible to hold out the truth with external peace and quietness.'"

"You sound as if you are quoting yourself," Chuck said with a grin.

"I am," Anne said coolly. "I helped Johnny write that sermon. We worked on it for two days. Harry helped, too. Methinks that is why I am here."

"What do you mean by that?" Dave demanded, staring at her as if he were trying to penetrate some twentieth-century consciousness he was sure was in her brain.

"I mean—to teach people that they cannot sit idly by and hope for the best," she said. "Harry knew that. Despite the Massachusetts Bay Charter, Master Winthrop and his friends, Masters Endicott and Dudley, were playing their own pipes. They were hoping that back home in England, King Charles would be unable to hear the tune. They were not only governing the Colony according to their own body of laws, which John-Luv and Master Ward helped frame, but they were following an interpretation of Scripture that would have got them hung if they had been in England." Anne shrugged. "Not that Harry and Johnny and I believed in Anglican doctrine, but as Johnny told Harry, 'We are not libertines or antinomians. We are only trying to let people think for themselves.'"

"What happened after the sermon?" Liz asked.

"Nothing," Anne shook her head slowly. "Master Winthrop outfoxed us. He knew that most of the congregation were whispering amens to everything Johnny said. If Master Winthrop had protested then, we might have immediately forced Master Wilson to step down, and Johnny and John-Luv could eventually have changed the thinking of the other ministers in the Colony. We should have boiled over, but we did not dare. So for the next six weeks, Master Winthrop let us simmer. Johnny refused to act without John-Luv, and John was like that Roman god Janus, looking both ways at once."

"Then on Friday, March 9th, the General Court met in Boston and without any warning, they summoned Johnny from Mt. Wolleystone to repeat certain passages of his Fast Day Sermon to them. They asked whether he truly believed what he had said. At the same time they picked out Stephen Greensmith, a lumber merchant and friend of ours, and fined him forty pounds because he had made the statement that all ministers except Masters Cotton and Wheelwright, and possibly Master Hooker, taught only a covenant of works. Johnny gave the Court a complete copy of his sermon, but they told him that he would have to remain in Boston over the weekend while they studied it.

"Even before Johnny had arrived, Harry told me that we were in trouble. The Court had insisted on questioning Johnny with no witnesses. The doors of the meetinghouse would be locked. Will Coddington called a meeting at my house that night, and more than fifty-five men and women arrived. Anne chuckled. "Obviously, Master Winthrop, who lived across the street, could see the hustle and bustle. We drew up a remonstrance and a petition demanding that the Court hold an open hearing, and we questioned whether the Court had any authority over a question of conscience. But the Court ignored the petition, and they informed Will Coddington and Harry that this matter was much more than a question of conscience.

"Monday morning, before the Court, Johnny demanded to know if the magistrates had found him guilty. 'Didst thou not know, even before thy sermon,' Master Dudley asked Johnny, 'that the ministers in this Colony preach a covenant of works?'

"Knowing that he would be accusing himself, Johnny refused to answer Master Dudley or any further questions from the Court. Finally, that afternoon, the Court was declared open to everybody, including the ministers in the Colony who had previously been called to Boston. Nigh onto everybody in town squeezed into the meetinghouse."

Speaking softly in a low, faraway voice, Anne wasn't really seeing us, although we were all listening to her attentively. She was voyaging on a sea of ancient memories. "I told Will later," she said, "that it was enough to make one puke. For three days the Court met from dawn to dusk. They were convinced that Johnny was a traitor and guilty of sedition. Harry and Will Coddington tried every tactic they knew to save Johnny, but the ministers quoted Scripture endlessly to each other and to the Court. Johnny listened to them with a grim smile without saying anything. As usual, John-Luv tried to balance on a tightrope, but he admitted that Johnny had implied that those walking in a covenant of works were enemies of Christ.

"Then, on the last day, the magistrates decided that while Johnny was guilty, they would withhold sentencing him until the next meeting of the Court. They were afraid to banish him. Nor did they dare silence him. They knew that the members of the Boston church were furious with them. So Master Winthrop suggested that they hold the next meeting of the Court in New Town, or Cambridge, as they named it later.

"Harry refused to put this motion to a vote, but Master Endicott did." Anne shrugged. "Master Winthrop was very clever. He knew that Master Shepherd, the new pastor at New Town, did not agree with Johnny, and he knew that it was not easy to get to New Town. It took all morning to sail up the Charles River, or even longer to go by way of Roxbury and Muddy River. Master Winthrop knew that he would have a better chance of being reelected governor, if many of the Boston freemen who were so angry with him could not get there, or did not have the time to influence the freemen from other towns.

"We had two months until election day. Will Aspinwall wrote a new petition favoring Johnny, and this time, after he traveled to most of the towns, he got sixty-four men from Boston and ten from other towns to sign it."

"Weren't you afraid to continue having meetings in your house?" Barbara asked.

Anne smiled. "I have told you. If you wish to overcome the enemies of Jesus, you fear not for your life."

"And you're not afraid of dying—even now?" It was obvious to me that Barb was pursuing her belief that Anne was a twentieth-century woman with a Napoleonic complex.

But Anne only smiled at her. "Once you have experienced death and have come back to life, you realize that dying is only one small section of the circle that we are all traveling."

"Why do you think you were reborn?" Liz asked trying to hide her skepticism.

"I am not *reborn,*" Anne said, startling all of us with her answer. "The Lord hath sent me to take up where I left off—to fight the anti-Christ, not with a sword but with love."

"How do you know?" Dave asked.

"The Lord speaketh to me."

Frowning, Liz shook her head. "I think I need another drink. I think we all do. Chuck can barbeque the steaks anytime that you're ready. Why don't we go out on the patio now? There's more room for flights of fancy out there."

"I want to hear what happened at New Town," Chuck told Anne as he was pouring her a third martini.

"Be careful," I warned her as she took it. "You'll get tipsy. They all think you're chasing pink elephants now."

But Anne was smiling at Chuck, who had found a Polaroid camera behind the bar and was aiming it at her. "Is he taking a picture?" she asked me as Chuck pushed the button and the camera flashed before I could warn him.

I watched him, fascinated, holding my breath, as Chuck waited for his picture to slide out of the camera. Saul hadn't tried a Polaroid. Would Chuck get a clear picture of Anne? He examined the picture and handed it dubiously to Anne. "You have to wait a minute," he said. "It's still developing." We all watched but the picture remained hazy. "I may not have had the right focus," he said. "Let me try again. I really want to preserve you for posterity this time around."

Four pictures later Chuck gave up. "The damn film must be outdated," he told Anne. "I can't seem to bring you into focus."

"Take a picture of Liz," I smiled at him. "I'm sure you'll have better luck."

Anne wasn't aware of it, but after I tried to explain to them that Saul and I had been unable to photograph or videotape Anne, their skepticism and disbelief grew almost pugnacious, as if they were psychologically unable to accept the possibility that Anne had truly arrived from another world. Were they foreshadowing what would happen when Anne appeared on the Sally Lane show? It made me nervous to think about it.

Dave and Barbara preceded us into the patio, and I noticed that Barb was talking rapidly to him in a low voice, obviously exhorting him to do something that he was dubious about.

"Barb hopes that you will bring Anne over to the Institute tomorrow," Dave said, as Anne stopped to watch Chuck, who was laying out six thick steaks and getting ready to barbecue them on a propane grill that vented into the patio fireplace.

"We'll give her a thorough physical examination," Dave said. "Electrocardiograms, electroencephalograms, urine analysis, blood tests, skin test. We can try a chest x-ray, and I can even try hypnosis to see if we can pinpoint the twentieth-century woman."

"No thanks," I told him grimly. "I'm not letting you or anyone treat Anne like a scientific freak. I don't care whether she lived before or not. She thinks she's resurrected. She hasn't struck a false note yet. That's enough for me."

"But maybe it's not enough for her," Barb said as Chuck and Anne joined us. "You should let her make her own decisions."

"Anne has made one decision," Chuck said, interrupting us. "She wants to dance. He showed us an Archive record, *Golden Dance Hits of 1600* that he had bought for the occasion. "The tile floor out here is great for dancing barefoot or in your stockings," he said. "In the summer it leads right out to the swimming pool. We've had occasional parties when the guests danced right into the pool without taking their clothes off."

"I love to feel water all over my body," Anne said smiling happily at him. "And I love dancing. When my heart's on fire dancing is the next best thing."

"What's the next best thing?" Dave asked, leering at her. He knew the answer before she said it.

"Thou art a doctor," Anne stared at him beguilingly. "I am sure that if thou thinketh about it, thou already knoweth what the best thing is."

I was more than a little shocked to hear Anne suddenly addressing Dave with her familiar *thou*, but I didn't make an issue over it. I was sure that Dave was well aware of her new familiarity with him.

"If you like to swim, we have a big indoor pool at the Institute," Dave said. "It's very soothing relaxation for our patients. I know that you were once a woman who was very interested in medicine. If Bob will bring you over tomorrow, we'll show you many things that we've learned about the human mind and body and how to keep it healthy."

Chuck had put his record on a turntable and our conversation was terminated by music flooding the patio from four speakers. I recognized the seventeenth-century dance called a courante with a fast one, two, three beat. Squealing with delight, Anne stepped out of her shoes and grabbed Dave's arm. "'Tis a dance from Paris," she said. "I will show you how to do it." They whirled together over the tiles in what was practically an old-fashioned waltz.

Beckoning to me from the kitchen, where she was preparing a salad to serve with the steak, Liz snorted at me. "Look at her. She's conning you, Bob. That's no seventeenth-century woman. I don't give a damn whether she can be photographed or not. You better watch out. That lady's got you by the balls."

I laughed. "Not only me, look at Dave and Chuck." They were passing Anne between them as they danced. "She's got them both spellbound." The record was now playing a volte. Swaying to the fast music, Anne was telling Dave that at the Court when men and women danced the volte the lady leaped into her partner's arms, and he held her by the hips twirling her in the air.

Dave offered to try, but Anne shook her head saucily. "Ladies wear very short dresses today. Robert doesn't like pantyhose. If thou whirled me in the air everyone could see my con and bum."

"I noticed that Liz and Barb were staring at her with pursed lips. "How do you keep your stockings up?" Liz asked.

Anne laughed. "With a silly lace thing that Robert bought me. It goes around my stomach."

"You and Bob seem to have become very intimate in less than a week," Liz said a little sourly.

Anne shrugged. "If the Lord drops you naked on a strange man's doorstep, He doesn't expect you to act like a virgin." She chuckled. "Robert knew that I had fifteen children. I got them not by being a modest dame."

Blithely unaware of the tension that she was creating with Liz and Barb, Anne was still listening to the music. She asked them if they knew how to dance the tangle. "It's a French dance," she said. "Harry Vane taught it to me at my house."

"You danced in Boston?" Chuck asked with raised eyebrows, as he flipped the steaks he was barbequing. "I thought Puritans didn't dance."

"Some did," Anne laughed, "behind closed doors and windows." Ignoring Liz's remark, "We're almost ready to eat," Anne told us that we should form a circle alternating ladies and men and hold hands. "Now we reverence each other," she said, "now bow, and with small steps keep time to the music. Now I am letting go of Robert's hand and I will slowly weave us together so that no one can move." When she had us intertwined in a knot, she grinned at us. "Now we sway against each other to the music, but only for a moment because it doth make some men too nervous."

"You may call it nervous," Dave said as he sat down next to the round table on the patio. "But I call it an erection. That dance is a sex tease."

"God made women to tease men," Anne said. "If they could not tease them, men would get too lazy in bed."

"You're obviously not a feminist," Barb said coldly. "If you are really going to appear on the Sally Lane show, you'd better not say things like that. Most women today don't like to think they are sex objects."

"Sex objects?" Anne, who was still having difficulty using a fork, scooped up a piece of steak with her spoon. "I knoweth that I have a con. A man has a pizzle. Methinks neither one objects to the other."

28

After an extended discussion of feminine equality during which Anne made it quite apparent that she always felt the equal of any man, Chuck finally got her back onto her previous life. "I'd like to hear what happened at the general elections in Cambridge," he said. "I know that Winthrop was reelected governor, but half of the Boston settlers were arguing with the other half. My history book reads like civil war in the making."

"In May, before the elections, it was worse than England had ever been," Anne smiled reminiscently. "Even before that, during April, Master Winthrop told Harry that he was very unhappy. 'Tis becoming as common here,' he told Harry, 'to distinguish between men and women whether they be under a covenant of grace or a covenant of works, as in other countries whether they be Protestants or Papists.'"

"Winthrop wrote that in his *Journal,*" Chuck said accusingly.

"Have you read Winthrop's *Journal?*" Liz demanded, obviously trying to trap Anne and prove that her knowledge was acquired second-hand.

"How could I?" Anne frowned at her. "Master Winthrop scarcely spoke to me. Until Robert told me yesterday, I knew not that Master Winthrop kept a journal. I can assure you that most of the people in Boston were not happy with Master Winthrop and it got much worse. When Peter Buckley was ordained at the Salem meetinghouse, neither Harry, John-Luv, nor Johnny went there to wish him a good ministry. But despite Master Winthrop, most of the freemen from Boston arrived in New Town early in the morning on May 17, 1637, before the Court of Elections was called into session. Will Aspinwall was determined to get our petition in favor of Johnny read before the election, and Harry tried to force the magistrates to consider the petition before the election. More than five hundred men, women, and children were milling around outside the meetinghouse. Most of us were agreeing with Harry, but then Master Wilson climbed out on the limb of a big oak tree and started to shout 'Proceed to the election. Proceed to the election. The new Court and governor will take care of the petition after that.'"

Anne shook her head. "They did, and we lost. Harry, by his own choice, was no longer governor. Master Winthrop was elected, and Master Dudley was made his deputy. Will Coddington was not reelected, nor was Richard Dummer, our friend from Newbury. When the results were announced, Edward, Will's brother, who had been one of the honor guard for Harry, was so angry that he, along with other flagbearers for the governor, threw their halberds on the ground and refused to escort Master Winthrop.

"The next day, back in Boston, Will Coddington called a meeting of the freemen and they agreed to defy the Court. They sent Harry, Will Coddington, and Atherton Hough back to New Town to represent us. But Master Winthrop refused to let them be seated. He claimed that all the Boston freemen had not been notified of the Boston election, and therefore the election was not valid."

Anne laughed. "So we immediately called another election and then the Court had to let them sit. One good thing happened. They let Master Wilson draw lots to see who would serve as chaplain on an expedition to fight the Pequods in Connecticut. Master Wilson lost, and he had to march with the militia. He did not return until August. Then the Court called Johnny before them once again, but this time Johnny frightened them. He refused to admit that he was guilty. He threatened to appeal their verdict to King Charles. 'If I be guilty of sedition,' he told them, 'do not wait. Put me to death now.' The Court refused to retract, but once again they deferred passing sentence on Johnny until the next meeting of the Court in August.

"But they were all aware that a shipload of Johnny's friends and mine were sailing from England and were due to arrive in Boston quite soon. They knew we would have many more people on our side, so Master Dudley proposed that they pass an alien law. Harry fought against it tooth and nail, but we only had three people on our side in the Court. The law was passed. New arrivals could not stay in the Colony more than three weeks. They could not purchase any lands or houses without permission of the local council and two magistrates."

"That was the kiss of death," I explained. "If you arrived in Boston in those days and couldn't get a little help from your friends, you couldn't survive the first year. Coming to New England would be like taking a trip to the moon, if it is ever colonized, and being rejected by those who got there ahead of you and live safely in huge plastic enclosures with their own oxygen."

"What happened during that summer?" Chuck asked. "It seems incredible to me that Winthrop didn't shut you and your brother-in-law up."

"I was very active," Anne said smiling. "For two weeks in June I stayed at our farm in Mt. Wolleystone helping Mary, Johnny's wife, until her baby, a dear little girl was born, but the truth is that Master Winthrop dared not trump our ace. Just so long as dear Harry remained in Boston, we were safe. To top it, Jimmy Ley, Lord Ley's son who was the Earl of Marlborough, arrived in Boston. He was five years younger than Harry, but Master Winthrop had always been very cautious with Harry and now there was another son of a royal family in Boston. Harry was already very incensed with Master Winthrop because of the alien act, and he warned Jimmy that he would quickly discover that Boston was no Utopia. 'People here are so concerned with their fortunes,' he told Jimmy, 'that most of the time they completely forget God and the Holy Spirit.'

"Harry convinced Jimmy to ignore Master Winthrop, and when Master Winthrop arrived back in Boston after a tour of the Colony that he had made, he discovered that Jimmy was staying at Sam Cole's Inn. Master Winthrop immediately tried to have Jimmy move into his own house, which was just down the street and where he would have a much nicer room, but Jimmy told him that he was quite happy where he was. Then, Mr. Winthrop announced a welcoming party for Lord Ley at his house, but the guest of honor never arrived."

Anne chuckled. "Early that morning Harry, Jimmy, Will, and I sailed across the bay to Sam Maverick's house on Noddle Island. By afternoon the Coddingtons and the Coggeshalls arrived, and at least ten other Bostonians with their wives. Jimmy learned that evening that not all of the Colonists were Puritans or acted like Masters Winthrop, Dudley, and Endicott."

Anne was silent for a moment as Liz served ice cream and we all noticed tears in her eyes. "I mean not to weary you with all this. I used to tell my mom, Bridget, who was always talking about what went on at the Court when Henry was king, 'Who cares? King Henry is dead and gone to Hell—if there is a Hell.'"

Anne sighed. "Those last days before Harry and Jimmy left for England were sad days. On August 3rd, I rode with them out to a ship that was waiting in the harbor. I told Harry that I would sorely miss him, and sometimes I wondered what I was fighting for. With him, I was alive and aware of the spirit dwelling within me. I loved Will, but I needed a friend to think with, and I could no longer count on John-Luv. Of course, I never told Harry that I had slept with John." She smiled at Liz's and Barb's tight-lipped expressions. "Actually I had not been betwixt John-Luv's legs for the past year."

"Are you telling us that you actually went to bed with John Cotton, the minister?" Liz asked. Her eyebrows were grim parentheses of doubt. "I can't believe that."

"I care not what you believe," Anne said coolly. "But I did, and I did again before I was called before the General Court, and quite a few times between November of 1637 and March of 1638, before we left for Portsmouth."

She laughed. "Dear Robert is nudging my foot. Methinks he is trying to tell me to keep my mouth closed. But I am not ashamed of loving John-Luv or Harry. I wil never forget my last day alone with Harry. Two days before he sailed, Harry took a long walk with me through the marshes on the Boston side of the Charles River. He was exceedingly wroth about the slaughter of the Pequods. Our little army of less than one hundred and fifty men, plus the Narragansetts, had killed more than seven hundred Pequods. The Narragansetts came back to Boston proudly displaying the hands and heads of the Pequods that they had severed. They had captured hundreds of Pequod women and children. They branded them so they could tell them from the Narragansetts and sold them as slaves. The magistrates were jubilant over the victory, but like Harry and me, John was horrified. He preached a sermon based on Numbers 27, which says that the rulers of the people should consult with the ministers before taking justice into their own hands.

"Talking, holding hands, Harry kept telling me for the hundredth time that I should return to England and escape the savagery of the Puritans, who were as ruthless with God's creatures as were the Indians. I knew that Harry and I would make love. We were alone in a world filled with egrets, gulls, tiny fish, and strange slimy creatures crawling out of the river to look around. Beneath our feet were thick, sun-washed grass and soft mud."

Anne smiled at Chuck. "I told you that I like to feel water all over my body, embracing me. A mud bath is a joy too. Harry coated me with mud, and I him, and I fashioned his pizzle into a huge black cannon pointing at the sky. 'Tis big enough to shoot Master Winthrop right out of Boston,' I told him. Harry thought that would be a terrible waste of powder from his cannon and balls. He held my muddy con and told me this was a happier place to go shooting. So after we carefully washed each other off in the river and stretched out naked together under the Lord's sun, Harry fired his cannon inside me." Anne laughed. "Not once, but three times that lovely afternoon."

"And you didn't get pregnant?" Barb asked, shaking her head in disbelief.

"I would have been overjoyed to have had Harry's child, but the Lord decided otherwise."

Liz joined the probe. "The history books say that you were pregnant at your trial. That was in November, just a few months after Harry Vane left."

"I was not pregnant at the Court trial in November," Anne said emphatically. "I got pregnant the next year in February, but the child formed in me was not Harry's seed nor Will's." She smiled sadly. "It left my womb September 12, 1638, two months before its time. Like John's love for me, it was not fully formed. I had been ill for nearly two weeks before it was born. Janey Hawkins was with me, but Will did not trust her medicine, nor mine. John Clarke, a doctor, lived near us. Unfortunately, he was present when my water broke and then the seed and the egg that never became a child poured out of me. John Clarke saw the pieces and lumps. He insisted on counting them. Twenty-seven. Some as big as a fist, some no bigger than the top of a thumb."

She shook her head. "I'm sorry. This is not nice mealtime conversation." She shrugged. "Janey and I knew that not all God sows, or lets his creatures sow, are born perfect. But men never blame themselves for strange events. I heard later that Doctor Clarke described the birth to Master Winthrop in horrible detail, and Master Winthrop told John-Luv. I heard that John agreed with him that it must be Satan's work, and that I was a witch. Then I heard that John had preached a sermon about it, and I grew very angry. I wrote him a letter and told him the truth. It was his child. He had seeded me in March in his own house, where I had been allowed to stay a week while he and Master Davenport tried to get me to repent of my heresies. It was a week I shall never forget, but I do not wish to remember it now." She smiled at Dave and changed the subject. "Thou art a doctor. Do not women have such births today?"

"How old were you?" Dave asked.

"Forty-six that July."

"After fifteen children, you were past childbearing. You had a menopausal conception. Doctors call it a hydatidiform mole." Dave nodded at me, and I knew he was thinking that Anne was a fascinating psychiatric case. "I really hope that you will bring Anne over to the Institute tomorrow," he said. "I'm sure that we could help her."

"Help me?" Anne stared at him.

"Help bring the two aspects of yourself together. I accept the fact that you have lived before as Anne Hutchinson. But somewhere inside you is a very real twentieth-century woman whom you are ignoring. We'll put the two aspects of yourself together and get you back to your present life. You may somewhere have a husband and a family who are worried about you."

"You do not believe me?" Anne said coldly. Her familiar *thou* had disappeared, and her voice was suddenly remote and disdainful.

"Of course I believe you. But not that you have risen from the grave."

"I never said that I had risen from the grave. My spirit, the light within me, was released from my body by fire. Like you, I believed not that I would ever return to earth in the same corruptible body. Being born again in a new body—reincarnation is easier to accept. But if the Lord can give a soul a new body, is it not possible, if he wished, that he could recreate a former body. In all the world are there not many people who resemble one another?"

"You may be right," Chuck said approvingly and trying to ease the tension. "I'm sure that even for God there are only so many variations on a theme. Of all the billions of bodies that have lived and disappeared from the earth, why shouldn't there be many bodies duplicating any of us? Statistically, enough time has passed. The averages for resurrection may be coming on line."

Dave chuckled. "I'm Jewish. I'm still waiting for the Messiah. But in the meantime, I would like to check you out at the Institute. You may be sure that if I don't do it and if you appear on television, you're going to be besieged by medical men."

Anne smiled. "I will let Robert decide if I should visit your bedlam for the insane."

"Does he own you?"

Her eyes twinkling, Anne stared at Dave. "Methinks he does. Without dear Robert, I would not be here. I am certain that the spirit within Robert is the same spirit that was within my husband, Will. Unlike you, Robert has taken me for better or worse."

I laughed. "All right, Dave," I said, "Anne and I will meet you tomorrow at the Institute in Cambridge. I'm going to take her to the First Parish Church in the morning. We can be there sometime later, between twelve-thirty and one. But you must agree to one condition: at no time do either you or Barb interview Anne alone or subject her to any of your gadgets unless I agree and unless I am present."

It was eleven o'clock. Chuck and Liz wanted Anne to continue her story, but I told them they would have to wait until another time.

"What makes you think there will be another time?" Liz asked me sardonically. I knew she was really asking how I was going to carry on a three-way romance when Emily got home. I didn't answer. How could I? I was living one day at a time.

29

I awoke early Sunday morning dimly aware that Anne's behind was no longer spooned into my stomach. Lying on her back, she was staring at the ceiling in what seemed like a self-induced trance. I asked her what she was thinking about. She didn't answer, but her hand slipped over my stomach and grapsed my penis, which immediately grew firm between her fingers.

"Speak not," she whispered. "Merge with me in the Holy Spirit."

Between her legs I was quickly immersed in the warmth of her vagina. Her eyes were closed and she lay silently beneath me. Lying in her arms for a long time, our breathing and heartbeats became matched rhythms. Her vaginal muscles nursed me ever so gently.

Finally she said, "Thank thee, dear Robert. Did you hear Him speaking?"

"What did He tell you?" I asked, thinking that she must be having some kind of mystical experience with her inner self, something that she called a revelation.

Eyes closed, she answered: "The voice saith to me, 'After eons of created time, which is less than the wink of an eye to me, my creatures still deny me. This is the choice I gave them. But denying me, they deny themselves. The time that is left to them is like unto a leaf on a tree."

She stared at me through tear-filled eyes. I kissed them a little dubiously. Making love to a woman who is communing with her maker is a shivery experience. "What did He look like?" I asked.

"I told thee," she said quietly. "The Lord and His Holy Spirit hath no image. To hear Him, thou must let thyself be a sponge absorbing His light and love." She kissed me fervently. "I pray that thou wilt learn how."

"Did He tell you why you are here?"

She nodded. "I must teach many people that there is time remaining. They can save themselves from those who deny the Lord. They must reject all leaders who would destroy them. They must lay down their arms and beat them into ploughshares."

"That's a very old song," I told her sadly. "Right out of Isaiah. Today, most of us have no arms to lay down, and we can't control the weapons and armies our governments torment us with."

"But people like thee and me make guns and cannons and bullets and powders, don't we?"

No one could deny that. "Every year the nations of the world spend trillions of dollars on missiles and nuclear bombs and airplanes and submarines and battleships."

"But the leaders make them not themselves!" Anne's eyes were dancing with the excitement of her still unexpressed idea. "Doth thou understand? That is why I have returned to earth. I must address the little people of the world—those that have no power—like many of those who came to my home to hear me. I must tell them they must no longer make weapons to kill each other. They must not let their governments make the weapons."

I was about to tell her that she was no David, that her resurrection was not the kind of slingshot that would destroy the Goliath of nuclear destruction looming over the world, but the telephone rang. Wondering who would be calling at seven-thirty in the morning, I answered it belligerently.

"It's Keith Munson." Keith was the minister of the First Parish Unitarian Universalist Church in Quincy. He apologized for calling so early, but when he said, "I hope I didn't interrupt anything between you and your lady friend," I'm sure that he was grinning. "Liz just phoned me. She's all excited about your guest from another world. She said that you were bringing her to church this morning. Liz said that last night she was about to tell all of you about the banishment of John Wheelwright, but you took her home. Chuck said you couldn't wait to get to bed with her."

"Chuck was daydreaming that he was going to take her to bed," I said sarcastically.

"It occurred to me," Keith said, and I noticed that he was being careful not to say her name, "that your friend might like to tell her story to the entire congregation—right from the pulpit."

"I gave a sermon on that subject last January," I said. "It's old hat." While I had no idea what new revelations she might make, I was pretty sure that Anne's version of the banishment of Wheelwright, the first minister of what was now the Quincy Unitarian Universalist Church, would probably shock some of the older members. Anne had already proved that she had no inhibitions about revealing details of her extramarital love life.

"But you weren't there," Keith laughed, "unless there're things you haven't told me about your previous life."

"I'm sure that you don't believe that she was there either."

Keith chuckled. "If I did, I'd have to find a new church. But I have an open mind."

I kept thinking I should tell him no, but then I remembered Dave Hedman's question to Anne, "Does he own you?" and Anne's conviction that she came with a special mission to earth. "She's not a Unitarian," I warned him. "But she's not afraid of people. It's up to her. But if she does agree, don't call the newspapers. This is for members only."

I gave Anne the phone and told her that Keith was a minister. She smiled into it as if he could see her and I knew that she was impressed. Listening to Keith trying to convince her, she kept nodding and she finally said, "I enjoy talking to people about the Lord and the Holy Spirit and God's grace." She looked at me. "Mr. Munson wants me to take his place in the pulpit and tell the people what happened in Boston before Johnny and I were banished. He wants us to come to his office before services so that we can become acquainted with one another."

Shrugging, I took the phone and told Keith that we would be there. I warned him that though Anne was not a Unitarian, her belief in the covenant of grace created a new kind of moral environment that evoked the kind of questions being asked by Jerry Falwell and the Southern Baptist evangelists. Can a society of humanists and Unitarian Universalists and people like Anne Hutchinson, who do not believe in Hell and damnation for their sins, and who do not constantly work and pray for their salvation because they think God has given it to them already—can such a society survive against the new Spartans, the Soviets, who in many respects are more puritanical than the founders of the Massachusetts Bay Colony were?

I was sure of one thing. Men and women might give lip service to Anne's loving God, and they might be momentarily astounded that God could resurrect one of His creations, but the only God who could make most people truly believe in Him was one who could hurl a thunderbolt at them and destroy them instantly.

I was trying to explain this to Anne when Saul and Susan Weiss arrived. I hadn't expected them so early. Anne was making breakfast, trying to assure me that I would like hasty pudding, which I discovered was simply cornmeal mixed with boiling salted water that turned into a mush when it was cooked for thirty minutes.

Watching her make the concoction, Susan, a laughing, brown-eyed woman with a sweet and naive oval face, told us that she was twenty-two. She was majoring in astrophysics at Boston University. She hugged Anne and told her, "Thank you for letting me come. I love Saul and sleep with him, but until Thursday when he met you at Lord & Taylor's, I wasn't sure that I would like living with a lawyer all my life. Most lawyers have no imagination. They live like gods in their tiny pragmatic world of rules and precedents and they think that is all there is. They think the world and the universe revolves around them. Saul surprised me. He still doesn't believe in God, but he believes in you. He can't stop talking about you. I think he loves you." She grinned at Anne. "I wouldn't share my man with every woman, but I'll share him with you."

While we were eating the hasty pudding covered with milk and sweetened with maple syrup, Susan told us that even though man had been studying the stars and the galaxies for thousands of years, we still didn't know very much about the cosmos. "If it all began," she said, "about fifteen billion years ago, with a big bang, then the people who wrote Genesis weren't too far from the truth—except for their timetable, and the length of time it took all life forms to evolve."

"Do you believe in God?" Anne asked. She was obviously fascinated with Susan.

Susan nodded. "Do you understand what a billion is? I don't. It would take your entire lifetime, day and night, to count to one billion. We now believe that the universe is fifteen billion years old and will probably continue for at least fifteen billion more years. In just one star out there, a minor one like the sun, there are a thousand billion, billion, billion, billion, billion, billion atoms to hold it together. In your body are a hundred trillion microscopic cells." Susan grinned at Anne. "Only God can understand numbers like that. But I'm not sure whether He cares how any aspect of Himself, including us, interact." She stared at Anne. "I can't believe that you are fifty-two. Saul is right. You have an inner glow," she sighed. "I want to believe you lived before. If somewhere there is a God who has some control over these overwhelming numbers, then I believe that the chance of anyone returning to life is not impossible."

Anne squeezed her hand. "I understand not your numbers. I can scarcely think of even one thousand. Methinks, thy God and mine are the same. I sense God's inner light shining in thee."

I told Saul and Susan what had happened last night at the Johnsons'. Saul wasn't pleased that I had agreed to let Dave Hedman examine Anne. "Anne's not something you can prove," he said. "She's something you believe in or you don't." Saul was happier when I told him that I wanted him and Susan to come with us and watch. He told us that he was even more dubious about the Sally Lane show. I explained that Anne was curious about both.

"I told Susan that Anne and you obviously need reinforcements," he said. "Anne simply doesn't know enough about this world, or how cynical people are. We've got to orient her before Sally Lane and the whole world try to dissect her."

I decided not to tell Saul and Susan about Anne's revelation this morning. Although I agreed with Saul that Anne seemed like an innocent lamb about to play with wolves, I reminded him, "She's a very cool lady. Wolves might frighten her, but men and women don't. She proved that at her trials."

30

We entered the church through the parish hall. Except for the choir, which we could hear practicing, there was no one in the sanctuary. Anne was awed by the stone temple, which was built of granite donated by John Adams and his son, John Quincy Adams, nearly two centuries ago. But the fact that two former presidents of the United States were buried in the crypt did not impress her. Presidents she understood not. But a choir singing joyful hymns and the sounds of an organ fascinated her.

"Johnny would be amazed," she told Keith, who was waiting for us in his office. "Everything changes. Johnny would not believe that there could be happy singing in such a grand church at Mt. Wolleystone. Even John-Luv would be surprised. This church is nearly as big as St. Botolph's in Old Boston."

She shrugged. "But Johnny would know that this was not his chapel of ease. We walked through the woods to his meetinghouse and when you got there you could see through the cracks in the walls and the benches we sat on were on a hard dirt floor." She smiled at Keith, who was shaking his head in astonishment. Her musical voice and the hypnotic warmth of her green eyes enveloped him.

Then to our surprise, she questioned Keith in some detail about Unitarians. He told her that the successor church to her meetinghouse, the First Church in Boston, still existed and was Unitarian Universalist. "Two hundred years after John Cotton wrote *The Way of the Congregational Churches Cleared,*" Keith said, "and for a period of nearly fifty years most everyone who lived in Boston no longer believed in the Trinity. But as you say, nothing lasts. Now there are very few Unitarians or Universalists. Jesus Christ and the Holy Ghost are back in style."

Anne shrugged, and it was obvious that she still wasn't afraid of challenging ministers. "But they are not three separate things, Master Munson. They are all manifestations of the Lord."

Keith smiled at her. "In a few minutes you can tell the congregation what you believe. Unitarian Universalists are open-minded. We may not believe you, but we won't banish you."

"I fear that I am not a learned preacher as you are."

"That's not the way I read it in the history books." Keith held up a book that was on his desk. "Chuck Johnson loaned me this. It was written by Edward Johnson, who Chuck says is another of his many Johnson relatives. Edward Johnson lived in Boston in the seventeenth century. 'These Sectaries,' Keith said, reading from the book (he still was not referring to Anne by name, as if saying her name would confirm her reality) 'these dissenters—especially the female sex—had many knacks to delude you with. They told revelations of things to come from the spirit. It was designed to weaken the word of the Lord in the mouth of his ministers . . .' 'Come along with me,' one man told Johnson, 'I'll bring you a woman that preaches better gospel than any of the black coats that have been to a Ninny-versity. A woman of another kind of spirit who hath many revelations of things to come. For my part, I'd rather hear such a woman speak from the mere motion of spirit, without any study at all, than to hear any of your learned scholars though they may be fuller of scripture.'"

Anne was smiling at him as he read. "The man who wrote that liked me not. But I had many friends who were not prejudiced because they loved me."

Before Saul, Susan, and I left them and went into the sanctuary to find a pew, I told Keith that we had a very busy schedule today and I didn't want to subject Anne to questions at the coffee hour after the service. But he wasn't sure that we could escape quickly. We found seats behind Chuck and Liz. A few minutes later as the voices in the choir faded away, Keith walked into the church. Holding Anne's arm, he led her to a chair beneath the pulpit.

There was a murmur of interest from the hundred or more members who were absorbed by Anne's smile and her classic beauty. But Keith waited to introduce her until he had completed the first part of the service. Then, guiding Anne up the stairs to the high pulpit that gave speakers who occupied it a sense of divine power—minor gods speaking for God—he showed Anne where to sit down. Momentarily, she was not visible while Keith introduced her.

"This morning, I have a surprise for you," he said. "Last night, the very pretty woman who is here in the pulpit with me, was a guest at the home of Elizabeth and Charles Johnson. According to Liz, who telephoned me early this morning, this woman knows more about the first minister of this church, John Wheelwright, than anyone alive. She is a friend of Bob Rimmer's. To be honest, I know very little about her or why she has come to Quincy. But I have decided on this Palm Sunday, rather than deliver a sermon on the theme of resurrection that is printed in your program, to let her tell you about herself and our first pastor, the Reverend John Wheelwright, whom she calls Johnny. She also knows a great deal about Reverend John Cotton, whom she calls John-Luv—suggesting a friendship with that Puritan preacher that seems to be intimate as well as ministerial."

Keith beamed down at the laughter. "I'm sure that very few Unitarian Universalists believe in the literal resurrection of Jesus or that you personally may return from the grave. But, according to Liz and Chuck, this woman, who claims she lived three hundred and fifty years ago here in Quincy and in Boston, may change your mind."

Anne stood up. Smiling confidently at the rapt faces beneath her, she said, "I am happy the Lord has brought me here. I am Anne Hutchinson. If a man had stood up in our meetinghouse in Boston between 1634 and 1638, when I lived there, and said, 'I am Jesus Christ, I have come here to save you,' Mr. Winthrop would have called his honor guard and had him evicted from the church and put in jail. As much as Puritans believed in Jesus, if this man had not admitted that he was lying, they might have hung him on Boston Common, or at the very least banished him from the Colony. They banished my brother-in-law, John Wheelwright, and me for much lesser heresies, which they called blasphemy and erroneous opinions. I am not Jesus Christ. And as you can see I am not a man. But whether you believe that I have returned from the grave or believe in Jesus, or believe as I do that God can only reveal Himself to us through an eternal Jesus whose image has been within us since He first created man and woman, doth not matter. Master Munson hath told me that the Lord speaketh directly to Unitarians. If that be so, I hope that you are aware of the inner light within you. Accepting God's grace maketh you and He one."

Anne smiled. "While dear Johnny was cautious about my revelations, I can assure you that like me, he believed that once you are deeply aware of God's inner light within you, His grace overflows for you and your salvation is assured. Mister Munson told me that I have only twenty minutes to speak to you. I know not what you may have heard or read about me, but I believe that a person reveals his love for God by his love for others. God manifested Jesus as a man to tell us this. And God feareth not when our spiritual love becomes mixed with an earthly love. Neither Master Winthrop, nor Master Dudley, nor most of the ministers in the Colony understood what loving truly meaneth, or that I could still love them although I told them they were not sealed in the spirit."

Anne paused. "But I did not love them with an earthly love as I did my husband, Will, and John-Luv. The truth is, though I have never told another soul, if I had not had an earthly love for John-Luv—Master Cotton—in addition to my Will, I would not have been able to resist dear Johnny. During many of the long days and nights we spent together studying Scripture, we were close to the point where our joy in Christ could easily have been consummated in bed." Anne smiled. "Not that Johnny and I could have lived together. Johnny was certain that two preachers under one roof would be one too many."

Ignoring the happy laughter, knowing she had her audience enraptured, Anne continued: "Last night, I told Master and Mistress Johnson about Johnny's Fast Day Sermon and how he finally was accused of blasphemy and sedition by the General Court. But the magistrates were afraid to pass sentence on him. They knew that most of the freemen of Boston believed that Johnny was a true minister of God.

"John-Luv was exceedingly unhappy with me. He kept telling me that because of my beliefs in an eternal Christ, I was partially to blame. He told me that I was sounding more and more like my friend Samuel Gorton, who had arrived in Boston a year before. But Sam did not stay there long. He went to Plymouth, not realizing that the Separatists would not tolerate a thinking person either.

"John-Luv never came to any meetings at my home, but he felt certain that I was giving my own version of his sermons and new meanings to the many friends who gathered in my home twice a week to discuss his and other ministers' sermons. He was certain that if Johnny were banished from Boston, it would be my fault. But I told him that he need not vex himself. It was obvious to all that he was protecting his own sweet arse. On Sunday, July 16, after his sermon, John-Luv spent an hour trying to prove that he and Master Wilson did not truly disagree. 'Faith in Christ is an empty urn filled with oil—meaning good works,' John told everybody, 'but the oil cannot be poured without the urn.' But the next week he switched himself completely around and admitted that 'a person must see nothing in himself, have nothing, do nothing, but to stand still and wait for Christ to do it all.'" Anne smiled. "If that confuseth you, so did it me because 'twas what I had told everybody that he had been saying all along."

"Master Shepherd and Master Buckley, ministers from Cambridge and Concord, told Master Winthrop that the only way to set matters straight was to call a synod, a conference of ministers from every town in the Colony and to keep it in a session until there was agreement on what was erroneous thinking and what was not. On August 30th, 1637, twenty-five ministers arrived, but they came not to Boston but New Town. Master Winthrop decided they should hold a synod there to avoid arguments with the Boston rebels like myself and Will Coddington and Will Aspinwall. Johnny and I knew that the purpose of the conference was to pin John-Luv down and determine if he was a heretic like Johnny. At the same time they could marshall more evidence against Johnny, who had refused to retract what he said about God's covenant of grace.

"Within the first week the ministers had compiled eighty-two opinions that they declared were either blasphemous, erroneous, or unsafe. Day after day, they assembled in the New Town meetinghouse, which was open to everyone who could find standing room, and they questioned each other and particularly Johnny and John-Luv. Throughout the proceedings, my name was never mentioned, although it was obvious to all the people from Boston that many of the errors were mine.

"I shall bore you not with all the errors, most of which no one understood and which I do not remember myself. But they were particularly incensed over Error 40, which propounded a testimony of the spirit and a voice into one's soul that is immediate and does not depend on the scriptural word or any knowledge of it. Another error that angered them was 'The revelation of a person's good estate, without reference to the Scriptures, is as clear to him or her as the voice of God from Heaven to Paul.' Another error stated that 'No minister can convey more of Christ to another person than he hath expressed himself' and another stated that 'The Holy Spirit doth not work in hypocrites because of gifts or graces. But in God's children, those who recognize the indwelling light, it is immediate.'"

Anne paused with a little chuckle. "To all of these supposed errors, I wanted to stand up and say amen, but I kept my mouth closed. I told Johnny that I could only laugh when they claimed that 'To take delight in the Holy service of God is to go whoring from God, or denying the resurrection of the body meant the kingdom of Heaven was at hand,' and if that was true, then men and women could go to bed with whomever they pleased without marrying. I wanted to tell them if that was what whoring and resurrection meant, then I was a whore and I believed in resurrection.

"Johnny told me that I was lucky that only freeman could speak or ask questions. Day after day, Johnny and I rode horseback to New Town from Boston. It surprised many of the ladies of the Colony, who had never seen a woman with her legs spread in a saddle. Some days the ministers got so angry with each other and with the freemen that Master Winthrop, who attended every session, warned them if a civil disturbance occurred among them this was no longer church business and the magistrates would take action.

"Right up to the last week in September, John-Luv managed to keep straddling the fence. He agreed that some sanctification occurred through good works and though it was not always apparent, good works were coexistent with the recognition of the Holy Spirit."

Anne paused. "Johnny was angry that they had spent so much time creating a tempest in a teapot. He refused to agree. He insisted that God gave his saving grace to saints and sinners alike. Then all of the ministers agreed, taking aim at me, that private meetings in private homes to discuss a minister's sermons or failings were disorderly and without rule. But Johnny told them that good ministers should not be afraid to learn what their congregation thought about the Lord and whether their preaching were true or not.

"So they accomplished what they had assembled to do. All the ministers except Johnny were in agreement. Four days later the magistrates startled everyone in the Colony by dissolving the Court that had just been elected in May and calling for a new election. Master Winthrop and Master Dudley were obviously hoping to get rid of any deputies who favored Johnny or me. Fifteen new deputies, nearly half the number on the Court, were elected. The only remaining friends Johnny and I had on the Court were John Coggeshall, Will Aspinwall, and Will Coddington. When the Court convened again on November 2nd, they were ready to cut off Johnny's head. Two weeks later, the night we buried poor Mary Dyer's half-formed baby, John warned me if I did not repent I was next on the agenda."

Anne paused and it was obvious that she had been watching the clock. "I have fifteen minutes left. I can see my dear friend Robert down there shaking his head and telling me to be careful what I say. But a few days ago in his home, I read in Master Winthrop's *Journal* the disgusting things he had written about Mary Dyer's baby. I will not repeat them to you. They would make you feel very ill. Though it now be like the snows of yesteryear, I should like to tell you quickly what happened that night.

"I loved Mary Dyer. She was only twenty-two, young enough to be my daughter. She was closer to me than any of my children except my dear son Francis. Mary was expecting her third child in the middle of December. I had already scolded her husband, William. ''Tis too soon,' I had told him. But of course by then it was too late. Poor Mary already had a child three years old, another one only two, and a baby seven months. 'After this one,' I told William. 'Tie a knot in your pizzle—or sleep in another bed.' But I could not in truth blame him. Mary was so beautiful. If I were a man, I would have wanted to play seesaw with her every night."

Anne grinned at the laughter. "My dear friend Robert telleth me that I have much to learn about your world, but I am happy to have learned one thing already. Playing seesaw hath not changed. Despite your many wonders, none are more wondrous than a man and woman merging their flesh with each other. But the Lord who hath made us doth not help us plant His seed, nor doth He always make sure that the earth we plant it in is ready to receive it. Two months before the baby was due, my friend Janey Hawkins, whom Master Winthrop, had he been a Papist, would have waved a cross at because he was sure that she was a witch, arrived at my front door at six o'clock in the evening. 'Mary is laboring,' Janey cried, 'and the poor baby is hipling.'"

"Janey and I ran all the way down High Street to Mary's little house next to the cow pond. It was bitterly cold, and I was shocked to find a neighbor's of Mary's, Betty Webb, was there, screaming and making more noise than Mary, who was moaning. Betty was not helping her or even tending the fire. I knew that unless we turned the baby and got it out of Mary's womb that she would die. I knew that we could not save the baby. Reaching deep within her, I found the baby's head and very slowly, while Janey spooned some strong liquors in Mary's mouth, I turned it."

Anne paused and we could all see tears streaming down her cheeks. Keith handed her his handkerchief. With a little sob, she continued. "I knew that my fingers were tearing the child apart but there was no stopping. An hour later Janey and I got it all out in bits and pieces.

"Watching us, Betty screamed, "Tis not human! 'Tis a monster! You must report it.'"

"'That's stupid,' I told her. 'Just keep your mouth shut. Mary miscarried. Many women do that and no record is kept. If it had come normally, it would not have lived. I care not what the laws of man may be. This is no man's business.' But Betty kept staring at the bloody mess and insisting that it was a birth that must be reported. Mary was finally asleep. William had appeared and was holding her hand, feeling wrought up about the problems he had caused. It was only six-thirty in the evening. I told them all to stay with Mary, and I walked more than a shivery mile up the hill to John-Luv's house to ask him what to do."

Anne paused and continued with a little sob. "I had not talked exceedingly much with John-Luv nor been alone with him for nearly three months, even though I probably kept him awake at night vexed about what I was saying about him. I knew that he perchance would have liked to spank me, but he could not help himself. He often told me, 'The only way I know how to seal thy mouth is with kisses.'

"That night, when he opened his door and took me into his study, even before I could tell him why I was there, he hugged and kissed me fervently. When I finally caught my breath and told him why I had come, and that we could not make love, he smiled forlornly. 'Dear Anne, thou art my *bête noir,*' he said. 'Thou must know that thou art in deep trouble. In two weeks when the Court reassembles, I am certain they are going to banish John Wheelwright along with Master Coggeshall and Master Aspinwall, and they may even try to get rid of Master Coddington, if they dare. After that, they are going to examine you and force you to tell in public what you truly believe.'

"John was trembling. He held me hard against him, his hands pressing my bum to him. 'I feareth that I may lose thee. If Mistress Webb doth not keep her mouth shut about Mary Dyer's baby and tells everybody that you and Goody Hawkins helped give birth to a monster, the Court will be sure that you are all witches.' He smiled limply at me, and tears were dribbling down his cheeks. 'Maybe 'tis true,' he said. 'Thou hast bewitched me for nearly ten years. I love thee, Anne. I will never testify against thee. Tonight I pray thee come back here with me. I need to lose myself in thee.'"

Anne sighed. "So with John's blessing and help we buried the remains of Mary's baby, and John-Luv tried to frighten Betty Webb so that she would keep her mouth shut. But a year later, when I was safely on the Isle of Aquiday, and Betty was repenting ever having known me, she told Master Winthrop what happened. They dug up the remains, and according to Master Winthrop, they found horns, claws, scales—the remains of a monster. Betty told them that when the baby died, Satan himself was present, and she could smell him, and Mary was shaking and shivering and everyone watching was vomiting and shitting.

"Two weeks later, on November 2nd, the new General Court met in New Town. Before the morning was over, the magistrates questioned whether Will Aspinwall and John Coggeshall had signed the petition favoring John Wheelwright, and whether having dishonored the Court they should be allowed to sit. An hour later only Will Coddington, whom they were still afraid of because he was very rich, remained on the Court to fight for Johnny and me. The Court then summoned Johnny from Mt. Wolleystone and me from Boston to appear the next Tuesday, November 7th.

"It was a cold, snowy day, and Johnny, who rode from Mt. Wolleystone to New Town, a three-hour journey, was late. Johnny insisted that the Court had not proved him guilty of either sedition or contempt, but the magistrates were not listening. Master Winthrop pronounced sentence for the Court. 'Master John Wheelwright,' he said, 'being formally convicted of contempt and sedition, and now justifying himself in his former practice, being to the disturbance of the civil peace, he is by the court disenfranchised, and banished, having fourteen days to settle his affairs, and if within that time he depart not the patent, he promises to render himself to Master Stoughton at his house, to be kept until he is disposed of.'"

Anne smiled at the congregation. "It was the same time in the morning as it is now, eleven-thirty. My turn was next. But I have not time to tell you about that. Thank you for hearing me. May you discover the light of God within you."

31

Thinking about it now, I am convinced that Anne's cool response to the mind-bending onslaught of the next forty-eight hours proved as conclusively as Dave Hedman's physical examination that Anne was in many ways beyond the human.

I had promised Dave that we would arrive in Cambridge at the Institute between twelve-thirty and one, but when Anne finished her little sermon there was no way to escape fifty or more spellbound Unitarians, many of whom were obviously shocked at her comfortable relationship with a nonjudgmental Holy Spirit within her.

She happily answered dozens of questions that covered every aspect of her previous life and the life of the Puritans in Boston. One woman asked her a question that hadn't occurred to me before, "How did you feel when you discovered that you were still alive?"

"I was exceedingly frightened," Anne told her. "First methought I must be waking from a terrible nightmare and that the Indians who had set me on fire were all part of a dream. Then, I thought that somehow I had escaped them but they might still be lurking in the shadows. But if it were a dream, why was I not waking in my own bed? Methinks, now, that dying is a stripping off of one's corruptible body. The inner light within you finally rejoins the everlasting light of the Lord. But, now, for reasons of His own, the Lord has poured me back into the mold that once was me and has given me back His light."

She smiled lovingly at me, and I knew it was time to leave before she went into greater detail. But it was too late. "Even so," she continued, "I would have perished in the cold March wind and snow, but then I saw a light in the window of a house. When my dear friend Robert opened the door, I knew that the Lord had chosen him for my protector."

"What were you wearing when Bob found you?" The questioner, a man, grinned at me.

Laughing, Anne said, "When you are born again, it will be as the first time. I was naked. The Lord doth not worry about clothes. Man does."

Finally, with Saul chauffeuring and Susan in the front seat, we drove to

Cambridge in my car. Susan was fascinated with Anne's story about Mary Dyer's baby. She couldn't believe that a year later Winthrop and the magistrates had dug up the remains. She told Anne that nearly fifty years after she died, Cotton Mather—son of John Cotton's wife, Sarah, by a second marriage after John had died—had spent a good part of his life persecuting witches. Cotton Mather thought witches were the Devil's legions incarnate, sent by the Devil "to blow up or pull down all the churches in New England."

"Most men, including Master Winthrop," Anne said, "were convinced that there were two kinds of women. The saintly ones like his wife Margaret, and the Eves and the Liliths like me and Janey Hawkins and Mary Dyer. Women like us were put on earth by the Lord to tempt good men like him and lead them to their destruction." Anne scowled at her thoughts. "Until I read a few days ago in Mr. Winthrop's *Journal*, I knew not how obsessed he was with the Devil and evil women."

While I listened to her amazed, Anne quoted verbatim from Winthrop's *Journal* what presumably were the words of the woman who had seen the premature birth of Mary Dyer's baby. 'It was a woman child, stillborn, about two months before the just time, having life a few hours before; it came hipling before she turned it.' Anne shrugged. "The *she* he mentions was me, and Master Winthrop knew it. 'It was of ordinary bigness. It had a face but no head and the ears stood upon the shoulders and were like an ape's. It had no forehead, but over the eyes were four horns, hard and sharp; two of them were above one inch long, the other two shorter, the eyes standing out, and the mouth also; the nose hooked upward; all over the breast and back it was full of sharp pricks and scales, like a thornback. The navel and belly, with the distinction of sex were where the back should be, and the back and hips were before where the belly should have been. Between the shoulders, it had two mouths, and in each of them was a piece of red flesh sticking out. It had arms and legs as other children, but instead of toes, it had, one each foot, three claws like a young fowl with sharp talons.'"

Susan listened to Anne horrified, and Saul kept muttering, "Good God." But as Saul turned the car into the grounds of the Hedman Psychiatric Institute, I was once again dubious. I knew that Anne had skimmed through Winthrop's *Journal*, but her ability to quote so perfectly something she had presumably read only once bothered me, and I told her so.

She kissed my cheek. "Dear Robert, thou still doth not believe me, doth thee? Why dost thou not question Master Winthrop? He wrote that a full year later, after Mary's miscarriage. Why should a man describe so precisely something that he never saw? Why should he listen to a silly woman like Betty Webb? I shall tell thee. Because he was terrified by women like me and Mary Dyer. We were not afraid of him, and we knew that many times when he kept staring at us what he was truly thinking. His pizzle was stirring in his pants."

Laughing heartily, Susan applauded her.

"Agreed," I said. "Winthrop was as fascinated by sex as a twentieth-century man. But that doesn't explain your excellent memory."

Anne patted my hand lovingly. "Thou truly art Will." She said. "Will could not believe that I could remember everything I read either. But 'tis true. All I have to do is think of the page I read something on and it comes back into my mind as if it were a real page. Then all I have to do is read it."

We were soon to discover even more startling things about Anne. As I have mentioned, Emily and I had known Dave Hedman for many years. The Institute was his own creation, and it is known and respected throughout the Western world for its successful treatment of many mental problems plaguing modern man. I knew that Dave had expanded the Institute from its original five-story brick hospital building, which offered limited accommodations for patients undergoing extensive treatments, to include fifty or more small cottages that had been integrated into the main building with landscaped walks. But I had not visited the place for more than five years, and I was surprised at the friendly country-club atmosphere of the grounds.

Dave and Barbara were waiting for us in the lobby. I introduced them to Susan and Saul. Leading us to the elevator, Dave told us that the dining room had been rebuilt on the top floor so that it overlooked a completely glass-enclosed swimming pool three floors below it, where all patients received various kinds of soothing water therapy.

"We're quieter here on weekends," Dave told us as we sat down for lunch at a table overlooking the pool, "but with the help of Barb, who can handle all the equipment and is an expert in biofeedback, plus a couple of nurses and a pathologist who is on duty, I'm sure we can give Anne a thorough checkup."

Dave smiled at her. "We're very informal here. I know that you were fascinated with medicine when you lived before," he said obviously trying to make her believe that he accepted her previous life. "But you're going to be amazed to discover how many things we've learned about the human body in the past three centuries. As we go through the various procedures I hope you will ask any questions that may be bothering you. We're going to take samples of your blood and urine, and by testing them we can tell a great deal about the state of your health. We're going to record your heart beats and brain waves and we're going to take an x-ray of your chest and take your blood pressure."

"Methinks you wish to discover whether I am lying," Anne said. Smiling coolly at him, she managed to pick up some chicken salad with her fork and hold it suspended, before she put it in her mouth. "I can save you time. Listen to the Lord within you, and you will know the truth."

"We believe you," Barbara said. "We believe that you are reliving a previous life. All that we would like to do is help you remember your present life."

"If you think she's lying, why don't you try a polygraph machine?" Saul asked.

"We don't have one," David said.

"Thank the Lord that there're some gadgets you don't believe in," I said sarcastically. "But you must admit that most psychiatrists are quick to label mystical experiences as disturbances in thought content. They even break them down into specific styles. There's *ineffability,* one's special experience that cannot be communicated to another. There's *noesis,* which covers revelations and the feeling that one has plumbed the mystery of the universe. There are *transient* and *passive mystical states,* and there's *unio mystica,* an oceanic feeling of oneness with the universe." I shrugged. "From your point of view, probably none of these are normal, and but they don't constitute lying to oneself. Anne thinks she's actually a seventeenth-century lady. But from your point of view, she is a little schizophrenic or has a hysterical disassociated personality."

Dave laughed. "Let's not get arguing the pros and cons of psychiatry," he said. "I told you I am interested in past-lives therapy. Later, I'll be happy to try hypnosis, but I can't work with an audience."

"Maybe she'll hypnotize you," Susan said. "She has me."

I tried to explain to Anne what hypnosis meant. "If Dave can establish a rapport with you, he can put your conscious brain to sleep and get you in touch with the person you really are."

"Do *you* know who you truly are?" Anne asked Dave.

Dave chuckled. "Sometimes I'm not sure."

Three hours later, although neither Dave nor Barbara would admit it, they were more than a little in awe of Anne. Before they led her from room to room in the hospital, they tried to convince me that it would be better if none of us were present since we would represent distracting elements during certain tests. Barbara pointed out that Anne would be wearing a hospital johnny. "It's a gown that doesn't cover you too well," she explained to Anne. "It may be embarrassing to expose yourself to strangers." Barbara gave me a sarcastic smile and gestured at Susan and Saul.

"Robert and Saul have seen me naked," Anne said calmly. "Susan is my friend, too." She smiled archly at a surprised Barbara. "Methinks they believe me and trust me. You and Dave do not. I wish them to be with me."

Anne was delighted when she saw her blood surge into a hypodermic needle. "I told thee," she said to Saul, "if thou cut me, I would bleed." Giving her urine in a jar to Barbara, she said, "I hope that you do not ask me to shit. I did that this morning."

But she didn't understand their surprise when they took her temperature and were unable to get normal oral readings of 98.6 degrees F. The thermometer climbed to 90 F and even after repeated attempts would go no higher. When they told her that they would like to do a rectal reading by inserting a thermometer in her anus, she giggled and told them that she was not embarrassed to show them her bum. "But no man nor woman hath ever touched me there." Her rectal readings were 90.8 F—still far below normal.

Dave admitted that her skin felt cooler than normal, something I could readily attest to, and he kept grumbling that she was so close to hypothermia that her brain shouldn't be functioning. But he finally gave up and strapped a blood-pressure cuff to her arm, and asked her if she knew how her heart pumped blood.

To the surprise of all of us, she nodded. "Papa had a book written by a man that John Calvin burnt at the stake. His name was Michael Servetus. I remember he wrote, 'In a wonderful way the subtle blood is conducted through a long passage from the right ventricle to the lungs where it is rendered light, because bright red in color, and it passes from a vein-like artery into an artery-like vein where it is finally carried into the left ventricle."

"Nice going," Dave chuckled. "That's how your blood becomes saturated with oxygen and keeps you alive. The pressure produced at the peak of the ventricular contraction of your heart is called systolic," he told her. "The resting resistance to that flow is called diastolic." Fascinated, Anne watched the gauge as he pumped the bulb and the instrument tightened on her arm.

"The myth is that a normal systolic pressure should be about 100 plus your chronological age." He told Anne. "But with a diastolic reading of 90, that would make you a little hypertensive. A good reading for you should be 140/90. Perfect would be 120/80." As he spoke, he stared silently at the reading he was getting with a puzzled expression on his face. He said nothing and tried again. Now Barbara was watching the gauge incredulously. Dave shrugged. "80/50," he said. "Impossible. Either the machine is broken or you're still in your adolescence."

"Why don't you admit it?" I demanded. "So far Anne is not responding like any normal human being."

"I'd like to keep her here for a few days," Dave smiled uncertainly. "Maybe she's a medical wonder."

Anne sat on an examining table, her hospital johnny dropped to her thighs. I knew that Dave was surprised at the youthful curve of her breasts. He put a stethoscope in her ears, and she listened silently to her heart sounds. "It goes lub-dub, lub-dub," she said, entranced.

"A doctor must learn to distinguish between the intensity and quality of heart vibrations," Dave told her. "There are valve-sounds, diastolic sounds, and systolic and diastolic murmurs. From them we can tell a great deal about the condition of your heart."

He took the stethoscope from her. Tapping her chest, telling her to breathe deeply, he listened and frowned at her. "Are you falling asleep?"

Wide-eyed, Anne's eyes enveloped him. "Nay. But I am suddenly deeply aware of the spirit within me."

Dave handed the stethoscope to Barbara and let her listen. She frowned at Anne. "Why are you slowing your heart beat?" she demanded. She took Anne's pulse and shook her head. "I can get only thirty beats a minute," she told Dave. "Yogis can do that, but they press their chin against their chest. Look at her. She's perfectly relaxed, almost in a trance." Barbara waved her hand in front of Anne's eyes, but she didn't blink.

"Are you aware of what you're doing?" Dave asked her. He listened again, sliding his stethoscope slowly over Anne's chest. "Some athletes have a slow pulse—it's called sinus bradycardia—but I never heard of any arrythmia like this. Are you consciously slowing your heart down?" he asked.

Anne shook her head negatively. "I knew Mashmono, an Indian sachem. He told his people that the time had come for him to rejoin the Great Spirit, and he did. He simply stopped breathing." She laughed. "But I never tried it."

They led Anne to a moving belt, which could be speeded up, and Dave told her that this was a stress test. But despite the fact that she was breathing a little more heavily, her heart beat climbed only to fifty beats a minute. Explaining to Anne that they wanted to observe the electrical waves created by the motion of her heart, they led her back to the examining table. With an ethereal expression on her face, her pubic area decorously covered, but the rest of her body exposed, she told Dave that dear Robert had told her all about electricity, and she was delighted to learn that there was some in her body.

Barbara pasted electrodes from the electrocardigraph machine to her right arm and left leg and chest while Dave explained to her that the machine would record various electrical waves from her body with a roving pen and he would show them to her when they finished.

Watching the machine through three separate recordings, during which they kept changing the positions of the electrodes, Dave finally said, "It's the damndest reading I have ever seen. Her PR interval is consistently 0.30 seconds. The QRS is 0.06 with no prolongation and the amplitude is amazing. As for the QT interval, it is long and the T-wave is nearly flat." He grinned at our bewilderment. "Without trying to explain what all that means, I can only tell you that you may be right. Anne has either arrived from another planet, or she's a medical curiosity. If her heart is any criterion, she could live forever."

A few minutes later, in another area of the hospital, they connected Anne to an electroencephalograph machine, which Barbara explained had been hooked to a biofeedback instrument. She explained to Anne that the human brain gives off electrical waves, too, which reflect various mental and environmental states, and that some people can learn how to control their brain waves. With the electrodes attached to her head, Anne quickly grasped that she could turn on a series of red, green, and blue lights as she changed her thought processes. Eyes open so that, according to Barbara, she couldn't easily achieve the "instant zen" of alpha activity, which was possible when a person kept his eyes closed, Anne stared at the lights while the machine was recording her brain waves.

The blue light came on and stayed lit. Barbara was delighted. "She's producing alpha waves—rhythms of thirteen cycles per second," she said. She was surprised at how quickly Anne learned how to turn on the green light, which had been coordinated to theta waves. But despite detailed instructions from Barbara, Anne was unable to turn on the red light or produce beta waves.

Barbara asked her how she felt when she was producing alpha waves. Anne smiled, "I was dissolved in my own light," she said. "I was not here."

Dave explained that alpha waves were associated with relaxation, concentration, and meditation. "They reflect a state of mental calmness," he said. "Theta waves are associated with drowsiness and dreaming. Beta waves indicate feelings of anxiety, tension, alertness." He shrugged at Anne. "Seemingly, you are a very cool lady—without a care in the world." He asked her to open her eyes wide and look up at him. "Now look upward, toward your eyebrows," he told her.

But Anne focused directly on him and her gaze held steady. She couldn't seem to move her eyeballs toward the top of her head. "Am I doing it?" she asked.

Chuckling, Dave shook his head. "Susan is probably right. Unless you can move your eyeballs upward and look at the top of your head, you're not going to be an subject for hypnosis." He shook his head. "But it doesn't correlate with with your alpha ability. People who can produce alpha waves are usually good subjects."

By four o'clock, when a nurse appeared with the pathologist's urine and blood analysis—Anne had type O—and neither study revealed anything unusual, Dave had taken two chest x-rays of Anne. Examining them he scowled at me and Saul. "You'll be happy to know that the goddamned things are fuzzy. You heard me tell her to stand still and hold her breath," he sighed. "She kept telling me that the metal was cold against her titties. She probably moved." He smiled at Anne. "How you could feel cold when you're so cool yourself is a mystery. Anyway, enough for today. You'd better get dressed."

"I know you still don't believe her," I told Dave when Anne had left with Susan to retrieve her clothes. "But you must admit that Anne has been very cooperative. Saul and I agree. You can help her. I don't want her to go through this again. A letter from you with the results you've had will help convince people that she's not lying."

"I'm not going to confirm that she's been resurrected," Dave frowned at me. "These tests don't prove anything—not until everybody and his brother has replicated them. My advice to you is to keep her completely out of the public eye. What the Hell is she going to accomplish if she appears on television with that bitch Sally Lane?"

"Nothing," I said. "I agree with you. But I am convinced that I shouldn't try to stop her. Like it or not, Anne believes that she has returned to earth to warn people that some kind of millennium is at hand."

"That's shit, and you know it!" Dave said. "Christ isn't about to appear out of Heaven riding a white charger with a flaming sword in hand."

"Anne's message is more subtle than that," I said. "She believes that man is about to create his own millennium. She believes that the Lord has sent her back—has re-created her—to tell His creatures that there's a way out of their own dilemma."

"What the Hell is that?"

"I'm not sure," I said. "But if millions of people really believe that she is resurrected and is directly in touch with the Lord, God alone know what may happen, or what she can accomplish."

"For Christ's sake," Dave said. "And I use Christ's name advisedly. Stop playing with fire. Keep in mind that I haven't proved anything one way or another. I'm not sticking my neck out. I think there's a rational explanation for the tests we have made. If you'd let her stay here for a few days, we could prove it. Whoever she is, your lady is a cool, probably calculating woman. I'm pretty damned sure that she's not the original Anne Hutchinson."

"Did it ever occur to you," Saul asked Dave, "that Anne exists because we need her to exist? Even you, Dr. Hedman—though you won't admit it— need a belief in an afterlife—resurrection or reincarnation. Our lives on earth only have meaning if there's something beyond."

"As one Jew to another," Dave grunted at Saul as we finally said goodbye, "I can tell you that I don't believe in any God who deliberately re-created anyone. You and Bob obviously disagree with me. That is your privilege. But don't try to be her apostles. Remember what happened to Peter and Paul."

To Dave's surprise, Anne hugged him. "Methinks that thou art more aware of thy inner light than thou pretendest," she said. "I thank thee for looking inside me and seeing the spirit within me. I hope thou wilt find it within thee too."

Reluctant to see her leave, Dave kissed her cheek. "You didn't have time to try our pool," he told her gruffly. "Come back and go swimming with me. You're a lovely illusion. Don't let anyone turn you into a mass delusion."

32

Tuesday morning at nine o'clock, prodded by another phone call from Sally Lane's program director confirming that we would be there, we drove Anne to the television station. Had I visualized the media explosion that Anne would unleash—worse than all the devils in Pandora's box—I'm sure that I would have heeded Dave Hedman's advice and tried to convince Anne of the dangers of a miracle-starved world.

Driving home from the Institute on Sunday, I should have realized that Anne's mission was coming into focus. She had silently watched the surging panorama of traffic, stoplights, storefronts, and restless people, When I asked her what she was thinking, she responded.

"About glass," she sighed and brushed her hand across the window. "We had two windows in our house in Boston," she said. "But a body could not see much through the glass. Now everywhere there is glass. From your houses and buildings and automobiles everyone can watch everyone else. But no one seems to smile or take time to tell each other, 'God be with you!'"

"We've exchanged companionship for privacy and loneliness," Saul said. "We no longer know how to be rugged individuals, like you were, and at the same time love other rugged individuals." He grinned at Anne in the rear mirror. "We need you to show us how."

"But what if I am like them?" Anne waved at people in a car that had stopped next to us waiting for a traffic light. Like animals in a cage they stared sullenly back at us with no sign of recognition. "Behind glass, people all seem to be illusions to each other. Maybe I too am an illusion." The flashing lights of oncoming cars revealed her tear-misted eyes.

"Remember the ghost of Hamlet's father," I said trying to sound light-hearted. "'Stay illusion,' Hamlet said. 'If thou hast any sound or voice speak to me.'" I held her hand, still trying to absorb the reality of Dave Hedman's examination of her. Anne was no ordinary woman. I was sure of it. "Tell Saul and Susan about your revelation last night," I told her. "Anne believes that she has come back to earth to save us from ourselves."

"How?" Saul asked.

"Before I tell thee, there is much I yet need to know. Thou and Robert tell me that everyone knows that this beautiful world, that the Lord created, is on the edge of man-made self-destruction. Why is it taking people so long to find God and love, and the wonder of Him endlessly giving his light and love to each of us? Why do men let their leaders tell them that they must bear arms against one another?" She sighed. "I told Master Winthrop and Master Dudley and all the magistrates and ministers, whom they had wrapped around their fingers, my judgment was not altered—although my expression of it may have changed. I will obey my God—not leaders who know him not."

"Sounds like civil disobedience to me," Saul said jubilantly. "Is that what God told you? Tonight or tomorrow you've got to meet Henry Thoreau. He probably got some of his ideas from you."

"Or from the Quakers," I said, afraid that Saul would put words she never thought into Anne's mouth. "But Anne never knew the Quakers either."

When we got home, at Saul's prodding I unearthed a dusty copy of Thoreau's essay on civil disobedience. Over my protest that Thoreau's message was written for another world and another time, Saul, Susan, and Anne skip-read it to each other.

"'That government is the best which governs not at all . . . the only obligation which I have a right to assume is to do at anytime what I think is right . . . Law never makes a man a whit more just,'—"or pay attention to God's laws," Anne added vehemently. "Master Winthrop tried to make man's laws equivalent to God's laws. 'Dost thou honor thy father and mother?' he asked me. And he tried to convince me that the State was my father and mother and that I must honor the magistrates because they were the leaders of the State, the same as if they were my father and mother." Anne grimaced. "Father, mother, or not I honor only the man or woman who is aware of the Lord within him."

Susan continued to read from Thoreau. "'A common and natural result of respect for the law is that you may see a file of soldiers—colonels, captains, corporals, privates all marching in a natural order over hill and dale to wars against their will. Aye, against their common sense . . . The mass of men serve the state thus, not as men mainly but as machines . . . They put themselves on the level with wood, earth and stones, and wooden men can perhaps be manufactured that will serve the purpose just as well.'"

Clapping enthusiastically, Anne took the book and with flaring nostrils read the words over again. Then she read on: "'Unjust laws exist. Shall we be content to obey them or shall we transgress them at once? I say break the law. Let your life be a counter-friction to to stop the machine . . . I was not born to be forced . . . I will breathe after my own fashion.'" Smiling agreement, Anne gave the book to Saul. "Methinks that Master Thoreau was a very wise man."

"But a dreamer," I said. "When your leaders tell you that it's your country, right or wrong, and they convince the majority to believe that what they think is right, you are forced to breathe after *their* fashion."

Anne shook her head defiantly. "I agreed with Roger Williams and Sam Gorton. They believed that the State hath no jurisdiction over the conscience of men."

Later, telling Susan how happy she was that they were going to stay with us in Quincy, she kissed them both good-night, and hoped that tomorrow they would continue to help her. "I love thee both," she said. "I am certain that we will find the way."

Snuggled in bed with me, although it was eleven o'clock, Anne was still charged up. She kept repeating Thoreau, proving, as she had with Winthrop's *Journal*, that once she read something she could recall it verbatim. Listening to her, I held her wrist and counted her heartbeats. Despite her excitement they were an even thirty to the minute. But I was no longer uneasy. Was I making love to an unearthly creature—a holy spirit? It didn't matter. The agnostic me had a cup that runneth over with love.

Knowing that for better or worse Thoreau was catalyzing her thinking and that Tuesday she would probably give Sally Lane a Quaker-style interpretation of her revelations, I told Anne that if she had lived fourteen years longer until she was sixty-six, she probably would have been in Newport, Rhode Island, when the first Quaker colonists, seven men and four women, arrived on the *Woodward,* which had left England some six weeks earlier with George Fox's blessing. Mary Dyer, who was in her mid-thirties at the time, no doubt welcomed them and recognized, in the Quaker philosophy of a creedless religion and a God-loving, self-governing society, many beliefs similar to Anne's.

"Had the Lord let you live until you were seventy-nine, you would probably have met George Fox. He was the founder of the religion which became known as Friends or Quakers, because they trembled and quaked with their love for God. He sailed to the Barbados in 1671 and six months later was in New York and then Rhode Island looking for a place to establish a Quaker colony."

Making what Anne called "talky love and blowing gently on a fire," which delighted her because it lasted "forever," we interspersed kisses and touches and I told her what little I knew about the Quakers. "George Fox was nineteen when you died," I said. "He blended the Familist belief in an indwelling spirit with a quieter approach than the Ranters. The Ranters insisted that man himself was God. Fox denied that. He never thought of himself as God, but he insisted that he was the son of God, and that God had many sons and daughters. Like you, he believed that the light of Christ is in everyone, and God's 'Amazing Grace' is His gift to all mankind.

"As for sin," I continued, cupping her vulva while she engulfed me with her loving sea-green eyes, "according to William Penn, who finally founded the first Quaker colony in Pennsylvania, from light came sight, with sight came sense and sorrow, but from sense and sorrow comes amendment to life. God sacrificed Christ, who assumed man's sins. Early Quakers believed that if you resist Christ as your sanctifier then His coming and suffering would not redeem you. If you accepted Him, you can achieve perfection from sin."

"'Tis just what I have been telling thee!" Like a happy child whose thinking has been confirmed, Anne clapped her hands. "I hope that there are many Quakers in America."

"Only a few hundred thousand," I told her. "And fewer every year. Their beliefs don't jibe with a world that puts Mammon before God. The Puritans hated them because, like you, they believed that they had direct access to God, and because their beliefs undermined the state and the power of the leaders. Among other things, they found God in loving communion with each other. In England and America they were whipped, beaten, had their ears and tongues cut off, and were hung, but like your friend Mary Dyer, they died loving their enemies. They believed that men and women should never swear nor take an oath, but like Jesus say 'yea, yea, or nay, nay.' Even today they will not bear arms against anyone. They will not respect one person over another. They will not doff their hat to another person. Unlike you, they used to call strangers, as well as loved ones, *thee* and *thou.* Like you, they do not believe in baptism, and their burials are very simple with no rituals and ostentation. They generally dress plainly, and they believe that marriage is an ordinancy of God, and only God can join man and woman together. So instead of authorizing priests or ministers to marry them, they marry themselves in the presence of friends and they do not exchange rings."

Nodding her head approvingly as she listened to me, Anne gave me a laughing kiss and told me it was time to come into her belly. "Except for no friends being present," she said as she lay on top of me, "that is how I married John-Luv, and that is the way that I will marry thee, if thou willst consent to become a bigamist."

Squeezing her hand resassuringly as Saul drove into the parking lot next to the television station on the Boston side of the Charles River, I couldn't help grinning at the insanity I was involved in. Monday, after breakfast, Anne and I had married each other. Grinning happily, our friends, Saul and Susan, listened to us exchange vows. "I love thee now and tomorrow. I will love thee and care for thee through time and wherever after in this life God may reunite us."

Then Saul reminded me that time was running out. "We should give your new wife a tour of America and the kind of world that she's living in before she confronts Sally Lane."

Using video cassettes, of which I have many, we skimmed through the actuality of World War II, and with a film called *Genocide,* we showed her the horror of man's inhumanity to man if a Hitler, or even a Winthrop, persisted in following his Utopian daydream. She quickly grasped the difference between democracy and communism, and why the Russians were afraid of religion. "Reading the Scriptures makes a body realize that the priests, the kings, and the prime ministers are not God," she said. "When you insist on your freedom to believe what you believe and you no longer worship any of them, that is democracy."

We showed her a film of nuclear-bomb testing and explained the fate of Hiroshima, and we followed that with a cassette depicting the U.S. landing on the moon and our most recent trips into space, whereby we were able to interweave all the people of the world with satellite transmissions and manufacture strange new products in space. We introduced her to computers and genetic engineering, and told her about the world's overpopulation and the problems of child care in America, where fifty percent of the women work in jobs far from where they raise their children. And Susan told her about divorce and marriage American style and premarital cohabitation and extramarital sex, and we even showed her a porn movie, which surprisingly didn't shock her at all. "Papa used to tell my Momma that people were ashamed of making love because they listened to men like Saint Augustine, who told them: '*inter faeces et urinam nascimur.*'" She laughed. "But Saint Augustine never told people that pissing and shitting was a miracle too." She grinned at me. "Pictures of men and women playing tick-tack make those who watch them want to play tick-tack, too. At the fairs in London, they sold pictures printed in Italy. Will had a collection of them engraved by a man named Romano. With each one was a little sonnet by a man named Aretino, and it explained what they were doing in the picture. I remember one. 'Place your leg, dearest, on my shoulder here—and take my truncheon in thy tender grasp.'" She laughed. "There were twelve more lines all describing a laughing woman lying on her back and a man inserting his pizzle into her con."

She sighed. "I understand not many of the things you have told me, especially why men and women make weapons to kill one another, but cannot bear to see themselves naked in each other's arms. Methinks the Lord is growing weary of His creatures. They loveth Him not and understand not that when they murder each other they are murdering Him."

Sally Lane's program director, Bill Vining, met us in the reception room of the television station. "Sally hasn't arrived yet," he told us, staring at Anne approvingly. "But with my research and her own inquisitive mind, Sally has become an expert on Anne Hutchinson."

He led us into a special studio that had been designed for a talk-show format. Gradually elevated seating, arranged in a semi-circle, could accommodate a live audience of several hundred people. Slightly below was a stage furnished like a comfortable living-room study with a sofa, three separate plush chairs, and a glass-top coffee table with fresh flowers set against a background of bookshelves filled casually with many knick-knacks and a few books. Having been a guest on "People Passion" a year before, I knew that Sally encouraged women's clubs and various groups of women to attend the daily show. In addition to taking a few telphone calls, she also gave the studio audience the opportunity to ask her guests a few questions. But now, as I stared at the empty seating uneasily, I had forgotten that in addition to a remote television audience, Anne would encounter a vociferous audience of women who had nothing else to do with their time except watch and bemoan the less predictable lives of the celebrities that Sally attracted.

"Sally told me that presumably Mrs. Hutchinson can't be photographed or imaged by a video camera." Vining smiled condescendingly at Saul and me and shrugged when Saul, omitting our nude experiments, told him in detail of our failures. Leading us to the stage, where we were to wait for Sally, he said, "I'm sure we'll solve the problem. We've got some expert cameramen and engineers here." He looked at his watch. "We've got an hour and a half before we let Sally's fans into the studio. Let's see what we can do."

Although I told him that neither Saul, Susan, nor I would appear on the show, Vining asked us to remain on the stage with Anne, whom he led to a wing-back chair. "Together you give the cameramen something to focus on," he said. He told the female assistant to round up Bill and Eddy, who manned the cameras for Sally's show. "We haven't told anyone in the studio yet that Mrs. Hutchinson can't be photographed," he told us. "But I'm sure that Bill and Eddy can solve any technical problems that you might have overlooked with a home-video camera." He waved at two men entering the studio and explained that they operated the cameras on different sides of the stage, switching the perspective back and forth between them and making the program more interesting to watch.

"As you can see," he told them, "our guest today, sitting in the wing chair, is a very beautiful woman. Sally and I called you in early because we want to make sure that all the young and old plumpies out in the boondocks who watch this show with their hair still in curlers or who schlump around in sloppy jeans or their nightgowns, become aware that at fifty-two a woman with class, like Mrs. Hutchinson, can turn a man on even if they can't." He grinned at Anne. "After the show, if you need any help getting reacquainted in your old home town, you can call on me anytime."

A half-hour later, along with the cameramen and several studio engineers, all perspiring in an air-conditioned room which had gradually filled up with station employees as the word got around, Vining gave up. "I don't know who the Hell you are, or where you came from," he told Anne, "but unless you turn off some invisible light that you're radiating we can't seem to get your face, arms, or legs on the monitors or on tape."

In the long shots, zoom shots, and closeups, Saul, Susan, and I could see ourselves on the television screens suspended from the ceiling. But Anne, watching and listening to the activity and obligingly changing position a dozen times, was even more ephemeral and ghostly that she had appeared in Saul's photographs or on my video screen. The powder-blue spring suit that she had picked out in Lord & Taylor's reproduced perfectly. But wearing it was a faceless woman. Her hair, her features, and the flesh on her neck, arms, and legs were transmitted like a warm misty fog drifting over the surface of cold ocean water. Everyone in the studio watching her was shiveringly aware that one aspect of this woman was as evanescent as a will-o-the wisp, or as mysterious as a dim light flashing from nowhere across a black sky. She was a person beyond our understanding of *homo sapiens*. Yet, contradicting the television image, there she sat on the stage, a warm, laughing woman whose limpid eyes and loving smile drew you to her like a physical embrace.

Sally Lane arrived in the middle of the confusion and quickly grasped the situation. "Forget it," she told Vining, "it's more convincing this way. We've still got half an hour to show time." She bussed Anne's cheek and told her, to Anne's amused laughter, "Bill didn't believe you, nor did I, but I try never to get caught with my pants down—like you did a few centuries ago. I alerted Tom Snelling, Jake Goldman, and Patsy Latik. They're here and ready to go." She explained to Anne that they were courtroom artists. "If people like them had been around when Winthrop and Cotton were putting you over the coals, we'd have had plenty of drawings of you, and every damned witness against you."

For the next half hour, while the studio filled with chattering women, young and old—a few accompanied by obviously retired husbands who stared dolefully at the overwhelming mass of effervescent female flesh—Sally sat on the stage with us. We watched the artists sketching full-color chalk drawings of Anne's face and shoulders. Each of them captured different perspectives and made remarkable likenesses of Anne, but none of them was able to catch the warm glow from her flesh that I was beginning to believe must be the inner light she so ardently believed in.

Coolly connecting Anne and herself to microphones so that the audience could hear the preliminaries, Sally told the illustrators that she wanted them to continue to draw Anne, capturing her expressions and moods, as the show progressed. She explained to her wide-eyed audience, that while they could see Mrs. Hutchinson, for some reason the video camera could not focus her. "Whether this is a verification from God that this is no ordinary woman, I do not know," she told them. "But in the next hour, on 'People Passion,' I hope we'll discover what or who motivates this woman. The artists you are watching will substitute for the cameras. They will do their best to capture the

beautiful woman you see before you. If you watch the monitors, you will see
the cameramen cutting back and forth between finished drawings and drawings in process to reveal the strange phenomenon of this beautiful but un-
photographible woman."

To Anne she said, "I never rehearse with my guests. You and I are going
to talk together for about an hour. Over a million people watch this show
and will make their own decision whether you really are the original Anne
Hutchinson and if so what miracle has brought you back to life. I will open
the show with a capsule biography of your life as we know it from historical
accounts. This will take two or three minutes. During the rest of the show,
with interruptions for commercials, I am going to probe and discover whether
you are for real or a phony, and whether this is all a big gimmick to get
national attention.

"To begin with, I am going to focus on your trials. I read them carefully.
I'm not sure that I undersatnd all that stuff about works and grace and
sanctification and justification, but I am going to make the point that anyone
who reads them not only will discover a very spunky lady who took on the
male establishment of Boston but also will wonder just exactly what your
relationship was to John Cotton. Why did he go all out and defend you in
the first trial before the General Court of Massachusetts and then six months
later condemn you as a dangerous woman in your church trial? We have a
big female audience out there who will want to hear your answers."

Sally laughed, "At the same time, I warn you, what you say may be used
against you. A slip of the tongue may reveal that you are not who you say
you are. Assuming that you will survive, without cracking up, during the last
fifteen minutes I will give you time to tell everyone why, after nearly two
thousand years, God has suddenly resurrected another person and why it is
you instead of the thousands of others who have lived before you and since."

Totally unflustered, a smile flickering on her lips, Anne said, "I understand not everything that you have been telling me. But I am not what you
call a gimmick. I am Anne Hutchinson. I may not be able to stop my tongue
from wagging, but I assure you it will slip not." Anne ignored my whispered
warning that she shouldn't discuss her sex life with John-Luv, or that if she
really trusted me she'd get up right now and bid Sally goodbye.

"It's too late, dear husband." She kissed my cheek. "I am very happy that
all these people came to hear me. That is why I am here on earth—not only
to tell them the truth about me, but what is going to happen to them if they
continue to deny the light and love within them." Anne smiled at the audience
who, hearing everything that we said, cheered her. I couldn't help wondering
if Anne were reliving centuries past when her home on Sentry Lane was
crowded with an equally enthusiastic audience of women waiting to hear her
latest interpretation of the Gospel.

33

At 12:28 Sally shooed us into front-row seats that had been reserved for us. She and Anne were alone on the stage waiting for a two-minute countdown to Sally Lane's "People Passion"—billed as New England's Most Controversial Television Show. Sally immediately created suspense by alerting her viewers that it was impossible to transmit Anne's features.

She assured them that this was no television stunt. "If you could actually see this woman in the flesh, as we can here in the studio, you might really believe that she is one of God's angels returned to earth."

The television cameraman intercut completed drawings of Anne and shots of the artists themselves drawing, as they continued to try to capture a likeness of Anne from different angles and with different expressions on her face. At the same time Sally gave a brief biography of Anne, which Bill Vining had probably extracted from the Encyclopedia Britannica. Then Sally moved rapidly into Anne's trials and asked her to explain what had been happening in Boston in 1637, three and a half centuries ago. "Why was Governor Winthrop afraid of you?" she demanded.

"He was not afraid only of me," Anne smiled at her. "But of John-Luv and Johnny, and Harry Vane, who had returned to England in August before my trial. Master Winthrop was also afraid of many other people in Boston and later on the Island of Aquiday, because we believed that God had given His grace to all without exception."

Sally quickly explained who the three men were. Then, with a slightly lascivious smile, she said, "We'll explore why Mrs. Hutchinson called Reverend Cotton, John-Luv, later. But first I'd like to ask you what you mean by grace and works."

"Grace is God's freely given love to all men and women," Anne told her with a little smile. "'Tis quite independent of any merit on our part but methinks that many people still believe like Master Winthrop did. They think that if they work hard and lead a good life, even though it includes killing their enemies, that their good works will justify them before the Lord and they will be saved and arrive safely in the Kingdom of Heaven."

"But you don't believe that," Sally said.

"I believe that *everyone* can experience God's grace, but men and women must become aware of the eternal Christ within them. For those who understand God's grace, the resurrection and second coming of Christ is continuous. The apostles who saw Christ were finally sealed in the spirit of God. But they were not the last. Resurrection is available to anyone who becomes aware of the light within him."

"Are you a born-again Christian?"

"I know not what you mean by born-again Christian. The light within you is within everyone. Christ asked for no temples or steeplehouses to be built for him."

"Don't you believe that there are sinners and evil persons in the world?"

"There is only one sin against God—not loving Him and not recognizing that His inner light dwelleth in all His creatures. Killing a fellowman, making war against men and women, as men have been doing for thousands of years—for whatever the reason—is a sorrow and a sin against God. All other sins are man-made sins. Men devise man-made laws to protect us against those who have not yet discovered the inner light and who do not follow the Golden Rule. But man-made laws are not *always* God's laws."

"You keep saying that Christ's resurrection is something a person must experience within himself," Sally said beginning to twist the knife. "But you insisted at your trials that you did not believe in the resurrection of the corruptible human body. That was one reason why you were banished. Obviously, you must have changed your mind."

"I still do not believe in resurrection of the human body." Anne smiled at Saul, Susan, and me, who were staring at her open-mouthed, wondering how she would explain her present reality. "I know very little of your world. I arrived at my dear friend Robert's house a week ago. I was stark naked. Robert took me in and clothed me. First I thought that I had been re-created in the same flesh that I had when I left this world three hundred and fifty years ago. But I have learned that my heart beats differently from yours, and my body temperature is different." She smiled at Sally, leaving her momentarily bewildered and then she laughed. "I still piss and shit, and I enjoy what Master Shakespeare called "country" matters and a happy flourish with the right man. Methinks the reason you cannot make me appear on your television is that God has brought me back to earth in a new form. Robert told me that almost everyone believes that we are all descended from the same species that produced monkeys. If God has improved on monkeys, could he not also improve on humans who love him?"

"I'm not going to ask you God's reason yet," Sally said, after a two-minute break for commercials. I could see that she was deftly steering Anne out of religious waters. "I'm sure that we'd all like to know about the real woman you once were. At your first trial on November 7th and 8th, 1637, which occurred immediately after your brother-in-law, John Wheelwright, was banished, for some reason your good friend, Reverend John Cotton, was not called as a witness until late on the second day. Bear with me, ladies, this calls for a bit more of the history books than we usually get into on 'People Passion.' When Governor Winthrop questioned Mr. Cotton, he said that he didn't think that he should be called as a witness against you. During the final hours of your trial, Mr. Cotton did his best to protect you. You told the court that the reason you came to Boston was that being without Mr. Cotton, your teacher, had been a great trouble unto you. But you said, even though the Lord had given you the bread of adversity and the waters of affliction, you knew that you would see your teacher once again. Then you blew it, Anne. You told the court that God spoke directly to you and that you had revelations. You must have known that the ministers wouldn't believe you. They were sure that all direct communication with the Lord, except those recorded in Scripture, had ceased.

"To top it off, my dear, you told the magistrates that they had better watch out. 'If you continue the course that you have begun,' you told them, 'you will bring a curse on you and your posterity. And the mouth of the Lord hath spoken it.' Despite the fact that you were pouring oil on troubled waters, John Cotton really tried to defend your revelations and told the court that somehow or other you might be saved by a miracle directly from the Lord.

"My question to you," Sally continued, sounding like a prosecuting attorney, "is why—six months later on March 15th and on March 22nd, 1638, at your church trial—John Cotton suddenly attacked you so strongly and after two days of hearings during which the magistrates questioned your heresies and erroneous beliefs, why did he tell the Court that up to that time he did not know that you believed the things that you were accused of? He even blamed it on his "sleepiness" that he had not corrected your views. At your church trial, he tossed you to the wolves and he agreed that you were a liar. Quoting Revelation he said, 'Whosoever loves and practices a lie are dogs and sorcerers and are sexually immoral and murderers and idolaters.' After excoriating you for ten minutes or more, he turned you over to Reverend John Wilson to complete your banishment and Wilson called you a leper and daughter of Satan and cast you out of the church in the name of Christ." Sally shook her head at Anne sorrowfully as if Anne must indeed be guilty of something. "But before you answer, I think we'd all like to know why you refer to John Cotton as John-Luv."

Tears running down her cheeks, Anne stared at Sally for several seconds. Her sob was audible and the cameramen panned over the artists' drawings as they sketched her sad expression. "I called him John-Luv because I loved him with all my body and all my soul, and he loved me." Anne smiled down at me through her tears.

"You were having an affair with him?" Sally demanded.

"I know not what you mean by affair." Anne said quietly. "In the many years I knew him in Old Boston and in the Colony, John-Luv and I joined our bodies many times. A week before the General Court trial John-Luv warned me that Johnny Wheelwright would be banished, and unless I were very careful I would be next. Lying in his arms in his study on Cotton Hill, while he was deep within my belly, he begged me that when I was called before the Court to be very cautious and modest. He told me, 'Like most men in the Colony, Master Winthrop believes that women that give themselves to reading and writing and preaching are meddling in things that are only proper for men. Much as I need thee and love thy body,' he said, 'much as we agree on God's gift of grace, I cannot ever say that thou speaketh the same as I. What I tell thee privately I can never say publicly.'"

Anne paused. "'I know that I am a woman questioning men,' I told John, 'and I know that most women dare not do that. I know that thou canst not defend me. But I canst not change my beliefs. I am sorry for the troubles I have brought thee. I love thee so much that I wanted everyone to love thee too and know your beautiful thoughts. I know that my love has become an affliction to thee. Thou must promise me,' I told John-Luv, 'that no matter what happens to me thou wilt not become tarred with the same brush. It would serve no purpose. If thou dost not deny me, I will deny thee.'" Anne smiled sadly at Sally. "I told John-Luv all these things two days before the Court called me before them. But John listened not to me. He sat with me at the trial and tried to protect me. I did not see him again until I was imprisoned in Roxbury for six months."

"You were banished on November 17th, 1637." Sally said. Bringing her listeners into Anne's world, she read her sentence from a paper. "'Mrs. Hutchinson, the wife of William Hutchinson, being convented for traducing the ministers and the ministry in this country and voluntarily declaring her revelations for her actions that she should be saved and the Court ruined, along with their posterity, thereupon shall be banished and committed to the home of Joseph Weld in Roxbury until the Court shall dispose of her.'" Sally paused and stared at Anne, who was nodding in agreement. "Your brother-in-law had already gone to New Hampshire, but the Court took pity on you and let you stay in Boston until spring. They knew it was nearly impossible to travel during the New England winter. Why weren't you permitted to return to your home?"

"In my home, they could not control who came to see me," Anne said. "They were still afraid that I might incite the Colony against them." She shrugged. "Like Master Wilson, Joseph Weld and his wife believed that the Devil himself slept in my bed. I could have told them that the Devil did not, but that John Cotton did, at least once a month." Anne smiled at the gasp of surprise from the audience.

"Where was your husband, Will? Wasn't he allowed to see you?" Sally demanded.

Anne nodded. "Will came as often as he could. In November he went to New Hampshire with Johnny and helped him move his family to Exeter. Then, despite the bad weather, knowing that we would have to leave Boston in March, he went to Pocasset on the Island to search for a new home for us."

"Was he aware that John Cotton was sleeping with you?"

Anne shrugged. "He knew that I cared for John-Luv. John kept telling him that if I would repent and ask the Court for leniency and if I would agree that works and grace were not independent of each other—as he was gradually saying—that I would be forgiven.

"But John never liked to face reality. Immediately after my trial, Will Baulston, and Will's brother, Ed Hutchinson, and fourteen other men were disenfranchised and fined various sums for signing a petition in favor of Johnny. They had already banished John Coggeshall and Will Aspinwall. Master Winthrop asked Will Coddington to denounce me. The magistrates were determined to get rid of anyone who had ever come to my house, and that included poor Will Dyer and Mary, Will Dinely, and Richard Gridley. But at the same time they were afraid there would be a rebellion in Boston, so they informed all householders who had signed the petition for Johnny, or who favored me, that they must 'turn in all guns, pistols, swords, powder and shot that they had in their possession or be fined ten pounds for every default.' But if anyone wished to acknowledge their sins in subscribing to such seditious beliefs, he would be exempted." Anne shrugged. "Master Winthrop was afraid that I thought I was a new Joan of Arc."

"Criticizing the government was an act of sedition." Then Sally laughed, speaking directly to her viewers, "We've come a long way, baby." She turned back to Anne. "Why didn't they try to get rid of Mr. Cotton?"

"They did. Master Winthrop told John-Luv that he was a 'stalking horse' and that I had made a dupe of him. John was walking a tightrope. No matter what he said publicly, many people still believed that he preached that our union with Christ was more important than works. Some of the magistrates even questioned whether he loved me more than God's covenants."

"When he was telling you all these things, where were you?" Sally asked after another commercial break. She was well aware that her viewers were more intrigued by Anne's sex life than by her religion or politics.

"In bed with John-Luv," Anne grinned provocatively into the cameras, which were still recording a ghostly woman. "I was given a room on the second floor of Master Weld's house next to the chimney. During the day I was allowed to come downstairs into the fireroom. But most of the time it was filled with people staring at me as if I were some kind of fearful demon, or they ignored me. It was too noisy to read or think. The only people who dared talk with me were ministers like Master Shepherd and Master Thomas Weld, and Master Eliot, who came frequently. I refused to talk with them while the Weld family were listening. So like the ladies at the King's Court, I entertained them in my bedroom."

Anne chuckled. "I was properly dressed, of course. Being alone with me made them very nervous. But they soon forgot that I was a woman, especially when I told them that they were the sinners—not me. And I continued to tell them that every day I was learning more from the Lord. I did not tell them that Sam Gorton had been writing to me from Plymouth. Master Winthrop feared Sam more than he did me and Johnny. Sam wanted to come to Boston and talk to me, but the only visitors I was permitted were my family and the ministers. Sam finally did come to Boston and he heard one of John-Luv's sermons. Right before the congregation, Sam challenged John and told him, 'If Christ lived eternally, he died eternally.' He also said that Christ was incarnate in Adam. Adam was made after God's image and God could only have one image.

"That made John very angry and he called Sam a snake and an adder. But I agreed with Sam, who wrote me: 'The doctrine which ties the death of Christ to one particular man in one time and in one age in the world, falsifies the death of Jesus Christ and sets man upon the law of works to achieve their salvation, by which law no man is justified.'" Anne smiled. "I told John-Luv that I was not alone in my beliefs, and I tried to convince him tha Sam Gorton was closer to his thinking than he dared to admit.

"Poor John. Until the last night that I spent with him in Boston in his house, he had almost given up trying to change my thinking. Making sure than no other minister would arrive and telling Mistress Weld that he had come to pray with me to repent my sins, he no sooner got the door closed and barred then he would be hugging me and kissing me and undressing me. But even while I was happily wagging my tail to keep the edge on his knife, he was reminding himself what Paul told the Romans: 'With the mind, I myself served the Lord: but with the flesh the law of sin.' Or he would moan from Galatians 5:17: 'The flesh lusteth against the spirit, and the spirit against the flesh, and these are contrary to each other.' And though he would listen to me while we were playing seesaw and finally forget the Scriptures, and I kept telling him that God loveth us most when we loveth each other, he would shake his head sadly at me and tell me that he had never read that in the Bible."

"So your lover felt guilty, but you didn't?" Sally said. "Why not—you were breaking the Seventh Commandment?"

"The Commandments were written by men," Anne smiled. "Most men cannot love without possessing. They understand not that a woman can love a man for himself, especially a man who can reach into her brain as well as her flesh, and not want to own him. But I did feel sorrowful about all the problems that I had caused John-Luv, and I was very sad that many thought he was a weak man who was in my power."

After another commercial break, during which Sally told the audience that in a few minutes she would be taking questions from the floor and by telephone, Sally continued. "You were excommunicated from the Boston church on Thursday, March 23rd, 1638," she said, once again assuming the role of prosecuting attorney. "Before the entire congregation of the Boston meetinghouse, many of the Colony's ministers, including Cotton, spent the entire afternoon questioning you about some twelve false opinions and vile errors held by you. At that meeting you didn't arrive until after John Cotton had preached his sermon. A Mr. Oliver stated that you told him that you hadn't been feeling too well, but when I read the transcript of this trial it seemed to me you were just as fiery as ever, and you didn't back down much from the beliefs you had held six months before. In fact, you finally admitted that some of your new beliefs had been acquired since your imprisonment.

"But then a week later you returned to the church for your final examination, and you were charged with ten more theological errors. To everyone's surprise, you suddenly admitted that you had been deeply deceived, and you agreed that some nine beliefs that you held were dangerous errors. But then after further questioning, no one believed you, including John Cotton, who agreed that you must be lying." Sally paused. "I'm sure that our viewers would like to know why, during the week of March 15th to March 22nd, you stayed in Cotton's house rather than your own home, which was only a quarter of a mile away. Why weren't you brought back to Roxbury to Joseph Weld's home? It looks to me as if Cotton and the Reverend John Davenport, who had just arrived from England and was lodging in Cotton's home, tried to save you. Did they help you write your retraction? Finally, since you've already told us that you went to bed with John Cotton in his own house, where was John Davenport and Cotton's wife, Sarah, while this was happening? Finally, were you pregnant at the church trial?"

Smiling coolly at her, Anne said, "I shall answer your last question first. I was not pregnant. I did not conceive until the last night I bedded with John. I knew when I finally arrived in Pocasset that I was not carring Will's child. I had my monthly flow after Will had gone to the Island. We did not go to bed again until early April." Anne shrugged. "But John's third baby did not live. I miscarried in September and was very ill for a month. As for finding time to be with John alone in his home, that was easy." She smiled. "Love will always find a way. I did not spend the night in John-Luv's bed, but several afternoons we prayed together for many hours in his study. Even if Will had been in Boston, the Court would not have let me go home. Being in the custody of two ministers was another matter. Master Winthrop would have liked nothing better than to have me tear out my hair and confess my evil ways in front of everyone. He told John that if I truly repented, my banishment could be revoked and eventually the church would accept me again. But first I must become a terrible example to everyone in the Colony of what happens to a person who is lured by Satan."

Anne sighed. "You keep asking why John spoke so harshly to me before the congregation. He had no choice. I had already told him he must reject me. Denouncing me was the only way that he could restore confidence in himself. While he lay in my arms, nursing my breast like a lost child, I kept telling him, 'Only thou, dear love, can make people aware that the Spirit within them is more important than works. The only way thou canst do it now is to play Master Wilson's game. Agree with him that I am an evil woman.' I told John that I would never change my beliefs or repent, but he could make it seem as if I had been lying and that I truly believed I was innocent before I was imprisoned. Poor John-Luv. He sobbed in my arms that he could not betray me. 'I love thee,' he told me, 'and I believe that thou art closer to God than I shall ever be.'

"'So live because thou loveth me,' I told him. 'Denying love when one loveth can be a victory too.'"

Noting that Sally was shaking her head dubiously, Anne paused. "I feareth that you believe me not."

"It's not easy," Sally said. "I can't believe that Cotton could have loved you, gone to bed with you, and then at your trial would have had the nerve to stand before the congregation and make the following statement, and I quote: 'Neither do I think that you have been unfaithful to your husband.' How could Cotton look you in the eye and say that when he had been sleeping with you so often for so many years?" Sally shook her head. "The ministers finally excommunicated you because they were convinced you were a liar. How do we know that you're not lying to us right now?" Sally had timed her question for the mid-show break and five minutes of commercials. She was well aware that nothing Anne could say would prove that Anne was telling the truth. But when they were finally off camera, she patted Anne's hand and told her, "I don't mean to be too rough on you. But you can be sure that the studio audience and the telephone callers will ask you tougher questions than that."

During the break, Sally acknowledged a woman in the audience who was waving her hand. "Make it quick," she said. "We'll be back with the show in a couple of minutes."

"You don't look like any Puritan woman to me," the woman stared belligerently at Anne. "You don't look a bit like your statue in front of the State House."

Anne smiled benignly at her. "I wasn't alive when the sculptor made that statue. When I lived in Boston there was no copper or iron to make statues. And there were no artists who had time to carve, or even whittle with wood."

Sally nodded at another woman who asked the familiar question. "If you really are resurrected, Mrs. Hutchinson, where are you living now? Who is supporting you? Where did you get that expensive dress that you're wearing?"

"We don't have time for the answer to that yet," Sally said ignoring many other fluttering hands. "We're going back on the air." Speaking to the television viewers, she said, "In the past half hour the woman sitting with me who calls herself Anne Hutchinson has turned history upside down. She has given us an intimate look into the private life of a famous woman and what seems like a plausible explanation for something that has bothered historians for years, namely, why the Reverend Cotton suddenly turned on Anne Hutchinson and denounced her. I have been unable to prove whether this woman is or isn't the real Anne Hutchinson. Frankly, she boggles my mind. I have difficulty accepting the idea of a woman who has returned from the grave." She smiled at Anne. "But before I open the telephone lines and also let the studio audience have a go at you, I want to give you a chance to tell us why you think that God has brought you back to life." She nodded at Anne. "Go ahead. We're all waiting with baited breath."

Sitting in her wing chair perfectly at ease, it was obvious that Anne was completely sure of herself. "Lest ye think that the Lord speaks to me alone," she said, "I first wish to tell ye that this is not so. The Lord speaks directly to any and all of his creatures, and He can be heard by anyone who will open his or her mind and heart and listen to Him. Jesus said, 'Behold I come as a thief in the night. Blessed is he that watches, and keeps his garments.' Jesus often spoke in parables. By *garments* He meant the spirit of God within ye, and when He said he who watches, He really meant all of us who are aware of the Holy Spirit within us. Jesus did not mean that He was coming at some future time. His coming to us—silent as a thief in the night—is continuous. It was not John, Jesus' beloved disciple, who wrote the Book of Revelation. It was written by John of Patmos. He did not understand the meaning of resurrection. He told stories about the second coming of Jesus to frighten people and make them fear the day when at a Hebrew city called Armageddon all the spirits and demons would bring all the kings of the world together on the final day. My Papa read me these stories, and he told me that the real Armageddon would be very different. Christ would not appear on a white horse, his eyes afire, his robe dipped in blood. What would really happen was that God would let His creatures, those who loveth Him not and who have followed false gods, destroy themselves. For thousands of years the Lord has sorrowfully watched while men and women everywhere bear arms against one another. God lets us make our own choices. We can follow the leaders who believe that they themselves are God or we can reject them and their false gods. Only one God created ye. He loveth ye. But if ye love Him not, He *will not* try to convince ye that ye should. He will not save ye. Ye are thine own enemy. Armageddon will be more horrible than any ye could imagine."

Anne paused. Her voice, warm, tender, but sounding almost on the verge of tears, and emerging from the smoky swirl around her face, had created a prophetic spine-tingling aura. "Seven days ago," she continued, "the Lord gaveth me life again. He brought me naked to the home of a loving man who hast given me food, clothing, and shelter. During the few days that I have walked the earth again, I have learned that my father was right. Men and women have continued to let God-hating men perfect weapons of self-destruction. Like ye and me, most men and women are as loving and caring of each other from birth to death as they have ever been. But in every nation of the world we, who are aware of the infinite light of God, are afraid to face the truth. We *are* our brother's keepers. We must show all our brothers and sisters that loving God is their only salvation. I have learned that kings and queens have disappeared from the world, but now ye have new communal and democratic ways of living together, yet which giveth more power to thy leaders than ever before.

"Like the kings before them, thy new leaders believe that God is on their side. And they believe that their particular nation is destined by God to be the most powerful nation in the world. I have learned that this nation which ye call the United States and a combination of other nations that is called the Union of Soviet Socialist Republics now dominate the world. I have learned that the leaders of these nations still think the same way that the kings and queens of England, France, and Spain did many centuries ago. They are convinced that their nation is the most favored nation in the eyes of God and will rule the world. The only difference is that the weapons ye now have are more deadly. Ye have missiles and terrible bombs, beyond my comprehension, and ships and airplanes and leaders who are ready to use them against each other and care not how many of God's creatures they murder. And I have learned that the God-loving people of the earth, like ye and me, are in despair. Ye know that the end of the world is coming, and ye believe that there is nothing that ye can do to prevent it.

"But ye are wrong. God hath given me life once again to tell ye who hear me that ye, the loving people of the world, can take command of thy lives and thine earth. The time has come for all loving men and women, God's creatures, who are aware of the spirit of love within them to arise! It matters not whether the spirit be called by the name of Christ or some other name. Silently as thieves in the night, you must refuse to make any weapons, or bear any arms that could kill another man or woman. Through me, the Lord is asking each of thee to take responsibility for thine earth. Repent that ye have let your leaders lead ye to the edge of Hell and damnation. Repent and rebel! Take back their power of life and death over thee. Take back a power that belongs to God alone. Ye must begin tomorrow. Rise up! Ye art Christ! Ye art the Second Coming, and it is now! The millennium is in thy hands. Call for a world fast against the murder of Christ within ye! Refuse to make the tiniest part of any weapon, any bomb, any ship, any airplane, any machine or instrument that can cause the death of another human being.

Through me the Lord is telling ye that if ye choose war and death, then God will let all His creatures on this planet perish forever. Through me the Lord is telling ye that there is a resurrection in life, but only for those who exalt the spirit within them and choose life. I have returned to help relight the fire of life within ye. Hear me. Choose life! Repent and rebel! Choose life and ye will live forever."

34

Even before Anne had finished, many of the two hundred women and a few men in the audience were nodding their heads and whispering "Amen! Amen!" Ignoring Sally's attempt to shush them, they began softly clapping. Then, to everyone's surprise, a young woman who had been brought into the studio in a wheelchair burst into tears and sobbed, "Dear Anne, I love you. I feel your love and God's love coursing through my body and my poor legs." Swaying, she held the arms of her wheelchair and slowly stood up. While the woman next to her, obviously her mother, moaned, "Oh, dear God, dear God! Chrissie hasn't walked for ten years," Chrissie staggered toward Anne.

Anne stepped down from the stage to catch her. Sitting on the step, she held the young woman in her arms and stroked her face.

"This is fantastic!" Sally yelled at the cameraman. "Don't miss it!"

She brushed Bill Vining, who had been waving at her frantically, aside. "There're a thousand telephone calls out there," he said, still trying to get her attention. "A lot of them are from people who think you've staged the whole thing." Forgetting that he had moved into camera range, he scowled at Anne, who now, along with Susan, was surrounded by the women in the studio.

"I don't give a damn what anyone thinks," Sally's voice had risen an octave, "this is real-life drama!" The cameraman closed in on Sally, revealing tears in her eyes. "I only wish that millions of you out there who are watching us, could actually see this madonna of a woman holding this child and telling her that God loves her."

She frowned at one of the assistants, who was waving a time-for-commercial sign at her. "Kill the commercials!" she yelled. "I don't care if we go into the next hour." Then she told the television audience, "I'm sorry that we couldn't take your calls. Our switchboard is swamped. But I can assure you that nothing you've seen today on 'People Passion,' or are watching right at this moment, has been cooked up by me. I'm sorry that our time is up. I wish you could be here and actually see this woman, instead of the drawings of her. Whether she is the original Anne Hutchinson, or not, no longer matters. I am overwhelmed. I am a believer. You have not only heard the voice of God speaking through this woman, but before your eyes you have seen a miracle."

Extracting Anne from the tearful, chattering women who encircled her and Chrissie, who had finally walked slowly back to her wheelchair, took more than an hour. Everyone wanted to touch and kiss Anne's unphotographicable face, and despite the heat from the studio lights they were amazed, when she held out her hand to them, or they kissed her cheek. "She's as cool as death," one woman marvelled.

They bombarded Anne with questions that ranged from her revelations —and several women told her that God often spoke to them—to how her husband really felt about John Cotton, to what Boston was like when she was living there, and whether, if she had been burned to ashes by the Indians, how could God give her back her body? And did she really believe that all of us who loved God would live after death? Quite a few were dubious that a Puritan woman could look so modern and pretty as she did, and one officious-looking woman, who said that she was a lawyer, questioned Chrissie in detail about her polio, and whether the real truth was that, even before her encounter with Mrs. Hutchinson, she'd been able to walk a little.

Chrissie denied it. She slowly stood up again and smiled radiantly at Anne. "I cannot walk around the block," she said, "but I will. Mrs. Hutchinson has awakened the spirit of God within me. She's a daughter of God. I am sure that like Jesus she can heal the sick and make the blind see."

"Are you going to perform other miracles?" one woman asked sarcastically.

"I did not perform this one," Anne said coolly. "The Lord did. We are all sons and daughters of God. When you are fully aware of his inner light within you, you can perform your own miracles."

Along with Susan and Saul, I had kept in the background and let Anne be the center of attention. But then, a man who identified himself as a nuclear-freeze activist asked Anne where he could get in touch with her. Smiling, Anne pointed to her "dear Robert," just as Sally walked back into the studio, and I was trying to tell him that Anne really wasn't a political activist.

"You can't keep her in a pumpkin shell," Sally said. "I'm sorry, Bob, but I've already told the press that she is living in Quincy with you. I just talked with Steve Carlson, the man you met at the Bay Tower Room. He watched the show. He wants Anne to appear on 'Wake Up America' Friday morning in New York. Lucy Sprague and Jack Varsi will give her an hour coast-to-coast interview. Steve assured me that the network will cancel a prime-time show Monday evening, if Anne will appear with an assorted panel of medical men, psychologists, and historians. All the networks and Cable News Network have been on the phone." Sally hugged Anne, who I was sure didn't realize that this kind of national exposure meant the end of her privacy and her temporary womb in my home. "You and your miracle will be shown on World News Tonight, on every network," she told Anne. "By midnight a hundred million Americans will have heard your message from God." Sally shook her head in wonder. "Repent and rebel—my God, that's a great slogan! It could unite the world against nuclear warfare."

Sally told Anne that the network would cover all her expenses to and in New York, including a two-bedroom suite at the Savoy Plaza overlooking Central Park. "It should be very exciting for you," she said. "You lived near New York City once. Throg's Neck, wasn't it? I think it was Dutch territory then and the Big Apple was called New Amsterdam. She smiled a little dubiously at Saul and Susan. "You can even bring your friends, and of course I'm sure Bob will go with you. This is Tuesday. You can either drive or fly down, but you must be at the studio by eight-thirty A.M. Friday morning."

"If I were she," I said sarcastically, "I'd forget the whole business and pray to God to make me totally invisible." I knew that Anne had no idea of what New York City, or exposure on national television meant. And I wasn't at all sure that I wanted to be involved. "We really need time to think it over," I told Sally, but Anne kept repeating "New Amsterdam, New Amsterdam—I remember William Kieft, the governor. After Will died he invited me to come to Dutch territory and live there. Methinks that I would like to see the place where I died."

It was impossible to tell Anne that she wouldn't recognize Pelham, New York, and certainly not New Amsterdam. But then Saul cast the die by telling Sally that if I were agreeable, he would be happy to drive all of us to New York. "You'll love it," he told Anne. "We'll take you on a tour of the city, and you can even see the Statue of Liberty."

We finally escaped the studio into the privacy of my car. It was three o'clock, and we still hadn't eaten lunch. I suggested Pier 4.

"Anne's not invisible yet," Susan said, not realizing that her words were portentous. "Keep in mind they never stopped showing drawings of her on the show. Someone is sure to recognize her. Saul and I can pick up pizza or Chinese food on the way home. I think we should hide out in Quincy while we can. We need time to talk." She told Anne that her problem was going to be that millions of Americans would love her so much that they wouldn't give her room to breathe. "They'll all want to touch you and hug you."

"But a lot of them won't try to suffocate you," I said. "They'll be convinced that you're a faker. They'll demand the ultimate repentance and *auto-da-fé*."

"What's that?" Anne asked.

"Self-immolation. This time the Indians won't burn you. You'll have to set yourself on fire to convince the nonbelievers."

Laughing, Saul told her that I was a pessimist. "You've done it, Anne," he said. "You've given the little guy something to think about. He or she can no longer pass the buck on nuclear war and nuclear weapons to their leaders. Every damn person in the world who helps to make bombs and missiles is responsible. It's really *three* R's. Repent for choosing death. Take responsibility for life. Rebel against those who don't." Saul was so enthusiastic that I had to warn him to keep watching the road, or he'd be personally repenting for choosing death.

But he couldn't contain the ideas bobbing in his brain. "Don't you realize what Anne can do?" he demanded. "Acting together, we can help her stop this nuclear-war insanity. We can make millions of workers realize that their leaders can't make nuclear weapons without them. Responsibility for a real nuclear freeze and a total disarmament begins with each one of us. If we don't actually help make weapons, we must refuse to support those who do make them. We must refuse to pay taxes. You and I and Susan can help Anne provide the leadership. We can show them how to rebel and take back the power of our own destruction from our leaders. Anne can call for a simultaneous World Fast Day, and a strike against all weapons of war. Imagine—a fast day to repent and a strike to rebel. Billions of dollars will pour in." Saul grinned in the rear-vision mirror at Anne. "You're going to need an organization and a manager. If Bob doesn't want the job, I'll take it."

"What is a strike?" Anne asked. "I know not that word."

"It's just what you asked for," Saul said. "It's right out of the Bible. Most people have no arms to lay down, but we can all lay down our tools and refuse to make them. We can strike for God."

"You're absolutely crazy," I told him. "Americans may hate war, but they aren't going to walk out on good-paying jobs, and the Russians will simply shoot down any dissenters in their country or send them to Siberia."

"Not when we've told them the truth," Saul said. "They might as well die now as later. Armagaddon. The reason Anne returned to earth is because God is fed up with all of us. Anne will convince them. We'll start right here in the United States. One guy striking would do no good. But a million Americans staying off the job—repenting and rebelling for just one day—will wake up the world. That's only the beginning. Our message will be that the leaders of the world must schedule a total-disarmament conference within a month. If not, we'll call for a World Strike and Fast Day, and we'll follow that with Fast and Strike Weeks—one week every month."

Saul shook his head grimly. "Believe me, we're not going to be alone. Thousands of people all over the world will join us. They'll realize that God has given us one last chance."

Although Anne listened to Saul with nods of approval, I was sure that she didn't understand the extent of his mania. When we finally turned off Wollaston Boulevard into Merrymount, I was sorry that I ever got involved with him or Sally Lane. Narragansett Road was jammed with automobiles and hundreds of people crowding the sidewalks. Near my house and in the driveway, we could see three police cars. Looking like guardians of Hell, with a subdued moan of their sirens and ominous revolving lights picking out strange white faces in the early nightfall, they seemed to be waiting for doomsday.

"My God!" Susan exclaimed in awe as Saul slowly inched the car down the street. "They're waiting for us."

"It's her. It's Anne Hutchinson," someone shouted, and there was cheering and enthusiastic shouts of "You tell 'em, Anne! We're with you, Anne!"

Reluctantly, Saul stopped the car and we were surrounded by men and women peering at us through the windows and yelling, "Anne! Anne! We heard you! We love you! Help save us! Oh God, look at her! She's really beautiful. She's an angel of God." Several cameras flashed at us through the windows, and someone shouted, "If you get a picture, I'll give you a hundred bucks for it."

Leaning out the window, Saul begged the crowd to stand back and let us turn into the driveway, which was blocked by two mobile television vans. For a moment we were at an impasse until the police broke through and made them back up. "You're a mighty popular lady, ma'am," one of the young cops grinned through the window at her. "I didn't see you on TV, but a lot of the boys at the station saw the drawings of you. Word got around pretty fast where you were living. Is it true that no one can take your picture?" He waved at several men carrying television cameras and mobile lighting. "Some of those guys don't believe it."

"Please clear the way for us into the house," I said. "We don't know these people. Some of them could be dangerous. I'm afraid for Mrs. Hutchinson."

The front lawn and driveway were a churning, swaying ocean of people pushing and shoving to get as close to Anne as they could. The car was now encircled by five other policemen, who were trying to keep them back. We could see several people on crutches. One man was in a wheelchair. Many old men and women were wrapped in overcoats and looked as if they had just been released from a nearby nursing home.

"They're expecting you to heal them," I told Anne, and I was afraid that whether she was responsible or not, there would be another miracle on my front lawn.

"They are God's creatures," Anne said and she was obviously delighted. "I fear them not."

The policemen finally escorted us to the front door past television cameramen and many people with still cameras.

"Thank thee for coming to see me," Anne kept saying as we moved through the crowd. "Love not me but the light of Christ within thee and me." She touched the extended hand of a man who seemed to be blind but who had been pushed to the front of the crowd and told that she was passing. "See God," she told him, and the man burst into tears. "His Kingdom is within thee."

Inside the front door, waiting for Saul, who finally got the car in the driveway, to join us, I asked Bill Murphy, one of the policemen who was wearing sergeant stripes, if they could disperse the crowd. In the living room, to my shock I realized that some of them were standing in the shrubbery peering at us through the front window.

"Get the Hell out of here," Murphy yelled, rapping on the window. He shrugged at me. "We can keep them off your property," he said. "But the streets and sidewalk are a public way." He grinned at Anne. "God knows what will happen here if you really perform miracles. If I were you," he told me, "I'd call up the station and get round-the-clock police protection. You'll have to pay, but I really think you should have a couple of men to keep the crowds away, and you have to face it. Inevitably you will attract some nuts and crackpots, who might be dangerous."

Within an hour I was an uneasy prisoner in my home. I was more than a little peeved with Saul, who told me that I should be happy. I was going to be almost as famous as Anne was. "Seriously," he asked, "what can you do about it? The fat's in the fire. You could tell Anne and Susan and me to get out of the house. I'm sure I could call any of the Boston hotels and they'll be happy to give us a suite—just for publicity." He grinned at me. "But I can see from your face that, problem or not, you don't want to lose Anne." He laughed. "History repeats itself. You're in the same spot John Cotton was. You're her 'dear Robert'—her protector. Are you going to toss her to the wolves like he did?" He gestured at Anne, who was trying to listen to us and at the same time hear Susan, who was questioning whether she really understood what was about to happen to her.

"You won't belong to yourself anymore," Susan was telling her. "If people really believe that God has recreated you, millions of them are going to arrive here, or wherever you are. They'll want to see you in person. They'll want to touch you. They'll even think that if they could only have a piece of your clothing, or a medal that you blessed, it might cure them of their miseries. You'll have to be protected from them or they might strip you naked in the streets. And there will be many people who will hate you and believe that not God, but Satan himself has sent you back to earth."

Anne smiled sadly at us. "I have no choice. Why else am I here? Time runneth out. I must bear whatever afflictions the Lord may wish." With a little sob she came into my arms. "I love thee, dear Robert, but I fear that I may cause you sorrow and trouble. Methinks thou shouldst renounce me like John-Luv did."

"Damn it," I said and hugged her. "Saul is right. Anyway, I'm not going to try to change history and turn you into a passive wife. But I know now how Cotton must have felt. But, Anne, you must keep one thing in mind. I married you yesterday, for better or worse, but you make me nervous when you keep saying that time runneth out. What do you mean?"

Kissing me tenderly, Anne sighed. "I asked the Lord if he will let me stay with thee until thou art weary of me." She smiled mischievously, "Thy wife may see to that."

Prophetically, as she spoke, I heard the phone ringing. I had turned on my answering machine, but thinking it might be Emily, I decided to pick it up.

It was Liz Johnson, who pitched her ball without preliminaries. "I've been trying to reach you for the past two hours, but all I could get was a busy signal. Emily had the same problem. She's been trying to call you all day," Liz said grimly. "I spared Emily the details of the Sally Lane show, but I presume that the miracle worker is still living with you."

Examining the answering machine while Liz ranted and prayed that I'd be over my Anne Hutchinson insanity before Emily got back next Tuesday, I was surprised to see that the tape, capable of storing fifty short messages, had been completely used. Before she hung up, Liz gave me the phone number of a hotel in Madrid where Emily and her friends were staying on the last lap of their art tour. They had just arrived from Rome and were spending two days exploring the Prado, after which they would fly to Amsterdam and then to London.

"If it won't disturb your new bed chum," Liz told me sarcastically, "Emily expects you to call her at midnight our time. It will be early morning in Spain."

I wondered what details Liz had spared Emily. Probably more than enough to provoke Liz's curiosity as to how the mouse was enjoying life while the cat was away. But my thoughts were interrupted by the phone ringing again. This time it was the voice of a woman who identified herself as Carol Anders. "Could I speak with Mrs. Hutchinson?" she pleaded in a tearful voice. "I'm sure that she can help my husband. He is only thirty-six and he is dying of cancer."

I gave the phone to Anne, who listened sympathetically. She told the woman that if there was to be a miracle it must be that she and her husband would make it possible by loving the light of God within them. Listening to her, I knew that the word was out. Anne Hutchinson was living with me. I had always had a listed telephone number. The reason the answering tape had run out was that between the time Anne had appeared on "People Passion" and now, less than three hours later, there must have been a continual stream of phone calls trying to reach her.

Saul had drawn the living-room curtains. While one policeman patrolled the front yard, and another the floodlit back yard, and we were aware of the incessant traffic on the street, we listened to the tape. It was filled with cries of help for Anne to cure people: believers in reincarnation who had lived before insisted that they must talk with her; spiritualists who wished to communicate with dead relatives; Jehovah's Witnesses, Seventh-Day Adventists, and members of the Unification Church, who were enthralled with Anne's concept of Armageddon. A famous Baptist evangelist, who hadn't seen the program but had been told about it, had called from Georgia and invited her to speak at his college, and there were ten or more men and women who insisted that they must meet with Anne immediately and promised that with their help millions of supporters and dollars could be marshalled for her Repent and Rebel crusade. And an anti-nuclear group was ready to hire Sullivan Stadium in Foxboro so that sixty thousand people could actually see Anne in person.

It was only beginning. By the time the six o'clock news came on, long cuts from the Sally Lane show were being shown on all three network stations. These were followed by seven o'clock World News Tonight and reports by the nation's foremost commentators, who balanced chuckles of disbelief and doubt with wide-eyed maybes and what-ifs. Drawing after drawing of Anne's face, poised, smiling, and tearful, were being freeze-framed on television screens from coast to coast. Like glorified pictures of a missing person that the world was searching for, Anne was inescapably identified. Thanks to Sally Lane, fifty million or more Americans knew that a beautiful woman, who had died some three hundred and fifty years ago, had returned to her home in Mt. Wollaston—Quincy, Massachusetts—and that she was living with her dear Robert, who might be a reincarnation of her husband Will.

Several commentators raised the question that would quickly become an undercurrent and would gradually infiltrate all discussions of Anne's Repent and Rebel scenario. Was it Soviet-inspired? If Americans and Western nations went on strike against war, wouldn't the Russians, who already had more military strength than any other nation, control the world? Might she not be in danger of terrorists, kidnappers, assassins, who would believe that her repent message was directed against them? Wouldn't they be encouraged by their governments to destroy her?

Responding to my "What the Hell are we going to do now?" Saul suggested that rather than disconnect my phone we put a message on the tape that precluded any response from the caller, but, in Saul's words, kept him on the hook. "We've got to put all this national enthusiasm to work," he told Anne, who was patting my hand soothingly while she nodded and beamed her approval of his suggestion.

The message they finally agreed on was Anne saying on tape, "Thank thee for calling. I love thee. I wish that I could be with thee in person. But we are united in a better way. We share the same inner light and spirit of a loving God within us. God loves us all. But each of us must help Him. Through me, God is telling thee that thou must save thyself and all His creatures. Thou must accept responsibility. Right now, directly or indirectly with the taxes thou payest, thou art telling thy leaders that thou condone man killing man. God is asking thou to repent and rebel. Refuse to build any weapon that can be used to destroy His creatures. Thou canst help create a triumphant crusade and bring the Kingdom of Heaven to earth. Thou must help all mankind become aware of the loving light of God within each person. I will speak again Friday morning from New York City on 'Wake Up America.' If thou wisheth to help financially, send thy donations to Anne Hutchinson, Post Office Box AH, Mt. Wollaston, Quincy, Massachusetts."

Elated, Saul promised that by morning he would coordinate the box number with the post office. "That message will be picked up by the networks within an hour," he said. "Within a week you'll have a headquarters in Boston with a complete office staff." He hugged Anne jubilantly. "The cradle of liberty will become the cradle of salvation. Three and a half centuries ago you built the creche and nursed the freedom baby right here."

Saul watched me shaking my head dubiously. "What's the matter?" he scowled at me. "Have you got cold feet? Don't you approve?"

"Sunday is Easter Sunday. But Anne isn't Jesus Christ," I said sarcastically. "And you're not Paul of Tarsus. You're either going to get her crucified and yourself beheaded or you'll make her ridiculous and then within a few weeks boring. Americans have a very short attention span. If you don't convince them to repent and rebel en masse, within two weeks your crusade will run out of gas. Look at cigarettes. Despite the warnings, millions of people are still smoking themselves to death."

"You can't equate smoking with nuclear warfare," Susan said, frowning at me.

I shrugged, "Why not?" Most people don't believe that they'll die from cigarettes or nuclear bombs."

Then to my surprise, Anne put in words what I was really afraid of. "Ye do not have to worry," she said. "Methinks that the Lord knew that Jesus had the same problem. If he had lived to an old age, he could not have assumed the sins of man. They believed him because he died before his time."

I knew that Anne was telling me, once again, that her time was limited and she probably knew what was going to happen to her. But Susan missed the implication. "Do you understand what running out of gas means?" she asked Anne.

Smiling, Anne nodded. "Gas is something wispy that has not settled down. It has assumed not its final shape. The Greeks called it *xaos.*"

"That's what I'm afraid of," I muttered, "chaos."

Afraid to leave the house to bring in dinner—a steady stream of cars and people were still passing by, some of them yelling, "Anne, Anne, please talk to us!" and a few shouting obscenities, "She's a fucking crazy old lady!"— Susan and Anne made a huge omelet filled with onions and peppers, which we embalmed with ketchup and washed down with several bottles of white wine. Our endless, what-shall-we-do discussion continued until eleven. Then we watched another reprise of Anne's television appearance on the late news. For the moment at least, as one commentator suggested, millions of Americans believed that God was once again proving that he existed.

Puttering around my bedroom half-naked, Anne and I were invaded by "our children"—Anne's laughing description of Saul and Susan, who swirled into the room in a see-through nightgown followed by Saul in jockey shorts. "We came to say goodnight and tell you not to worry," they said, and Saul hugged Anne affectionately and Susan gave me a daughterly kiss.

I was finally alone with Anne. Wearing a black satin nightgown that Miss Green or she had picked out at Lord & Taylor's and that clung provocatively to her breasts and hips, she blithely grinned at me. "Liz Johnson told thee that thy wife is in Spain. Methinks that is a miracle."

"You mean that my wife is a miracle?"

"No—that we are not at war with Spain, and thy telephone can reach across that big ocean. Art thou going to call her?"

I wasn't too enthusiastic about calling Emily with Anne lying voluptuously in bed beside me, but I had no choice. Hoping that Anne wouldn't start talking the moment that Emily answered, I called the overseas operator. It occurred to me that if Liz hadn't already told Emily that Anne was living in her house and sleeping in her bed, she probably had implied it. But I wasn't prepared for Emily's sleepy, sarcastic, "Good morning, lover. I learn something new about you every day. I didn't know that you were a necrophiliac."

"It's not good morning here," I said grouchily, wondering how much she knew.

"Is your just-back-from-the-grave girlfriend in bed with you?"

"She's not a girl," I said. "She's a fifty-two-year-old woman. I suppose that Liz has told you some lurid stories about her." As I spoke, I was surprised to feel Anne's hand softly caressing my stomach and lingering over my genitals. She was holding my penis in the air and staring at it gravely.

"All Liz told me," Emily said, "is that you are being your usually naive and sappy self. We all saw your Anne on Spanish television last night. You can cut out the crap. Maybe she can't be photographed, but she doesn't look like the mother of fifteen kids to me. Does she perform miracles in bed too?"

"Don't worry, I don't need any miracles yet," I said, staring at my appendage, which was now pointing at the ceiling without Anne's help. "I'd forgotten about the miracle of satellite transmission," I told Emily. "I'm astounded that Anne has already appeared on European television."

"Are you going to leave me for her?" she asked, altogether too sweetly. "My painting group thinks that you may be ready to be born again with Jesus and Anne."

"Anne's gone to New York," I said, ignoring the fact that she was now slowly kissing her way down my chest. "You don't have to worry about her. Anne's on her own trip. What's the reaction to her in Spain?"

"The prime minister has already told King Juan Carlos that she should be invited here. He hopes to snatch her out of Queen Elizabeth's arms. This is a Catholic country. They believe in miracles. Please, dear Robert," Emily paused with a sarcastic little laugh, "I believe in miracles, too, but I think it will be a miracle if you are at the airport next Tuesday to bring me home."

I assured Emily that I would be there and said goodbye.

"Methinks thou tells lies, too," Anne said. "Thou told Emily that I was already in New York. Thou didst not let me talk with her. I wanted to thank her for sharing thee." Kissing me with a hundred tiny kisses, she slid on top of me and leaned on her elbows and stared at me with tears in her eyes. "I've been thinking about Will and Pocasset and the Island," she said. "I lived there longer than I lived in Boston. Can we go there in your automobile on the way to New York? I would like to see it again."

35

At breakfast I asked Saul and Susan if they'd like to escape from our prison. "Anne would like to see Portsmouth, Rhode Island, where she lived for five years after she was banished," I told them. "I'll call Steve Carlson and tell him that we'll be in New York at the Plaza late Thursday. If we can get out of here without being followed, the four of us can vanish for about thirty hours. I'm sure we can find a hideout for the night in Rhode Island."

Susan and Saul were delighted. "I can drive there in a couple of hours," he said. "But when we come back, we've got to find another hideout in Boston for Anne." Saul grinned at me and nudged Anne. "You look like a lost soul," he said to me. "How are you going to live without her?"

I shrugged but decided not to bare my lost soul. Dave Hedman had warned me that I wasn't facing reality. I still hoped that somehow, after Emily got home, I could weave her and Anne into a tranquil domestic existence. But I hadn't yet assimilated the celebrity factor, which leaves no room for tranquility, or the inevitable clash of two women over one man— even if one woman "cared not" about ownership rights or might have arrived from another world.

Saul verbalized my thoughts. "How would you feel," he asked Anne, who had told him that I had talked with Emily last night, "if Will brought another woman into your home and told you that he had married her too?"

Anne knew that Saul was teasing her. Her eyes flooded with tears, but she managed to smile. "Will loved me—so I would love her. I loveth Robert, so I loveth Emily, too. I would have told Emily last night, but Robert wanted me not to speak to her." She tossed the question to Susan. "What wouldst thou think if Saul loved another woman?"

Susan laughed, "It would depend on the woman." She nuzzled Anne's cheek. "I'd share Saul with you, anytime."

Saul blushed. "You don't have to worry. Anne prefers older men. But you're all forgetting the real problem. It's not sex; it's religion. With Anne living here, Bob and his wife would be driven crazy." He pointed out the window. "It's only nine o'clock and there must be a hundred people out there already. The place is becoming a shrine." He shrugged, "Or maybe circus is a better word. Anyway, for Anne's protection I think we should leave as quickly as possible. No one should know where we're going. I'll tell the police that we're driving Anne to the airport to catch a plane to New York."

Checking, I quickly discovered that Anne's resurrection was still being rehashed on the early morning radio news and television. To our surprise, and unknown to us, at least two additional prime-time network television specials, originating in New York City, wanted to feature Anne Hutchinson next week. She was being tentatively scheduled for Sunday and Monday nights. According to one commentator, during the next few days several local radio and TV shows would offer an analysis and discussion of Christian beliefs in resurrection, Armageddon, and reincarnation, the latter as experienced by well-known movie personalities such as Shirley McClaine.

I found a large suitcase for Anne, who decided that she would bring all her new clothes with her and not leave them for Emily to find.

By ten-thirty, beds made, breakfast dishes washed so, as Susan said laughing, "Emily couldn't complain of the mess that Bob's friends had made," we were ready to leave. I had cleared with the police that I wanted them to continue to patrol the house until Monday. Two friendly cops cleared a path through a cheering, pleading crowd. "Please let Anne talk with us," they kept saying. "We love you, Anne."

"Love the light of God within ye, and ye will love me," Anne told them as she waved at them through the open car window.

We were finally in the clear. Saul drove out of Quincy, and I was relieved to see that no one was following us.

"We've got world enough and time," Saul said, watching my worried expression in the rear-view mirror. "And two women who love us—what more can you ask?"

"For time to stop," I laughed, "at least until I can absorb this—and that will take the rest of my lifetime."

"We've still got a problem," Susan said. "Even if I had never seen Anne, I'd still recognize her from those drawings on television. Wherever we stop for lunch, or stay the night, someone is sure to spot her." We were passing the Braintree Shopping Plaza as she spoke. "I've got a great idea," she said excitedly. "Anne needs a disguise. Can you afford a wig?" she asked me.

Twenty minutes later, while Saul and Anne waited for us in the car, Susan and I had selected a shoulder-length wig with natural looking black hair and a pair of stylish sunglasses. Trying them on in the car, Anne was as giggly and excited as a schoolgirl.

"You look like Sophia Loren, an Italian movie star," Susan told her.

"Methinks I could appear in Court," Anne said, examining herself in the car mirror. "King Charles would quickly choose me as a lady-in-waiting to his wife." She sighed. "But alas, I do not like the spectacles. I cannot see God's sunshine."

"Elizabeth is queen now," I said, surveying the transformation a little sourly. "Her son is Charles. I'm sure that he wouldn't keep you waiting. You'll have to wear sunglasses."

Susan agreed, "Bob is right. Your big green eyes will give you away." Susan looked at her a little worriedly. "Even so, with your new sexy hairdo and your clear skin almost glowing you're going to attract a lot of attention."

"She looks like Mata Hari," Saul laughed. "Or an expensive lady of the night."

Snuggled beside me in the back seat, Anne patted my middle. "Methinks that my wig makes you more excited than a belt with garters." She pulled back her skirt to show me. "I wore it today to keep my stockings up."

I told Saul to take Route 24 to Portsmouth. "I think it approximates the sixty-mile trail through the woods that Anne took in April of 1638."

It was now a high-speed expressway, bypassing the cities of Brockton and Taunton and most of Fall River. Soon we were passing many patches of virgin forest. Anne asked Saul if he could drive a little slower. "It maketh my brain whirl to go this fast. I cannot remember anything I see." She shook her head. "And that thing you call a radio—doth it never stop talking and making music? Methinks that today men and women listen to so much noise that they no longer can hear the Lord talk to them."

Chuckling, Saul turned the radio off, and I told Anne to tell them how she had got lost in the forest and been guided to Pocasset by her friend Miantonomo, a sachem of the Narragansetts.

"We don't think of Rhode Island as an island today," I told Anne before she began. In case you're not up on your history," I said to Saul and Susan, "Roger Williams had been banished from the Colony even before Anne arrived in Boston. He settled in the northern area in a place called Mooshausick by the Indians. Miantonomo sold it to him and twelve other men for thirty pounds. He renamed it Providence, 'because of God's merciful providence in my distress.' And he said it would always be a shelter for those distressed in conscience. In the south were several islands in Narragansett Bay occupied by the Indians. The biggest of them was known as the Isle of Aquiday. It's about ten miles long and about eight miles wide at the widest point. Today it is connected to Massachusetts by a bridge across the Sakonnet River. In Anne's day they used boats to get back and forth to the island. The first settlement was in Pocasset, which Anne and her friends renamed Portsmouth. What's now called Newport, which is about ten miles south of Portsmouth, was called Aquidneck."

"The Separatists, in Plymouth, insisted that the Island belonged to them," Anne said. "But Master Winthrop claimed that the charter that King James had given him for the Massachusetts Bay Colony included the Island and gave the Bay Colony complete jurisdiction over the entire area, including Providence."

"When did it become Rhode Island?" Saul asked.

"Not until March 1644," I said. "Roger Williams finally received a patent from Parliament. Williams called it Rhode Island after the Greek island of Rhodes. From the beginning, it was the only place in the New World that offered freedom of thought and belief. Williams stated that submission on Rhode Island was not to be to a particular belief in God, but only to 'civil things' affecting the public good."

Anne was delighted to learn that a little more than a year after her death Rhode Island was free of Master Winthrop. "I was afraid that it would never happen," she said. "I wish that I had lived to see it. Before I left Aquiday and settled on Long Island with the Dutch, I wrote Harry Vane and begged him to come back and help us. Harry knew that Masters Weld and Peters, who detested me, were in London trying to convince Parliament to expand the Massachusetts Bay Charter to include all the islands and land adjoining Narragansett Bay. I was fearful that once again Master Winthrop and Master Dudley would try to own my body and soul."

"They had a charter that predated Roger Williams, or else they forged one," I said. "In 1643, before you died and before Williams went to England—and with Harry Vane's help got the Rhode Island charter—Winthrop claimed he had one. Evidently he was afraid to use it because he thought it might be a fake—something that Weld and Peters had cooked up themselves and that the king had never actually seen."

"I read that you were pregnant at the church trial," Susan said. She had been watching miles of still undeveloped land. She pointed out the window of the car. "How did you ever walk so far?"

Anne smiled. "I wasn't visibly pregnant," she said. "But as I told Sally Lane, John-Luv's seed was in me. He put it there two weeks before I left Boston. But that it was growing, I knew it not, not until late April when I was living on the Island." She shrugged. "I was frightened in the forest, but vexation and anticipation are often harder things to bear than actuality. I well knew that Pocasset was a long way, but I had no other choice. I was banished. I had to leave my dear home in Boston. When I finally faced the truth, I began to feel better every day. On March 28th I corralled my family. Francis was eighteen years, Bridget nineteen, Anne and Mary were eleven and ten, Katherine was eight. They helped me with William, who was six, and Susanna, who was only three. Little Zuriel was only a year old, and we took turns carrying him. Richard, who was twenty-two, agreed to stay in Boston to take care of the house. Edward had gone south to look for a new home for us with Will and had not returned. We sailed across the bay to our plantation at Mt. Wolleystone. I knew that Will and nineteen other men banished from the colony, including Will Coddington, John Coggeshall, Will Aspinwall, Will's brother Ed, my son Ed, and my son-in-law, Tommy Savage, had all met at Will Coddington's house on March 7th, the week before I was excommunicated. They signed a compact which read: 'In the presence of Jehovah, we do solemnly incorporate ourselves into a body politic, and with His help we will submit our persons, lives and estates unto our Lord Jesus Christ, and to all those perfect and absolute laws of His given us in His holy word of truth to be guided and judged thereby.'"

"That 'body politic' was the beginning of our Constitution," Saul said. "But your menfolks hung onto their theocracy."

"It was a mistake," Anne said. "I told Will that it sounded as if Master Winthrop had written it. Although I loved Will Coddington, I was not overjoyed when they named him judge, which was the same as governor. Master Coddington was autocratic enough without the title. As it turned out, I was right. But when they signed the compact, they knew not whether they would settle on Long Island in Dutch territory or at Delaware Bay. Will thought I should go to New Hampshire with Johnny's wife, Mary, and Will's mother until they were sure where they were going to settle. When they found the right place, Will told me that he would build us a new home and then I could join them.

"But before I left Mt. Wolleystone, Edward came back from the Island with good news. Roger Williams had finally made an agreement with Miantonomo and Canonicus to sell the Isle of Aquiday to our group of families. Miantonomo knew that Harry Vane and I were good friends, and he loved Harry like a brother. Will even told him that Harry might come back to the Island and be the chief sachem."

Anne chuckled. "That was my doing. Will knew that I wrote to Harry once a week. Harry had finally found a woman, Frances Wray—a daughter of Sir Christopher Wray. They were married in 1639. Harry told me that he could do more for the Colony in England than he could in America, but he kept writing me that I should come to England with Will." Anne grinned at me. "Harry wrote me that I would like his wife, but he needed me for jollity and to stimulate his head and heart."

For a moment Anne silently watched the stretches of woodland we were passing. "I believe not what I am seeing," she said in a hushed voice. "There is a wide road miles ahead of us with deep woods on either side. They are like the forest that I walked through with my family, but the trees are not so tall. It was April then, as it is now, and the buds were dancing happily in the breeze. Like me, they were glad to be alive again. Before I got to Pocasset, Miantonomo told me that the Narragansetts had sold the Island to us for forty fathoms of white beads—wampum—twenty hoes, and ten English coats, which they much admired. We finally arrived at a wide river that the Indians called Sakonnet. They ferried us across in canoes. We could see people on the other side waving to us but it took us nearly all day to get there.

"When I finally walked into the meadow in Pocasset, Will saw me and the children. All of us, and our friends, danced for joy and hugged each other. Like Hagar and Ishmael, Will and I, once again, had wandered in the wilderness. Feeling sad that John-Luv would never see his son again, I held Zuriel up in the air. Like Hagar, I heard the angel of God calling unto me: 'Arise, lift up the lad, and hold him in thine hand, for I will make him a great nation.'"

36

We stopped for lunch at Valle's, a roadside restaurant close to the Rhode Island border. The waitress was fascinated with our black-haired companion. She kept staring at Anne, and I saw her whisper to several other waitresses. They obviously thought she must be a movie star, but no one recognized her from the Sally Lane show.

"Where did you live with all your kids?" Susan asked her after we had ordered salads and sandwiches.

"Will and Ed dug out a cellar for our house. We covered the hole with canvas at night and slept on the ground under it. We had a tent for the older children. When we wanted to get away from them, Will and I slept under the stars and played seesaw in the marsh grass. Every day I thanked God for Will, and I worked with him to build our new home. I liked Pocasset. I am like a water nymph. I was born in Alford near the sea, and all my life I was never far from it. Summer nights we bathed in the Great Cove, and although I am certain that Will knew that the coming child was not his, he washed my swollen belly tenderly. One night he told me that his only complaint was that he could not understand how a man who cared for me, and was my teacher, could turn his back on me.

"By August my belly was so big that I was getting in my own way. Will tried to stop me, but I continued to work every day. I wanted our house to be finished before the baby was born. But then in September I was suddenly feeling very poorly. I was in my seventh month." Anne smiled at me. "I knew not, until thy friend Dave Hedman told me Saturday night, that I had nothing left in my body to fertilize a man's seed properly."

"Winthrop described Anne's premature birth in his *Journal*," I told Saul and Susan. "His description was based on what her doctor, John Clarke, had presumably told him. The details are so nauseating that James Hosmer eliminated them from his edition of the *Journal*."

"Was John Clarke a friend of Winthrop?" Susan asked.

"Methinks not," Anne grimaced. "He moved to the Island to escape from him. He told me: 'I thought it not strange to see men differ about matters of Heaven, for I expect no less upon earth. But to see that they were not able to bear each other in their different understandings and consciences, and here—in these utmost parts of the world—cannot live peaceably together, passeth all understanding.'"

She shrugged, "But John was a man, and I would never have asked for his help. Mary Dyer and Janey Hawkins were with me, but John had settled close by. Even though he was a chirguen, like many men he was made nervous by the humors that emergeth from a woman's body. I am certain that he believed that women harbor evil spirits. The next day, after the birth, someone—I know not whom—was returning to Boston and John must have told him that the child was not formed. Whoever it was, told John-Luv. The next Lecture Day John told the congregation that the unformed birth 'signified my error in denying inherent righteousness, and saying that all was in Christ in us and nothing of ours in faith and love.'

"When Master Winthrop heard about it, he was certain that Satan had fathered my child. He sent a messenger from Boston to John Clarke to get all the details." Anne scowled. "Methinks that John was still awed by Master Winthrop. When Master Winthrop gave John Clarke's answer to John-Luv, he preached another sermon and told everyone in Boston that I had given birth to twenty-seven monstrous little devils. I was very angry, and I wrote him a letter and told him that it was he who should ask the Lord's forgiveness. I told him that the child within me had not been seeded in love and that was why the Lord had not let his seed take form in me." Anne shook her head sadly. "John did not answer me."

Never mind," I told Susan, who gave Anne a quick sympathetic hug, "Winthrop was right about one thing. Anne *had* unleashed a lot of female devils. Lady Deborah Moody, a wealthy woman who lived in Salem, was against the baptism of infants, and she followed Anne's teachings. Winthrop reports that she was quickly banished and moved to Long Island. Another woman refused to bow her head when Jesus' name was mentioned, but insisted that faith in Jesus overrode the laws of all magistrates and ministers. She was whipped on her bare buttocks and had a cleft stick put in her mouth. And according to Winthrop, who recorded the mischief all these women were causing, Roger Williams made things worse. He told the ladies in Providence that they were at liberty to attend all religious meetings whether their husbands did or not. One man named Verin refused to let his wife go alone, and Williams' congregation told him that if he wouldn't give his wife her freedom, he should let her go to some other man who would treat her better."

Anne watched silently while the waitress served us, and then she said, "Master Winthrop never stopped complaining about me to Roger Williams and anyone else, including John-Luv, who would listen to him. The poor man finally made himself sick with the fever and no doubt blamed it on me. In January of 1639 there was a terrible storm in Boston followed by earthquakes, which lasted three days. Master Winthrop told everyone that I had caused them by praying to the Holy Ghost, but in the process Satan had taken over and my house had started to shake from an earthquake. Master Winthrop could not believe that Roger had become an Anabaptist, or that my sister Katherine had baptized him. I wrote a letter to Master Oliver telling him that he should advise the congregation that I was not responsible for the storm or the earthquakes and to tell them the truth. The Lord was not happy with them for excommunicating me.

"Will told me that I should not send the letter, and I finally did not, but by this time I was at odds with Will Coddington. Our friend, Sam Gorton, and his wife, who I told Sally Lane had written me when I was a prisoner in Master Weld's house, and with whom Will and I had often stayed in England when we were on our way to London, got into a fracas with the Separatists from Plymouth. Sam and his family had lived there for three years. The reason that Sam went to Plymouth was because he was certain that he could never live in the same town with people like Master Dudley and Master Winthrop. But the Separatists were uneasy about him too. Finally, when Sam was preaching that Christ's image was present in Adam and the Lord had given us Jesus, who redeemed Adam's sin for all mankind forever, they were totally horrified. They gave Sam fourteen days to leave their jurisdiction.

"Where else could Sam go but to the Isle of Errors? He arrived in Portsmouth in 1641, and Will and I had a two-day welcoming party for him. Will Coddington came not—nor showed his face. He did not fancy Sam, who he said should learn to keep his mouth shut and not always speak his piece.

"'Twasn't long before Sam was in trouble again," Anne laughed. "This time it was over a cow. Sam's maid let Sam's cow roam in Goody Fenshaw's pasture, and the cow ate a few bushel of her maize. Goody was incensed, particularly because when she complained, Sam's maid kicked her in the bum. Sam defended his maid and called Goody and the magistrates a bunch of asses." Anne shrugged. "Of course Master Winthrop heard about it and wrote to Will Coddington that Will must be deluded by the Devil himself if he would tolerate such nonsense from a blasphemer like Sam Gorton. It all ended with Will deciding that Sam should be whipped. When Sam was stripped to his bum in the marketplace, Will's friends were yelling, 'Ye that are for the King lay hold on Gorton,' and Sam's friends, insisting that Will should be whipped instead of Sam, were yelling the same thing except to lay hold on Coddington. Sam got his arse warmed in public, and he decided to leave the Isle. He settled not far away in Shawomet. He and a few others bought the land from Miantomono, but another Indian named Pumham, a very scurrilous man, said that the land belonged to him."

Anne shook her head. "Before I left for Long Island, Master Winthrop was threatening to send an army down to Shawomet and put an end to Sam's career."

"He finally did. But Sam went back to England," I told them, "and Shawomet is now called Warwick."

"Will Coddington was very unhappy that after nearly a year we had built no meetinghouse in Pocasset," Anne said. "In truth, we were too busy planting crops and building our new homes to worry about a steeplehouse. I told Will Coddington that, for myself, I no longer believed that anyone who was truly aware of the spirit of Jesus within them needed sermons on Sundays and Lecture Days, or a steeplehouse where the women sat on one side and the men on the other and there was always some deacon or elder walking up and down the aisle prodding them to stay awake. Meetings of a few friends in their own homes, who shared their problems and their lives, were more meaningful than a church filled with restless people, each arguing that his own belief was the only way to know God.

"I told Will Coddington that the best thing that ever happened to me was that I was cast out of the Boston church. I was weary of organized religious bodies, and I believed no longer in the magistrates either. The best governors were those who governed least, and kept their noses out of people's lives and what they did in private in their beds. It was no concern of theirs whether a person believed in God or Jesus or not. Harry Vane agreed with me and so did Sam Gorton. I told Will Coddington that I was very unhappy about his treatment of Sam Gorton, and that he was acting like an ancient Hebrew. He was not our Moses, and the truth was that he was becoming more theocratic than Master Winthrop.

"My Will agreed with me, and for a while Will Coddington would not converse with either of us. He kept insisting that 'manifest preaching against the Law of God tends to civil disturbances.' Then in April he went up to Boston for several weeks, and he admitted to Master Winthrop that he had been at some fault in the near-rebellion. By the time he returned on April 28, I had convinced Will and most of the freemen that we must get rid of him." Anne laughed. "Master Coddington could not believe what was happening to him. All the signers of the original covenant insisted on a new election. My Will was elected governor, and they signed a new compact: 'We whose names are underwritten do acknowledge ourselves loyal subjects of his Majesty King Charles, and in his name do bind ourselves in a civil body politic, and do submit to his laws according to matters of justice.'"

"*Civil* is the key word," Saul said excitedly. "The church and state were finally separated in Rhode Island, and God took a back seat. What did Coddington think of that?"

"God did *not* take a back seat!" Anne expostulated. "His spirit of love would always guide us in making civil laws. I told Will Coddington that it was beyond all question that he would soon see the light, but he thought that we would destroy ourselves. He and John and Mary Coggeshall, Will and Mary Dyer, and few other families decided to move south to the fishing port called Aquidneck. The Coggeshalls and the Dyers were not angry with Will or me, or Will Coddington either. The truth was that Portsmouth was becoming very crowded and everyone needed more land and space."

Anne smiled. "A year later Will Coddington changed his mind and agreed that the Isle should be governed by a new covenant. My Will was delighted. We rode horseback to Aquidneck. When we got there, I hugged both Wills and told Will Coddington that Will and I agreed that he should become governor of the entire Island again. My Will told him that being governor was the blackest job he had ever had. 'I care not whether men always follow the Scriptures,' he told Will Coddington, 'but truth is I have no patience with blockheads.' Will Coddington agreed with me that our motto should be *amor vincet omnia,* and no one should be accounted delinquent for doctrine.

"Will Coddington got a meetinghouse raised at Aquidneck, but we never built one at Portsmouth whilst I lived there," Anne chuckled. "A year after Master Coddington's church was finished, the congregation had a new disagreement. Half of them decided to become Baptists. I told my Will that we had caused it. The Islanders had repented for not loving God, but they would always rebel against anyone who insisted that their particular way of loving God was the only way."

Anne was silent for a moment, watching people at other tables in the restaurant, many of whom were staring back at her.

"Winthrop didn't quit," I reminded her. "I read that on March 6, 1640, nearly two years later, Captain Edward Gibbons, Will Hibbens, and John Oliver, whom Thomas Weld referred to 'as men of a lovely and winning spirit and most likely to prevail,' arrived in Portsmouth and called for a church meeting to tell people that the churches of Aquiday were still under the jurisdiction of the elders of the Boston church."

"They were surprised," Anne chuckled, "because there was no church. They went from house to house trying to find out what was happening. Then they located Will in his shop and told him that he was still a member of the Boston church. Will could not believe his ears. He gave them short shrift. 'Go home,' he roared at them. 'Tell Master Winthrop that I believe not in churches. I am more tied to my wife than to any church. She is a dear saint and a true servant of God.'"

Anne laughed. "Will told me later that it was too bad that they had not sent John Cotton. He would have kicked John's arse once for me and twice for himself. But the men from Boston did not give up. The next day they got up their courage and essayed me."

"'We have a message for thee from the Lord,' they said.

"Scarcely believing that the sniveling lot of them dared to speak to Satan's daughter, I asked, 'Which Lord do you mean?'"

"'We came in the name of one Lord that is God,' Master Oliver said bashfully.

"I knew that he was the only one who had signed our petition for Johnny Wheelwright. To his surprise, I hugged him. 'So far we agree,' I said. 'But where do not agree, let it be set down.'

"I thanked them for coming, and pointed to the pot of soup on the fire. 'It was made by a witch,' I laughed at them, 'but if you are not afraid to break bread with us, you are welcome to sup.'

"They were too hungry to be vexed about dining with the Devil's daughter. They remained the night and slept on the floor of the fireroom. They kept telling me that they had a message for me from the Church of Christ in Boston, but I told them that the only Church of Christ I knew was within me."

Anne laughed. "I never got their message. When they returned to Boston, they told John-Luv what I had said. My son, Richard, wrote me that John told the congregation, 'Once they'—meaning Will and me—'were in covenant with our church. They were with us as a wife to her husband. But now, like a harlot, the wife has gone after her own covenant.' The Boston church decided that all of us on the Island 'were heathens and publicans.' But they still did not give up. I received a letter from Elder Leverett. 'What has become of the light you once shined in these parts?' he asked, and he called me a railer and reviler.

"I answered him: 'If it were a true light, in which you say I did once shine, I am sure that the author thereof and the maintainer of it is God, and it shall break forth into a more perfect day. But when I was with you, I discovered that the best light in yourself to be darkness, as you yourself confessed to me in your parlor. And if what you call railing and reviling were a truth of God acted by Him through me, take heed because you have called the spirit of God a railer and reviler.'"

As Anne was speaking, I noticed that she was entranced by several dishes of ice cream being brought to a table near us. "It's only one o'clock," I said. "Anne is having a love affair with strawberry ice cream. We can be in Portsmouth in about ten minutes but dessert comes first."

"Dost thou think I was a railer and reviler?" Anne grinned at me, as she slowly ate her ice cream, letting each spoonful melt in her mouth.

"You still are. But now you're railing against war and reviling the makers of weapons," I laughed. "But don't worry about it. It fits your style. The world needs railers—people who dare to stand up and contest the insanities of their leaders."

"What did your children think of you?" Susan asked.

"When I spoke my mind I made my oldest boys, Edward and Richard, exceedingly anxious. But sweet Francis was like me. The elders of the Boston church continued to write to him. They told him that despite his mother he was still a member of the church. He wrote Elder Leverett a letter and told him that in his opinion 'the ministers had made the church no better than a strumpet or whore who espoused their beliefs.'

"He should have kept silent. But as the mother does, so doth the son. Forgetting what he had written, in the summer of 1641 he decided to return to Boston with his friend, Will Collins. He wanted to see Edward and Richard and his sister Faith at Mt. Wolleystone, but methinks that he found Portsmouth very dull, and he and Will wanted some excitement." Anne shook her head and lapped the ice cream in her spoon. "They found their excitement. They stayed in Sam Cole's tavern almost directly across the street from Master Winthrop's house."

"Wasn't Will Collins married to your daughter Anne?" I asked.

She nodded. "Anne was only sixteen, but Will Collins told Anne that he loved her because she could argue Scripture and contest magistracy as well as her mother. Will was a joyous lad. But he and Francis should have known better than to go back to Boston.

"Will Collins had arrived from Barbados in 1639. He had to leave that island because he had preached that King Charles was not much better than the king of Babylon. All the king wanted from the colonies, Will preached, was greater wealth for himself. When Will got to Boston, he soon discovered that he could not be happy living there either—so he removed to Hartford. Then he, too, wrote Thomas Leverett a letter saying that he had departed Boston because he could not tolerate the governors of the Bay Colony, who behaved as though they were Hebrew prophets. He told him the only true magistracy in the world was the awareness of Christ within a person, and he insisted that there were no true Gentile churches since the apostles' time and that no church should now ordain ministers who were not sealed in the spirit.

"Everyone was sure that I had bewitched Will Collins and made him say such things, but 'twas not true. I knew him not when he wrote that letter," Anne laughed. "He came to Aquiday a year later because only on the Isle of Errors could he say what he thought. But meanwhile, back in Boston, Master Winthrop soon learned that Will and Francis were drinking and having a merry old time at Sam Cole's tavern. Master Winthrop, who had read both their letters, sent a messenger and told them they must appear before the Governor's Council on the morrow. Being happily soused, they told the messenger he could use his message on his arse. The next day a constable arrested them, but Will and Francis nearly convinced the constable, a young man named Anthony Stoddard, that he had no right to arrest them. Instead of putting them in prison Anthony told Master Winthrop, 'Sir, I think you ought not deal with brothers on matters of this kind, other than in a church way. A magistrate should not deal with a member of the church before the church proceedeth with him."

Anne chuckled. "Master Winthrop did not take kindly to that thought. Poor Anthony—with Will's and Francis's help he had put his foot in his mouth. The Council forced Anthony to repent and fined him a few shillings. But they fined Will Collins four hundred pounds and Francis fifty pounds.

Can you imagine that? 'Twas more money than they could earn in a year, and they had to remain in prison until they could give security for it. Master Winthrop stated that the reason for such a large fine was that their family—signifying me—had cost the Colony so great a deal of money. To resolve my heresies had required a council of ministers, and that, together with my imprisonment, had cost the Colony well over five hundred pounds."

Anne put down her spoon and looked regretfully at the empty ice cream dish. "Francis refused to ask for money from us or from his brothers. After three months in prison, Master Winthrop abated the fine to forty pounds for Will and twenty pounds for Francis, but they would not let us pay. 'We will stay in prison until doomsday,' they wrote Will. But the truth was that they were not too much inconvenienced. Many friends visited them every day, and they were constantly railing and reviling against the magistrates and ministers." Anne grinned. "Master Winthrop finally decided that too many people had agreed with them. He said that it was costing too much money to keep them prisoners. He let them go after six months and told them that if they returned to Boston, it would be on pain of death."

37

Back in the car, a few minutes later, we passed a sign: "Welcome to Rhode Island, The Ocean State." Clapping her hands in astonishment, Anne said, "'Tis an amazing world. I believe it and still I do not. We are here the same day we left Mt. Wolleystone, and we stopped to eat for nearly an hour."

We crossed the Sakonnet River bridge, high above the half-mile of water that separates the Island from the mainland. In the distance we could see the Mount Hope bridge. "It connects the Island with Providence," I told Anne. "And it makes it possible for people who live in Connecticut and New York to get to Cape Cod within five or six hours by automobile."

"It sticks in my heart. This is another world," Anne said, and she shook her head thoughtfully. "And this is another Island that I have come back to."

Saul saw an exit from the highway going south to Portsmouth, and we were soon driving down the tree-lined main street of the town. "Do you recognize the place?" he asked. We were passing rows of one-story development houses followed by the inevitable clusters of stores and service stations sandwiched between older homes, none of which dated back to the original settlement.

Anne stared mutely at the passing scene and there were tears in her eyes. The thought crossed my mind that the real sting of death is to be resurrected and discover how impermanent you and your possessions are. Then I noticed a sign, "Portsmouth Public Library," before an attractive one-story white buiding set back on a green lawn.

I told Saul to stop. "I don't think that Anne should go in and ask about herself," I said grinning at her. "But you and Susan may discover something. Most libraries have old records. See if you can find out where she lived. We'll wait in the car."

Twenty minutes later, they emerged from the building with big smiles on their faces. "The librarian was great," Saul said waving a sheaf of legal-size paper. "She not only had a book with the town records from 1638—we copied about twenty pages through the year 1643—but she also had a copy of an ancient land map, which we copied." He handed the sheets and the map to Anne. "All is not lost. You left a mark here. There's a school named after you, and on a road called Old Boyd's Lane there is a monument, near a stream called Founder's Brook. It probably provided fresh water for the first settlers."

"It's a good thing you didn't come in with us," Susan told Anne. "We're not the first. The librarian is well aware of you. They've had phone calls from all over the country. Newspapers, *Time, Newsweek,* historians, and even a television producer have called. He told the librarian that you were going to be on a panel show Monday night." Susan grinned at me: "That's not on our schedule. You're going to have a problem getting back to Boston to meet your wife on Tuesday."

"One day at a time," I said and smiled at Anne, who was waving a copy of the map.

"Look!" she said. "It's all here. All the names of the freemen are on the map, and it shows where their land was. Here's the field facing the Great Cove. Will and his brother, Sam, bought that land. There's the spring where John and Mary Coggeshall lived, and behind them Randall Holden. Over there near the pond is Will Coddington's land, and next to it John Clarke's and Will Baulston's." Anne smiled at Saul and Susan, and her eyes were dancing with delight. "Oh, thank thee both for finding this."

"We also found a more recent map of Portsmouth, and copied that," Saul said. "If we superimpose it on this one, we can probably find the exact spot. But first let's take a look at Old Boyd's Lane."

Although the librarian had told him how to get there, a half-hour later we were still looking. Then to our dismay we discovered that we had been driving back and forth past it. A dirt road, totally unmarked, it was flanked by a seedy-looking building surrounded by gravel trucks and road-building equipment on one side, and a farm house on the other. "It looks like a dump," Susan said, as we walked up an unmown path next to the construction-company building.

It wasn't quite a dump. In a moment of zeal, half a century ago, the town fathers must have remembered the first settlers and fastened a bronze plaque to a granite outcropping near a brook that was still bubbling past. Long forgotten by most of the citizens of Portsmouth, it was set in the middle of a tree-lined grass plot and enclosed with a fieldstone fence.

I read the inscription aloud. "1638-1936. Erected to honor the memory and perpetuate the spirit and ideals of the founders of the first government in the world to allow and to insure its citizens civil and religious liberty on this site in the year 1638." That was followed by *The Portsmouth Compact,* the original "Body Politic" document that had been signed by Coddington, Hutchinson, Clarke, and sixteen other men.

"After what Anne has told us, I think they put the wrong compact on the plaque," Saul said. "They didn't get civil liberty—freedom from religion— until Will became governor."

Anne shrugged. "It matters not. I prefer to see the river and the Great Cove."

A few minutes later we were parked near a sea wall in an area called Island Park. Even though no homes remained from the seventeenth century, there were still several acres of open land, and it was possible to imagine what Pocasset had looked like three hundred and fifty years ago in this area.

"This is the Great Cove," Anne said pointing to a basin of churning water a half-mile across. "The river goes up the east side of the Island to the Atlantic and Cape Cod on the other side." She watched the waves pounding against the seawall. "There was no protection from the water then. Our home was back there a half-mile, but sometimes the water filled the marshes in front of us." She grinned at us. "I told thee that Will and I played tick-tack here many a night."

While Anne and I walked the shore road for a few minutes, Saul and Susan pored over the town records. When we returned to the car, Susan told us that she had found a copy of the first recorded town meeting. "It was on May 16, 1638," she said. "The first law they passed was: 'That none shall be received as inhabitants or freemen to build upon the Island, but shall be received in and by consent of the bodye, and do submit to the Government that is or shall be established according to the word of God.'"

Like an archaeologist who had found lost biblical tablets, Susan couldn't contain her excitement. "There were thirteen men at that meeting, and one of the original signers was your Will."

"I was there," Anne said. "The ladies could listen but could not speak except in whispers to their men. They decided that they would build a town near the spring they had discovered. Later in June they put a price of two shillings an acre on the land."

"That's right," Susan said, "I just read that to Saul. In that first meeting they agreed that 'every inhabitant of the Island should be provided with one musket, one pound of powder, twenty bullets and two fadems of match with sword and rest and bandeliers."

"What are fadems of match and bandeliers?" Saul asked.

"Fadems are flints to spark the powder," Anne said, "and a bandelier is a strip of leather to wear around the head." She sighed. "We trusted not the Indians, nor the Massachusetts Bay magistrates. We had meetings once a week, and if any of the freemen did not repair to the public meeting to treat upon public affairs, or failed to heed public warnings, or a beating of the drum, in less than one quarter of an hour, they had to forfeit twelve pence." She laughed. "I remember at one meeting they summoned eight young men because they were rioting and boozing. The poor boys had nothing else to do, and there were very few young women on the Island. They made the boys sit in the stocks all one day for punishment. At another meeting they decided to have military training for every man between sixteen and fifty." She smiled.

"Methinks the training ground was next to the brook we just saw. At that meeting Will's brother Ed was appointed bread baker for the plantation."

Despite the fun we were having reading the old records and confirming them with Anne, I reminded them that it was getting late. "We have to find a place to stay for the night." Pointing to the area where Anne lived, I hugged her. "We got here fast enough but we have no blankets to roll up in, and as you can see there's no place to camp out. I think we should drive to Newport. There're many nice hotels in that area."

In motion once again, I told Anne that if she wanted to see Pelham, New York, the town she had migrated to after leaving Portsmouth, we could drive there on the way back from New York City. "I need to think about that," she said doubtfully. "I lived there less than a year. I feareth the memory. But if the Lord wishes I will go back."

I know now that I should have asked her what the Lord had to do with it, but Saul was wondering aloud why Anne had finally decided to leave Portsmouth and go to Long Island.

"By June of 1642," she answered, "both Will and I agreed that we would never find peace of mind on the island. The magistrates in Boston kept insisting that all the land in Narragansett Bay belonged to the Bay Colony, and there were rumors that eventually they would send a company of soldiers to capture Sam Gorton and the others who had defied their ruling. It had been a stormy winter, and Will and I were looking forward to the warm months. He was in his shop attached to our house. I heard him groan and call for me. I found him on the floor. He was having severe pains in his chest." Anne shook her head sadly. "I pulled him into my arms, and he said, 'Dear Anne, methinks the Lord wants me. I loveth thee and I am not sorry that we came here. But I feareth that Winthrop and his friend Uncas will take over the island. Go with John.'" Anne suppressed a little sob. "He spoke of John Throckmorton. Will had a second attack the following day, and he died. He was only fifty-six. We had met Master Throckmorton, who was a Baptist and lived near Providence, through my sister Katherine and her husband. John Throckmorton was out of all patience with the incessant meddling of the Massachusetts colonists. He was planning to leave for New Netherlands with thirty other families in August.

"I would not have gone with them but that that rascal Jack Underhill arrived to pay his respects to Will. Jack had married a Dutchwoman and was moving to Dutch territory with her. He, too, was certain it was only a matter of time before Master Winthrop would get his hands on me again. Jack told me that the governor of New Netherlands, William Kieft, was selling land to any of the English who wished to settle there. What he did not tell us, and what Master Throckmorton never knew, was that Governor Kieft owned not the land. He was selling land that belonged to the Mohegans and keeping the money for himself."

Anne shrugged. "I was without a man, and I was afraid. My son Samuel decided to stay on the Island because he was in love with a girl. Richard had gone back to London. Edward had made his truce with Master Winthrop and was living in Boston, and Faith and Tommy Savage were farming at Mt. Wolleystone and keeping their own counsel about religion. Francis was twenty-two and he wanted to go. Anne was only sixteen, but she was her mother's daughter. And *her* husband, Will, after spending six months in Boston jail was convinced that we were all in danger from the magistrates in Boston. So they came with us. Mary was fifteen, Katherine was thirteen, William was eleven, and they helped me with Susanna, who was nine, and Zuriel, who was only six. We all met in Aquidneck and Master Throckmorton found a captain who owned a fishing boat. He sailed us across the bay to Dutch territory. I remember we passed a point of land on the other side, and then sailed into a little harbor."

"Probably Point Judith," I said, "and Snug Harbor."

Anne shrugged. "I know not their names. Not knowing exactly where we would settle, we finally walked more than a hundred miles toward New Amsterdam. It took us nearly a month. The younger children got tired and every day we had to catch fish or game to eat."

As we approached Newport, Susan told Anne that tonight, after we found a hotel, we could wander through the many shops near the harbor, and we could take a ride out Ocean Drive and Bellevue Avenue so that we could see the Breakers, The Marble House, The Elms, Rose Cliff, and other beautiful estates that were equal to any palaces in London or on the continent.

"They were built by multimillionaires, now long dead," she told Anne, and then she said teasingly, "I'm sure they would give all their millions to come back to life again. But they'd be shocked to see what has happened to their possessions. They're now owned by a Preservation Society, which keeps them open to show poor Americans how rich ones lived. Like your Mr. Winthrop, the original owners thought they were building good estates." Susan laughed. "They tried to achieve salvation through work, too—most often, the backbreaking work and sweat of others."

We passed the Treadway Inn, a hotel built in a seventeenth-century style that overlooks Newport harbor. I told Saul that maybe we could find rooms there for the night. He checked the registration desk and returned to the car with a big grin on his face. "We've got adjoining rooms on the third floor, each with a balcony overlooking the harbor," he said. "I decided to register for all of us. Believe it or not," he said to Anne, who burst into laughter, "you are my mother and Bob is my father—Mr. and Mrs. Roger Dremler."

"Who am I?" Susan demanded.

"You're my wife. You and I are taking the old folks on a little vacation. I know you don't like to think of yourself as a senior citizen," he told me, "but

I was afraid to use your name. By now half of America is aware that Anne has been living in your house. Right now, no one knows that Anne has two apostles—Susan and me."

Saul held out his Visa Card. "We're on credit. But unless Anne gets some sponsors and the money starts to roll in, you'll have to pay the bill, Bob."

Behind her wig and sunglasses Anne was shaking with laughter, and she was delighted when she saw the lobby. "'Tis a lovely tavern."

As we crossed the lobby near the registration desk, she clung to my arm, telling me that she feared she might trip because she couldn't see very well through her glasses. I noticed the clerk grimace at us as we passed.

"You don't look like the kind of woman he expected," I told Anne in the elevator. "He probably thinks I'm a wealthy old swinger who has picked up a call girl for the night."

Inside the room Anne stared out the balcony window at the cold grey water of Narragansett Bay. Susan unlocked the connecting doors. Snapping Anne out of her reverie, she danced merrily around the room with her. Then laughing like schoolgirls, they flopped together on one of the two king-sized beds.

"Why do we needeth two rooms with four beds?" Anne asked amazed. "One of these beds is big enough for two people."

"It makes Americans feel rich if they have a big bed all to themselves," I said. "They call them king- and queen-size. People who sleep alone in them pretend that they're royalty."

We were safe—at least for the moment. I unpacked a bottle of Beefeaters I had brought, along with vermouth. I showed the Beefeater, one of the English king's guards, on the bottle to Anne and made us martinis on the rocks. Saul turned on the television to see what was happening.

A few minutes later we quickly found out. Anne was at the top of the six o'clock news, during which drawings of her face appeared in shot after shot. After a summary of her appearance on the Sally Lane show, a newscaster, standing on the front lawn of my house announced: "I am standing near the home of Robert Rimmer, a novelist who was popular in the late 1960s. This is where Mrs. Anne Hutchinson has spent the past eight days. Mrs. Hutchinson, who some people are now calling the woman God sent back to earth, flew to New York at eleven o'clock this morning, according to police who are guarding the house. With her and the author are a young male and female companions, who have not been identified. They were expected to arrive at the Plaza this afternoon, and Mrs. Hutchinson is scheduled to appear on 'Wake Up America' Friday morning followed by other personal television appearances all next week."

"How the Hell did they find out where we were staying in New York?" I groaned.

"Sally Lane or Steve Carlson," Saul shrugged. "Who else?"

I didn't have time to answer. After a still picture of me, which had been taken twenty years ago, had been cut in, the view shifted to the front entrance of the Plaza, and a female commentator said, "This is Jessica Southworth in New York City. As you can see, the Plaza is under siege. Inside and out there must be three or four thousand people waiting to get a glimpse of Mrs. Hutchinson, the woman who for some unknown reason can't be photographed in real life. But the question of the moment—intriguing everyone—is where is she now? If she flew to New York City from Boston, she should have arrived here long ago. This woman is rapidly sending the country on a religious binge, turning millions of people into believers. To add to the mystery, it was discovered this morning that last Sunday Mrs. Hutchinson spoke to a small congregation at the First Church in Quincy. The members of this church claim that her brother-in-law, John Wheelwright, was their first minister."

"Women can't keep secrets," I said. "Liz Johnson must have told them."

The cameraman roved over thousands of faces staring up at him while Jessica continued. "Later the same day, for some unknown reason Mrs. Hutchinson was taken to the Hedman Psychiatric Institute. Carl Philby is standing by right now in Cambridge, Massachusetts, to give you his impressions."

The camera switched to Philby and the grounds of the Institute and Anne squealed in astonishment. "'Tis the same place that you took me," she pointed at the screen, "and that is Barbara, Dave's woman."

"We don't deny that Mrs. Hutchinson visited us last Sunday," Barbara was telling Carl Philby. "She came here under no compulsion. We gave her a fairly complete physical examination. While Doctor Hedman does not wish to go into details—medical ethics, you realize—he admits that some of her tests were quite surprising."

"Did they indicate that Mrs. Hutchinson might be something other than human?" Philby asked. "A woman who has somehow returned from the grave?"

"We know very little about death," Barbara said, "but we are quite positive that when the heart stops beating, the human body will disintegrate. Whether it can be reconstituted or whether there is a God who does that is another matter. Doctor Hedman agrees. More things are possible in the world than we have dreamed of."

"But not probable," Philby said as the camera closed back on him. "On the other hand, there is more here than meets the eye. Doctor Hedman refused to be interviewed, but rumors persist that Mrs. Hutchinson's body temperature and her heartbeats are subnormal or, depending on how you look at it, supernormal. In addition, of course, no one thus far has been able to obtain a true photographic image of her."

A commentator on a competing channel named two New York hospitals who had offered to check any findings of the Hedman Institute and give Mrs. Hutchinson a thorough examination. In addition, the commentator reiterated, "Mrs. Hutchinson will probably appear on additional prime-time television shows to explain her Repent and Rebel philosophy, which presumably were the words of God Himself.

"While no formal announcement has been made," he concluded, "it was learned today that the President is quite fascinated with Mrs. Hutchinson's idea of Armageddon. If no doubts arise in the next few days as to her authenticity, he may be forced to invite her to the White House. One thing is sure: at the present stage of arms negotiations any strike that would curtail our arms production and endanger our national defense policy could prove to be a sticky wicket."

I snapped off the television while Susan was trying to explain to Anne what the White House meant. "I hope you realize that we have a Hell of a mess on our hands," I told them gloomily. "We can't just drive up to the hotel and tell the doorman Anne Hutchinson is here—take the car. She needs police and bodyguards to protect her from the mob.

"There's a populist, deeply felt reaction to her that may scare the government." I reminded Susan and Saul of Father Jerry Popielusko, the Polish priest who had challenged the Russian-supported government of Poland and supported the Solidarity movement. "The KGB probably kidnapped and murdered him. Anne is challenging our national defense policy," I said. "No President is going to agree to her Repent and Rebel scenario. If necessary, the C.I.A. would arrange for some nut to assassinate her."

Anne was listening to me with a faraway smile, and I can't help wondering now if she already knew what was going to happen to her.

It was six-thirty. I dialed Steve Carlson in New York and reached him just before he left his office. "It was a great idea for you to disappear for the day," he said enthusiastically. "It helps build the excitement. We expect an all-time record for viewers on the 'Wake Up America' show. Everybody loves Anne. She's more exciting than the President—and he'll probably have to talk to her. I've kept my mouth shut about your trip, but where the Hell are you right now?"

"Never mind," I told him. "We just watched the six o'clock news. Anne isn't president yet, and the C.I.A. or some other group may decide that she's undermining our foreign policy. We haven't got Secret Service protection, and we're not driving Anne up to the hotel into a crowd like we just saw on television." I sighed. "If Anne would listen to me, we wouldn't arrive at all. Someone who loves war better than God might try to take a potshot at her."

"Calm down," Carlson said soothingly. "I'll meet you with a limousine. When are you going to arrive?"

"Around four. We might come by way of Hutchinson River Parkway," I said, "and stop at Pelham—but that's not definite. Anne may decide that going home again isn't very entertaining."

Carlson told me that he would meet us at an uptown garage, not far from Grant's Tomb, and he gave me the address. "Stop worrying," he said. "I'll have some professional bodyguards with me, and we'll get into the hotel through the celebrity entrance."

Feeling relieved, I made myself another martini and sat on the bed beside Anne, where she and Susan, propped up by pillows, had listened to me. "Thank thee, dear Robert," Anne said. "I love thee. Thou truly art my dear Will. Thou feareth things that shall never happen. No one is going to take a *potshot,* as you call it, at me. Methinks that when I go, it will be quickly, the way I came. Please be not sad—we still have much time." Smiling happily, she handed me her glass. "I would fancy another of those London gins."

"Okay," I said, deliberately deciding not to probe her. I figured that we had about fifteen hours before she belonged to the world. "It's early. We can shower and continue to float on the breeze from the Beefeaters ginmill. We can have dinner in the hotel and then go shopping across the street in the Brick Market Place, where there are quaint little shops selling everything from reproductions of colonial gadgets to the famous Newport pineapple."

Anne laughed. "And then we can all return here and climb into bed. But I wish not to sleep alone."

After a silly hour, during which Anne and I discovered that we could fit into the oversized bathtub together—but not do much washing—our "children" pounded on the connecting door and told us that if we preferred to stay in the room, it was all right with them.

In the lobby, Susan changed her mind about eating. A whisper of spring was in the air. It was a night to walk around and look in shops, which would remain open for only another hour. Anne agreed. It was too early to dine. She told Susan about the Bay Tower Room, where we didn't have dinner until nine. Maybe this tavern would have an orchestra, too, and we could dance.

"I greatly fancy dancing," she said. She grinned at me. "Especially with thee. We can hold each other close and feel each other's body."

"But tonight you must not sing," I warned her. "And you must not talk with *anyone* in the shops or the dining room."

We were sure that no one would recognize Anne, who was reluctantly wearing her wig and dark sunglasses, but Saul and Susan agreed that she should not speak to anyone. Her warm caressing voice with its seventeenth-century lilt and word usages would instantly identify her.

Anne protested. "I am learning how to speak your way and say *don't* instead of *dost thou not,* and *I think* instead of *methinks."* She shrugged. "But if thou wisheth, I will speak French."

"Please," I hugged her, "the safest thing is not to speak in front of strangers at all."

But twenty minutes later, a stranger spoke to Anne, and although I wasn't aware of it then, he foreshadowed the coming events.

Fascinated by the feminine enjoyment of what Saul and I called "junk gifts and gadgets," we tagged along behind Susan and Anne, who became totally involved in shops filled with stuffed teddy bears, cast-iron and pewter reproductions of colonial ephemera, candles in an endless variety of sizes and shapes, yarn shops, dress shops, and even a shop that specialized in rich chocolate concoctions. I bought a pound for future eating and told them it was time for dinner.

Following Susan and Anne out of the shopping area as they led the way back to the Inn, we were in the midst of a crowd of late shoppers. Both Saul and I saw a man in his early fifties with a carefully trimmed beard that finished in a devil's point below his chin. Passing Susan and Anne, he nodded at Anne with a cool smile. The lights from the shops reflected his burning stare and flashed directly at Anne. "You still do not preach what the Apostle commands," he said in a hollow voice and vanished in the crowd.

I heard Anne gasp, and I ran to close the gap between us, but for a moment—and Saul verified it later—Anne disappeared. *Disappeared* is not the right word. For a little more than thirty seconds, she was invisible—even to Susan.

When we questioned her, she shook her head and it was obvious that she was unaware that momentarily she couldn't be seen. "That seemeth quite silly," she said, but she was trembling and clung to my arm. "I am sure that I vanished not. But that man frightened me. He looked just like Master Winthrop." She smiled at our open-mouthed astonishment.

"What does the Apostle command?" Susan demanded, trying to appear nonchalant and not reveal that she didn't believe in ghosts or that another resurrection was possible.

Shaking, Anne clung to her. "To stay at home. Master Winthrop told me that at my trial. Women should stay at home." She shook her head defiantly. "No matter. I fear him not."

Susan, Saul, and I were more dubious than Anne was. Many men wore beards today, we assured her, but we had to admit that we had heard his strange warning. However, Anne had no doubts. Governor John Winthrop was her nemesis, and she believed that he could—if for some reason, the Lord was willing—pursue her across the centuries.

At dinner in the hotel she insisted that all the gin we had drunk had nothing to do with it. We weren't hallucinating. "That really was Master Winthrop," she said. "Methinks his spirit is very comfortable in your world." Then she merrily told us that she would forget Leviticus. She would try lobster and one more martini.

Later, back in the room, she stood naked on the balcony overlooking the harbor of Narragansett Bay. Shivering beside her, wondering if she would disappear again if I embraced her, I kissed her and asked if she were cold.

"No, dear Robert," she said and pressed her cool belly and breasts against me. "I feel the earth turning toward the sun. Perchance it will melt the spirit of Master Winthrop."

38

During my last bittersweet days with Anne, I began to think that she might be right about one thing. Perhaps I *was* a reincarnation of Will Hutchinson. Like Will, I loved her, but like he probably had been, I was appalled by her stubborn sense of destiny. Her almost childish belief that God loved her and was on her side was once again leading to her destruction.

Because I didn't believe that playing the activist game would succeed any better today than it had in her first life—and the truth was that I would have preferred to play Peter and keep her in a pumpkin shell—I became a passive dissenter. But Susan, and particularly Saul, insisted that Anne's three R's—responsibility, repent, and rebel—were more important for the future of mankind than reading, 'riting and 'rithmetic. Along with Anne, they only laughed when I added "railing and reviling."

Thursday morning we drove past the estates of the robber barons and took a quick tour of the Breakers. Finally on our way to New York City, I told Anne that a hundred years ago the very rich had tried to emulate the culture of Europe. "They built their palaces in Newport because they could sail here from New York City on their yachts. There were no automobiles then, and the poor could not see how idly they wasted their money."

Anne was not surprised. "'Twas no different in London or in Boston when I lived there. Many of the Puritans loved money and power more than they loved God."

It was two o'clock when we passed New Haven, and I knew that we didn't have time to explore Pelham Bay, or take Anne into the city on the Hutchinson River Parkway. Actually, when I had mentioned stopping, Anne had seemed uneasy. "I can wait," she said moodily. "I'm not sure the Lord wishes me to go back there again."

As Steve Carlson had promised, he was waiting for us at the Uptown Garage when we arrived. A few minutes before we got there, Susan, who I was discovering was as politically astute as Saul, suggested that Anne should hide her wig and sunglasses in her traveling bag.

"No one—except the apparition we think we saw last night—knows your disguise," she said. "Evidently Mr. Carlson is going to bring us into the hotel through a private entrance. Even if you are recognized going in, the chances are good, if you wear your wig, the four of us can get *out* of the hotel without being recognized."

I objected, thinking that Anne's disguise might be the only way we could get through the crowds at the Plaza undetected. But Susan was right. When we drove into the garage, Carlson stepped out of an extended black limousine and greeted us. He was wearing a pin-striped suit and, with a dusting of gray in his black hair and moustache, he was the model of the cool, top-brass generals who are paid millions to achieve superior television ratings. With him was a young blonde secretary, Lisa Carr, who was equally cool and efficient, and two burly guards whom Steve introduced as Hank and Buck.

"They're assigned to you for your entire stay in the city," he told us as I introduced Susan and Saul as Anne's mentors and apostles without further explanation.

Behind black-tinted glasses, Hank drove us downtown in the limousine to an office building on West 58th Street, which he explained was connected by an underground passage to the hotel. A few people on the sidewalk paid no attention to us. Cadillac limousines were as common as fire hydrants in the city. Following Hank on the celebrity route, with Buck bringing up the rear, we passed laundries, kitchens, a bakery and storage rooms. I remembered pictures of Robert Kennedy, shot and lying on the floor dying as he had traversed a similar route in a Los Angeles hotel.

Holding Anne's arm, Steve told her that she was even more beautiful than the night he had first seen her in the Bay Tower Room. "If all else fails," he told her laughing, "I'll be happy to manage your acting and singing career." It was obvious that Steve couldn't care less if Anne "bombed" or turned out to be a fraud. At the moment, she was a top attraction with a commercial television time value of a couple of hundred thousand dollars a minute. But Anne didn't understand the irony, and she was happily telling him that she enjoyed singing and was amazed that one's voice could be saved like dried apples and salted fish and be enjoyed later.

A smiling hotel manager, wearing a morning coat, greeted us at the service elevators. "We're delighted that you're staying with us, Mrs. Hutchinson," he told her, "but please help us serve you best. Don't leave the hotel through the lobby or without your guards. The crowds are bigger today than they were yesterday." Assuming that I was her manager, he handed me a deep silver dish filled with envelopes and messages. "Mr. Carlson told us that all telephone calls to Mrs. Hutchinson would be filtered through special telephone operators provided by the network. As you will see on these messages, the operators are taking phone numbers, and you can return any calls that you wish on your private room lines."

The elevator opened on one of the top floors and he led us down the hall to a two-bedroom suite, exquisitely furnished in eighteenth-century style. It overlooked Central Park. "Special room attendants have been assigned for any services you may require," he said, and he pointed to the wet bar. "If there are any liquors lacking that you may prefer, please let me know. Mr. Carlson has told me that he is providing you with two guards." He nodded at Hank and Buck. "They will provide a floor watch. We could have shut off all rooms on this floor, but that would have been very expensive, and you do have this side of the hotel to yourself." Looking at me quizzically he said, "I presume that two bedrooms are sufficient, but if you require an additional bedroom, we can open up another room."

Even before he left, Steve was behind the bar taking drink orders. "I know that you must all be tired," he said, "but there are a few things I'd like to straighten out before Lisa and I leave. First, I hope you won't leave the hotel tonight. You can order dinner right here in this attractive living room. I haven't been able to coordinate our plans with you or Mrs. Hutchinson, but we certainly hope that you will stay until the middle of next week, at least."

He smiled at Anne. "You may not be aware of it but practically overnight you have become internationally famous. Segments of the Sally Lane show, or all of it, have been shown in practically every country of the world—even in Moscow. The Pope and the Patriarch of the Greek Orthodox Church are cautious, but they admit that God works in curious ways. Whether you are truly resurrected or not, they agree that all men and women should take responsibility for permitting nuclear weapons to be built, and repenting is inspirational. But the Pope is not so sure about rebelling. Nevertheless, you've made billions of people aware of where responsibility lies. It's a great idea," Steve said as he poured himself another martini. "In the aggregate we can stop all wars and potential nuclear destruction—if we really want to."

At Anne's request, he had given her a glass of white wine. He and Lisa raised their martinis in a salute to her. "But I think you should know," he said, "that personally I'm out on a limb. Most of my colleagues are sure that I'm going to fall flat on my ass on this one. I'm really counting on you, Anne. I hope you can pull it off for a couple of shows at least without anything going wrong." He smiled at her without immediately qualifying what that might be. "There are plenty of doubters. The Kremlin has denounced you as a fraud. The President issued a statement an hour ago that until your resurrection has been proved medically beyond any doubt, people should listen to you cautiously. And he warned that any strike against armament makers in these crucial times would be considered an act of sedition."

"You've come full circle, Anne," I told her grimly. "Three hundred and fifty years ago you were banished as an enemy of the state."

Anne smiled patiently at me. "I told thee, dear Robert, perchance that is why I am here. If man and woman still loveth not, then magistracy signifieth nothing."

Steve shrugged. "Don't count on it. The government is still in charge. If the politicians think that you're dangerous, they won't banish you this time. You can count on it. They'll find some way to shut you up. Quite a few evangelical groups, along with Mormons and several Catholic archbishops, have questioned your sexual morality and your defamation of the character of a famous man like John Cotton. To be perfectly honest with you, Mrs. Hutchinson, they can't believe that a preacher, especially a woman who disobeys some of God's commandments, can brazenly insist that God speaks to her." Steve chuckled. "Or that the Lord would be happy with anyone who sings dirty songs. You should know that Prudence Awkley, who heard you at the Bay Tower Room, has told the press that you sang smutty songs, and she has denounced you as a charlatan trading on the venerable name of a great lady."

"What Steve is trying to tell you," Lisa said, "is that tomorrow on 'Wake Up America,' Lucy Sprague and Jack Varsi will inevitably concentrate on your love life with John Cotton and whether you were involved with Harry Vane."

Lisa nodded at me. "And whether you are sleeping with Mr. Rimmer. Whether you realize it or not, because of his writings condoning premarital sex and adultery, your protector has a somewhat questionable reputation."

"Evidently Anne alluded to Harry Vane when she spoke at the First Church in Quincy," Lisa couldn't help grinning. "He was a governor of Massachusetts and everyone's been rushing to the library for history books. Rumors in England, at the time, were that Harry Vane came home in disgrace, because he got both Anne and Mary Dyer pregnant, and they both gave birth to monsters. Reading Roger Williams between the lines, you can reach your own conclusion. He wrote to Winthrop that 'the eyes of some are so earnestly fixed on Harry Vane that Mrs. Hutchinson professeth, if he not come back to New England, she must return to Old England.'"

"This is silly prattle," Anne said quietly. "I fear not questions about whom I have loved. I have hurt no man nor his family by any manner of loving. God judgeth not those who truly loveth."

None of us were sure that the world would buy that belief, but it was obvious that whether Mr. Winthrop—or someone disguised as him—was following her or not, or was trying, once again, to exact retribution, Anne wasn't going to be deflected.

Steve told her that he had convinced the top three competing networks to pool the cost of maintaining her and her staff while we were in the city. He smiled at Anne. "Right at the moment, you're hotter than the President, but you're not a public employee yet. I didn't want to be greedy, so I decided to share the wealth. If Anne is willing to appear on three different prime-time shows we have scheduled on different networks, we will pay Anne one hundred thousand dollars an appearance. Keep in mind that ordinarily we don't pay authors, or anyone who has something to gain or who is trying to sell the public something. In one sense that *is* what Anne is doing." He shrugged at her. "I know it may sound mercenary, but a hundred grand is the price for a true resurrection. If it should be discovered that you were actually born in this century, you will forfeit all fees."

I was sure that Anne didn't understand the meaning of so many dollars, but she knew what he meant by being born in this century. "The Lord knows why I am here," she told him, "believe Him."

Steve laughed. "I don't know whether I believe Him, but you can count on it that I'm praying to Him. In addition to tomorrow, we have you tentatively scheduled for two special one-hour shows Sunday and Monday nights in prime time. That gives you plenty of free time. You're going to need it. Every local radio talkshow in town wants you, reporters from all the newspapers and the major magazines headquartered here in the city want to interview you. Hundreds of photographers insist that they are sure that they can get a clear picture of you, and a couple of well-known artists have volunteered to paint your portrait." He gestured at the box of messages. "What you do with that stuff is up to you."

"The Mayor talked with us this morning," Lisa said, "and the Governor is in town. They're waiting and watching. If nothing goes wrong, I think you'll be invited to a special reception Saturday night. You're obviously great publicity for the Big Apple." She grinned. "The Governor may even want to apologize for what happened to you when you lived in Pelham three centuries ago."

Before they left, Lisa excused herself to use the bathroom, and Steve made himself another drink for the road. Then, like us, I saw him staring at Anne bewilderedly for a moment. He was trying to tell her that ordinarily she wouldn't have to be at the studio tomorrow until six-thirty. But several studio cameramen were convinced that they could televise her without any ghosts, and he had to give them time to prove it. He said the word *ghosts* as Anne was telling him that she understood not why they could not take her picture. She most certainly wasn't a ghost.

As she was speaking, Steve rubbed his eyes and shook his head as if he was trying to clear his vision. "Where the Hell are you?" he demanded. "I can hear you but I can't see you."

Susan, Saul, and I said nothing, but we were aware that for the second time during a lapse of less than three seconds Anne had actually disappeared from our sight and then returned.

Steve laughed. "Christ Almighty," he said as Lisa returned, "I guess I've got to face it and get glasses—or stop drinking."

Before he left, Steve questioned us about the Hedman Institute and tried to convince us that it would be great publicity if a New York hospital would confirm its findings—whatever they might be. But I told Anne that she didn't have to expose herself to further medical investigation. "I'm sure that they won't be able to photograph you," I told her. "That should be proof enough."

I had never told Saul or Susan that Anne's skin seemed strangely cool to my touch, and often when I was alone with her her heart beat so slowly—even when we were making love—that if it hadn't been for her open-eyed smile and happy laughter I would have wondered if she were in a trance or not fully alive. Now, within the last twenty-four hours, the three of us had become aware of her occasional invisibility, but none of us could really think or react to her differently. She still was a vibrant and loving woman who made a profound impression on all who spoke to—or even only saw—her.

When she appeared (if I can use that word to describe her ethereal vision on "Wake Up America"), the amazed and bewildered cameramen were unable to bring her into sharp focus. There was no live audience, but this time there were four artists sketching her as she spoke. Lucy Sprague and Jack Varsi probed every aspect of her life, trying unsuccessfully to make her admit something that would identify her as a twentieth-century woman. When Lucy delved into her relationships with John Cotton, Harry Vane, and even me—I had once again politely declined to appear with Anne—Anne quickly defused her. "A man or woman canst be ashamed of simple lust, but not of love. If thou truly lovest a person, thou canst not harm anyone that ye love. I have opened my life and the light within me to more than one man. Ashamed I am not. If thou truly loveth a person, the gift to him or her of thy body harms no one." Then she quoted Jesus' parable of the lamp: "'Is a lamp brought in to be under a bushel, or under a bed, and not on a stand? For there is nothing hid except to be made manifest, nor is anything secret, except to come to light. If any men or women have ears to hear, let them hear this.'"

That night, after listening to Saul review the many invitations she had received, Anne agreed to accept an invitation to speak at St. Patrick's on Sunday. Tuesday she would appear at a luncheon sponsored by the National Organization of Women.

She finally slid into bed beside me. She was well aware that I was distancing myself from what I disparagingly referred to as her campaign to be chosen secretary of state. Like a weeping angel, she whispered, "Forgive me, dear Robert, I canst not help myself. As I told Will long ago, I must do what the Lord asketh. Whatever happens—even if it be true, as thou believest, that I am tilting at windmills—I will always love thee."

I told her I was disappointed mostly because we wouldn't be driving back to Boston together. "I have to meet Emily Tuesday morning," I said, "but I told Saul that he could take the car. I will fly back. You can drive back together through Pelham, if you wish." I smiled at her sadly. "I'm sure that it won't be much different from Portsmouth. Up until now most people had forgotten you."

She was kissing me fervently, and I could feel her cool skin in my arms.

"Are you cold?" I asked, wondering as I had many times how her flesh could feel so cool without her wanting more blankets. But kneeling naked over me, while I kissed her breasts and caressed her back, she was oblivious to the room's cool temperature.

"I care not if I do not see my last home again," she said, and then stretching out on top of me, she sighed moodily. "But methinks the Lord wishes me to go there."

"You haven't told me much about the months that you lived in New Amsterdam," I said. "According to the history books you and your family were the only English, or Dutch, slaughtered by the Indians in that period. Why did they choose you?"

"I shall tell thee later." She smiled at me. "I can feel thee pressing against my con. Tonight, I need to be with thee. Come into my belly. My life is thy life."

Did she disappear again while we were making love? I think so, but I cannot be sure. After a long time, I opened my eyes. I was still big within her. I could feel her but she was weightless. Or was I dreaming? Perhaps, in our laughing joy, we had disappeared into each other.

39

Saturday morning at nine o'clock, Susan and Saul piled into bed with us and, bursting with laughter, told Anne that she had done it. We were all invited to the Mayor's reception at seven and later to a private dinner with him and a few other government officials.

"After seeing you yesterday on 'Wake Up America,' the Mayor's a believer." Saul blithely hugged a half-naked Anne, who stared sleepily at him as she sat up in bed. "You've got a lot of things to decide," he said. "There are call-back messages from the Archbishop and from rabbis and priests and ministers too numerous to mention. Three publishers will pay a fortune for your autobiography, two motion-picture producers want you to star in a movie based on your life. Three different promotion outfits want the exclusive rights to Anne Hutchinson sweatshirts and Repent and Rebel buttons and anything else they can dream up to sell the public—all with drawings of you on them. Portrait painters can't wait to paint your picture. A senator and a congressman, from different parties, have invited you to Washington, or if you can't come there, they'll fly up here Monday. The people who run SANE, the Freeze, and the Council for a Livable World want to talk with you as soon as possible." Saul grinned at her. "There's so much more that even thinking about it makes me dizzy."

It was obvious to me that, other than at bedtime, I would have little opportunity to be alone with Anne. "I really think she needs to escape for awhile," I told Susan and Saul. "Anne needs to see the city—and not from the back seat of a limousine. It will give her some idea of what she's getting into."

Although I didn't say it, not only did I want to be alone with Anne for one more day but I also wanted to give her some idea of the immensity of her self-imposed mission. I still couldn't accept the fact that she was directed by God to do anything. Thinking about it now, I hope, if she had been, that the Lord hasn't decided the mission was accomplished. But I was sure of one thing. Leaders and prophets have passed through here by the dozens and were hailed and forgotten within a few months. In New York City alone there are millions of people who are well aware that it is the meeting place for nations that have never been united on very much.

While these thoughts were passing through my mind, I remembered Anne's wig. "We can be out of the hotel by ten-thirty," I told her. "No one has any current photographs of me. We'll look like a couple of affluent tourists. We've got four or five hours before the insanity begins again. I'd like to show you the city from the top of the World Trade Center. Maybe we can have lunch in the restaurant, Windows on the World, and you should certainly see the Statue of Liberty."

Neither Saul nor Susan were too enthusiastic, but I assured them that with Hank and Buck's help, and using the celebrity entrance, we could emerge on West Fifty-Ninth Street and be quickly lost in the crowd. After a quick breakfast served in the room, Susan and Saul, like dutiful children, hugged us and told us to be careful. "And please don't forget to come back," Susan said. "We need you too."

Buck and Hank followed us out of the hotel at a respectable distance. Near Central Park I flagged a horse and cabbie and waved goodbye to them. I told Anne that I was going to take her on a scenic tour of Central Park. It was a crisp spring day and all the trees were celebrating their own resurrection.

The whiskered old man sitting above us on the buckboard grinned at Anne and obligingly provided us with a blanket. "Nice day for a trip in the country," he said and asked where we wanted to go. "Take us wherever you like," Anne told him, delighted to return to a world where the horsepower was really horse. She grinned at me. "We don't care if we never return."

Behind the wheezy horse and enjoying the clop-clop of its hooves, we were like young lovers. Holding hands, and then when that was not enough, we breathed the cool clean air and kissed while our fingers searched out each other's bodies under the blanket and under our clothes. In a kind of ecstatic touching of breasts and genitals, we found our inner light together.

Finally, coming back to a dreamy reality, I told Anne that we should be thankful the original governors of the colony had had the foresight to save a vast portion of land that was now known as Manhattan from the City of New Amsterdam, which had never stopped growing—now toward heaven, since there was no more room to spread horizontally.

To my surprise, she told me she had visited New Amsterdam several times in 1643. She had met William Kieft, the governor from Holland and he had shown her the fort overlooking the harbor and a new one they were erecting on the Palisades to repel either Englishmen or Indians, if either decided to go to war against the Dutch.

"It was a very busy place," Anne said. "And it was much bigger than Boston."

"It still is," I said. "Your friend Roger Williams left from New Amsterdam harbor when he went to England to get a charter for the Colony of Rhode Island. He was afraid to go back to Boston for fear that Winthrop would put him in jail."

It occurred to me that, rather than return to West Fifty-Ninth Street, the cabbie could drop us off at Fifth Avenue and West One Hundred Tenth, where we could take a taxi to Battery Park. There Anne could see what had happened in three centuries to the harbor and even take a look at the Statue of Liberty through a telescope.

But we still had a way to go and there was no hurry. "Master Winthrop," she was telling me, "was very angry with the Dutch for selling arms to the Indians. All of the magistrates in the Massachusetts Colony believed that Connecticut belonged to them. But the Dutch did not agree with them. To make matters more confusing, a man named Andrew Forrester arrived from London and told Master Kieft that he was an agent for Lady Sterling, whose husband had died after the King had given him title to the Long Island. Thus the island belonged to her. The Dutch did not fancy the English knocking at their back door. Master Forrester was arrested, put in jail, and finally sent back to England. I know not what happened to him. At the same time, Jack Underhill, who was always in trouble personally, declared war on the Dutch because he was certain that the Dutch were in league with the Indians and they would soon drive all the English out of New Netherlands."

Anne shrugged. "When I finally reached a settlement, which had been started by Lady Deborah Moody on the western end of the Long Island, I decided that I loathed ferries and I was weary of islands. But I wanted to be near the ocean."

"Thomas Weld wrote that you lived and died at a place called Hell's Gate," I said. "He thought it was an appropriate place for the demise of a woeful woman."

"Master Weld was wrong," Anne said. "John Throckmorton had chosen land on the mainland, and I gave him money that Will and I had saved. He bought me a piece of land that curved out on the bay. John's house and a Master Cornhill's were nearby. Thou hast told me that the place is now called Pelham. My land had a river on one side. The Sands family lived a half-mile away, and John Sands helped Francis and Will Collins build our house. It was a very pretty place, but, alas, we lived not long enough to harvest our first crop. Many Indians lived around us, and I learned from them and Jack Underhill, who was always dropping by, hoping that I would play see-saw with him, that Miantonomo was in trouble.

Anne shook her head. "Poor Miantonomo. His good friend Sam Gorton meant only to make him happy. He gave Miantonomo a suit of armor, which Miantonomo loved. But then, Punham, another Narragansett, claimed that the land Miantonomo had sold Sam in truth belonged to him. A man named Benedict Arnold decided that Sam should be evicted, and he told Master Winthrop that Punham had been cheated. That is all that Master Winthrop needed. He wanted to prove that the Massachusetts Colony had jurisdiction over the Island and Shawomet, where Sam lived, as well as Providence. The magistrates summoned Sam and Miantonomo to appear in Boston. Sam refused to go. He wrote Governor Winthrop a long letter and called him the 'Idol General, and a Satan who was trying to transform himself into an angel of light.'

"But Miantonomo went to Boston anyway to prove that Punham was lying and was an evil Indian as well. By this time, Master Winthrop, who was afraid of both the Indians and the Dutch, as well as blasphemers like me, had convinced the colonists at Plymouth, Hartford, and New Haven, to join with Boston and create an overall government called the United Colonies of New England. Their main duty was to raise a militia and be prepared to defend themselves. He told the freemen of the United Colonies that Miantonomo was a friend of Sam Gorton and me, and he insisted that we were all hatching a plot to overthrow the government and to kill most of the English. But, by my troth, that was not the truth. Because they had no proof that Miantonomo was involved, they let him go free. But Master Winthrop now had a new friend, Uncas, chief of the Mohegans, who were always warring with the Narragansetts."

Anne shrugged. "I cannot prove it, but methinks that Master Winthrop put a price on Miantonomo's head and told Uncas that he would be well rewarded. In July of 1643, Miantonomo was captured by Uncas." Anne smiled sadly. "Poor Miantonomo—he could not run fast enough because he was wearing Sam Gorton's suit of armor."

We had arrived at the northeastern end of Central Park. I flagged a taxi and told the cabbie to take us down to the Battery by way of the Franklin Roosevelt Drive. Inside Anne hugged me. "I love horses," she said. "But I like taxis with motors, too. I am delighting in this blessed day with thee."

I told her to speak softly so that the driver couldn't hear her. She snuggled close to me, and, although I had read it in the history books, I asked her what had happened to Miantonomo.

"Uncas sent a message to Master Winthrop and asked what he should do with him." Anne sighed. "Miantonomo had been our friend, and he had helped us in the war against the Pequods. Now he was the Colony's enemy. Master Winthrop said he must die. Uncas split his head open with a tomahawk at Norwich, Connecticut, and ate a piece of his flesh. He told his tribe that it was very sweet."

"How did you know that?"

"The Mohegans told my neighbor, Thomas Cornhill, who was in Hartford when it happened in July of 1643. Six weeks later a hundred or more Mohegans were circling my house dancing a war dance. They were still carrying Miantonomo's head. I told thee about that the first night I came to your house," she shivered. "From death by fire to death by ice. You saved me from freezing."

"You said that Uncas was their leader. How did you know him?"

"He camped near us one summer when we were in Portsmouth. He told Will that the Big White Sachem at Shawmut—meaning Master Winthrop—had told him that I was an exceedingly bad woman filled with devils. I knew when I saw him in front of my house there was no help in pleading with him. His face was stained with red and black juices. 'Me kill Miantonomo,' he said. 'Big White Sachem not like evil woman. Me kill her friend. Now me kill her.'" Anne sighed. "He grabbed me by the hair and I fainted. When I came to life again it was growing dark. I had been stripped naked and tied to a tree trunk. I could see my poor Anne's head and Will's on a notched stick, but I could not see their bodies." She shuddered. "I screamed and screamed. Searing red and yellow flames engulfed me and were followed by a bright white light, into which I disappeared."

I held her sobbing in my arms, and I could see the taxi driver staring curiously at us in his mirror. We passed the United Nations buildings, and I tried to tell Anne that since World War II, the leaders of the nations of the world had gathered here to try and resolve world economic and political problems, and hopefully to continue to talk together rather than declare war on each other.

"But thou toldst me that right at this moment wars are being fought all over the world."

"The world hasn't changed that much," I said. "Like the Narragansetts and the United Colonies of New England, the nations of the world still refuse to walk a mile wearing the other fellow's moccasins." I kissed her wet eyes.

"Methinks if I had been Jesus, I would not have had his courage," she said. "I would have stayed in Galilee. It would be easier—right now—to run away with you and to fish for men's souls in a smaller lake."

The driver stopped at Battery Park. Grinning happily at his tip as he drove away, I heard him say, "Another old meshuganah with a young broad."

"It's very strange," Anne said, as I led her toward a telescope on the walk overlooking the harbor. "Although he never spake a word of kindness to me, methinks that Master Winthrop needed me. Perchance, he still does."

Wondering if it were true that the leaders of the world couldn't survive without enemies and victims, I pointed out the Statue of Liberty to Anne and put a quarter in one of the telescopes so that she could see it better.

"It's a hundred and fifty-three feet high," I told her, as she peered at it and gasped in amazement. "It was given to us by France a hundred years ago to commemorate the alliance of France and America in the Revolutionary War. About a hundred years after you died, Englishmen stopped fighting the French and the Indians, and went to war against each other. The Englishmen who lived in Boston and Philadelphia believed that they were taxed unfairly without representation in the English Parliament. Listening to his generals and not his saner advisers, the King, whose name was George, dispatched thousands of English soldiers and German mercenaries to America to show who was boss. It was France's great opportunity to stick a knife in England's back, which they did, by helping us win the war against the King." I grinned at her. "Whatever else you may say about the French and English, at least they had good ancestors like you who believed in liberty."

Smiling, Anne said, "Methinks that it is abundantly estimable that Liberty is a woman leading the way with a torch in her hand. That should surprise Governor Winthrop."

Her calm acceptance that Winthrop might be around to see the statue made me a little uneasy. I concentrated on trying to recapture the past history of the city for her while she watched the modern ships moving in and out of the river. But the immensity of the city towering behind us was just as impossible for her to absorb as Mr. Winthrop's possible resurrection was for me.

Later when we were having lunch in Windows on the World overlooking Manhattan on the top of the World Trade Center, she shook her head sadly and asked, "Can so much happen in five lifetimes? The Lord must grieve that His creatures, who can do all these things, still have not learned to love one another." She sighed. "When I came here, the streets were mud and filled with slops, and pigs and animals were running loose. The men and women from Holland spoke a language I understood not. Where are the Dutch now?"

"Drowned in a tidal wave of immigrants from Europe." I laughed. "You can find your company of Jews here, a few million of them, and many more Italians, Irishmen, Greeks, Slavs, Blacks, Hispanics, and now Arabs and Vietnamese, who came here by the millions in the past hundred years."

In a taxi on the way back to the hotel, we passed Rockefeller Center. We still had a couple of hours and it suddenly occurred to me that Anne might like to see people skating in the middle of the city. Afterwards we could walk back to the hotel. A few minutes later I would wonder if I were actually making the decisions, or was I being maneuvered by powers beyond my comprehension?

Standing in Rockefeller Plaza, overlooking the skaters, Anne clapped enthusiastically at a pretty young woman who was figure skating in an abbreviated costume that revealed her underpants when she gracefully raised one leg high in the air and floated on her momentum.

Then Anne clutched my arm. "Oh, dear Lord!" she moaned. "Why is he following me?" She pointed across the pavilion to a bearded man, who was aiming what looked like an expensive camera in our direction.

Almost as she uttered the words, the man moved off into the crowd. "It's not the same man," I said and hugged her. But I wasn't sure. I could feel her trembling against me.

"It was Master Winthrop," she said as we walked on Fifth Avenue back to the hotel. "I know that it was, but why? Oh, I wish the Lord would tell me why." She looked at me sadly. "Methinks, as Master Shakespeare wrote, I am 'on a whirligig in time that brings in his revenges.'"

"Maybe it's a carrousel," I said and explained to her what a carrousel was. "Merry-go-round or not, I am glad to be on it with you."

"Dost thou think that, like Saul, he was trying to take my picture?"

I laughed and tried to cheer her up. "I don't think it was Winthrop. You've been trying to live in two worlds at once. Your mind is rebelling. If it were really Winthrop, how did he recognize you? Everytime you've seen him you've been wearing a wig and sunglasses. Anyway, stop worrying. No one has been able to take your picture yet. And who taught Winthrop how to use a camera?"

Anne looked at me with raised eyebrows. "Maybe someone is teaching him things, the same way thou art teaching me."

40

I flew back to Boston Monday night after a special hour and a half television feature during which two doctors—one a psychiatrist, the other an internist—plus a minister, a priest, a specialist in Colonial history, and a lawyer acting as moderator interrogated Anne.

Like every overexposed celebrity or politician, Anne had discovered at the Mayor's reception and three previous television shows, plus an appearance at St. Patrick's and innumerable one-to-one meetings with people that she had agreed to talk with, that she was becoming bored and impatient. Answering the same old questions over and over again, she told me, "It giveth me the feeling that I am listening to someone else talking."

Saul told her that she must be careful. She was scowling at people who asked her intimate questions about her extramarital sex life or tried to question the validity of her resurrection. All she really wanted to talk about was the essential reason that the Lord had brought her back to life. She told the Mayor that, unlike Jesus, she did not die for man's sins. "I died because men hated each other and still do. I am the Lord's warning to the people of the world. There will be no resurrection, no further life for anyone who loveth not the Lord and the Lord's people. The Lord will not save ye from thyself."

Dining with ten other guests of the Mayor, she had told everyone at the table, "Methinks, many of ye care not for love, but ye relish the details of adultery and what the lovers are doing with their coyntes and pizzles." Then she had smiled. "Mine answer to how ye can love another person in addition to the one ye are married to is quite simple: do it not, if it makes ye feel guilty. Save thy guilt and repentance for not loving the light of the Lord within ye."

Amusingly, she was happier at St. Patrick's, where the cathedral was packed but in which, in good high-church style, there was no chance for rebuttal either during the ceremony or the sermon. Instead, she charmed everyone by telling them that she hoped both her father, Francis Marbury, and her good friend John Cotton could see her enjoying the bell, book, and candle, which was one way of finding the Lord within oneself.

Thousands of people were in total awe of her but not the panel that Steve Carlson assembled on Monday night, which more than one morning newspaper heralded as an "Is she or ain't she" spectacular. The two women and four men assumed a "Sixty Minute" approach, which often gave the impression that the person being interviewed was guilty until he or she proved himself innocent.

Sitting in a semicircle, with Anne in the center, the panel shot questions at her from both sides. Although the cameramen were still only capturing a hazy glow and the television monitor obscured her features at times, I knew that to Saul, Susan, and me, at least, Anne seemed a little weary and short-tempered.

At one point she told the lawyer, Frank Gaines, who acted both as devil's advocate and moderator, "Thou maketh me feel as if I am in the twelfth century instead of the twentieth century. Thou forgeteth that I was burned for my heresies three hundred and fifty years ago. Methinks thou wouldst take pleasure in doing it again."

"It's difficult to believe that you have returned from the dead," the minister, Reverend Waggert, replied. "We can't help but wonder whether you are trading on this assumption. You seem to be telling the American people that through you the Lord is telling all of us that our only salvation lies in a strike against the armament makers. You must be aware that you're inciting people to rebellion against the state. I can assure you that many of us consider this just as dangerous to the welfare of this country as the original Anne Hutchinson's belief that, through God, Jesus Christ has forgiven man for all his sins, past, present and future."

"I am Anne Hutchinson," Anne said. "And that was and is my belief. Thou seemeth to be saying that the Lord approves of guns and powder and killing one's enemies. Methinks, Master Waggert, that this never was the preaching of Jesus. Jesus knew that one must rail against evil. He said, 'I bring not peace but a sword.' But thou understand not that Jesus' sword was not a weapon of iron but loving words and gentle actions that disturbeth the mind better than any sword—especially the minds of those who think the Lord is on their side when they wage war on each other."

"Aren't you contradicting your beliefs that the church and state should be separated?" Father Leahy, the priest, asked.

Anne laughed. "I think not. The government should not interfere with religion, but if the magistrates and the men and women ruling the country loveth not God, then those of us who are aware of the light within us must show the way. I am telling the people that the Lord loveth them. But He will never force them to love Him."

I listened to Anne, fascinated, but the idea of a God who grieved but would take no responsibility for man's behavior was difficult for everyone on the panel to cope with. They questioned Anne about mass starvation, especially in Ethiopia, and Saul and I smiled at Anne's answer as we suddenly realized that we had briefed her better than we thought.

"It's not the Lord's fault that his creatures die of hunger," Anne told them, "or that they died in one of your wars because some were Jews and some men hated Jews. It is man's fault. Man loveth himself and his weapons more than the Lord. The problems of men, whether they be of death through stavation or death because of hatred, are problems that God expects His creatures to solve themselves, and there is only one way to do that."

"Why has God chosen you?" Father Leahy asked.

"He chose *thee*," Anne said, startling him by her blithe response. "But thou hear Him not, or if thou does thou art afraid to act. If like me, thou or Master Waggert were truly born again, I am well-nigh certain that thou wouldst finally believe and do what the Lord asketh. If those who say they love the Lord wish to kill me again, it will be to their own sorrow. Whatever may happen to me, I fear it not. I am here to tell ye that there is only one way that God's creatures can save themselves from their own Armageddon. Each one of ye must take responsibility. Repent and rebel!"

Trying a different tact, Harold Cornsby, the historian, after several questions about Puritan manners and mores, smiled coolly at Anne. It was obvious that he thought he could trap her. "I am sure you must be aware," he said, "that the fact of your prior existence is crucial to whether people really believe what you are telling them. Basically, you are saying that God is standing by, expecting that we will destroy each other and this earth unless we believe that you are actually resurrected and can communicate with the Almighty." He smiled condescendingly. "Many preachers and evangelists, including Reverend Waggert, have told us similar things, but even today the Pope doesn't claim your kind of credentials."

Cornsby took a sheet of paper out of his pocket. "I am holding a copy of a letter that Anne Hutchinson wrote to Thomas Leverett in 1639. This letter and the copy have been authenticated by a Boston historical society. A table is being placed in front of you so that you can write comfortably. I am going to read you a sentence from this letter, and I'd like to have you write the sentence as I read it to you. We will then compare the original with what you have written. Do you have any objection?"

Imagining the baited breath of eighty milllon television viewers watching this neatly conceived drama, I nudged Saul. "Now *we* better start praying."

As Cornsby finished, Frank Gaines handed Anne a felt-tip pen, and asked again if she had any objections.

Anne stared curiously at the pen. "I have no objections, but I seeth no ink."

Gaines took the cap off the pen and showed her the point. Smiling, Anne tested it with her finger. "'Tis amazing," she said softly. "I never saw a quill with the ink inside." She leaned over and quickly scrawled something on the paper and gave it to Gaines. He held it up and the camera closed in on it. In a cursive style of writing she had written, "I am Anne Hutchinson."

Looking a little disconcerted, Cornsby dictated, and while the camera peered over her shoulder and her ghostly fingers were holding a clearly defined pen, Anne wrote: "And if what you call railing and reviling were a truth of God, acted by Him through me, then you have called the spirit of God a railer and reviler."

Shrugging, Cornsby held up his copy. It was an exact match. After a sharp intake of breath and gasps of "My God," everyone in the studio, who had come in from various offices to see her, applauded.

After an hour and a half of more questions in this vein and questions decrying the morality of a woman who had carnal knowledge of three men in one lifetime, and now presumably was sleeping with another one, the middle-aged female internist, Doctor Thomas, who was sitting next to Anne, demanded to know why she had refused to submit to another physical examination.

Summing up for the panel, she said, "We are all impressed by your scriptural knowledge and your belief in a God who watches and weeps but will not act against His creatures. But the reality is that if Jesus Himself reappeared, I am afraid that He would have a difficult time proving that He was actually Jesus."

As she was speaking, she reached over and took Anne's hand in an obvious attempt to feel her skin and take her pulse. Anne didn't pull away, but smiled benignly at her. But then, within what was less than a three-second gap, once again Anne disappeared. Doctor Thomas stared totally bewildered in her direction and said hollowly, "I can't see you! What's happening? Where are you?"

A cold shivery silence hung over the studio as we watched the technicians and cameramen fumbling with their cameras in disbelief. Was Anne's momentary disappearance one more proof that she was really an emissary of the Lord? It was such a brief time that I'm sure each of us wondered if it were our own hallucination. But before they could evaluate it, Anne was thanking the panel and the program was over.

I'm sure now that our temporary inability to see Anne was a by-product of our doubt, and it was counterbalanced by her laughing conviction that her disappearance was in the eye of the beholder.

Three hours after the show I was back home in Quincy. Narragansett Road was deserted. A lonely police watchman greeted me when I got out of the taxi from the airport and asked me how Mrs. Hutchinson was doing. I told him that he could go home and watch the reruns on late television. I wouldn't need police protection until Anne returned. Saying it, I wondered if she would ever return, and I crossed my fingers.

Knowing that I couldn't get a direct phone call through to Anne at the

Plaza, I had told Saul before I left to call me after midnight when I was sure I would be home. While I puttered around the lonely house, memories of the past two weeks unreeled in my mind. Would I ever look at the rug near the fireplace without seeing her lying naked on the floor? Would I ever get into bed without thinking of her blending herself into me, physically and mentally, as she told me about her life—a life of love for God and God's creatures?

Tomorrow I would have to explain to Emily that I too had taken a long trip. Would she ever understand that I had traversed the centuries and had become inextricably involved with another woman? A dream woman?

Wondering uneasily if I could ever sleep in this bed without feeling Anne's cool flesh pressed against me, I was jarred back to reality by the telephone ringing.

Anne's voice breathed warmly in my ear. Sounding both happy to hear me and a little melancholy, she said, "Dear Robert, art thou as lonely for me as I for thee?"

I assured her that I was.

"Wherever thou art, I am," she said—words I will never forget. "I am beside thee now. I cannot believe that thou art already back at Mt. Wolleystone. Only three hours ago I kissed thee goodbye. When you left in that taxi to fly home in an airplane, I cried. It is hard to believe that man can fly and loveth not God." She sighed. "I should have come home with thee. I am afraid to sleep alone. Boston is my home. I ran away once and tried to live near this New Amsterdam Apple. But I shall not do it again. Saul and Susan agree with me. Those who loveth the Lord will come to me wherever I am."

Saul got on an extension phone. "Anne is lost without you," he said. "She's decided that she's weary of television. The politicians who want her to come to Washington will have to come to Boston. Steve Carlson has agreed to help us set up a national Repent and Rebel Committee with headquarters in Boston and locations in every city throughout the country. We're going to leave here early in the morning. Hank and Buck will drive us uptown in the limousine to your car. I told Anne that Pelham will be like Portsmouth. Her former life is gone and mostly forgotten. If there're going to be any monuments to her, they'll erect them now. But unless she changes her mind, she keeps telling us that the Lord wants her to complete the cycle of her former life. We'll drive home via the Hutchinson River Parkway, and we'll look around Pelham Bay Park for awhile. We should be back in Quincy by three."

I could hear Saul chuckle. "I hope that your wife Emily has a sense of humor. Your new wife, Anne, will have to stay with you for a few days. You just heard her. She's afraid to sleep alone."

Tuesday morning, I awoke with an indefinable uneasiness. It wasn't caused by worry of how I would manage a compatible existence with both Anne and Emily. I was sure that Anne would captivate Emily, and they would be friends. Centuries ago Anne had attracted many women who depended on her. Even though she had loved John Cotton, and Sarah had probably been aware of her husband's love for Anne, Sarah had never felt threatened by her.

No, I had a different feeling of something impending, something about to happen that I might be able to avoid. It was similar to a feeling that occasionally occurred to me when I decided that today, when I got behind the wheel of my car, I had better not daydream. I was sure to get into an accident if I drove so automatically that when I arrived, I couldn't remember how I got there.

Driving Emily's car to the International section of the airport where Emily and her friends were expected to arrive at one o'clock, I turned on the radio to hear the noon news. A few seconds later, I listened in horror to the commentator, whose voice was shaking with excitement. "This morning about an hour ago, a strange motor accident occurred near Pelham Bay Park, New York. Presumably Anne Hutchinson was involved. At this moment no one knows what has become of her.

"Last night more than eighty million people watched Mrs. Hutchinson on television. Once again, she couldn't be photographed, and viewers received a striking demonstration that she must indeed have returned from the dead.

"This morning, presumably in disguise, Mrs. Hutchinson was being driven back to Boston by a young man and woman, who claim that they are close friends of hers and had accompanied her to New York. The Cadillac with Massachusetts plates that she was riding in was side-swiped by a passing trailer truck. The car catapulted over an embankment and rolled over a few times. Miraculously, Saul Dremler, a student at Boston University, who was driving the car, and his friend, Susan Weiss, got out before the car exploded and burst into flames.

Dremler insisted that the driver of the trailer truck seemed to be racing him. The driver had passed him twice and, according to Dremler, kept forcing them over to the edge of the road. The second time, Dremler swerved to avoid hitting the trailer, but it glanced off the Cadillac and he lost control of the car. Battered and badly burned, Dremler was trying to open the back door of the car when the police and firetrucks arrived. Dremler told the police and medics, who took him and Susan Weiss to a local hospital, that Anne Hutchinson had been sitting in the back seat of the car. But a thorough search by firemen, who finally put out the flames, revealed no charred body or bones.

"Although it seems improbable that Mrs. Hutchinson could have escaped from the car, as yet no one has see her in the vicinity of the accident. Fearing that she might be wandering around in a daze, and might not be recognizable since she was wearing a wig, police have issued an alert.

"To add to the mystery, coincident or not, the holocaust occurred close to the area where Mrs. Hutchinson and her children were torched by Indians three centuries ago.

"The driver of the trailer truck, a man in his middle sixties, who was identified as Thomas Dudley, was unharmed. He insisted that he tried to pass the Cadillac several times but that the driver kept swerving to the center of the road. He told police that he could see the occupants of the car, and he was sure from their actions, that they had either been drinking or were on drugs. Told that one of the occupants of the car was Mrs. Hutchinson, the driver shrugged and said, 'I saw her last night on television. The woman was obviously on some kind of weird trip.'"

Waiting for Emily to clear Customs and emerge through the closed door designed to keep returning tourists from passing contraband to confederates, I was oblivious to the hundreds of people waiting for relatives or friends to rush into their arms, thankful that they were back in America. I was drowning in a profound sense of loss for a woman from another world—a woman I loved, and I was scarcely aware of a man who pressed a small envelope into my hand. Before I could question him, he disappeared into the crowd. But his afterimage was etched into my brain. I had seen those burning eyes and pointed beard before. Shaking, I opened the envelope. Inside was a three-by-five, sharp and clear snapshot of Anne at Rockefeller Center. On the back in a flowing script was written: "Be she from God or Satan, methinks this is a woman who haunted some men for eternity. J.W."

Dazed, a bright light flashed through my brain, and I could hear Anne saying, "Wherever thou art, I am here."

I smiled at Emily, who was running toward me and I hugged her. "Welcome home. I've missed you."

She looked at me searchingly. "Are the tears in your eyes for me? Where's Anne?"

I shrugged. "I'm not sure." And I smiled sadly, "within me, perhaps."

ANNE HUTCHINSON'S TRIALS

Anne was called before the General Court of Massachusetts on November 7th, 1637, for two days. Five months later, after she had been imprisoned during the winter in the home of Joseph Weld, in Roxbury, she was forced to appear before the members of the First Church of Boston on March 15th and March 22nd.

Her trials were called "examinations," and the accusers were both judges and jury. She was banished by the General Court and excommunicated by her church. The original transcript of these trials, which was taken down in a kind of shorthand and later printed that way, do not exist in most libraries.

Fortunately, the American historian, Charles Francis Adams, realized the significance of the Antinomian Controversy and preserved both trials, Winthrop's *Short Story,* and Cotton's *The Way Cleared* in a book titled *Antinomianism in the Massachusetts Bay Colony,* published under the auspices of the Prince Society. This book, which was long out of print, was republished by Burt Franklin in 1967, but it is almost impossible to find on library shelves, and the trials in the original format are difficult to read and almost incomprehensible.

After completing *The Resurrection of Anne Hutchinson* and her "true" description of early colonial life and religious beliefs, the reader may find the complete transcription of both trials fascinating and the interplay of politics and religion easy to understand, with many modern implications. The cast of characters and my identification of particular people whose names do not appear in the original transcripts, and my interpretation of the emotional responses of various people help convey the drama of these trials. I have also interwoven John Winthrop's own report of Anne's "examination," which contains some additional conversation not reported in the "official" transcript. Other than modification of a particular word here and there, the elimination of *F* for *S* in certain words, the use of *you* throughout, and modern punctuation to fit the actual speech patterns, these are the words that Anne and her contemporaries spoke three and a half centuries ago. They reflect many religious, political, and church and state problems that still exist.

THE FIRST TRIAL OF ANNE HUTCHINSON

Before the General Court of the Province of Massachusetts Bay
November 7-8, 1637

Anne Hutchinson kept no diaries or journals. There are no drawings or pictures of her. Practically everything that is known about her is derived from her two trials and the *Journals* that John Winthrop kept, in which he views her not in friendship but as a religious and political problem and as a woman whom her husband should have silenced. In addition to his *Journals*, Winthrop wrote a book, which was not published until several years later in England, attempting to vindicate himself. Titled *A Short Story of the Rise, and the Ruin of Antinomiasts, Familists and Libertines*, it covers the reasons for the banishment of Anne Hutchinson as well as John Wheelwright. It also contains a slightly different transcript of the first portion of the trial, which was preserved by Thomas Hutchinson in his book *The History of the Massachusetts Bay Colony*, which was written nearly a hundred years later.

John Cotton also addressed himself to the problem of Anne's banishment in a pamphlet, *The Way for the Congregational Churches Cleared*, but neither in this pamphlet nor in his voluminous sermons does he clear up the mystery of Anne's attachment to him.

All other information about Anne, her life in England until she was forty, and her seven years in Rhode Island after the second trial are suppositions based on a sentence here and there in *Journals* and other documents.

Neither Cotton Mather, a great-grandson of John Cotton, nor Thomas Hutchinson, Anne's own great-grandson, who wrote about her in their histories many years later, were very sympathetic to her. In 1896, nearly two hundred and fifty years later, the transcript of the *Second Church Trial of Anne Hutchinson* was discovered, and for the first time Charles Francis Adams, in one section of his *Three Episodes of Massachusetts History* (1892) (after publication of the Church Trial first published in 1888, see page 372), treated her in a more friendly way, and he excoriated John Cotton for betraying her.

The Court was assembled in the Meetinghouse in New Town (Cambridge), Massachusetts. The following trial took place after the banishment of John Wheelwright, Anne Hutchinson's brother-in-law, earlier that morning. There is no detailed transcript of Wheelwright's appearance before the Court. But as a minister of the Gospel he had already made his heretical beliefs quite clear in his sermons. The Meetinghouse was on Spring Street in Cambridge, and was difficult to get to from Boston except by a day's journey through Roxbury. The Meetinghouse, whose pastor was Thomas Shepherd, could accommodate less than two hundred people sitting on backless benches. It was a thatched-roof building, totally unheated.

The magistrates would have worn cloaks of heavy black wool and their badges of office. The congregation who crowded into the church were dressed in woolen and leather garments. The ladies wore caps and gowns of "sad colors," which means colors of dark red, green, grey, or blue, and the men wore breeches, doublets, and great coats.

The magistrates and deputies were gathered on a slightly raised podium beneath a pulpit at the front of the Meetinghouse. Sitting in a row, they faced Anne Hutchinson. For staging, so that the audience can see Anne's face, the members of the Court sitting behind a table should be at the left side of the stage with some of the deputies in a circle facing Anne, who would be standing and/or sitting center stage. The time of the first day is approximately 1:00 P.M. Anne's husband, Will, and some of her children were in the congregation, but none of them were called as witnesses. The eight ministers would be dressed in black gowns and Geneva bands. Outside, it might have been snowing.

Cast in Order of Speaking Appearance

GOVERNOR JOHN WINTHROP

Raised in an illustrious family in England, he studied law and was a justice of the peace at 18. Appointed governor of the Colony by the original adventurers under a Charter received from King Charles in 1629, he lost the second election to Thomas Dudley, who thought Winthrop was too lenient in prosecuting wrongdoers. He and Dudley were friendly enemies most of their lives. At the time of the trial, after the current governor, Sir Harry Vane, who sided with Anne Hutchinson, had left the Colony and returned to England, Winthrop was reelected governor, largely because of his opposition to Anne Hutchinson. He had arrived in the Colony on the *Arbella* in 1629, along with Thomas Dudley and John Wilson, and he was instrumental along with them in choosing Boston as the main site of the new colony. He wore a Van Dyke beard. At the time of the trial he was 49 years old and would live until 1649. A year before his death, a somewhat disappointed man, he refused to sign another order for banishment that Dudley put before him.

ANNE HUTCHINSON

Born in Alford, England, she lived in London, England, during her teens. When her father, Francis Marbury, a minister, died, her mother, Bridget Dryden (of noble heritage), moved back to Alford, where Anne married Will Hutchinson in 1612 when she was 20. Between 1612 and 1634, when she and Will came to New England aboard the *Griffin,* Anne had fifteen children. None of them died in childbirth, but three of them died between 1629 and 1630, when England was swept by fevers and the Black Death. She arrived in Boston in 1634 with her entire surviving family, except

Edward, her oldest son, who had preceded her to Boston on the *Griffin* the year before with John Cotton. During her twenty years in Alford, she attended fairs in Old Boston about twenty-two miles from Alford, and listened to John Cotton preach. She admits in her trial that she left England for the Colony because she was desolate without her teacher. At the time of the trial Anne was 46. There are no drawings or pictures of her but she probably had a light complexion and was fairly tall. She was murdered by the Mohegan Indians in 1643, seven years after she was banished, in New York, where she had fled, believing that the Bay Colony was going to extend its jurisdiction to Rhode Island, where she had been living. Some people believe that Uncas, sachem of the Mohegans, who had murdered Miantonomo, sachem of the Narragansetts, under an agreement with Winthrop, Dudley, and magistrates of the Colony, may have been encouraged to get rid of Anne Hutchinson too.

JOHN ENDICOTT

A flamboyant man who wore a goatee, he arrived in Salem before the Colony had a charter and was elected governor. Fast-talking, impulsive, he had the cross cut out of the King's flag in Salem because it was a symbol of popery. For attacking the magistrates and challenging their primacy in the Colony, he was admonished and unable to hold office for a year. In 1642 he led an expedition to Mt. Wolleystone, a few miles from Boston, captured Thomas Morton, who had been previously evicted by the Pilgrims but had returned to New England. He burnt down Morton's house and imprisoned him. At the time of the trial Endicott had been reinstated and was captain of the Massachusetts Bay militia, and he was 49. He tried to pass a law insisting that women wear veils in church, and later made it a law that men must not wear beards or let their hair grow below their ears. He lived until 1665.

SIMON BRADSTREET

A deputy on the General Court, he was the son-in-law of Thomas Dudley. His wife, Anne Bradstreet, became known as the first American poet. He was 34 at the time of the trial. He served as governor of the Colony from 1679 to 1686. He lived until 1697.

DEPUTY GOVERNOR THOMAS DUDLEY

A hard-nosed, gruff, heavily built man, he received a captaincy from Queen Elizabeth and fought in the seige of Amiens under Henry the Fourth in 1597. He was steward to the Earl of Northumberland and could, as a warrior, wear the white plume of Navarre. When he arrived in the Colony he was 54. At the time of the trial he was 61. He lived until 1653, and was governor of the Colony four different times.

HUGH PETERS

Minister at Salem. A fleshy, red-faced man, he arrived in the Colony in 1635. He returned to England in 1641 with Thomas Weld and became chaplain to Oliver Cromwell. During the Restoration he was apprehended as one of those responsible for the beheading of King Charles. He was hung in England in 1660. His wife went insane and returned to the Colony, where she was supported by the magistrates. He was 38 at the time of the trial.

JOHN WILSON

Minister of the First Church, Boston, he arrived in 1629 on the same ship John Winthrop left England on, the *Griffin*. His wife, the widow of a wealthy man, John Mansfield, was afraid to make the trip. He returned to England in 1631 and again in 1635 and finally persuaded her to come to America. He was 49 at the time of the trial and lived until 1667. He was "resurrected" by Nathaniel Hawthorne and appears in *The Scarlet Letter*.

GEORGE PHILLIPS

Minister at Watertown. Presumably Anne had never heard him preach, although she indicated she had. At the time of the trial he was about 45. He lived until 1644.

THOMAS WELD

Minister at Roxbury. Although he had been driven out of England by Archbishop Thomas Laud for his heretical views, he practiced the same kind of vindictiveness on Anne. He returned to England in 1662 and became impoverished. At the time of the trial he was about 47.

ZACHARIAH SYMMES

Minister at Charlestown. He first met Anne en route to America aboard the *Griffin,* and just as soon as he arrived in Boston he reported her deviational thinking to Thomas Dudley and John Cotton, thereby delaying Anne's admittance to the church for more than a week after her husband, Will, had been accepted. At the time of the trial he was probably in his 40s.

THOMAS SHEPHERD

Minister at New Town (Cambridge). A frail, poor-complexioned man, he is known to history because he wrote his memoirs, part of which have survived. He disassociated himself from John Wheelwright's beliefs long before Wheelwright was banished. He was married three times. His third wife, Margaret, survived him and married his colleague, Jonathan Mitchell. He was 33 at the time of the trial, and he lived until 1649.

JOHN ELIOT

Minister at Roxbury along with Thomas Weld. Deeply interested in missionary work among the Indians, he learned their language and wrote an Indian grammar and translated several books of the Bible into their language. He was 33 at the time of the trial and lived until 1694.

NATHANIEL WARD

Minister at Ipswich. He was not present at the trial but was referred to as a friend of Thomas Dudley, and one who had certain knowledge of Anne's heretical beliefs. He was the author of *The Simple Cobbler of Agawam,* which, among other things, decried women's fashions. He was 67 at the time of the trial. He lived until 1653.

INCREASE NOWELL

Secretary to the General Court, he lived in Charlestown. At the time of the trials he was in his 50s. He died poor in 1655.

RICHARD BROWN

An elder in the Watertown church.

ROGER HARLAKENDEN

Deputy to the Court. He did not live in Boston. A friend of Thomas Shepherd, he was 28 at the time of the trial. He lived another year, to 1638, and died of the pox.

JOHN HUMFREY

Deputy. One of the six original founders of the Colony, he lived in Swampscott. He returned to England in 1641 when his home was destroyed by fire. He was in his 40s at the time of the trial.

ISRAEL STOUGHTON

Deputy, but not from Boston. He was a merchant.

NATHANIEL BISHOP

Deputy, who arrived in the Colony in 1634.

JOHN COGGESHALL

Deputy, but not from Boston. Probably in his 40s. He was disenfranchised after the trial and threatened with banishment. Before he died, along with William Aspinwall, who moved to Rhode Island, he became a Quaker, a religion that Anne did not know of, but which reflected many of her religious beliefs.

WILLIAM COLBURN

Elder of the First Church, Boston. In his 40s at the time of the trial. He lived
until 1662.

THOMAS LEVERETT

Elder of the First Church of Boston, he was in his 40s at the time of the trial.
He lived until 1674.

WILLIAM BARTHOLOMEW

Anne and Will Hutchinson lived with the Bartholomews in London before
departing for America on the *Griffin*. He was probably in his 50s, and a
merchant in the Colony.

JOHN COTTON

Teacher at the First Church in Boston. He arrived in the Colony in 1633
when he was 45. One of the most important Puritan ministers in England.
After preaching twenty years at St. Botolph's in Old Boston, he was
driven into hiding for not conforming to the practices of the Church of
England as proclaimed by Archbishop Thomas Laud. He was 48 at the
time of the trial and lived until 1652. He is buried in King's Chapel in
Boston near John Winthrop's grave.

RICHARD COLICUTT

Deputy from Dorchester.

WILLIAM CODDINGTON

Deputy from Boston. Coddington was one of the wealthiest men in the
Colony. His was the only brick home in Boston. Although he sided with
Anne Hutchinson, he was not banished, probably because Winthrop respected his wealth. He was unwilling to live in the Colony under Winthrop and left Boston after the trial. He became governor of Rhode
Island. Will Hutchinson succeeded him as governor of Rhode Island for
a short time, because of a charge that he was ruling Rhode Island with
the same lack of religious freedom that Winthrop had instituted. Under
Anne's influence Coddington and her husband patched up their differences, and Coddington became governor again. He was 37 at the time of
the trial and lived until 1678.

WILLIAM JENNISON

Deputy from Watertown.

GOVERNOR JOHN WINTHROP

Mrs. Hutchinson, you are called here as one of those who have troubled the peace of the Commonwealth and the churches. You are known to be a woman who hath great flare in promoting and divulging of those opinions that are the causes of this trouble. You are known to be nearly joined not only in affinity and affection with some of those that the court has already taken notice of and passed judgment on, but you have spoken divers things as we have been informed, very prejudicial to the honor of our churches and their ministers.

In addition, you have maintained a meeting, an assembly in your house that hath been condemned by the General Assembly of Ministers as a thing not tolerable nor comely in the sight of God, nor fitting to your sex. And notwithstanding that it was cried down you have continued the same. Therefore, we have thought it good to send for you and understand how things are. And, if you may be in an erroneous way, we may reduce you so that you may become a profitable member here among us. Otherwise, if you be obstinate in your course, then the court may take such course that you may trouble us no further. Therefore, I would entreat you to express whether you do not assent, in practice, to those opinions and factions that have been handled in this court already. That is to say whether you justify Mr. Wheelwright's sermon and the petition.

ANNE HUTCHINSON
(Standing, facing the magistrates)

I am called to hear and to answer such things as I am accused of. But I hear nothing laid to my charge. *(She appears quite calm but determined to present her case in her own way.)*

WINTHROP
(Exasperated)

I have told you some already and more I can tell you.

ANNE

Name one, Sir.

WINTHROP

Have I not named some already? Have you countenanced, or will you justify these seditious practices which you have heard censured in this court?

ANNE
(Sticking to her guns)
What have I said and done?

WINTHROP
That you did harbor and countenance these parties in the faction—and for your doings that you have already heard of.

ANNE
That's a matter of conscience, Sir. Do you ask me upon a point
of conscience?

WINTHROP
No. Your conscience you may keep to yourself. But in this case, if
you must countenance and encourage those that transgress the
Law,* you must be called to question for it. And that is not your
conscience, but your practice of it. Your conscience must be kept
or it will be kept for you.

ANNE
(Teasingly)
Must I then entertain the saints?—because I must keep my con-
science.

WINTHROP
(Scowling and changing tack)
If one brother should commit a felony or treason and come to
another brother's house, if he knows that he is guilty and conceals
him, he is guilty likewise. It is conscience to entertain him. But if
his conscience comes into the act so that he gives countenance to
him and entertainment, he has broken the law and is guilty, too.

ANNE
(Puzzled)
What Law hath they transgressed—the Law of God?

WINTHROP
The Fifth Commandment. These seditious practices of theirs have
cast reproach and dishonor upon the Fathers of the Commonwealth.

The essence of the Law in a Christian theocracy is the Ten Commandments,
or Decalogue.

ANNE

In what particular?

WINTHROP

Why in this—among the rest—where the Lord does say "Honor thy father and mother." That includes all authority.

ANNE
(Shaking her head)

Aye, Sir—in the Lord.

WINTHROP

You have broken this honor and given countenance to them.

ANNE
(Frowning)

In entertaining those, did I entertain against the Law? For there is the problem. Or did I converse against what God has appointed?

WINTHROP
(Slowly and sternly)

You have justified Mr. Wheelwright and his sermon for which you now know that he has been convicted of sedition. You have likewise countenanced and encouraged those that put their hand to a petition for Mr. Wheelwright. You cannot deny that you have joined with them in this action.

ANNE
(Boldly)

In what action have I joined?

WINTHROP

You cannot deny that you had your hand in the petition.

ANNE
(Questioningly)

Suppose I had set my hand to the petition? What then?

WINTHROP

You have counselled them.

ANNE

How?

WINTHROP

Why, in entertaining and conversing with them.

ANNE

What breach of the Law is that, Sir?

WINTHROP
(Angrily)

I just told you. The dishonoring of your parents.

ANNE

But let's suppose I do fear the Lord and my parents, may I not entertain people who fear the Lord because my parents will not give me leave?

WINTHROP
(Patiently as possible)

If they are fathers of the Commonwealth, and your friends are of another religion, and you entertain them, then you are dishonoring your parents and are justly punishable.

ANNE
(Agreeing with a smile)

If I entertain them and they have dishonored their parents, I do.

WINTHROP

By countenancing them above others, you honor them.

ANNE

I only put honor on them as children of God, and as they do honor the Lord.

WINTHROP
(More than a little vexed)

We do not mean to discurse with those of your sex. But rather to tell you that you do adhere unto them, and you do endeavor to set forward this faction, and thus you do dishonor us.

ANNE
(A little shrilly)

I acknowledge no such thing. Neither do I think that I ever put any dishonor upon you.

WINTHROP

(Sharply)

What say you to the weekly public meetings at your house? Can you show a warrant for them?

ANNE

(Quickly and confidently)

It is just as lawful for me to do so, as it is for all your practices. Can you find a warrant for yourself and condemn me for the same thing? The reason for my taking it up was when I first came to this land, because I did not go to such meetings, it was presently reported that I did not allow such meetings in my house but held them unlawful. Therefore in that regard, people said that I was proud and despised all ordinances. Then a friend came and told me of it. So, to prevent such opinions, I invited people to my home. But it was a practice before I came; therefore I was not the first.

WINTHROP

Appealing to our practice needs no confutation. There are private meetings indeed and still are in many places of a few neighbors, and they are useful for the increase of love and edification. But none so public and frequent as yours. Yours are of another nature. They have been evil, and there is no good warrant to justify yours. If your gatherings had answered to the former, they would not have been offensive. But I tell you that your meetings were not of women alone, but of another kind. Many times there were men among you.

ANNE

(Nervously)

There never was a man among us.

WINTHROP

(Pleased with her answer)

Assuming that there were no men at your meetings, and you agree that there is no warrant for your doings, why do you continue on such a course?

ANNE

I believe that there is a clear rule in Titus, Chapter 2, that elder women should instruct the younger. So I must have a time wherein I must do it.

WINTHROP
(Sharply)

All this I grant you but as the Apostle means—privately and upon occasion. He gives no warrant for such meetings as may suit your purpose. For what purpose do you, Mrs. Hutchinson, call a company together from their other business so that they may be taught by you? You take it upon yourself to teach many that are elder than yourself. Do you teach them what the Apostle commands: namely, "to stay at home?"

ANNE
(Wearily)

Will you please answer this and I will yield. Tell me what the rules are. Then, I will willingly submit to the truth. If they come to my house to be instructed in the ways of God, what rule do I have to send them away?

WINTHROP

You must have a rule for it, else you cannot do it in faith. *(Pausing for effect.)* Yet you have a plain rule against it. I will not permit a woman to teach!

ANNE
(Shrugging)

In that case I suppose I break a rule. But by that is meant the teaching of men.

WINTHROP

Exactly, and you do not do so, here? Suppose a hundred men came unto you to be instructed? Will you agree to instruct them, too?

ANNE
(Warily)

No, Sir, because for my reason. They are men.

WINTHROP
(Shrugging disgustedly)

Men and women are one for all of that. But suppose that a man should come and say, "Mrs. Hutchinson, I hear that you are a good woman that God has given his grace to. In the word of God, I pray instruct me a little." Ought you instruct this man?

ANNE

(Thoughtfully)

I think I may *(pausing)*. If you do not think it lawful for me to teach women—then why do you call me to teach the Court?

WINTHROP

(Trying not to shout)

We do not call you to teach the Court. But rather to lay open yourself. It is clear that what is meant is not the teaching of men but the teaching in public.

ANNE

(Coolly)

It is said in the Bible: "I will pour my spirit upon your daughters and they will prophesy." If God give me the gift of prophecy, I may use it. I desire that you would set me down rules by which I may send away those who come to me, and thus have peace in so doing.

WINTHROP

You must show *your* rules, if you want to receive them.

ANNE

I have done so.

WINTHROP

I deny it.

ANNE

I told you for me, it is a rule.

WINTHROP

(Seething)

First, the Apostle tells us that prophecy long ago in those extraordinary times, and the gifts and miracles of tongues, were common to many as well as the gift of prophecy. Second, in teaching your children, you may exercise your gift of prophecy, but only *that* is within your calling.

ANNE

(Nodding in agreement)

I teach not within a public congregation. But the men of Berea, Acts 17:2, were commended for examining Paul's doctrine. We do no more at our meetings than read the notes of our teacher's sermons, and then reason about them by searching the Scriptures.

WINTHROP

You have departed from the nature of your meetings. We will show your offense in them. You do not as the Bereans, search the Scripture for confirming the delivered truths, but you open up your teacher's points. You declare his meaning, and correct wherein you think he has failed. By this means you abase the honor and authority of the public ministry and advance your own gifts—as if the ministers could not deliver these matters so clearly to their hearer's capacity as you yourself.

ANNE

Prove that—that anybody doth that!

WINTHROP

You are a woman of most note and of the best abilities. If some agree with you, it is by your teaching and example. But you do not show upon what authority you take it upon yourself to be a public instructor.

(Noticing that Anne is quite weary from standing and appears faint, Winthrop tells her to sit down.)

ANNE
(Trying to get a grip on herself)
Here is my authority. In Acts 18:24-26, Aquila and Priscilla took upon themselves to instruct Apollos more perfectly. He was a man of good parts. But they, being better instructed, taught him.

WINTHROP
(Smiling sarcastically)
See how your argument stands. Priscilla with her husband took Apollos home to instruct him *privately*. But Mistress Hutchinson *without* her husband, may teach fifty or eighty.

ANNE
I call them not. But if they come to me, I may instruct them.

WINTHROP
Yet you show us not a rule.

ANNE

I have given you two places in Scriptures.

WINTHROP

But neither of them will refute your practices.

ANNE

(Sarcastically)

Must I show my name written in the Scriptures?

WINTHROP

You must show that which must be equivalent. Seeing that your ministry is public, you obviously would have them receive your instructions as coming from such sources.

ANNE

They must not take it as it comes from me, but as it comes from the Lord Jesus Christ. If I took upon myself a public ministry, I would break a rule. But not in my exercising a gift of prophecy.

JOHN ENDICOTT

(No longer able to restrain himself)

You're saying that there are some Laws of the Bible that you abide by. I think there is a contradiction in your words. What rule for your activities do your offer? Only that it is a custom in Boston?

ANNE

(Grimly)

No, Sir—that isn't a rule for me. If you look upon a rule, Titus is the rule for me. If you convince me that Titus is no rule, then I'll yield.

WINTHROP

You know that ordinarily there is no rule that crosses another, but this rule crosses one in Corinthians. You must take it in this sense. Elder women must instruct the younger about their business and to love their husbands. But never to make them clash.

ANNE

(Smiling)

I believe that is meant for public occasions.

WINTHROP
(Scowling)

Have you no more to say, but this?

ANNE

I have said sufficient about my activities.

WINTHROP

(Slowly, pronouncing his words carefully)

Your course is not to be suffered by us. Besides we find such activities as yours to be greatly prejudicial to the State. Your meetings seduce many honest persons that are called to those meetings. Your opinions, being known to be different from the word of God, may seduce many simple souls that believe in you. Besides, the problems which hath come of late, come from none but such as those who have frequented your meetings. So that now they have flown away from their magistrates and ministers. But only since they have come to you. Besides that, it will not stand well with the Commonwealth that families should be neglected by so many neighbors and dames, and so much time spent with you. We see no rule of God for this, and we do not see that anyone should have authority to set up any exercises besides what the authorities have already set up. For what hurt comes from this, you are guilty of, and we for suffering you.

ANNE
(Nervously)

Sir, I do not believe that to be so.

WINTHROP

Well, that's how we see it. We must therefore put you away, or stop you from maintaining this course.

ANNE

If you have a rule for it, from God's word, you may.

WINTHROP
(Wrathfully)

We are *your* judges, and not you *ours*. We must compel you to it!

ANNE

If it please, by your authority to stop me, I will freely let you, for I am subject to your authority.

SIMON BRADSTREET
(Smiling at Thomas Dudley, his father-in-law)
I would ask a question of Mrs. Hutchinson. Do you think this is lawful? If you agree, then all other women, who do not follow you, are in sin?

ANNE
(Smiling at Bradstreet)
I conceive that mine is a freewill offering.

BRADSTREET
If it be freewill, then you ought to forbear it because it gives offense.

ANNE
Sir, in regard to myself, I could. But for others, I do not see light, but I shall consider it further.

BRADSTREET
I'm not against all women's meetings, but do you consider them lawful?

DEPUTY GOVERNOR THOMAS DUDLEY
(Interrupting)
Much hath been spoken here concerning Mrs. Hutchinson's meetings. Among other answers, she saith that men come not to her home. Therefore I would put to her this one question. Was there never any man at your meetings?

WINTHROP
(Waving his hand)
There were two meeings kept at the Hutchinson house.

DUDLEY
How were there two meetings?

ANNE
Aye, Sir, I shall not equivocate. There is a meeting of men and women, and there is a meeting only for women.

DUDLEY
Are they both continual?

ANNE

No. On occasion they are deferred.

ENDICOTT

Who teaches at the men's meetings—none but men? Do not women teach sometimes?

ANNE

Never as I heard. Not one.

DUDLEY
(Ominously)

I would go a little deeper with Mrs. Hutchinson. About three years ago we were all in peace. From the time that Mrs. Hutchinson arrived here she hath made a disturbance. And some who came over with her on the same ship did inform me what she was thinking as soon as she landed. I, then being governor, dealt with Mr. John Wilson, the pastor, and Mr. John Cotton, the teacher of the First Meetinghouse, and asked them to inquire of her what her opinions might be.

Then, I was satisfied that she held nothing different from us. But within the next year and a half after she had vented divers of her strange opinions and had made friends in the country, at length, it seems, that Mr. Cotton and Mr. Harry Vane believed the way she did. Mr. Cotton hath cleared himself that he was not of her mind. But now it appears, because of this woman's meetings, that Mrs. Hutchinson hath so forestalled the minds of many that resorted to her meetings that she hath become a potent party in this country.

Now, all these things hath shaken the foundation. If she, in particular, hath disparaged our ministers in the land, insisting that they have preached a covenant of works and only Mr. Cotton hath preached a covenant of grace—why—this is not to be suffered! And therefore, she is undermining the foundation. It being found by this Court that she has, and that Mrs. Hutchinson is she who hath depraved all the ministers, and hath been the cause of what hath come about, we must support the foundation or the building will fall.

ANNE

I pray, Sir. Prove it, that I have said that they preached nothing but a covenant of works.

DUDLEY
(Smirking)
Nothing but a covenant of works? Why even a Jesuit may preach the truth, sometimes.

ANNE
Did I ever say that they preached a covenant of works?

DUDLEY
If they do not preach a covenant of grace, clearly then, they must preach a covenant of works.

ANNE
No, Sir. One may preach a covenant of grace more clearly than another. So I said.

DUDLEY
We are not considering that now, but rather your position.

ANNE
(Adamantly)
Prove it, Sir. Prove, what you say I said.

DUDLEY
We are asking you: when they do preach a covenant of works, are they preaching the truth?

ANNE
Yes, Sir, but when they preach of covenant of works for salvation, this is not the truth.

DUDLEY
(Aggravated)
I do but ask you this: when the ministers do preach a covenant of works, do they preach a way of salvation?

ANNE
(Nervously)
I did not come hither to answer questions of that sort.

DUDLEY
Because you will deny the thing.

ANNE

Aye, but that is to be proved first.

DUDLEY

I will make it plain. You said that the ministers did preach a covenant of works.

ANNE

I deny that!

DUDLEY

You said that they were not able ministers of the New Testament and that only Mr. Cotton was.

ANNE

If I ever spake that, I proved it by God's word.

(There is much commotion and cross-conversation in the court.)

COURT CLERK
(Trying to restore order)

Very well. Very well.

ANNE
(Tears in her eyes)

If someone shall come to me in private, and desire me seriously to tell them what I thought of such and such a person, I must either speak false or true in my answer.

DUDLEY

Likewise I shall prove that you said that the Gospel both in the spirit and the words hold forth nothing but a convenant of works and that all that do not hold as you do are in a covenant of works.

ANNE

I deny that. For if I should so say, I would speak against my own judgment.

ENDICOTT
(Sternly)

I desire to speak. It seems that Mrs. Hutchinson seems to lay something against those who are to witness against her.

WINTHROP

And I would add this: it is obvious to the court that Mrs. Hutchinson can tell when to speak and when to hold her tongue, especially upon answers to questions when we ask her to tell her thoughts about the desires that she wishes to be pardoned.

ANNE

(Staring forlornly at the assembled ministers)

It is one thing for me to come before a public magistracy, and there to speak what they would have me speak. It's something else when a man comes to me in a way of friendship and I speak privately to him. There is a difference in that.

WINTHROP

(Shrugging)

What if the discussion be the same?

HUGH PETERS

(Standing and waving for attention)

We will hold our tongues unless the court commands us to speak. If it does we shall answer Mrs. Hutchinson, notwithstanding that some of our brethren are very unwilling to answer.

WINTHROP

Mrs. Hutchinson's statement was not spoken in a corner but in a public assembly. Though things she mentions were spoken in private. Since they are now coming to our attention, we will deal with them in public.

PETERS

(Commanding attention with his mellifluous voice)

We shall give you a fair account of what was said. We do not desire that we come as informers against this gentlewoman, but only as it may be serviceable for the country and posterity to give you a brief account. This gentlewoman was of suspicion from the day of her arrival in this country, not only that she was a woman difficult in her opinions but was of an intemperate spirit. What happened at her landing, I do not well remember, but as soon as Mr. Vane and ourselves arrived, this controversy began. Some of our brethren had been given a bad reflection by Mrs. Hutchinson, and suffered from this reflection that we taught a covenant of works, not according to the Gospel, instead of a covenant of grace. Hearing this, we did address ourselves to Mr. Cotton, the teacher of the Boston church. The court which was then assembled was aware of these things, and that this gentlewoman was the chief agent thereof. We asked Mr. Cotton to tell us wherein the difference lay between him and us, and he suggested that the dissension did arise from this gentlewoman. He said that he thought it not according to God to bring this to the attention of the magistrates but to take some other course.

So we thought it very good to send for this gentlewoman, and she came willingly. At the very first we gave her notice of such reports that we had heard where she did conceive our ministry to be different from the ministry of the Gospel, and that we taught under a covenant of works, etc. If this were her table talk, we desired her to clear herself and speak plainly. She was very tender at first. But some of our brethren did desire to test her, and thereupon her words were: "The fear of man is but a snare. Why should I be afraid of you?" These were her words. I did then take it upon myself to ask her this question. "What difference do you conceive to be between your teacher and us?" She did not request that we should preserve her from danger or that we should be silent. Briefly, she told me that there was a wide and broad difference between our brother, Mr. Cotton, and ourselves. I desired to know the difference. She answered that he preaches a covenant of grace and we a covenant of works, and that we are not able ministers of the New Testament and know no more than the Apostles did before the resurrection of Christ. I did then put to her: What do you conceive of such a brother? She answered that he hath not the seal of the spirit. And other things. But generally the frame of her belief was this. She did conceive that we were not able ministers of the Gospel.

The next day our Brother Cotton told us he was sorry that she should have laid us under a covenant of works and he wished that she had not done so. The elders being present, we did charge them with her, and Mr. Cotton said that he would speak further with her. But after some time she answered that we had gone only so as the Apostles had before Christ's ascension. Since then some of us have gone to her with tears in our eyes to change her mind.

ANNE
(Calmly but pointedly)
If Mr. Wilson would show his writings to you, you would see what I actually said. Many things that have been said are not as reported.

JOHN WILSON

Sister Hutchinson, the writings you speak of, I have them not. And this I must say. I did write down all that was said and passed between one and another at our meeting with you. But I say what is written I will avouch.

DUDLEY

I desire that the other elders will confirm what Mr. Peters hath said.

THOMAS WELD
(Standing up pontifically)

Being asked by the honored Court, I agree that that which our Brother Hugh Peters hath spoken was the truth, and things were said as he hath related about the occasion of calling this sister, and the passages that took place among us. I keep asking myself why she did cast such aspersions upon the ministers of the country. We are poor sinful men, and for ourselves cared not. The precious doctrine that we held forth, we could not but grieve to hear it so blasphemed. She was at that time sparing in her speech. I need not repeat things that have been truly related. She said, "The fear of man is a snare," and therefore, "I will speak freely." And she spoke her judgment and mind freely as was before related, saying that Mr. Cotton did preach a covenant of grace and we a covenant of works. And I remember that she said we could not preach a covenant of grace because we were not sealed, and that we were not able ministers of the New Testament anymore than were the disciples before the resurrection of Christ.

GEORGE PHILLIPS

For my part, I had little to do with these things. I was not privy to the complaint which our Brother Peters hath mentioned. But they asked me to go along with them, telling me that they must deal with her. At first she was unwilling to answer, but at length she said there was a great deal of difference between Mr. Cotton and us. Upon this, Mr. Cotton told her that he could have wished that she had not said that. Being asked of particulars, she did pick out Mr. Shepherd, and said that he did not preach a covenant of grace clearly, or did our Brother Weld. Then I asked her about myself—since she had spoken rashly of them all—because I knew she had never heard me preach at all. She likewise said that I was not an able minister of the New Testament, and the reason was the same. We were not sealed.

ZACHARIAH SYMMES
(Snidely)

For my part, being called to speak in this case to discharge the relationship wherein I stand to the Commonwealth, and for that which I stand unto God, I shall speak briefly. Of my acquaintance with this person, I had none in our native country. I had occasion to be in her company on the *Griffin* before we arrived in the Colony, and I did perceive that she did slight the ministers of the Word of God. It so fell out that we were often in the great cabin together. She did seem to agree with the labors of Mr. Lothrop and myself, but she had her own secret opinion on things we said. The main thing was about the evidencing of good estate, and among the rest about that place in the Gospel of John concerning the love of the brethren. That which I took notice of was the corruptness and narrowness of her opinions, which I doubted not, and I told her so. But she said when she came to Boston there would something more be seen than I said. Many speeches were cast about and abused. Imitating our Savior, she said, "I have many things to say but you cannot bear to hear them now." After we arrived, knowing that she desired to be admitted as a member of the church, I was present, and Mr. Cotton did give me full satisfaction in the things I had questioned about her. As for the things that have been here spoken, as far as I can remember they are the truth. When I asked her what she thought about me she said, "Alas, you knew my mind long ago." Yet I do think myself disparaged by her testimony. I would not trouble the Court except for one thing. Neither Mr. Dudley nor Mr. Haines were unaware of the problem, after I had given them notice about her thinking.

WILSON

I desire that you would give me leave to speak this word because of what has been said concerning her admission as a member of the Church. There was some difficulty made, but in her answers she gave full satisfaction to Mr. Cotton and myself. For example she did not deny justification by sanctification, but only said that justification must be first. Mr. Cotton told her that if she were of that mind, he would not protest her admittance to the church. For we thought that it was a point of order that did not make much difference. We hoped that she would hold with us in that truth as well as the other.

THOMAS SHEPHERD

I am loth to speak in this assembly concerning this gentlewoman in question, but I can do no less than speak what my conscience speaks unto me. I take it a man's wisdom to conceal personal reproaches. Concerning the reproaches of the ministry in this country, there hath been many. And this hath been my thoughts about that. Let them speak what they will, not only against persons but also against the ministry. Let us strive to speak to the consciences of men, knowing that if we had the truth with us we shall not need to prove our words by our practice or our ministry to the hearts of people. But they shall speak for us. And therefore, I am satisfied that my brethren and myself agree on that. Now for that which concerns this gentlewoman at this time, I do not well remember every particular. I do remember that the purpose of our meeting with her was to satisfy ourselves on some points. In the process, Mrs. Hutchinson was asked to speak her thoughts concerning the ministers of the Bay. I do remember that she said that we were not able ministers of the New Testament. I listened to her particulars, and she gave myself as an example, and hearing me preach at a lecture when I gave some ways whereby a Christian might come to an assurance of God's love. But she said that I was not sealed, and I asked her why she said so, and she said, "Because you put love for an evidence." Now I am sure that she was in error in this speech for if assurance be a holy estate, then I am sure that there are not graces wanting to evidence it.

JOHN ELIOT

I am also loth to spend further time. Therefore I shall be content to what hath been said. Our brethren did entreat us to write down what things hath been spoken, and I have it in writing, therefore I do avouch it.

SHEPHERD

I desire to speak this word. It may have been but a slip of the tongue. I hope she will be sorry for it, and then we shall be glad.

DUDLEY
(Speaking directly and coldly to Anne)

I called these witnesses and you deny them. You see that they proved this and you deny this. But it is clear. You said that they preached a covenant of works and that they were not able ministers of the New Testament. Now there were two other things that you did affirm, which are that the Scriptures, in the letter of them, hold forth nothing but a covenant of works, and likewise that those who are under a covenant of works cannot be saved.

ANNE

Prove that I said so.

WINTHROP

Did you say so?

ANNE

No, Sir. It is your conclusion.

DUDLEY

Then why am I charging you, if you deny what is so fully proved?

WINTHROP
(Before Anne can answer)
Here are six undeniable ministers who say it is true, and yet you deny that you did say that they did preach a covenant of works and that they were not able ministers of the Gospel. It appears plainly that you have spoken it, but you say that it was drawn from you in way of friendship, and you did protest then that it was out of conscience that you spake and you said: "The fear of man is but a snare. Wherefore should I be afraid? I will speak plainly and freely."

ANNE
(Shaken but determined)
I absolutely deny that the first question was thus answered by me to them. They thought that I did conceive there was a difference between them and Mr. Cotton. At first I was somewhat reserved and then Mr. Peters told me: "I pray that you answer the question directly and as plainly as you desire so that we can tell you our minds, Mrs. Hutchinson." He said, "We come for plain dealing and telling you our hearts." Then, I told him that I would deal as plainly as I could. They saith that I said that they were under a covenant of works, following the state of the Apostles, but these two speeches contradict one another. I may have said that they might preach a covenant of works as did the Apostles, but to preach a covenant of works and be under a convenant of works is another business.

DUDLEY
There are six witnesses to prove what you said and yet you deny it.

ANNE

I deny that these were the first words that were spoken.

WINTHROP

You make the case worse for you when you clearly show that the reason for opening your mind was not to satisfy them but to satisfy your own conscience.

PETERS
(A little too oilily)

We do not desire to be so strict before the court with the gentlewoman about times and seasons, whether first or after. But it was said.

DUDLEY
(To Anne)

As for the other thing that I have mentioned about the letter of the Scripture, you insisted that it offers nothing but a covenant of works, and for believing in the latter we are also in a state of damnation, or to that effect. These two things you also deny. About three quarters of a year ago, I heard what you were claiming. The person is not here, but he will affirm if need be that he did hear you so say in so many words. He set it down under his hand, and I can bring it forth when the Court pleases. His name is subscribed to both of these things and upon my peril be it, if I bring you not what he wrote, and bring Mr. Nathaniel Ward himself to confirm it.

WINTHROP
(Glaring at Anne)

What say you to this? Though nothing be directly proved as yet, you may hear it to be.

ANNE
(Firmly, without trepidation)

I acknowledge saying the words of the Apostles to the Corinthians to Mr. Ward, and I told him that they were all ministers of the letter and not of the spirit, and they did preach a covenant of works. Upon his telling me that there was no such Scripture, I fetched the Bible and showed him the place: 2 Corinthians 3:6. He said that was the letter of the Law. "No," I told him, "it is the letter of the Gospel."

WINTHROP
(Bored)
You have said this more than once.

ANNE
Then, upon further discussion about proving a good estate and showing it by the manifestation of the spirit, Mr. Ward did acknowledge that was the quickest way. "But yet," he said, "will you not acknowledge that which we believe, too, so that we may have hope?" "No, truly," I told him, "I can't even if that be the way to Hell."

(It has grown so dark in the Meetinghouse that it is hard for people to see one another. Despite the cloak she is wearing, Anne is shivering.)

WINTHROP
Mrs. Hutchinson, as you can see the Court hath labored to bring you to acknowledge the error of your ways so that you might be reduced. But the time now grows late. We shall therefore give you a little more time to consider it, and therefore desire that you attend the Court again in the morning.

(Will Hutchinson, who has been sitting silently on a bench in the crowded congregation, along with a dozen friends, walks toward Anne as the governor and deputy governor, led by the halberd bearers, and followed by the ministers and deputies, file out of the Meetinghouse.)

(The next morning)

WINTHROP
We proceeded last night as far as we could in hearing this cause of Mrs. Hutchinson. There were divers things laid to her charge, including her ordinary meetings about religious exercises, her speeches in derogation of the ministers among us, and the weakening of the hands and hearts of the people toward them. We heard sufficient proof made of that which she is accused, and the point concerning the ministry that they did preach a covenant of works, when others did preach a covenant of grace. We know that she said they were no able ministers of the New Testament and that they did not have the seal of the spirit. And we know that this was spoken, not as pretended in a private conference

with her, but she spoke out her feelings and quoted Scripture as her warrant, alleging that the fear of man is a snare. And she told them that God had given her calling to do so and she would speak freely. Some other speeches she used, were that the Scripture set forth a covenant of works, and this she offered to be proved by probable grounds. If there be anything else that the Court hath to say, it may speak.

ANNE

It seems to me that the ministers have come here in their own cause. Now, the Lord hath said that an oath is the end of all controversy. Although there be sufficient number of witnesses, yet they are not speaking, according to what I said. I desire that they speak upon oath.

WINTHROP
(A little startled)
It is in the liberty of the Court whether to amend an oath or not. It is not in this case as in a case with a jury. If they be satisfied they have spoken sufficiently, we can proceed.

ANNE

When I went home last night I perused some notes about what Mr. Wilson did actually write and I find things not to be as hath been alleged.

WINTHROP

Where are these writings?

ANNE

I don't have Mr. Wilson's actual writings. It may be that Mr. Wilson hath them.

WINTHROP
(Nodding to John Wilson)
Are there notes or instructions that you can give us, Mr. Wilson?

JOHN WILSON

I do say that Mr. Vane told me to copy the discourse out, which I did. Whether it be in Mr. Vane's handwriting or someone else's I know not. My own copy is somewhat imperfect but I could make it perfect with a little pains.

WINTHROP
(Speaking to Anne)
For that which you allege as an exception against the elders is vain and untrue. They are not prosecutors in this case, but have been called here as witnesses in the cause.

ANNE
(Nearly in tears)
But they are witnesses only to their own cause.

WINTHROP
It is not their cause, but the cause of the whole country. They were unwilling that it should happen, but they came for the glory and honor of God.

ANNE
(Determined)
But it is the Lord's ordinance that an oath should be the end of all strife. Therefore they should confirm what they say about me under oath.

BRADSTREET
(Showing off before his father-in-law)
Mrs. Hutchinson, these are but circumstances and adjuncts to the problem. If they admit that they do mistake you in your speeches, you would make them sin. Especially, if you urge them to swear.

ANNE
(Coldly)
That may be. But if they accuse me, I desire it may be upon oath.

WINTHROP
(Shrugging)
If the Court is not satisfied, they may have an oath.

INCREASE NOWELL
I think it convenient that the country also should be satisfied, because I do affirm that things which are spoken in private are carried abroad to the public, and as a result they do undervalue the ministers of the congregations.

RICHARD BROWN
I desire to speak. If I mistake not, an oath is of an high nature and

is not to be taken but in a controversy. For my part I am afraid of an oath, and I fear that we shall take God's name in vain, unless we may take the witness of these men without an oath.

ENDICOTT

I think that ministers are so well known to us that we need not take an oath from them. But, indeed, an oath is the end of all strife.

ANNE
(Amused)
There are some here who will take their oaths to the contrary.

ENDICOTT
(With pursed lips)
Then it shall go under the name of controversy. Therefore we desire to see the notes and also those who will swear.

WINTHROP
Let those who are not satisfied in the Court speak.

(Many voices from the Court say: "We are not satisfied.")

WINTHROP
I will say this to Mrs. Hutchinson: if the ministers take an oath, will you sit down satisfied?

ANNE
(Shaking her head)
Notwithstanding oaths, I can't be satisfied against my own conscience.

ISRAEL STOUGHTON
I am fully satisfied that the ministers do speak the truth. But now in regard to censure I dare not hold up my hand to that. Because this is a court of justice, and I cannot satisfy myself to proceed so far in the way of justice. Therefore, I should desire an oath in this and as in all other things. I do but speak to prevent offence. If I should not hold up my hand, it is because no oath has been given.

PETERS
(After conferring with the other ministers)
We are ready to speak, if we can see a way of God in it.

(Here there is a parley between Dudley and Stoughton about the oath.)

ENDICOTT
(Commenting on the discussion)
If they will not be satisfied with a testimony, an oath will be in vain.

STOUGHTON
I am persuaded that Mrs. Hutchinson and many other Godly-minded people will be satisfied without an oath.

ANNE
(Disagreeing vehemently)
An oath, Sir, is the end of all strife—and it is God's ordinance.

ENDICOTT
(Bitterly)
It shows what respect she hath for the ministers' words. Further, pray see your argument. You ask for words that were written and yet Mr. Wilson saith that he wrote not at all. And now you will not believe these ministers without an oath.

ANNE
(Warily)
Mr. Wilson did say that which he told the governor was the truth. But not all the truth.

WILSON
I did say that, so far as I did take notes that they were true.

ROGER HARLAKENDEN
I would have the spectators take note that the Court doth not suspect the evidence that has been given so far. But we see that whatever evidence is brought will not satisfy, for they are agreed upon this thing. Therefore, I think you will not be unwilling to give your oaths.

WINTHROP
I see no necessity of oath in this case, seeing that it is true and the substance of the matter being confirmed by man. Yet so that all may be satisfied, if the elders will take an oath, they shall have it given to them.

DUDLEY

Let us join things together that Mrs. Hutchinson may know for what they will give their oaths.

ANNE
(Coolly)

I will prove by what Mr. Wilson hath written that they never heard me say such a thing.

SYMMES

We desire to have the paper and have it read.

HARLAKENDEN

I'm still persuaded that it is the truth the elders do say, and therefore I do not see it necessary now to call them to oath.

WINTHROP

We cannot charge anything of untruth upon them.

HARLAKENDEN

Besides, Mrs. Hutchinson doth say that they are not able ministers to the New Testament.

ANNE
(Smiling grimly)

They need not swear to that!

DUDLEY

Will you admit it then?

ANNE

I will neither deny it or say it.

DUDLEY

You must do one.

ANNE

After they have taken an oath, I will make good what I say.

WINTHROP

Let us restate the case, then we may know what to do. That which is laid to Mrs. Hutchinson's charge is this: that she traduced

the magistrates and ministers of this jurisdiction; that she hath
said that the ministers preached a covenant of works and Mr.
Cotton a covenant of grace; and that they were not able ministers
of the Gospel. She excuses these charges because she said she
made them in a private conference and with a promise of secrecy.
But now it is charged that the reason they sent for her was that
she made such charges her table talk, and she told them that the
fear of man was a snare and she would not be afraid of them.

ANNE
(Agreeing)
This that you have spoken I desire that they take their oath
upon.

WINTHROP
To do so would put the reverend elders in this position: that they
deliver upon oath only that which they can remember themselves.

ENDICOTT
(A little exasperated)
But you lifted up our eyes to Heaven as if you were asking God
to witness that you did not come to entrap anyone, and yet you
will not have them swear.

HARLAKENDEN
(To Anne)
Put any statement unto them and see what they say.

ANNE
(Patiently)
They say that I said that the fear of man is a snare, and why
should I be afraid? When I came unto them, they were urging
many things unto me, and I was slow to answer at first, but at
length this Scripture came into my mind—Proverbs 29:15: "The
fear of man bringeth a snare, but whoso pursueth the truth in the
Lord shall be safe."

HARLAKENDEN
There's no essential difference.

WINTHROP
I remember that the testimony was this.

ANNE
(Impatiently)
Aye, that is the thing I do deny. They were my words. But they
were not spoken at first, as they do allege.

PETERS
We cannot remember what comes first and last. We do agree that
an oath is the end of all strife, and we are tender of it. Yet the
main thing against her is that she hath charged us to be unable
ministers of the Gospel and to preach a covenant of works.

WINTHROP
You are correct and the Court is clear. We are all satisfied that is
the truth. But because we wish to eliminate all doubts, we desire
that you satisfy the spectators by oath.

NATHANIEL BISHOP
I desire to know, before they be put to oath, whether their testimony be of validity.

DUDLEY
(Exasperated)
What do you mean to trouble the Court with such questions?
Mark what a flourish Mrs. Hutchinson put upon testimony. She
said she has witnesses to disprove what was said, and yet there is
no man to bear witness.

ANNE
If you will not question them on that, it doesn't help me.

ELIOT
We desire to know of her, and her witnesses, what they deny—
and then we shall speak upon oath. I know nothing we have
spoken but what we may swear to.

SYMMES
(Nastily)
Aye, and more than we have spoken to!

STOUGHTON
I would be glad that an oath be given so that the person to be
condemned should be satisfied in her own conscience. And I

would say the same for my conscience, if I should join in the censure.

JOHN COGGESHALL
I desire to speak a word. It is desired that the elders should confer with Mr. Cotton before they swear.

WINTHROP
(Determined not to bring John Cotton's beliefs into question)
Shall we not believe so many elders in this case? We know the mind of Mr. Cotton without his testimony.

ENDICOTT
I'll tell you what I think, Mr. Coggeshall. This attitude of yours is further casting dirt upon the faces of the judges.

HARLAKENDEN
Mrs. Hutchinson's attitude does the same, for she doth not object to any essential thing, but depends upon circumstances, and would have them sworn.

ANNE
(Angrily)
This I would say unto them. For as much as it was affirmed by Deputy Governor Dudley that he would bring proof of these things, and the elders that they would bring proof in their own causes, therefore I ask that the particular witnesses swear to the things that they speak.

WINTHROP
The elders do not know what an oath is—nor, since it is an ordinance of God, whether it should be used.

ANNE
That is the reason I ask it, and because Mr. Dudley spoke of witnesses, I desire to have them here present.

WILLIAM COLBURN
We desire that Mr. Cotton, our teacher, may be called to hear what is said.

(Winthrop asks John Cotton to come forward. He does and sits beside Anne, smiling sympathetically at her.)

ENDICOTT
(Frowning unhappily at them)
This could cast blame upon the ministers. *(He shrugs.)* Well, whatsoever Mr. Cotton will or can say, we will still believe the other ministers.

ELIOT AND SHEPHERD
(Speaking to Cotton)
We desire to see light as to why we should take an oath.

STOUGHTON
(A little testily)
Because it is the end of all strife, and I think you ought to swear and put an end to the matter.

PETERS
(Coldly)
Our oath would not be to satisfy Mrs. Hutchinson, but the Court.

ENDICOTT
The assembly here will be satisfied by it.

DUDLEY
If the Colony will not be satisfied, you must swear.

SHEPHERD
In my opinion, the Colony doth not require it.

DUDLEY
Let Mrs. Hutchinson's witnesses be called.

WINTHROP
Who are they?

ANNE
Mr. Leverett, Mr. John Cotton, and Mr. John Coggeshall.

WINTHROP
(Surprised)
Mr. Coggeshall was not present.

COGGESHALL
Yes, I was but I preferred to be silent until I was called.

WINTHROP
(Staring angrily at him)
Will you, Mr. Coggeshall, tell the court that she did not say
these things?

COGGESHALL
(Placidly)
Yes. I dare say that she did not say all the things that they accuse
her of.

PETERS
(Blustering)
How dare you look at the Court and say such a thing.

COGGESHALL
(Abashed and suddenly backtracking)
If Mr. Peters takes it upon himself to forbid me, I shall be silent.

STOUGHTON
(Trying to be fair)
Aye, but she intended that you speak.

WINTHROP
(Turning to Thomas Leverett)
Well, Mr. Leverett, what were her words. I pray you speak.

THOMAS LEVERETT
(A little piously)
To my best remembrance, when the elders did send for Mrs.
Hutchinson, Mr. Peters did with such vehemence and entreaty
urge her to tell them what difference there was between Mr.
Cotton and them. After his urging of her she said: "The fear of
man is a snare but they that trust in God shall be safe." And
being asked what the difference was, she did answer that they did
not preach a covenant of grace so clearly as Mr. Cotton did, and
she gave this reason: Like the Apostles, they were for a time
without the spirit and until they received witness of the spirit they
could not preach a covenant of grace so clearly.

WINTHROP
Do you remember that she said that they were not able ministers
of the New Testament?

ANNE

(Interrupting)

Mr. Weld and I had an hour's discourse near the window, and then I spoke it, if I spoke it at all.

WELD

Will you affirm that in the Court? Did not I say unto you, Mrs. Hutchinson, before the elders, when I mentioned the words, you then asked for proof? Was not my answer to you before the Court, leave it there. If I cannot prove it, you shall be blameless.

ANNE

(Pleading)

Yes, I remember that I spoke. But do you not remember that I came afterwards to the window when you were writing, and I spoke to you privately?

WELD

(Adamant)

No, truly.

ANNE

(Near tears)

But I do very well.

WINTHROP

Mr. Cotton, the court desires that you declare what you remember of the conference at the time and the things now in question.

JOHN COTTON

(Staring coolly at the magistrates)

I did not think I should be called to bear witness in this case, and therefore I have not labored to remember what was done. But the greatest occurrence that made an impression upon me was to this purpose. The elders told her what they had heard—that she had spoken some condemning words about their ministry. Among other things they did pray her to answer how she thought their ministry was different from mine. *(He looks at Anne sorrowfully.)* But how she made such comparison, I am ignorant. But I was sorry that a comparison should be made between me and my brethren, and told them how uncomfortable I felt about it that she told them that they did not hold forth a covenant of grace as I did. Wherein did we differ, I asked them? She told them that they did hold forth with a seal of the spirit as I do. "Where is the difference there?" they asked her. "Well," said she, speaking to I know not whom, "you preach about a seal of the spirit upon works, and he upon free grace without works, or without respect to a work. Mr. Cotton preaches the seal of the spirit upon free grace and you upon work. I told Mrs. Hutchinson that I was very sorry that she made comparisons between my ministry and theirs, and she had said more than I could myself. I would rather that she had put us in fellowship with them and not have made a discrepancy between us. She insisted that she found a difference. After that there were some speeches that morning about other things. I do remember that I used as an example the story of Thomas Bilney in Fox's *Book of the Martyrs* and how freely the spirit witnessed unto him without any respect unto work—as he himself professed. *(He pauses and smiles at Anne.)*

If you can put me in mind of anything, I will speak about it. But this was the sum of the difference. It did seem to me, so ill-taken as it is now, that our brethren did say that they would not believe reports about Mrs. Hutchinson as they had done, and unless it were mentioned further, that they would speak no more about it. But some of them did, and some said they were less satisfied than they had been before. But I must say that I did not hear her saying that they were under a covenant of works, nor that she said they did preach a covenant of works.

WINTHROP
(Shaking his head unhappily)
You said that you do not remember. But can you really say that she did speak so?

COTTON
(Smiling as if it does not matter)
I do remember that she looked upon them as Apostles before the ascension of Jesus Christ.

PETERS
I humbly desire to remind our reverend teacher. May it please you to remember whether she said that we were not sealed with the spirit of grace? Therefore, we could not preach a covenant of grace. And that she said further: "You may do it in your judgment but not from your experience." And she spoke plainly that we were not sealed.

COTTON
(Still hedging)

You do remind me that she was asked by you, "Why can't we preach a covenant of grace?" And she answered: "Because you can preach no more than you know"—or that was the gist of her words. But that she actually said that you could not preach a covenant of grace, I do not remember such a thing. I remember well, however, that she said you were not sealed with the seal of the spirit.

PETERS
(Disgusted)

There was brought up that day, a double seal which never was.

COTTON

I know very well that Mrs. Hutchinson took the seal of the spirit as meaning the full assurance of God's favor through the Holy Ghost, and there is a place in Ephesians that doth hold out that seal.

PETERS

So that was the basis of our discourse concerning the great seal and the little seal?

COTTON

To that purpose I remember somebody speaking of the difference between the witness of the spirit and the seal of the spirit. Someone made a distinction between a broad seal and a little seal. Our Brother Wheelwright replied: "If you will have it so, be it so."

ANNE
(Shaking her head)

Mr. Ward said that.

(She is greeted by a chorus of most of the ministers: "No. Mr. Wheelwright said it!"*)*

COTTON
(Agreeing with Anne)

No. It was not Brother Wheelwright's speech, but one of your own expressions.

PETERS

I'm sure it was Mr. Wheelwright.

COTTON
(Determinedly)
Under favor, I do not remember that.

PETERS
(Sarcastically)
Therefore her answer clears it in your judgment, but not in your experience.

ANNE
(To Peters)
My name is precious and you affirm a thing I utterly deny.

DUDLEY
(Sarcastically)
You should have brought the book with you.

NOWELL

The witness does not answer that which you are asking.

WINTHROP
(Wearily)
I do not see that we need their testimony any further. Mr. Cotton hath expressed what he remembers, and what made an impression on him, and so I think the other elders remember that which made an impression on them.

WELD

I told Mrs. Hutchinson when it came to her disagreement, why did you let us go thus long and never tell us of it?

WINTHROP

I wonder too why the elders shouldn't have convinced the elders of the congregation to have dealt with her, if they saw some cause.

COTTON

Brother Weld and Brother Shepherd, I did explain to you both that I understood her speech as expressing herself to you that she did think that some of your preaching was not pertinent to the seal of the spirit.

DUDLEY

But they agree that Mrs. Hutchinson did say that they were not able ministers of the New Testament.

COTTON

I still do not remember that.

ANNE

(Unable to contain herself any longer)

If you please give me leave, I shall give you the basis of what I know to be true. Being much troubled to see the falseness of the Church of England, I almost could have turned Separatist. Finally, I kept a day of solemn meditation and pondering on the Bible. This Scripture kept occurring to me: "He that denies Jesus Christ to come back in the flesh is anti-Christ." I kept thinking of this and in considering the papists, I knew that they did not deny Him to return in the flesh. Nor did we deny Him. Who then was the anti-Christ? Were only the Turks anti-Christ? The Lord knows that I cannot interpret Scripture; He must by His prophetical office reveal it to me. So after being dissatisfied in these questionings, the Lord was pleased to bring me to this Scripture out of Hebrews. "He that denies the testament denies the testator." And thereby He did reveal to me and let me see that those who did not teach the new covenant had the spirit of anti-Christ. And as a result He did reveal the ministry unto me. And ever since, I believe that the Lord has shown me which is the clear ministry and which is wrong. Since that time, I confess that I have seen the difference, and He hath let me distinguish between the voice of my beloved Jesus and the voice of Moses, the voice of John the Baptist and the voice of the anti-Christ. For all those voices are spoken of in Scripture. Now, if you do condemn me for speaking what in my conscience I know to be the truth, I must commit myself unto the Lord.

NOWELL

(Coldly curious)

How did you know that that was the spirit?

ANNE

(With a touch of impertinence)

How did Abraham know that it was God that bid him offer his son when that was a breach of the Sixth Commandment?

DUDLEY
(Emphatically)

By an immediate voice.

ANNE

(Triumphantly)

So to me by an immediate revelation!

DUDLEY

(Totally astounded)

How? What do you mean by revelation?

ANNE

(Oblivious to the fact that she's sealing her fate)

By the voice of His spirit to my soul. I will give you another Scripture—Jeremiah 46:27-28—where the Lord showed me what He would do for me and the rest of His servants. After He was pleased to reveal Himself to me I did presently, like Abraham, run to Hagar. After that He did let me know the atheism in my own heart. And I begged the Lord that it might not remain in my own heart. And finally He did show me (a twelvemonth after) that which I told you about before. Ever since, I have been confident of the things He hath revealed to me. In another place, Daniel 7, He showed me the sitting of the judgment and the standing of all high and low before the Lord, and how thrones and kingdoms were cast down before Him. When Mr. Cotton went to New England, it was a great trouble unto me, and then my brother, Mr. Wheelwright, was unable to preach either. I was then much troubled concerning the ministry under which I lived. But then that verse in the 30th chapter of Isaiah came to my mind: "Though the Lord give thee the bread of adversity and waters of affliction, yet shall not thy teachers be removed into corners any more, but thine eyes shall see thy teachers." The Lord *(she pauses and smiles bravely at John Cotton)* giving me this promise, and there being none left in England that I was able to believe, I could not rest, but I must come hither. And that verse in Isaiah did much follow me—and the bread of adversity and the waters of affliction that the Lord gave me because of the lying about me in this place. But I did remember Daniel, and the Lord did show me that, although I meet with affliction, I am the same with God who delivered Daniel out of the lion's den. Therefore I ask you to think about it. For you see, this Scripture foretold this day, and therefore I desire that you, as you tender the Lord and the church and

the commonwealth, to consider and think about what you will do
to me.

(She pauses again and sobs.) You have power over my body
and soul, and assure yourselves of that, but if you do as much in
your lies to put Jesus Christ from you, and if you continue in this
course that you have begun, you will bring a curse upon you and
your posterity! And the mouth of the Lord hath spoken it!

DUDLEY
(Shaking his head ominously)
What is this Scripture that she quotes?

STOUGHTON
"Behold I turn away from you."

ANNE
(Regaining her composure and smiling tenuously at Cotton)
But having seen that which is invisible, I fear not what man can
do unto me.

WINTHROP
(In shock)
Daniel was delivered by a miracle. Are you saying that you will
be so delivered too?

ANNE
(Fearlessly)
I do so speak it before the court. I believe that the Lord will
deliver me by his providence!

HARLAKENDEN
I may read the Scripture—and the most glorious hypocrite may
read them—and still go down to Hell!

ANNE
(Sadly)
It may be so.

WILLIAM BARTHOLOMEW
(Pompously)
I would remind Mrs. Hutchinson about one thing. She, knowing
that I did know her opinions, when she stayed at my house in
London prior to her departure on the *Griffin,* was afraid I think,

or loth, to reveal herself unto me. But on shipboard when we came within sight of Boston and looking upon the meanness of the place, I remember she uttered these words: "If I had not had a sure prophecy that England would be destroyed, my heart would shake to have come here." Now it seemed to me at the time a very strange thing that she so prophesied.

ANNE
(In a faraway voice)
I do not remember that I looked down upon the meanness of the place, nor did it discourage me because I knew that the bounds of my habitation here were predetermined.

BARTHOLOMEW
As a member of the Court, I fear her revelations will lead many astray.

WINTHROP
Have you heard of any other of her revelations?

BARTHOLOMEW
(Altogether too nice)
For my part I am sorry to see her here, and I have nothing against her, but I only spoke to reveal what manner of spirit Mrs. Hutchinson is. I remember once when I was walking through St. Paul's churchyard in England with her, she was very inquisitive about revelations, and she told me that never had any great thing happened to her but that it was revealed to her beforehand.

ANNE
(Her hands clasped over her breast)
I still say the same thing.

BARTHOLOMEW
(Slyly)
And she also told me that the only reason she came to New England was for Mr. Cotton's sake. As for Mr. Thomas Hooker, as I remember, she told me that she did not like his spirit. But she spoke of a sermon of his in the Low Countries wherein he said: "It was revealed to me yesterday that England should be destroyed." She took notice of that passage and it was very acceptable to her.

COTTON

(A little shocked)

One thing, Mr. Bartholomew, let me entreat you to remember. Why did you never say anything about this to me?

WINTHROP

We're not concerned with that.

BARTHOLOMEW

I remember also that Mrs. Hutchinson's eldest daughter said when we were aboard ship that she had had a revelation that a young man in the ship would be saved. Only he must walk in the ways of her mother, Mrs. Hutchinson.

SYMMES

I would say something to that effect. She told me, "What would you say if we should arrive in New England within three weeks?" I reproved her vehemently for such speculations.

ELIOT

I do not think that speech of Mr. Hooker's which they quote is of his mind or judgment.

SYMMES

I would entreat Mrs. Hutchinson to remember that the Lord will teach the humble. I have spoken of it before, and therefore I will not pursue it, but I do desire her to consider of the many revelations that she hath spoken to her husband. *(He shrugs.)* But I will not enlarge upon it.

ENDICOTT

(Judgmentally)

I would have a word or two, with your leave, of that which hath thus far been revealed to the Court. I have heard many reports of Mrs. Hutchinson's revelations, but now I see that Mrs. Hutchinson actually doth maintain some by her discourse here today. And I think it is a special providence of God that we have heard what she hath said. Now, there is revelation, by which you can see that she doth expect a miracle. She said that she now suffers—but let us do what we will, she shall be delivered by a miracle. I hope that the Court take notice of her vanity of that, and the heat of her spirit. Since her reverend teacher, Mr. Cotton, is here, I ask that he would please speak freely whether he doth defend such speeches or revelations as have been spoken of here. He thus will make us feel more confident.

COTTON
(Trying desperately to extricate Anne)
May it please you, Sir, there are two sorts of revelations here, both of which may tend to danger in more ways than one. And there is another sort of which the Apostle prays, that the believing Ephesians may be partakers of, and these are such as are breathed by the spirit of God, and are never dispensed but in a word of God and according to a word of God. Although the word *revelation* is rare in common speech, and we make it uncouth in ordinary expressions, nevertheless, being understood in a Scriptural sense, I think that some revelations are not only lawful but such as Christians may receive and God bear witness to in His word. Usually He doth express it in the ministry of the word, and doth accompany it by His spirit. Or it may be in the reading of the word in some chapter or verse when it may come to a person flying upon the wings of the spirit.

ENDICOTT
I understand you but I desire that you give your judgment of Mrs. Hutchinson, and what she hath said. Do you believe in the circumstances thereof, of this kind of revelation?

COTTON
I would ask whether by miracle she doth mean a work above nature, or by some wonderful providence of what is often called a miracle in the Psalms.

ANNE
(Smiling at Cotton with tears in her eyes)
I desire to answer our teacher. You know, Sir, what Mr. Endicott doth declare, even though he doth not admit it himself. No matter what happens to me at the present time, I would not expect that the Court should believe that I think Mr. Cotton will save me.

DUDLEY
(Peeved)
I still ask Mr. Cotton to tell us whether he approves of Mrs. Hutchinson's revelations as she hath expressed them.

COTTON

(Hopelessly)

I know not whether I do understand her. But this I will say: if she doth expect a deliverance in a way of providence, then I cannot deny the possibility.

DUDLEY

(Frowning)

No, Sir, that is not what we are asking about.

COTTON

(Shrugging, knowing he is trapped)

If it be by way of a miracle, then I would suspect it.

DUDLEY

Do you believe that her revelations are true?

COTTON

That she may have some special providence of God to help her is a thing I cannot bear witness against.

DUDLEY

(Angrily)

Good Sir, all I am asking is whether her revelations be of God or not.

COTTON

I would have to know whether the sentence of the Court will bring her any calamity, and then I should know whether she expects to be delivered of the calamity by a miracle or by the providence of God.

ANNE

(Trying to save the day)

If some calamity shall come unto me, I expect to be delivered by a providence of God.

WINTHROP

The charges against Mrs. Hutchinson are now somewhat different. I see a marvellous providence of God that have brought things to pass as they are now. We have been disputing in this trial of different things, and now the mercy of God, by a providence, hath answered our desires and made Mrs. Hutchinson lay open herself and admit all of these disturbances arise from her revelations. But we do not accept such revelations from one Scripture or another. For with such revelations there is no need for the ministry to explain the word of God, nor any call of God to Mrs. Hutchinson by His word, which is already written. The basis of her revelations is the immediate revelation of the spirit and not of the word. And that is how she hath very much abused the Colony, teaching them that they shall look for revelations and are not bound to the ministry for the word of God. Instead she teaches that God will teach them by immediate revelations, and this hath been the basis of all these tumults and troubles. Personally, I wish that all those who trouble us were cut off from us. For this is the thing which hath been the root of all this mischief.

COURT
(Unanimously)
We all agree with you.

WINTHROP
Aye, it here is the most desperate kind of enthusiasm in the world. Nothing but a word **comes** into her mind, but then an application is made of it which has nothing to do with the real meaning. And it is *her* revelation even if it is impossible that the word and the spirit should speak the same thing.

ENDICOTT
I would speak to Mr. Cotton. I am sympathetic toward you, Sir, and I know that much weighs upon you in this particular. But your answers do not free you from the way your last answer was intended. Therefore I beseech you that you be pleased to speak your opinions about the way Mrs. Hutchinson has spoken about her revelations. And the Court wants to know whether you do witness for her or against her.

COTTON
(Uneasily)
I repeat what I said, Sir. My answer is plain. If she doth look for deliverance from the hand of God by His providence, and her revelation be in a word, or in accordance with a word—that I cannot deny.

ENDICOTT
You give me satisfaction.

DUDLEY
(Exasperated)
No! No! He gives me none at all!

COTTON
(Trying to appease him)
But if it be by way of a miracle or revelation *without* the word,
then I do not assent to it but look upon it as a delusion, and I
think she does also, as I understand her.

DUDLEY
Sir, you weary me and do not satisfy me.

COTTON
(Placating, but determined)
I pray, Sir, give me leave to express myself. In the sense that she
speaks, I do dare bear witness against it.

NOWELL
I think hers is a devilish delusion.

WINTHROP
Of all the revelations that I ever read I never read the equal of
this. Neither the Anabaptists or the Enthusiasts professed anything like this.

COTTON
But, as you know, Sir, their revelations broach new matters of
faith and doctrine.

WINTHROP
(Harshly)
So does Mrs. Hutchinson. The Lord knows what her revelations
may breed if they are let alone. I do acknowledge that there are
such revelations as do concur with the word of the Bible, but hers
hath not been of this nature.

DUDLEY
(Grimly)
I have never heard such revelations as these, even among the
Anabaptists. I am very sorry that Mr. Cotton should try to justify
her.

PETERS
(Smugly)
I can say the same. Mrs. Hutchinson's beliefs come close to the Enthusiasts. I think Mr. Cotton's belief that she may look for deliverance from the hand of God by His providence in a day of trouble is disputable.

WINTHROP
Her beliefs overthrow all of ours.

DUDLEY
These disturbances that have spread in Germany in the past have all been based upon revelations. As they have vented them, they have stirred up their believers to take arms against their princes, and to cut each other's throats. And these have been the fruits of their revelations. Whether the Devil may be inspiring the same ideas in their hearts here, I know not. But I am fully persuaded that Mrs. Hutchinson is deluded by the Devil. Because the spirit of God speaks the truth in those who believe in Him.

WINTHROP
(Nodding ponderously)
I am persuaded that any revelations bring forth delusions.

ALL THE COURT EXCEPT A FEW MINISTERS
We all believe it, too! We all believe it!

ENDICOTT
I suppose that all the world is wondering where the basis of all these troubles among us lies.

ELIOT
I still believe that *there is* expectation of things promised in the Bible, but to have a particular revelation of things that will occur, there is no such thing in the Scripture.

WINTHROP
But we will not limit the word of God.

RICHARD COLLICUT
It is a great burden to us that we do not agree with Mr. Cotton and that he should justify Mrs. Hutchinson's revelations. I would entreat him to answer about the destruction of England.

WINTHROP

Mr. Cotton was not called here to answer to anything. *(He points at Anne.)* We are to deal with the party standing before us.

BARTHOLOMEW

My wife hath told me that Mr. Wheelwright was not acquainted with Mrs. Hutchinson's beliefs until she imparted them to him.

RICHARD BROWN

(Jumping to his feet)

Inasmuch as I am called to speak for myself, I would therefore try to speak the mind of my brethren. Although we have had sufficient ground for censure before, now that Mrs. Hutchinson has vented herself, I find many flat contradictions in the Scriptures about what she says, especially in Hebrews. God at sundry times may have spoken to our fathers. For my part, I understand that Scripture and other Scriptures of the Lord Jesus Christ. And also the Apostle writing to Timothy, that the Scriptures are able to make one perfect. Mrs. Hutchinson evidently thinks differently. Therefore, I agree with the brethren. I think that she deserves no less a censure than has already been passed on Mr. Wheelwright. But even something more. For what she says is the foundation of all mischief and all those bastardly things which have been overthrowing our government. They have all come from this cursed fountain.

WINTHROP

(Taking charge)

Seeing that the Court hath declared itself and hearing what hath been laid to the charge of Mrs. Hutchinson, and especially by what, by the providence of God, she hath declared, freely without being asked, it therefore be the mind of the Court, looking at her as the cause of all our troubles, that they would now consider what should be done with her.

CODDINGTON

(Interrupting)

I do think that you are going to censure her. Therefore I desire to speak a word.

WINTHROP

I pray you, speak.

CODDINGTON

There is only one thing objected to in her meetings. What if she had desired to edify her own family in her own meetings at home, may no one else be present?

WINTHROP
(Disgustedly)

If you have nothing else to say but that, Mr. Coddington, it is a pity that you should interrupt our proceedings to censure her.

CODDINGTON
(More than a little angry)

I would say much more, Sir. Another thing you lay to her charge is her speech to the elders. Now, I have not seen any clear witness against her. You know that it is a rule of Court that no man may be a judge and accuser, too. I do not speak to disparage our elders and their callings, but I have not heard anything that they accuse her of and actually witnessed against her. Therefore, I do not see how she should be censured for that. And for the other thing that she hath mentioned occasionally about the spirit of God, you know that the spirit of God witnesses with our spirit, and you know that there is no truth in Scripture but God bears witness to it by His spirit. Therefore, I would entreat you to consider whether those things you have alleged against her deserve such censure as you are about to pass—be it banishment or imprisonment. And I repeat, there is nothing proved here by the elders—only that she said that they did not teach a covenant of grace as clearly as Mr. Cotton does, and that they were in the same state as the Apostles before the ascension of Christ. This was not meant offensively nor does it imply any wrong to them.

WINTHROP
(Wearily)

You are repeating all that has been said formerly. Anyway, her own speeches are ground enough for us to proceed.

CODDINGTON

I beseech you, do not force things along too fast. For I, for my part, do not see any equity in the Court in all of your proceedings. There is no law of God that she hath broken, nor any law of the country that she hath broken. Therefore she deserves no censure. And if she did say that the elders preach as the Apostles did, what is wrong with that? For it is without question that the Apostles did preach a covenant of grace, though without conviction, until they received a manifestation of the spirit. Therefore, I pray that you consider what you do, for in this case no law of God or man is broken.

HARLAKENDEN

Things thus spoken will stick. I would therefore tell the assembly before it is too late, to take notice that there are none here who condemn the meetings of Christian women, but not in such way and for such ends that it is to be detested. And even if the matter of the elders and Mrs. Hutchinson be resolved, there is still sufficient here in addition to condemn her. I shall speak no further.

DUDLEY
(Impatiently, wanting his dinner)

We shall all be sick from fasting.

WILLIAM COLBURN

I dissent from a censure of banishment.

STOUGHTON

The censure that the Court is about to pass, is, in my conscience, just what she deserves. But because she asked for witnesses and there were none in the way of witnessing, therefore I desire then that no offence be taken, if I personally *do not* formally condemn her. She hath not formally been convicted as she would have if the witnesses had taken oaths.

CODDINGTON
(Very determined)

That is my conscience, also. As Solomon saith, every man is partial to his own cause, and there are none here who accuse her except the elders, and she spoke nothing to them except in private. I do not know why they made the thing public. Secret things ought to be spoken in secret, and public things in public. Therefore, I think that they have broken the rule of God's word.

WINTHROP
(Angrily)

What is spoken in the presence of many cannot be kept secret.

CODDINGTON

She spoke to but few and in private.

WINTHROP
(Ignoring him)
Since Mr. Stoughton is not satisfied, and to the end that all
scruples will be removed, the Court desires the elders to take their
oaths.

*(There is great whispering among the ministers. Some draw back,
others try to push them on.)*

ELIOT
If the Court calls us to swear, we will swear.

STOUGHTON
There are two things that I would like to clear my conscience of.
First, to hear what they testify to under oath and second——

WINTHROP
(Interrupting)
An oath is required of you, Mr. Weld, and you, Mr. Eliot. *(Pausing, as they rise.)* We shall give their oaths. *(Mr. Weld, Mr. Eliot,
and Mr. Peters, also hold up their hands.)* You shall swear to the
truth and nothing but the truth as far as you know, so help you
God. What do you remember of her? Pray speak.

ELIOT
I do remember and I have it written. That which she spake first,
before anything else was said, was that the fear of man is a snare,
why should she be afraid? She would speak freely. The question
being asked whether there was a difference between Mr. Cotton
and us, she said there was a broad difference. I would not stick
upon the exact words, but the thing she said was that Mr. Cotton
did preach a covenant of grace, and we of works. And she gave
this reason: "To put a work in point of evidence is revealing upon
a work." We then did labor to convince her that our doctrine was
the same as Mr. Cotton's. She said no, because we were not
sealed. That is all I shall say.

WINTHROP
What say you, Mr. Weld?

WELD
I will speak to the facts themselves. These two things I am fully
clear in. She did make a difference in three things. The first I'm

not so sure about, but she said this and I am fully sure of it—that we were not able ministers of the New Testament and that we were not clear in our experience because we were not sealed.

ELIOT

I do further remember this, also. She said that we were not able ministers of the Gospel because we were like the Apostles before the ascension.

CODDINGTON

(Sarcastically)

This was, I hope, no disparagement to you.

WINTHROP

(Smirking)

Well, we've seen in this Court that Mrs. Hutchinson doth continually say and unsay things.

PETERS

(In a whining tone)

I was much aggrieved that she should say that our ministry was illegal. Upon which we had a meeting, as you know, and she told us the same thing—that here was a broad difference between Mr. Cotton and us. Now, if Mr. Cotton did preach things more clearly than us, it was our grief that we did not preach a covenant of grace so clearly as he did.

CODDINGTON

(Grinning)

Why was it wrong to say that you were not able ministers of the New Testament, or that you were like the Apostles? Methinks, the comparisons were very good!

WINTHROP

(to John Cotton)

Do you remember her saying that she should be delivered from this calamity?

COTTON

(Still trying to pacify him)

I remember that she said she would be delivered by God's providence, but whether or not or at another time, she knew not.

PETERS
(Shaking his head)
I must admit that I never thought Mr. Cotton would take her part.

STOUGHTON
I tell you now that these oaths do convince me. I am fully satisfied that her words were pernicious, and her attitude is the same.

WINTHROP
(Pounding his hammer)
The Court hath already declared themselves satisfied concerning the things you have heard, and concerning the troublesomeness of Mrs. Hutchinson's spirit and the danger of her course among us which is not to be suffered. Therefore if it is the mind of the Court that Mrs. Hutchinson, for these things that have been witnessed before us, is unfit for our society and if it is the mind of the Court that she shall be banished out of liberties and imprisoned until she can be sent away. Let those in agreement hold up their hands. *(All but three do.)* Those that are contrary minded hold up theirs. *(Only Mr. Coddington and Mr. Colburn do.)*

WILLIAM JENNISON
I cannot hold up my hand one way or the other, and I will give my reason if the Court require it.

WINTHROP
(Ignoring him)
Mrs. Hutchinson, you have heard the sentence of the Court. You are banished from our jurisdiction as being a woman not fit for our society, and you are to be imprisoned until the Court shall send you away.

ANNE
(Tears running down her cheeks)
I desire to know wherefore I am banished.

WINTHROP
Say no more. The Court knows why and it is satisfied.

THE EXCOMMUNICATION
OF ANNE HUTCHINSON
The Trial Held in the First Church
of Boston on March 15 and March 22, 1638

The following transcript of Anne Hutchinson's second trial was probably recorded by Robert Keyane, a Boston merchant who functioned as church secretary. In colonial days most sermons and church proceedings were recorded in a longhand kind of shorthand. Spellings varied from recorder to recorder since there was no agreement on how to spell English words. The transcript, covering more than fifty-six quarto pages in manuscript, was kept in a huge leather-bound book in the church pulpit. The book itself has disappeared. In 1771, it was copied by Ezra Stiles, who was then a minister and later became president of Yale. This manuscript did not see print—and few people knew of its existence—until another hundred years passed. It was published October 11, 1888, as part of the proceedings of the Massachusetts Historical Society. Without the background provided by this trial, biographers of Anne Hutchinson, until this time, were writing only from hearsay about these terrible days of her life.

The Meetinghouse where the trial took place was built in 1632; it was probably enlarged to accommodate at least a thousand persons. It was an open-raftered building with a bell tower and thatched roof; it had mud and wattle sides. Wooden, backless benches filled the sanctuary. Facing the congregation was the pulpit and seats for the elders of the church, all raised high enough on a platform so that they could watch and be seen by the entire congregation. The first rows were reserved for the freemen and the wealthy people of the Colony, and the people of "meane condition and weak parts" sat from the middle to the far rear. During the trial, Anne no doubt faced her accusers. It will be noted that during this trial nonmembers of the church, who could not vote, were asked to sit at one side so that a count of the members' votes could be quickly determined.

Many of the men who tried Anne before the General Court were also present at the excommunication trial. The following people may have been present at the earlier General Court trial, but they did not speak. They are presented in their order of appearance.

EDWARD HUTCHINSON

Anne's first son. He arrived in Boston in 1633 on the same ship, the *Griffin,* brought John Cotton and his wife Sarah to the Colony. He returned to England in 1636 to marry Katherine Humley. Later, he became a town assessor and a sergeant in the militia. After the trial he went Rhode Island with the rest of the Hutchinsons, but returned to Boston before Anne's death. He was 25 years old at the time of the trial. A captain in the Massachusetts Bay militia, he was killed by the Indians in King Philip's War, in 1675.

THOMAS SAVAGE

Anne's son-in-law. A tailor, he had just married Anne's daughter, Faith. At the time of the trial he was about 25.

JOHN DAVENPORT

Driven out of England by Archbishop Laud, he arrived in the Colony in 1637, a year before the excommunication trial. He lived in John Cotton's home at the time of the trial. In 1638 he moved to New Haven and helped develop the colony there, which was under the Massachusetts Bay Colony's jurisdiction. He was 40 at the time of the trial. He lived until 1668.

PETER BUCKLEY

Minister at Concord. He was in his late 40s at the time of the trial. He lived until 1652.

EDWARD GIBBONS

He arrived in the Colony in 1628, or perhaps earlier, with Captain Wollaston (and Thomas Morton). He applied for church membership at Salem but being of "jocund temper," he was denied. Soon after, he was admitted to the Boston church. In his 40s at the time of the trial, he was a wealthy tradesman. Later he lost 2,500 pounds in a deal at St. John's, Nova Scotia, and was "quite undone." An equivalent sum in today's dollars would be twenty times, or well over one hundred and fifty thousand dollars.

RICHARD MATHER

Minister at Dorchester. He arrived in the Colony in 1635. At the time of the trial he was about 31. He lived until 1689. When John Cotton died in 1652, he married Sarah Cotton, his second wife. Increase Mather was their son and the famous Cotton Mather, of witchcraft fame, their grandson.

RICHARD SCOTT

The husband of Katherine Marbury, Anne's fiery sister. Later, in Rhode Island, Katherine rejected the Church of England and became an active Baptist for a while. Still later, she was a Quaker who, along with Mary Dyer, harassed John Winthrop with her beliefs. Anne had no knowledge of the Quaker religion. Its English founder, George Fox, was only 14 at the time of her trial.

FAITH SAVAGE and KATHERINE HUTCHINSON were probably present at the trial with their husbands, but Will Hutchinson had left the Colony, along with William Coddington, William Coggeshall, William Aspinwall, Ned Hutchinson (Will's brother), William Colburn, Samuel Wilbore, John Porter, Dr. John Clarke, Randall Holden, and others who had signed a petition to exonerate John Wheelwright and were now under censure, banished, and fined by the General Court. They were obviously believers in Anne Hutchinson and her interpretation of the Scriptures, but they had been banished before her trial.

JOHN WILSON
(Surveying the nearly 200 people in the Meetinghouse)
We have heard this day, very sweetly, that we are to cast down all our crowns at the feet of Jesus Christ. So let every one be content to deny all relations of father, mother, sister, brother, friend, and enemy and cast down all our crowns. And any judgments or opinions that we have taken up may be cast down at the feet of Christ. Let all be carried by the rules of God's Word, and let all be tried by those rules. And if there be any error, let no one rejoice. None but the Devils in Hell will rejoice. But in our own proceedings, this day, lift up the name of Jesus Christ. And so let us proceed, in love, in this day's proceedings.

THOMAS OLIVER
(Ruling elder of the church)
I am here to acquaint this congregation that whereas our Sister Hutchinson was not here at the beginning of this exercise that it was not out of contempt or neglect to the ordinances, but rather because she has long been under sickness. She is so weak that she conceives herself not fit, nor able, to have been here for the entire meeting. This message was sent to the elders.

THOMAS LEVERETT
(An elder of the church)
I request that all those who are members of the congregation draw as near together as they can and in such places that they may be distinguished from nonmembers of the congregation. Thus when there is consent or dissent to the things which shall be discussed, we may know how they do express themselves either in the allowing of them or the condemning of them.

Sister Hutchinson, there are divers opinions laid to your charge by Mr. Thomas Shepherd of the church at New Town, and Mr. Frost. I must request you, in the name of the church, to declare whether you hold these opinions or renounce them as they are read to you:

1. That the souls (Eccles. 3:18-21) of all men by nature are mortal.

2. That those that are united to Christ (1 Cor. 6:19) have two bodies, one existing and a new body, and you knew not how Christ should be united to our fleshly bodies.

3. That our bodies shall not rise (1 Cor. 15:44) with Christ Jesus, at least not the same bodies as on the last day.

4. That the resurrection mentioned in 1 Corinthians 15 is not

our personal resurrection but is rather of our union with Christ Jesus.

5. That there are no created graces in the human nature of Christ, nor in believers after union.

6. That you believe there is no Scripture to warrant that Christ is now in Heaven in his human nature.

7. That the disciples were not converted at Christ's death.

8. That there is no Kingdom of Heaven except for Christ Jesus.

9. That the first thing we receive for our assurance is our election.

These are alleged against you by Mr. Shepherd. The following are alleged against you by Mr. Thomas Weld and Mr. John Eliot of the church at Roxbury.

1. That sanctification can be no evidence of a good estate in no wise.

2. That your revelations about future events are to be believed, as well as the Scripture because the Holy Ghost did bless both.

3. That you believe Abraham was not in a saving estate until he offered Isaac, and despite the firmness of God's election, he might have perished eternally insofar as works of grace were within him.

4. That any hypocrite may evince the righteousness of Adam and still perish.

5. That we are not bound to the Law—not as a rule of life.

6. That not being bound to the Law of the Bible, no transgression of the Law is sinful.

It is desired by the church, Sister Hutchinson, that you tell us whether these are opinions of yours.

ANNE HUTCHINSON

If these be errors, and they are mine, then I ought to agree. But if they are not mine and they are from Christ Jesus, then they are not my responsibility. But I do desire that the church respond to one question. By what rule of the Bible, when these elders came to me in private to ask satisfaction on some points and they do profess, in the sight of God, that they did not come to entrap nor ensnare me, but were speaking to me and expressing dissatisfaction with my ideas—by what rule they bring it all out publicly before the church? After they have perfectly dealt with me, and they had supposedly come to search for the truth, then afterwards to bear witness against me, I think that is a breach of church law, especially to bring these matters before the congregation until they have dealt with me in private.

JOHN COTTON
(Agreeing)
To answer you. If there be any plain breach of church rule, you may be dealt with publicly. But if there not be a manifest breach of rule, then the church hath not the power to make an inquisition in a doubtful case.

THOMAS SHEPHERD
I desire to ask this question of Mrs. Hutchinson. Does she accuse any of us of such a breach of rule?

ANNE
(Sarcastically)
I simply asked a question. There was none with me but myself to testify. I may not accuse an elder without two or three witnesses.

COTTON
Brother Shepherd, if you can express anything that concerns this matter, you shall do well to give God glory, and speak.

SHEPHERD
The first time I spoke with Mrs. Hutchinson, I was staying in town all night before going home to New Town, and I was importuned by some friends to go and see Mrs. Hutchinson. And so I did go to ask further satisfaction from her about the speeches that she had used in Court which I did not well understand. At my second visit to her, being sent by special providences of God, I did tell her that I came not to entrap her, nor had I any other thought, nor did I know how I could deal more lovingly with this your sister, than to bring her thus before you. And whereas she said that we did not deal with her fairly, I must need say that I never came to her but I bear witness and left some thoughts behind me against her opinions. Yet I did not publish anything concerning our conferences but kept it in my own breast. But seeing the fluency of her tongue, and her willingness to open herself and divulge her opinions, and sow her seed in us who are but strangers on the highway to her—and therefore can do much more to lead astray those who agreed with her, for I account her a very dangerous woman who sows her corrupt opinions to the

infection of many—and more the reason you have to watch out for her—therefore, at my third visit, I told her I came to deal with her and labor to reduce her errors. Therefore I do marvel that she says we bring her into public before I dealt with her in private (Heb. 4:12).

ANNE

I did not believe many of the things that I am accused of, but only did ask Mr. Shepherd questions (Eccles. 3:18-21).

SHEPHERD

I would have the congregation know that the vilest errors that ever were brought into this church were brought in by some of Mrs. Hutchinson's beliefs.

COTTON

(Ignoring Anne's pitiful expression)

Brother, we agree with you. Therefore, Sister Hutchinson, it will be most satisfactory to the congregation if you will answer the things that are objected to against you—in order.

ANNE

(Standing and ignoring Cotton's searching glance)

I desire that they be read.

COTTON

The first opinion that you are charged with is: "That the souls of all men by nature are mortal and die like the beasts." For that you cite Ecclesiastes 3:18-21. *(He stares sadly at her.)*

ANNE

I think it should be understood that the spirit that God gives us returns, not the body.

COTTON

That verse says that the spirit ascends upwards; so also does Ecclesiastes 12:7. Man's spirit doth not return to dust as man's body does, but to God. The soul of man is immortal.

ANNE

Every man consists of soul and body. "Adam dieth not except his soul and body dieth." In Hebrews 4, the verse saith: "The word of God pierce even soul and spirit." The word is lively. It makes a distinction between soul and spirit. So then, the spirit that God gives man returns to God indeed, but the soul dies. That is the spirit that Ecclesiastes speaks of and not of the soul (Luke 19:10).

COTTON
(Quite calmly)
But don't you see, if you hold that Adam's soul and body dies and was not restored in you by Christ Jesus, it overthrows our redemption. Both soul and body are bought with a price (Luke 19:10). "I come to seek and save what is lost" (1 Cor. 6).

ANNE
(Shaking her head)
I acknowledge that I may be redeemed from my vain conversation and other redemptions. But it is nowhere said that God came to redeem the seed of Adam, but rather the seed of Abraham.

WILSON
(Entering the fray)
I ask before you tell us your belief that you would seriously consider what is meant by 1 Corinthians 6: "The spirit of God needs no redemption." The verse speaks there not of God's spirit but of our spirits."

ANNE
(Shrugging)
I cannot speak about the spirit of God, but I do ask my conscience: How can a thing that is immortally miserable be immortally happy?

COTTON
He that makes us miserable can make us happy.

ANNE
(Smiling through her tears)
I desire to hear God speak this and not man. Show me where there is any Scripture that says that.

COTTON
(Trying to extricate her)
You do not say that the soul is not immortal, but rather that this immortality is purchased from Christ?

ANNE

(Gratefully)

Aye, Sir.

COTTON

Yet, Ecclesiastes proves that the soul is the gift of God and it hath no relation to such fading and destroying matter as is our body is made of (Matt. 10:28, I Thess. 5:23).

ANNE

(Bewildered)

Do you believe that Jesus' natural life has gone into Heaven and that we shall go into Heaven with our natural life?

COTTON

(Patiently)

There is a soul that is immortal (Matt: 10:28). Our nature shall go into Heaven—but not our corrupt nature.

ANNE

(A little triumphantly)

Then you have not a soul and spirit that shall be saved. I ask you, answer this. In I Thessalonians 5:23 it says: "I pray God your whole spirit and soul and body be preserved blameless unto the coming of our Lord Jesus Christ." And also it says in Psalms that God hath redeemed his soul from Hell.

COTTON

Sister, do not shut your eyes against the truth. All these places prove that the soul is immortal.

ANNE

(Determined)

The spirit is immortal indeed, but prove that the soul is. That place in Matthew which you bring up about the casting of the soul into Hell, really means the spirit.

COTTON

(Nodding patiently)

These are principles of Christian faith and I do not deny them. But the spirit is sometimes used to mean the conscience, and for the gifts of the spirit that makes the soul fit for God's service.

ANNE

The Holy Ghost makes this distinction between the soul and
body, not I.

COTTON
(Still trying)

But don't you see that if wicked men have the immortality of their
souls purchased for them by Christ, then Devils have immortality
purchased by Christ also.

GOVERNOR JOHN WINTHROP
(No longer able to sit back and listen)

She thinketh that the soul was annihilated by the judgment that
was sentenced on Adam. Her error springs from her mistaking of
the curse of God. The curse doth not imply annihilation of the
soul and body, but only a dissolution of the soul and body.

ANNE
(Nodding hopelessly)

I will take that into consideration, for it is of more weight to me
than anything which has been spoken thus far.

WINTHROP
(Delighted to teach her)

As the body remains an earthly substance after dissolution, so the
soul remains a spiritual substance after the curse, even though we
cannot see what substance it is turned into after dissolution.

JOHN ELIOT
(Coldly)

But she thinks that the soul is nothing but a breath, and so
vanishes. I pray put that to her.

ANNE

I think that the soul be nothing but light.

WILSON
(Frowning)

If the soul be but a breath, then why doth Christ say that a man's
soul is better than the whole world?

COTTON

The sum of her opinion is that the souls of men by creation are no other nor better than the souls of beasts which die. The souls of men are mortal, but they are made immortal by the redemption of Christ Jesus. So it is obvious that the soul is immortal through creation. And most people believe that the souls of the wicked are cast into Hell forever, and the souls of the Godly are kept in a blameless frame until they achieve immortal glory.

LEVERETT
(To the congregation)

The church wishes to ask whether what you have heard gives you satisfaction and sufficient light on the point in question.

SERGEANT THOMAS SAVAGE

My feeling is, seeing that the church is not accusing her of this opinion, but only one person is, whether we should express our consent or dissent, especially since Mrs. Hutchinson is not satisfied or convinced. The congregation should have time to consider it further.

WILSON
(Scowling at Anne's son-in-law)

It was usual in former times when any blasphemy or idolatry was revealed that the congregation would rend their garments and tear their hair in signs of loathing. For surely, if we deny the resurrection of the body, we turn into Epicureans. We can eat and drink and do anything we wish, for tomorrow we die, never to return. All the priests of Baal pleaded for Baal, but finally Elijah proved the Lord to be God. If anyone was doubtful and was not satisfied and believed that Baal was still God, should one man's scruple or doubt hold back the rest of the congregation who are satisfied—and cry out as one that the Lord is God, and the Lord is the only Lord?

WINTHROP
(Coldly)

The whole congregation but one brother is sufficiently satisfied that what we have said about this point is sufficient. Therefore let us proceed to the next error of Mrs. Hutchinson.

WILSON

I want to hear our sister speak to what becomes of our spirit when our bodies die, for I think she contradicts herself.

ANNE
(A little defiantly)
I spoke of the spirit that God gave us—that returns to God who
gave it to us.

COTTON
(Speaking warningly to Savage)
We are not here to listen to family affection. For the Scriptures
tell us we are to forsake father, mother, wife, and children for
Christ Jesus (1 Cor. 5:12).

WILSON
(Agreeing)
A person who will not confess to Me before men, she I will not
confess before Our Father, which is in Heaven. This is the rule of
God by which the church should proceed.

COTTON
(Looking coldly at Anne)
You have heard from Sergeant Savage how far natural affection
doth prevail with children to speak for their mother. Therefore, it
concerns everyone in the congregation to take heed how they link
themselves with any who hold such damnable errors. I am sorry
that any of our brethren be so brought up that they have not
heard of the immortality of the soul.

WINTHROP
(Impatiently)
I am surprised that there should be any doubt in this belief which
is practiced in all churches. We should ask some sign from the
congregation whether what hath been spoken does give satisfaction to the members or not, so that we may proceed.

COTTON
(Trying to elicit the right answer from Anne)
I would ask our sister this question. Is the soul and body immor-
tal? (1 Pet. 3:19).

ANNE
(Smiling sadly at him)
It is more than I know. How do we prove that both one's soul
and body are saved?

WILSON
(Sanctimoniously)
I pray God keep *your* whole body and soul blameless to salvation.

ANNE
(Coolly)
It is said that they are kept blameless to the coming of Christ Jesus, not to salvation.

WILSON
(Trying to get her out on a limb)
What do you mean by the coming of Jesus Christ?

ANNE
The coming of Christ means His coming to us in union (Rom. 6:4).

WILSON
I think such a belief is dangerous and damnable—nothing less than Sadducism and atheism, and therefore to be detested.

ANNE
If you are saying my belief is an error, then I desire to know for what error I have been punished. I am sure this is not an error, and there never was such an expression by me on this particular subject.

(For the most part the church members show themselves satisfied with what has been spoken. Lifting up their hands, they show their agreement that this is not an error, and Anne smiles hopefully at them.)

JOHN DAVENPORT
(A little testily)
When it comes to a case of testimony and a bearing of witness to the truth of God, the truth is often cried down. Then it is the time to speak. This question of the immortality of the soul is not new but an ancient heresy. For disbelievers it is most censurable, because it betrays a libertine philosophy of life. This point was once disputed for a whole day before Adrian the Pope, who like a beast concluded: "He that speaks for the immortality of the soul speaks most like the Scriptures, but he that speaks of the mortality

of the soul speaks most to my mind and my desires." So it
amounts to this: They that speak for the mortality of the soul
speak most for licentiousness and sinful liberty. Questioning this,
as hath been said, from natural affection and not from any scruple
of the conscience, has made some of the congregation wonder
whether they may express their judgment by vote or not. I think
that it is according to the rule, and do not see how we can bear
witness to the truth or against any error except by showing our
assent or dissent, either by silence or a lifting up of hands. Matthew 18 says: in the case of offenders against the church rule, and
if they will not accept the church belief, let them be declared
heathens or publicans. Now what is meant by the church? No! It
is plain that it is the whole church. Now how can a church
express itself except by their votes or their silence? So was an
incestuous person cast out in 1 Corinthians 5. How shall the
churches show their consent except that they express it one way
or the other? Therefore, I believe that there should be no scruple
about this.

COTTON
(Smiling at Anne and trying not to sigh)
We come to the second point. You say, Mrs. Hutchinson, that
through the redemption that Christ purchased for us, the soul is
immortal, but our creation is mortal.

ANNE
(Nodding)
The soul is immortal by redemption.

COTTON
(Shaking his head sadly)
You have no Scripture to prove this. Therefore you ought not to
prostitute your faith to anyone or try to convince them of your
own invention. You have heard plain statements against your
beliefs. The spirits of wicked men are in Hell and the souls of the
faithful in Heaven.

DAVENPORT
(Nodding in agreement)
And a soul may be immortal and not be miserable. But the curse
is this: misery is annexed to immortality. Immortality is a gift to
the spirit of man in his very being. The soul cannot have immortality in itself except for God from whom it hath its being.

ANNE

(Smiling appreciatively at him)

I thank the Lord now I have light. I see a great deal more now by Mr. Davenport's explanation.

COTTON

(Happily)

Then you will deny what you have said previously on this point?

ANNE

(Dubiously)

So far as I understand what Mr. Davenport has said. But I pray, let someone answer this: How is the soul immortal by creation?

DAVENPORT

(Pointing out the obvious)

It is immortal as the angels are by creation.

ANNE

(Still confused)

But if the soul be immortal by Christ, how can the soul die? The curse of Adam saith that the day you eat the forbidden fruit, you shall know death.

DAVENPORT

(Patiently)

The soul doth not die. Only the person of Adam—not his soul. But the person of Adam is redeemed by Christ Jesus. By contrast, the angels and the devils are immortal, not by Christ's redemption of us, but by nature and creation.

COTTON

(Nodding in agreement)

Sister Hutchinson, this comparison should certainly be familiar to you.

DAVENPORT

You must distinguish between the life of the soul and the life of the body. The life of the body is mortal but the life of the soul is immortal. Ecclesiastes 12. The spirit and the soul are similar. Isaiah 53:10: "Thou [God] shalt make his [Jesus] soul an offering for sin."

ANNE
(Smiling hopefully)
I think I am clear on this now!

DAVENPORT
Then you renounce what you previously said on these points?

ANNE
Yes, I do—thinking about souls as Mr. Davenport doth. That
was my mistake. I took soul for life.

DAVENPORT
(A little too pleased that his pupil believes him)
You see, the spirit is not a third substance, but rather the bent
and inclination of the soul and all the faculties thereof. The spirit
is not a substance suffering from the soul. The spirit mentioned in
Ecclesiastes is actually the soul. The spirit returning to God that
gave it means the soul or the substance thereof.

ANNE
(Lifting up her eyes to him and Cotton)
I do not differ from Mr. Davenport as he expresses himself.

DAVENPORT
(Still teaching)
The spirit referrred to in Thessalonians is as a bias to the soul.

WILSON
(A little unhappy that things are going so well)
But the question remains as to whether the spirit in Thessalonians
is immortal or not.

DAVENPORT
(A little aggravated by him)
The way *spirit* is used in Ecclesiastes is the same as soul. The way
spirit is referred to in Thessalonians, spirit is not a substance of
the soul but a quality of it. The soul which Christ mentions in
Matthew—"He cast both soul and body into Hell"—there, by
soul, is not meant spirit, but soul.

ANNE
(Still questioning)
May I speak plainly and ask whether the souls of men are immor-

tal by generation or are mortal, and so fade away like the soul of a beast? Now that Mr. Davenport has discussed, it is clearer to me. For God, through him, hath given me some understanding.

COTTON
(Changing the subject slightly)

Sister, will you speak to this? Do you conceive that the divine and gracious qualities of the souls of believers are immortal or not, and shall go with the soul into Heaven? Do you think that the evil qualities of souls of wicked men and their evil dispositions shall go with their souls into Hell or not?

ANNE
(Shaking her head sadly)

I know not presently what to say to this.

DAVENPORT

But you do agree with the first two questions that the coming of Christ (mentioned in Thessalonians) to the soul does not mean that Christ comes in union with us—but refers to His coming on the day of judgment?

ANNE
(Sighing)

I do not acknowledge it to be an error, but rather a mistake. And I do acknowledge my expression of the thought to be erroneous. But my judgment was not erroneous. I believed, before, as you did. But I could not express it so well. But with these things: (John 12. Corinthians 4:16). Actually, it seems that when men believe, they have a new body. Then they really have two bodies.

COTTON

Do you mean that they have an outward body—one of sin and death—and an inward body of grace?

ANNE

I mean as the Scripture means (1 Cor. 4).

COTTON
(Very much the teacher)

You say that you do not know whether Jesus Christ be united to this body of ours through our soul or our fleshly bodies. Therein lies your doubt and the absurdity of it. Remember that both our

soul and body are united to Christ. In our spiritual estate our
body is a sanctified instrument to hear and to be holy. And Christ
is also united to that body which we have made the body of a
harlot "sown in corruption." But our bodies are temples of the
Holy Ghost before we had become harlots.

ANNE
(Beseeching him with a forlorn expression)
I really would like you to speak to that place in 1 Corinthians 15:
37, 44, for I still question whether the body that dies shall rise
again.

DAVENPORT
The same body that is sown—that same body will rise again. It is
sown as a natural body but it shall rise as a spiritual body.

ANNE
(Shaking her head)
We all rise in Christ Jesus. But Romans 6 shows that Christ died.

DAVENPORT
That is another kind of death. But speaking first of our death, it
is clear that he raises us in the same body, and not another body,
for substance.

ANNE
I still question whether our body be sown or not.

DAVENPORT
(Sternly)
When I die, then my body is sown and turned into corruption
and dust. But that dust which is sown shall rise again in a body.

ANNE
(Persistently, while both Davenport and Cotton frown at her)
Then please explain Romans 6:2-7. There is no death of a child of
God, but a putting of our Tabernacle. Rev. 20.

DAVENPORT
The death and resurrection that is spoken of in these places is not
a natural death, nor a natural resurrection, but a spiritual one.
But the death mentioned in 1 Corinthians 15 is a natural and
bodily death and resurrection.

ANNE
(Trying a different tack)

There is another place in Revelations where a first resurrection is mentioned.

DAVENPORT
(Trying to keep his temper)

There is no first and second resurrection of one and the same body for that implies a second resurrection. Now, some believe that the resurrection of the martyrs and others is a spiritual resurrection, as explained in Romans 6, which we can enjoy in this life. But 1 Corinthians 15 refers to a bodily resurrection after this life. Are you clear on that point?

ANNE
(Shaking her head hopelessly)

No, not yet.

PETER BUCKLEY
(Impatiently)

I would like to ask Mrs. Hutchinson whether she believes in any other resurrection, other than that of union to Christ Jesus. And I would also like to ask her whether she believes in the foul, gross, filthy abominable opinions held by the Familists (Job 19: 25, Phil. 3) of a sharing of wives in a community of women.

ANNE
(Shaking her head slowly)

I hold it not, but I believe in Christ. But answer this: "I know thou hast a devil." That was the judgment they made against Christ when he told them: "He who believes in me shall not die." But I do believe that Christ Jesus is united to our earthly bodies.

WILSON
(Totally shocked)

God forbid!

DAVENPORT
(To Anne)

You are avoiding Mr. Buckley's question. But he states a right principle. If resurrection does not exist, then marriage does not exist. And it is a serious business. For if resurrection does not exist, and marriage does not exist, then if there is any union between men and women, it is in communal sharing.

ANNE
(Glancing quickly at Cotton)
If such practices or conclusion can be drawn from my beliefs, then
I must abandon them, for I abhor the idea of wife sharing.

WINTHROP
(Austerely)
The Familists do not try to evade the question, for they practice
wife sharing and they deny the resurrection to prove their belief in
a community of women and to justify their wickedness. It is a
dangerous error!

LEVERETT
But our sister does not deny the resurrection of the body.

ANNE
No.

ZACHARIAH SYMMES
(Waving his hand angrily)
But you do deny the resurrection of the same body that dies. To
prove that the same body that dies shall rise again I refer you to
Job 19:25.

ANNE
But that is what I am questioning. I do not think that the body
that dies shall rise again.

DAVENPORT
(Puzzled)
But you tell us of a new body and of two other bodies, which
makes three. Which of these three bodies do you believe shall rise
again?

ELIOT
(Disgustedly and after conferring with the other ministers)
We are completely dissatisfied with her answer and we think it is
very dangerous to dispute this question so long in this congregation. Mrs. Hutchinson, by her answers, doth not admit it is an
error. But with a mistake so gross and such dangerous ideas, we
much fear her spirit.

BUCKLEY

(Standing up and pointing a finger at Anne)

In Hebrews 6:1 the Holy Ghost states that the denying of the resurrection is the denying of the fundamental truth of religion. Therefore, for anyone to insist that there is no resurrection, I think is very dangerous heresy, and we should treat them as the dangerous heretics that they are.

SYMMES

(To Anne)

I ask that you respond to one more: I Corinthians 13. "If there be no resurrection, then our faith is vain and our preaching is useless, and all is vain."

ANNE

(Determined)

I agree that if there is no resurrection, then all is in vain—both preaching and everything. I do not deny resurrection, but I question that the body shall rise. I believe that it will only arise in Christ Jesus and that we shall all rise.

WINTHROP

(Indignantly)

I want to ask Mrs. Hutchinson a question. It is said that when Christ arose, many of the dead bodies of the saints also arose from their graves and accompanied Christ to the Holy City. Now, I would like to know just what those bodies that rose were. Aren't they the same bodies that were dead and laid in their graves?

ANNE

(Smiling fleetingly)

I do not know. They may be the same bodies.

WINTHROP

(Triumphantly)

Then that proves the point!

ANNE

(Frowning)

But I'm not clear on the point. I cannot yet believe that Christ is united to these fleshly bodies. But if he be not united to our fleshly bodies, then those bodies cannot rise.

DAVENPORT

The fleshly bodies of the wicked are not united to Christ, yet you say that they shall rise again.

ANNE

But they shall rise to condemnation.

DAVENPORT
(Shrugging)

That is true. But the bodies of the saints shall rise to salvation.

HUGH PETERS
(Snidely, sure that he will catch her)

I would like to ask Mrs. Hutchinson whether she thinks the actual bodies of Moses, Elijah, and Enoch were taken up into Heaven or not?

ANNE
(Taking her life in her hands)

I know not that, but I doubt the former much more than this.

DAVENPORT
(Astonished)

These are beliefs that cannot be borne. They shake the very foundation of our faith and tend to overthrow all religion. They are not slight matters but of great weight and consequence.

WILSON

If the congregation is satisfied with the questions that have been asked, and they are convinced in their judgments that these are errors, let them express it by the usual sign of holding up their hands and that they also agree that these are gross and damnable heresies. And because it is very late and there are many things yet to go over, the church thinks that it is best to reserve further discussion with our sister until a week from now, on Thursday, the next Lecture Day.

EDWARD HUTCHINSON
(Jumping up and waving his hand)

I would like to know by what rule I am to express myself in assent or dissent. My mother is not yet convinced, but I hope that eventually she will not shut her eyes against any new understandings.

WILSON
(Sarcastically)

Brother Hutchinson, you may well ask another question: Whether God will confess you before His Father which is in Heaven? Since now, you refuse to confess His truth before men, even though it be against your own mother.

DAVENPORT
(Warningly)

You are not to be led by natural affection but must declare your opinion for the truth or against error, even though it be held by your own mother. The question is not whether the arguments are weighty enough to convince your mother, but whether you have learned enough to satisfy your conscience that these are errors.

HUTCHINSON
(Shruggingly sadly at Anne)

Then I agree with them, so far as I know there is a resurrection.

SHEPHERD
(Grimly, pretending charity toward Anne)

If there be any in this congregation who do hold the same opinions as Mrs. Hutchinson, I advise them to take this warning: for the hand of the Lord will find you out. As for Mrs. Hutchinson, I would ask her to consider by what spirit and light she is led, for she hath often boasted that her guidance by God's spirit and her revelations are as true as the Scriptures. Now, she hath confessed her mistake in the first two points because of the clarification that she hath received from Mr. Davenport. Since her spirit has led her into some errors, I hope that she will see the rest to be errors and question herself and realize that it is not God's spirit but her own spirit that hath guided her thus far, and it is a spirit of delusion and error. For my part, I must admit that I did not know what better course to take than this, wherein I might show more love to her soul, by bringing her before this congregation of which she is a member, so that she could answer to these dangerous and fearful errors which she drank in her mind. You, this congregation, under God, who have care of her soul, may now deal with her for these errors and watch more carefully over her in the future, and try to reclaim her. For she has a most dangerous spirit, and no doubt with her fluent tongue and forwardness in saying what she thinks, she will seduce and draw many away from the truth, especially women of her own sex.

WILSON

If the congregation be satisfied with what hath been said and they believe that we ought to proceed to admonition, we will take their silence for consent. If any be otherwise minded, they may express themselves.

SAVAGE

For my part I am still not satisfied. Neither do I know any rule by which the church must proceed to admonition. Keep in mind that in most churches some errors or mistakes have been held. In truth, in the Church of Corinth, there were many unsound opinions, and in particular some people held the same opinion as my mother about the resurrection. It appears in Paul's arguments in the 15th chapter of Corinthians, and yet we do not read that the church admonished them for their beliefs. Actually, in point of fact, in such a case as incest, the church did proceed to excommunication, because it was such a gross and abominable act, but they never did excommunicate for one's beliefs. My mother is not being accused for any such heinous acts but only for opinions on which she was seeking information and understanding. And she did not peremptorily hold them. I cannot consent that the church should proceed to admonish her for this.

COTTON
(Sternly and determined to resolve the issue)

Although your mother is not accused of anything in point of fact, nor for my own part do I believe there is any cause for her thinking, yet she may be holding errors of dangerous and of worse consequences than if they were actually matters of practice. Therefore I do not see why the church might not proceed to admonition. You say that she seeks light and understanding and does not hold her beliefs peremptorily, but you've heard many pains taken and many arguments brought, not only from ourselves but from diverse elders of the church, which hath satisfied the assembly here and which she was in no way able to contest, and yet she doth persist in her opinion. In addition you should know that the Apostle Paul did admonish Himenus and Philetus on many similar opinions of this nature that they held. Since the Apostle did admonish them for their beliefs, you are doing a very evil thing out of your natural, but not religious, affection to hinder the church in its proceedings. In addition, you are the means to harden your mother's heart in these dangerous opinions and thus keep her from repentence. I pray you think about it.

LIEUTENANT EDWARD GIBBONS
(A handsome man, he smiles affectionately at Anne)

I ask to leave the congregation with one thought. Not that I would open my mouth in the least way to hinder the church proceedings, or in any way of God. I look at our sister as a lost woman, and I bless God to see the pains that have been taken with her to reduce her. But I would simply propose this to the congregation's consideration, seeing that admonition is one of the greatest censures that a church can pronounce against any offenders and one of the last next to excommunication—and also seeing that God hath already turned her heart about so that she could see her error or mistake as she calls it, in some of the points—I ask whether the congregation had not better wait a little longer and see if God will help her to see the rest of her errors and acknowledge them. In which case, the church would have no occasion to censure her.

SYMMES
(Stormily)

I am much grieved to hear so many in this congregation stand up and declare themselves unwilling that Mrs. Hutchinson should be proceeded against for such dangerous errors. I fear that if by any means it should be discovered in England that here in New England and in such a congregation there was so much spoken and so many questions raised about so plain an article of our faith as resurrection is, it would be one of the greatest dishonors to Jesus Christ and reproach to these churches that hath occurred since we arrived here.

DAVENPORT
(Trying to calm him)

I think it is appropriate that if any of the brethren have any doubts about their beliefs about this or any other point, then it shall be discussed until their doubts are removed. If these brethren, who disagree with the church in proceeding to admonition, would but consider that admonition is an ordinance of God and sanctified by Him for this very purpose as a special and powerful means to convince the offending party with the arguments and reasons given, then they would not oppose it. The lack of that consideration is the reason for the present doubt.

OLIVER

I would like to be satisfied about one thing and I am glad that I have such a good opportunity to propound my own doubts at such a time when God hath furnished us with such a group of elders and men of distinction from the other churches in the Colony who may help me resolve the same. I wish to ask how the church may proceed to any censure when all the members do not consent thereto, and whether the church hath not the power to censure those also who do hinder the church proceedings.

COTTON
(The voice of reason)
I think the brethren should be satisfied. The congregation should so far as possible remove all doubts that may arise so that the congregation may proceed with unanimous consent in the act to be done. If the church do take pains and do bring arguments that satisfy the whole congregation, it should be sufficient to dispel all doubts. Yet, if some brethren persist in their dissent, with no good reason except for their own, or out of natural affection for a relative, then the church should not delay its proceedings for that reason.

DAVENPORT
So far as I can see the church is satisfied. I perceive that no one doth oppose the church, except two or three of whom are tied to Mrs. Hutchinson by natural relationship. The others who have spoken did not contest it except as matter of conscience and they have received satisfaction. Therefore, I see nothing that should hinder us.

OLIVER
I want to suggest one thing to the congregation before you proceed to admonition. I do thank God to see so much care and faithfulness shown to the soul of this sister. It doth rejoice my soul to see so many pains taken and so many effectual arguments brought to convince her that her errors are leading her astray. It is no less a grief to my spirit to hear these brethren speak so much and to question the proceedings of the church—when the way of God is obviously at hand. Therefore, I would suggest this, seeing that all the proceedings of the churches of Jesus Christ actually function according to the pattern of the original church, and from the beginning the pattern was that things in the church should be done unanimously with an open heart and soul, then any and every act done by the congregation should be as the act of one person. Therefore, I ask if it is not appropriate that we put these

two brethren under admonition along with their mother, so that
we may proceed without any further opposition.

WILSON

I think you speak very well. It is very appropriate.

COTTON

(Looking sadly at Anne for a moment before he speaks)
I do in the first place bless the Lord, and thank in my own name,
and in the name of our church all the brethren and elders of this
church and other churches for their care and faithfulness in watching over our churches, and for bringing to light what we ourselves
have not been so ready to see in the opinions of our own members, and to take such pains to prevent any of our members from
going astray. I ask that their faithful and watchful care of us may
be continued. I doubt not but our Lord Jesus Christ, who is head
of the whole church, will make their hearts thankful. I confess
that I have not been ready to believe reports against Mrs. Hutchinson for want of sufficient testimony to prove the charges against
her. But now you have proceeded in the way of God and do bring
such testimony, and do reveal the truth of what has already been
shown, it would be our sin, if we did not all join in the same action against her. Therefore, first I will direct my speech and admonition to you who are her son and son-in-law, Edward Hutchinson and Thomas Savage. Though natural affection may lead
you to speak in defense of your mother and to take her part and
seek to keep up her credit and respect—which may be lawful and
commendable in some cases and at sometimes—yet, I would remind you, that in the cause of God, you are neither to follow
father nor mother, sister nor brother, but to say to all of them as
Levi did, "What have we to do with them?" Although the reputation of your mother be dear to you, and you hold her name in
high regard, the care and honor of Christ Jesus should outweigh
all other considerations. *(He stares at Anne sorrowfully and his
eyes are moist.)*

In truth, as you have heard, you must cast down your mother's name and reputation, though it be the chief glory that either
yourselves or your mother hath. Put them at the feet of Jesus
Christ and let them be trampled upon so that His glory may be
exalted. And I do admonish you both in the name of Jesus Christ
and of His church to consider how badly you have performed
toward your mother this day. You are guilty of hardening her
heart and nourishing her in unsound opinions. By your pleadings

for her, you have hindered the proceedings of the church against her, which God hath directed us to take, to heal her soul and which God might have blessed and made more effectual to her, had you not intercepted our course. Instead of acting as loving natural children, you have proved to be vipers who eat through the very bowels of your mother, to her ruin. If God doth not graciously stop you, I warn you both and admonish you in the Lord to desist from such a course, and ask yourself how by your flattery and mourning over her, and applauding of her opinions, and agreeing with her, when you are at home, whether you do hinder the work of repentance in her and keep her from seeing the evil in herself. Instead you should look to Jesus Christ and ask your mother with all faithful and grateful counsel, how you might bring her to see the wrong of her ways and prevent her from the path she is following. If you did that, you would be acting as faithful children indeed. If you do otherwise, watch out—for the Lord will bring you to account for it!

Next I wish to speak to the sisters of our own congregation, many of whom I fear have been too much seduced and led astray by Mrs. Hutchinson. I admonish all of you in the Lord to look in yourselves and to make sure that you accept nothing for which hath not the stamp of the word of God on it. I doubt not that some of you have also received much good from the meetings held by our sister and in your conversations with her. You may have even received help in your spiritual estates and have been saved from resting upon any duties, or works of righteousness of your own. But let me say this to you all and all the sisters of other congregations, let not the good you have received from her make you accept everything for good that comes from her. For as you have seen she is but a woman, and many unsound and dangerous principles are held by her. Therefore whatsoever good you have received, own it and keep it carefully, but if you have drunk in with this good, any evil or poison, make speed to vomit it up again and to repent of it and take care that you do not harden her in any way by pitying her, or confirming her in her opinions. Rather pray to God for her and deal faithfully with her soul in bearing witness against any unsound things that she hath tried to make you believe. *(He turns and looks wearily at Anne for a moment. When he speaks he sounds like a father reprimanding a daughter with tears in his voice.)*

And now, Sister Hutchinson, let me address myself to you. May the Lord put fit words in my mouth and carry them into your soul for good. It is true that when you first came into this country, we heard some things of your beliefs from Mr. Symmes that you had vented when you were aboard the *Griffin*. And when you came before the church to be accepted as a member, we had some discussion about your beliefs. You gave us satisfaction and after a warning and some delay you were received among us. Since your admission—and I would speak of it to God's glory— you were an instrument of doing some good among us. You have been helpful to many and saved them from unsound beliefs and principles, and you have shown them how to build their good estates upon their own duties and performances, or upon the righteousnes of the Law. And the Lord has endowed you with a good mind and body to instruct your children and servants and be helpful to your husband in the governing of your family. The Lord hath given you a sharp apprehension and a ready utterance and the ability to express yourself in the cause of God. I would deal with you as Christ Jesus deals with His churches when he admonishes them. You should take a vow and recall the good things that He hath bestowed upon you. Yet, notwithstanding, we do have a few things against you and in some sense they are not a few, but rather of great weight and heavy nature with dangerous consequences. Therefore let me warn you and admonish you in the name of Jesus Christ to consider seriously the dishonor that you have brought unto God by these unsound tenets of yours. They are far greater than all the honor you have brought to God, and the evil of your beliefs doth outweigh all the good you have done. Consider how many poor souls you have misled, and how you have conveyed the poison of your unsound principles into the hearts of many from whom they may never be erased again. Consider, in the fear of God, that this one error of yours— denying the resurrection of our bodies—you are doing your ut- most to destroy the foundation of religion and our faith. In truth, all our preachings that you have heard, and all our suffering for our beliefs are in vain. If there is no resurrection, then everything is in vain, and we, of all people, are the most miserable. Think about it. If resurrection does not exist *(Cotton is now speaking softly, his eyes avoiding direct contact with Anne's)*, you cannot evade the arguments that have been pressed upon you by Brother Buckley and others, reminding you about the filthy sin of sharing wives in a community of women, and all promiscuous coming together of men and women and without distinction of the rela- tionship of marriage that will necessarily follow. Though I have not heard, and neither do I think that you have been unfaithful to your husband in your marriage covenant, yet that would follow upon it. For it is the very argument that the Sadduces bring to our Savior Christ against the resurrection. And it is the argument that the Anabaptists and Familists bring to prove the lawfulness of sharing all women in common. And so, more dangerous evils and uncleanness and other sins arise from your beliefs than you do now perceive——

ANNE

(Interrupting him, brushing tears from her eyes)
Please let me ask you one thing before you continue. I would not interrupt you except I am feeling poorly. I fear that I may forget to mention it when you have finished.

COTTON

(A little nervously)
You have leave to speak.

ANNE

(Her eyes are boring into his)
All I would say is that I did not hold any of these beliefs before my imprisonment.

COTTON

(Fully aware of her meaning)
I confess I did not know that you believed any of these things until today. But it may be it was because of my sleepiness and want of watchful care over you. But I hope you see the danger of your beliefs, and how God hath left you to yourself to fall into these dangerous evils. But I must say that I have often feared the soaring of your spirits and your being so puffed up with your own ego. It is God's justice to abase you and leave you in this desperate plight. For the Lord frowns upon all the children of pride and delights and brings them low. And so the other things that you believe about the mortality of the soul by nature, and that Christ is not united to bodies, and that by the resurrection is meant Christ appearing within us in union—all these are of dangerous consequence and open the doors to Epicureanism and libertinism. If you are right, then come let us eat and drink, for tomorrow we die. Let us neither fear Hell or the loss of Heaven. Let us believe that there are neither angels nor spirits. Why should we care if our souls perish and die like beasts?

Nay, though *you* might not believe these things, yet if you do ask questions about them and discuss them as doubtful, others will hear you and they will conclude positively that there may be some truth in it, if Mrs. Hutchinson is doubtful. If people like yourself, who have great portions of wisdom and understanding, and if well-known Christians question these things, many people will believe that this is something that needs further search and inquiry. So your beliefs spread like gangrene and leprosy and infect people far and near, and they eat at the very bowels of religion and hath so infected our churches that God knows when it will be cured.

Therefore, so that I may conclude, I do admonish you and also charge you in the name of Christ Jesus, in whose place I stand, and in the name of the church, which hath given me this duty that you should sadly consider the hand of God against you, and the great hurt that you have done to the churches and the great dishonor that you have brought to Jesus Christ and the evil that you have done to many a poor soul and you should beg God to let you repent for it. And in your heart you should give satisfaction to the churches you have offended, and you should bewail your weakness in the sight of the Lord that you may be pardoned. And you should consider the great dishonor you have brought upon this church of ours of which you are a member, and how you have brought us all under suspicion and censure by holding and maintaining these errors. Therefore, I beg you think of it and be jealous of your own spirit, and take heed of how you have leavened the hearts of young women with such unsound and dangerous principles. And you should labor to save them from the snares, as the opportunity arises, to which you have drawn them. So I pray the Lord will bring into your soul what I have spoken in His name.

SHEPHERD
(Agreeing and heaping more coals on Anne's head)
Lest crowns should be set upon her head in this day of humiliation, I ask leave to speak one word before the assembly breaks up. It was of no little affliction and grief to my spirit to hear Mrs. Hutchinson's last words. It was difficult for me, Brother Cotton, not to interrupt you by speaking in the middle of your censure of her, which she ought to have listened to with fear and trembling. But it was a total astonishment for me to hear her affirm such a horrible and untrue falsehood, in the midst of such a solemn ordinance of Jesus Christ, and before this assembly and in the face of the church. She said that she held none of the beliefs before her imprisonment. And she well knows that she expressed

this thought to me when I was with her and talked to her about her beliefs. She fluently and forwardly expressed herself to me, and she told me that if I had come to her before her imprisonment, she would have revealed herself more fully to me and declared many other things about her beliefs. I am sorry that Mrs. Hutchinson should so far forget herself. It shows but little fruit for all the pains I took with her. This makes me fear the unsoundness of her heart more than anything else.

ELIOT

The same trouble and grief with her occurred to me.

(It is now so dark in the Meeting House it is difficult to see.)

WILSON

Sister Hutchinson, I require you in the name of the church to present yourself here again on our next Lecture Day, a week from today, to give your answers to such other things as this church or the elders of the other churches may charge you with, concerning your opinions and beliefs, and whether you hold them still or will revoke them.

Following is Anne Hutchinson's second examination in the First Boston Church on Thursday, Lecture Day, after the sermon on March 22, 1638, before all the elders of the other churches, the members of the congregation, and other people of the Colony. During the week which intervened she was not permitted to return to her home on Sentry Lane (now School Street in Boston), but was confined in John Cotton's home on what is now known as Beacon Hill, within ten minutes' walking distance of her own home. Presumably, during this time John Cotton and John Davenport, who was living in Cotton's house until he went to New Haven, spent a great deal of time trying to correct Anne Hutchinson's heretical beliefs.

LEVERETT

Sister Hutchinson, you are now to make further answers to the charges against you. But first I would have the members of our church draw together so that they may express their consent or dissent to the things at hand which most concern them.

Mrs. Hutchinson, the additional beliefs you are accused of holding are these:

1. Those who have union with Christ shall not arise in their own bodies.

2. The resurrection in 1 Corinthians does not refer to our resurrection on the last day but to our union with Christ Jesus.

3. That grace is not achieved in believers after union with Christ, but, after union, Christ accepts our grace into Himself.

4. That union in Christ does not create grace.

5. That there is an indwelling spirit of Christ even before our union with him, but we may not realize this.

It is further charged that you believe:

6. That your revelations about future events are as infallible as the Scriptures themselves. And that you are bound to believe them as well as the Scriptures because the Holy Ghost is the author of both.

7. That sanctification is no evidence of a good estate.

8. That union to Jesus Christ is not by faith in works.

9. That a hypocrite may have Adam's righteous beliefs in works and still perish.

10. That we have no grace in ourselves but only achieve it through Christ, and there is no inherent righteousness achieved by works.

To the first three of these charges at New Town, you gave no satisfaction. Therefore, an admonition was passed against you. Therefore, now, you are to give us further satisfaction concerning your beliefs.

ANNE
(Pitifully pale, reading from a paper)

1. The first thing I wish to say is that I do acknowledge that I was deeply deceived, and these beliefs were very dangerous (1 Cor. 19:18). *(There is a hush and surprise on the faces of the elders.)*

2. I never doubted that the soul was immortal, but I do renounce the belief that the soul was redeemed for eternal pain.

3. I acknowledge my mistake that believers have two bodies. I now realize that the Apostle in 1 Corinthians 6:14-15 speaks of persons in one place and bodies in another and that they are the same.

4. I acknowledge, and I thank God, that I see better now that Christ is united to our fleshly bodies as explained in 1 Corinthians 6:18-19. I do acknowledge that the same body that lies in the grave shall rise again, and I renounce my former belief as erroneous (Isa. 11:2).

5. As for there being no grace in believers, I ask that it be

understood that I meant that it is not in us, but flows from Christ. And I do not acknowledge that we have any grace that accompanies our salvation before our union with Christ.

6. I also agree that Christ Jesus hath grace created in Him (Isa. 11:2; 2 Pet. 4:24; Col. 3:10).

7. I do see good evidence that Christ's mansion is in Heaven, as well as in His body.

8. I have studied some Scriptures that satisfy me that the spirit of Adam is righteousness and holiness, and I admit that was a dangerous error which I held.

9. I agree that the word of the Bible is the rule of life and I acknowledge anything else to be a hateful error which opens the door to licentiousness, and I believe in the Law of the Bible over our life, and if we do anything contrary to it, it is a grievous sin.

LEVERETT
Do you have answers to Mr. Weld's charges?

ANNE
(Still reading)
1. I agree that sanctification cannot be an evidence, but only as it flows to us from Christ and is witnessed to us by the spirit.

2. Concerning those Scriptures that I quoted in Court to censure those hearing me, I confess that I spoke rashly and out of heat of my spirit, unadvisedly. I am very sorry for my irreverent atittude to the magistrates and ministers, and I am heartily sorry that anything I have said would have contradicted the elders of the Colony.

3. I agree that the command to believe is part of the doctrine of the Gospel.

4. I acknowledge that there is no promise of God's election but assurance and there is no hope for forgiveness such as hypocrites might think. But, in truth, I never believed such a thing anyway.

LEVERETT
It seems that you did but later you denied it.

ANNE
(Continuing to read)
5. I do not believe that a hypocrite can attain Adam's righteousness.

6. I believe that we are slow to act in spiritual things unless

we are influenced by Christ *(putting the paper down)*. But I deny that I ever said that one is not bound by the Law of the Bible or that it is no transgression to break the Law. I agree that any breach of the Law is a sin, and a hateful error.

WILSON

Sister Hutchinson, there is one thing that it will be necessary for you to answer and which you objected to at our last meeting. It being so late, we could not pursue the subject and that is this: You denied that you believed any of these things before your imprisonment. But Mr. Shepherd alleged to you that you had expressed these things to him, and more, before you were confined to the home of Joseph Weld in Roxbury.

ANNE
(Speaking softly as if she has been coached)
Since I have confessed my sins, I think it needful to acknowledge how I came first to fall into these errors. Instead of looking into myself, I questioned the ministers. I should have known that my dissemblings would do no good. I spoke rashly and unadvisedly. I should not have condoned the slighting of ministers, nor the Scriptures, nor anything that is established by God. If Mr. Shepherd doth really believe that I had anything like this in my mind, then he is deceived. It was never in my heart to slight any man. All I wanted to say is that man should know his place and not assume the authority of God.

LEVERETT

So that the assembly may know what is transpiring, our Honorable Governor Winthrop has suggested that it is appropriate that someone should express what Mrs. Hutchinson hath said to the congregation, many of whom cannot hear her.

COTTON
(Who has helped put the words in her mouth)
The sum of what she has said is this: She did not fall into these gross and fundamental errors until she was imprisoned in Roxbury. The basis was this: the miscarriage and disrespect that she showed the magistrates when she was in Court was caused by a rash spirit that often leads one into errors. She doth utterly retract and condemn herself for her attitude, and she confesseth the root of it all was the overweaning pride and spirit. As for her slighting the ministers, she is heartily sorry. And for her particular response

in her speech to the disgrace of Mr. Shepherd, she is sorry for it and asks all that she has offended to pray to God to give her the heart to be more humble.

SHEPHERD
(Sarcastically)
Mrs. Hutchinson may be admitting shame and confusion because of her gross and damnable errors, but she casts shame upon others and tells them they are mistaken, and she turns aside many of those gross errors with a shrug and slight answer and says, "your mistake." I fear it doth not reflect true repentance, and I confess that I am wholly dissatisfied in her response to some of the errors. Any heretic may bring a sly interpretation upon any of the errors, and yet believe them to their death. Therefore, I am unsatisfied. I should be glad to see any repentence in her that would give me satisfaction.

ELIOT
Mrs. Hutchinson did affirm to me, as she did to Mr. Shepherd, that if we had come to her before her restraint, or imprisonment, she could and would have told us many things about union with Christ Jesus, but now we had shut and debarred ourselves from her understanding by impressing and proceeding against her. But she did quote some Scriptures to me.

SHEPHERD
(Very unforgiving)
She spoke of many things which she now calls a mistake, and she said that in our union with Christ, He takes all the grace He finds in us and absorbs us into Himself.

COTTON
Sister, was there not a time when you believed that there was no distinct grace inherent in us but all was in Christ Jesus?

ANNE
(Nodding as if she is hypnotized)
I did not understand the word *inherent* as Mr. Davenport can tell you. He showed me my mistake in the meaning of *inherent*.

ELIOT
(Harshly)
We are still not satisfied with what she says. Why should she now

say that she never did deny the inherence of grace in us as subjects? When she was pressed by us, she denied that there were any
graces inherent in Christ Himself.

SHEPHERD

She did not deny the word *inherent* but denied the very possibility
itself when I asked her if she did believe that the spirit of God was
in believers.

ANNE

I admit my words may have sounded that way, but it was never
my judgment.

DAVENPORT
(Prodding her gently)
It is important that you answer clearly to these things.

ELIOT

She did not answer clearly to me about her belief that there is no
difference between the grace that is in hypocrites and that which
is in saints.

COTTON
(Smiling reassuringly)
There are two things that should be cleared, Mrs. Hutchinson.
First, what do you believe now, and second, what did you believe
then?

ANNE
(Suddenly becoming herself again)
My judgment is not altered, although my expression of it has
changed.

WILSON
(Shocked)
What you say is most dangerous! If your judgment in all this is
not changed but only your expression of it, your words are contrary to the truth.

SYMMES
(Piously)
I should be glad to see any humiliation in Mrs. Hutchinson, but I
am afraid that she shall jump about. There are no new things she

saith, but she has always held them. She needs to be humbled for her former doctrines and her abuse of divers Scriptures. If she believes nothing different, she ought to be humbled for what she formerly believed. For example, she saith: "A Christian is dead to all spiritual acting after they are united to Christ, and only that through grace." She hath quoted that place in Isaiah: "That all flesh is grass and a poor withering thing," and many other similar things.

PETERS

We did think that she should have humbled herself for denying grace today. Her beliefs are dangerous and fundamental, and as such, put down the Articles of Religion by denying the resurrection and faith and all sanctification. She has forced some elders to make whole sermons about faith, as if faith could never hold up her head again in this country, and or has happened in our native country.

DEPUTY GOVERNOR THOMAS DUDLEY

It is obvious that Mrs. Hutchinson's repentance is only for beliefs held since her imprisonment. But before her imprisonment, according to her, she was in good condition and held no errors and she did a great deal of good to many. Now I know of no harm that Mrs. Hutchinson hath done since her confinement; therefore I think that her repentance will be worse than her errors. For by repenting she shall draw attention to herself. How can any heretic in the world ask for more? As for her form of recantation, her repentence is written down on paper. *(He stares coldly at Cotton and Davenport.)*

Whether she had any help in writing it, I know not and will not now inquire. But it is certain that repentance is not on her countenance, and no one can see it there, I think. Therefore, I mention this only to remind the elders to ask her whether she actually did hold any errors prior to her imprisonment.

THOMAS WELD

I must mention that long before this, she hath said to me, when I spoke about grace, that she could not pray for faith, nor for patience and the like. When I asked her if she would confirm that, I took out my pen and ink so I could write it down, and then she turned it around this way. "I will not pray for patience but for the God of patience."

WINTHROP

I would like to remind Mrs. Hutchinson of a paper that she sent to me, wherein she did very much slight faith.

ANNE

Those papers were not written by me.

PETERS
(Fishing for trouble)

I would say this: When I was once speaking to her about the woman of Ely, she did exceedingly praise her to be a woman in a thousand, and hardly any like her. Yet, we all know that the woman of Ely is a dangerous woman and preaches grievous things and fearful errors. But when I told Mrs. Hutchinson that there were divers worthy and godly women among us, she inferred that she was better than so many Jews. So I believe that she has vile thoughts about us and thinks us to be nothing but a company of Jews, and that God has converted us to Judaism.

ANNE

I only told you what I had heard about the woman of Ely. I knew her not and never saw her.

WILSON
(Seething)

I must say this, and if I did not say it I could not satisfy my own conscience. You now say that the cause and root of these errors was the reason for your slighting of the magistrates and your irreverent attitude toward them. Though I think that was a great sin, and it may be one reason why God has abandoned you, but that is not all! For I fear and believe there is another greater sin, and that was your slighting of God's faithful ministers, and condemning them and crying them down as nobodies. You say that one reason was that men should not assume the authority of God, but you do have a high and honorable esteem of them. I do not deny that, but it may be that you only have a high and honorable esteem for one or two of them—*(he glances coldly at John Cotton)* such as Mr. Cotton and the like. And I think you were actually setting yourself up in the ministry, above others, so that you might be extolled and admired and followed after, and so that you might be one of the great prophets and undertake to expound Scripture, and interpret other men's sayings and sermons as you see fit. Therefore, I believe that your iniquity hath found you out.

Before, if anyone tried to deal with you about anything, you demanded witnesses and for accusers who can prove what they say about you. But now God hath left you to yourself and you have confessed what you previously asked witnesses to prove. It grieves me that you should so mince your dangerous, foul, and damnable heresies for which you have so wickedly abandoned God and have done so much harm.

SHEPHERD
(Emphatically)
I think it is needless for anyone to say more, and useless. The case against her is plain, and we have heard enough witnesses.

ELIOT
Some people acknowledge the gift of the Word and its fruits. But they deny grace, and they acknowledge the acting of the spirit. By such distinctions I could deny all of the repentance that she has written down and read to us. She would do better to express herself plainly and what her judgment is now in all of these things.

ANNE
(Staring at Cotton with tears in her eyes)
Mr. Cotton knows my judgment, for I never kept my judgment from him.

DUDLEY
(Smirking at Cotton)
I do remember that when she was examined by the court with six questions and articles, that she said she believed nothing but what Mr. Cotton believed.

WELD
I can attest to that. For when I spoke with her she told me that she and Mr. Cotton were of one mind, and she believed no more than Mr. Cotton did in these things. When I told her that lately she seemed to have changed her opinions and I told her that Mr. Cotton had written some things expressly against the opinions that she held, she still insisted that there was no difference between Mr. Cotton and herself.

OLIVER
I remember the time that Mrs. Hutchinson did plead for created graces, and did acknowledge them and stood for them, but now

since she hath used these expressions in a way of dislike and she hath said, "I have prayed for *grace* as much as *works.*" Now, if you do not really deny created graces in us, then explain those words.

ANNE

I confess that I have denied the word *grace*—but not the feeling itself, and when I said that I prayed for grace as much as works, I meant only in seeking comfort from them.

SYMMES
(Grimly)

On board ship, you may remember that you said you were offended at the expression *growing in grace* and laying up a stock of grace. You said that all grace is in Christ Jesus.

WILSON
(Angrily)

I know that she hath said it and she hath affirmed dogmatically that the grace of God is not in us and we have no grace in us but only from the righteousness of Christ that he imputes in us, and she saith that if there be any grace acting in us it is only Christ that acts (Isa. 53; Gal. 2).

RICHARD MATHER

Mrs. Hutchinson may remember speaking with me and telling me that she denied all grace to be in us and that there was neither faith, nor knowledge, nor gifts of grace, nor life itself but all is in Christ Jesus. She quoted some Scriptures to prove her opinions that before union there was grace and faith in us, but not after union with Christ. She quoted Romans 11: "If thou stands by faith, be not high-minded but fear, lest thou also be cut off." And she saith: "Before union there is faith, and thou liveth by faith, and works, but if you be full of pride, you shall be cut off, for knowledge is not within us but in Christ." She quoted Isaiah 53: "By his knowledge shall my righteous servant justify many." Then she insisted: "We are justified by His knowledge that is in Christ, but not by our knowlege or faith" (Gal. 2). Mrs. Hutchinson told me, "I live—but not I, but Jesus Christ lives in me." Therefore, I do wonder that she doth so far forget herself as to deny that she did formerly hold this opinion and denied that gifts and graces are within us.

PETERS

I would ask Mrs. Hutchinson, in the name of the Lord, that she search in her heart further to help her repent. For though she hath confessed some things, her confession is far short of what it should be and therefore *(speaking directly to her):*

1. I feel that you are not well-principled and grounded in your own catechism.

2. I would recommend this for your consideration. You have stepped out of your place. You would rather be a husband than a wife. You would rather be a preacher than a hearer. You would rather be a magistrate than a subject. So you thought to achieve all these things in church and in the commonwealth, and you did not expect to be humbled for this.

WINTHROP
(Pontifically)

Seeing that many sisters in this congregation have built their beliefs upon her experience, I think it would be very expedient and much to God's glory, if Mrs. Hutchinson would declare just what her estate is, or wherein her good estate may be. It cannot be achieved by the immersion into Christ Jesus, because the estate that she held before the elders was not by immersion into Christ. She insisted that a man may be immersed in Christ and still fall away from a good estate.

WELD
(Ignoring him)

I ask that we may proceed.

SHEPHERD
(Nodding to Weld but interrupting)

You not only have to deal with a woman today who holds diverse, erroneous opinions but also with one who never had any true grace in her heart, and that is by her own admission! Truly, today, she has shown herself to be a notorious imposter. It is a trick of the greatest subtlety as was ever offered in the church, to tell everyone that there is no grace in the saints. Now she hath dared to tell us that all this time she hath not altered her judgment but only her words and expression of it. *(Pauses and thunders):*

I would have you question whether Mrs. Hutchinson was ever in a state of grace or not, especially in view of her horrible untruths that she hath affirmed before the congregation and which have been proved by many witnesses. Yet she hath not confessed it before the Lord. I would have the congregation judge whether there was ever any grace in her heart or not, or whether a spirit of glory fills her because of the cause she professeth. If the cause were good for which she suffers, and she doth not suffer as an evil doer, then the spirit of glory and Christ shall rest upon her as Peter hath said. But if, in her imprisonment, God hath left her so sure of herself, and as she hath now confessed, she never held any of these opinions until her imprisonment, which she thinks was a time of humiliation and persecution, then Peter hath said, her sufferings are not for good, because an evil spirit hath not left her in this time of humiliatation. *(Surveying the congregation):*

For this reason, I think you must deal with her not only for her opinions but also as one who should be questioned whether she ever was in a good estate. Keep in mind that the basis of her beliefs have been built upon feigned and fantastical revelations which she admitted in court: one being about the certain destruction of old England, and another for the ruin of this country and all the people here for banishing her. Therefore, I pray too that you consider all the women and others who have been led astray by her and doted so much upon her and her beliefs.

PETERS
(Sarcastically)

We are still not satisfied with her repentance as she hath expressed it, especially because she blames her censure and her imprisonment as the cause of all her errors—as if she were innocent before.

WILSON
(Oratorically, sounding like God Himself)

I cannot but reverence and adore the wise hand of God in this thing, and I cannot but acknowledge that the Lord is just in leaving our sister to pride and lying and because of high spirits to fall into errors and many unsound judgments. I look upon her as a dangerous instrument of the Devil raised up by Satan among us—to create divisions and contentions and to take away our hearts and affections for one another! Before she arrived, there was much love and union and sweet agreement among us. But since she came, all love and union hath disappeared and there hath been censuring and judging and condemning of one another. I do believe all of these woeful conflicts come from this source, and if the foundation be unsound and corrupt, then must the building fall. The misgovernment of this woman's tongue hath been a great cause of disorder, which was not designed for the ministry of the Bible, either here or elsewhere, but to set up herself and to draw disciples after her. Therefore, she saith one thing today and another thing tomorrow. She speaks falsely and doubtfully and dully, while we try to speak the truth plainfully to one another. *(Pausing for effect and glancing at the congregation to see their reaction.)*

I do therefore believe that in point of religion and doctrine she destroys the foundation. Woe be to that soul that builds upon such bottoms! Our souls should abhor and be loath to see that she has come so far short of repentance. Therefore I think since she was liable to admonition before, we should now proceed to excommunication from our church to ease ourselves of such a member. Especially for her untruths and lies that she was always of the same judgment but she hath only altered her words. Therefore I leave it to the church to consider how safe it is to suffer such a schismatical and unsound member among us, and one who stands guilty of such foul falsehood. Consider whether it be faithful to Christ Jesus, or whether it attests to His honor to keep such a one any longer among us. If the blind lead the blind, whither shall we go? Consider whether we can or whether we may continue to suffer her as she goes on seducing to seduce, deceiving to deceive, lying to lie, and continuing to condemn authority and magistracy. We would sin against God if we should not put away from us such an evil woman, guilty of such foul evils. If anyone in the church be of another mind, let them express themselves, if she may not be separated from this congregation of the Lord.

OLIVER
(Trying to slow things down)
I did not think that the church would have come this far so soon, especially since I talked with Mrs. Hutchinson this morning, and I saw her come so freely to her confession of her sin in condemning the magistrates and ministers.

ELIOT
(Staring at Anne and then Cotton)
It is a wonderful wisdom of God to let those fall by the side who have upheld these opinions, and let her fall into such lies as she hath done this day. For she hath maintained all her error by lying, and telling us that she believed nothing but what Mr. Cotton did, and that he and she were of one judgment. We have cast many out of our church for these opinions.

COTTON

(Avoiding Anne's searching look)

The matter is now translated. Last Thursday she was dealt with on points of doctrine. Today she has been dealt with on points of practice. It belongs to the pastor's office and Mr. Wilson to instruct and correct in righteousness when an open lie is persisted in, in the face of the congregation and has been exposed by witnesses. I do not know how to satisfy myself except as Revelation 22:15 saith: "Whosoever loves and practices a lie are dogs and sorcerers and sexually immoral and murderers and idolators." Therefore, although she hath confessed that she understands many of the things which she held to be errors and has admitted that they proceeded from false pride of spirit, yet I believe that her pride is still working in her heart and is not healed. And she is keeping secret some unsound opinions. God hath let her fall into a manifest lie, and actually tell lies. Therefore, as we received her as a member among us, we are bound upon this basis to remove her and not to retain her any longer, because she doth prevaricate with words and tells us that her judgment is of one thing but her words and expression of it another.

DAVENPORT

(Nodding sadly)

God will not bear with mixtures of this kind. Therefore, Mrs. Hutchinson, you must freely confess the truth, and take shame of yourself that God may have the glory. But I fear that God will not let you see your sin until an ordinance of God hath taken place against you. So, it seems that God had a purpose to continue in His course of judgment against you.

UNIDENTIFIED CHURCH MEMBER

(With a slight show of indignation)

I would like to know how this church may proceed to excommunication when the Scripture telleth us that he who confesseth and forsaketh sin shall have mercy. Why should we not bear with patience the contrary-minded?

COTTON

(Firmly and grimly)

By a confession of sin, the Scriptures mean with all the aggravations of it. These hath not appeared to us. By bearing with the contrary-minded is meant of those who are without sin.

RICHARD SCOTT
(Standing near Anne, his arm around her)
I have scruples about this which keep me from approving of excommunication of Mrs. Hutchinson. I would like to know whether it be not better to give her a little time to consider things that are devised against her. Because right now she is not convinced that she was lying, and in her distraction she cannot recollect her thoughts.

COTTON
(Adamantly, wanting to get it over with)
It is not on a point of doctrine that we must be patient with her. We are willing to deal with her on a point of practice that she was telling and believing a lie. On that point, there is no way to delay proceedings.

SHEPHERD
I perceive that it is the desire of many members to stay Mrs. Hutchinson's excommunication and to put her under a second admonition. But for a person to tell a lie, and make a lie, and to maintain a lie, and to do it on a day of humiliation in the sight of God and before such a congregation as this, I would ask the members whether it is really for the honor of God and the honor of his church to be patient with such a gross offender.

MATHER
The Apostle tells us that a heretic, after one or two admonitions, should be cut out like gangrene. Since she hath been admonished already, why should not the church proceed?

LEVERETT
The word of the Bible is: After once or twice by a copulative. A man that is a heretic, after the first and second admonition, reject! Titus 3:10.

DUDLEY
(Impatiently)
I would answer this to Mr. Leverett and his objection that there have not been two admonitions. Mrs. Hutchinson hath been dealt with and admonished not once, twice, or thrice but many times by private brethren, by elders, and by other congregations, and by her own church. Therefore that should not be a scruple. Besides, I

think that text doth not speak of admonition by the church but rather private admonition.

ANOTHER UNIDENTIFIED MEMBER OF THE CHURCH

I would like to know if the church proceeds against her, whether it be for doctrine or for her lie. If for her lie, I consent. If it be for her doctrine, she hath renounced that as erroneous, and I would want more light on the subject to go along with the church.

WILSON

For my part, if the church proceeds, I think it is and should be for her errors of opinion as well as for the point of practice. For although she hath made some show of repentance, it doth not seem to be cordial or sincere. Like that of Achan: he did confess and acknowledge his sin, yet Joshua, by agreement with God, did proceed against him. Also in Corinthians, as soon as the Apostle heard of the sin committed against them, he wrote a letter, "To cast them out, forthwith—and without delay!"

COTTON

(Arguing)

To further cast out any need for delay and what rule you have for it, in point of practice there hath been a comparable proceeding. Acts 5: "As soon as ever Ananias hath told a lie, the church cast them out."

WILSON

*(After the church has been polled by a raising of hands,
in a stern hollow voice)*

The church consenting, we will now proceed. Inasmuch as you, Mrs. Hutchinson, have highly transgressed and offended, and inasmuch as you have in many ways troubled the church with your errors, and have drawn away many a poor soul, and inasmuch as you have upheld your revelations, and inasmuch as you have told a lie, therefore, in the name of our Lord Jesus Christ and in the name of the church, I do not only pronounce you worthy to be cast out, but also I do cast you out in the name of Christ! I do deliver you up to Satan! That you may learn no more to blaspheme, to seduce and to lie. And I do account you from this time forth to be a heathen and a publican, and so to be looked upon by all the brethren and sisters of this congregation and of others. I command you, in the name of Jesus Christ of this church, as a leper to withdraw yourself out of this congregation! And since you have despised and condemned the holy ordinances of God and turned your back on them, so you may now have no part in them or benefit by them.

(In silence, the entire congregation watches Anne Hutchinson trembling but holding her head erect. While the congregation stares at her, she walks down the aisle of the church. As she passes Mary Dyer, Mary stands up, slips her arm around Anne, and walks with her to the door. They pass a man who snarls at her: "The Lord sanctifies this unto you!")

ANNE
(Smiling at him through tears)
The Lord judgeth not as man judgeth. Better to be cast out of the church than to deny Christ.